"Are you all right?" She moved to his side and brushed her fingers over the knot on his forehead.

He caught her hand and held it for a moment before letting her go. "I was just thinking of all that needs to be done. I'll ride in with you in the morning and pick up seed. It may be a week before I'll have the field ready, but I'll want the seeds when I do."

"Stop thinking about work, husband, and come to bed." He'd worked twice as hard as she had today, and she was exhausted. She moved to her side of the bed and climbed in. He did the same.

He lifted his arm and she lay an inch away from him. After a few minutes he shifted to face her and touched her cheek with his hand. "It was a good day, Valerie," he said so low she wondered if he knew he'd said the words aloud. "The best I've had in longer than I remember."

"I'm glad," she added. "I feel like we've got a strong plan, and for the first time in years, I seemed to be working toward a goal of more than just existing."

His hand traced her jaw and moved to the lace at her throat, then slowly trailed down the front of her gown, touching the tiny pearl buttons that ran from just below her chin to her waist. There had to be thirty buttons. It might as well have been thirty locks between the two of them.

"What are you doing?" she asked, afraid he'd tell her to lift her gown.

"I'm getting my mind off work by thinking you have way too many buttons to unbutton," he said as his hand stopped moving just between her breasts. "I feel your heart pounding, Valerie. Tell me to stop if you don't want this, but I find I do like touching you."

**Collections by Jodi Thomas, Linda Broday,
Phyliss Miranda, and DeWanna Pace**

GIVE ME A TEXAN

GIVE ME A COWBOY

GIVE ME A TEXAS RANGER

GIVE ME A TEXAS OUTLAW

A TEXAS CHRISTMAS

BE MY TEXAS VALENTINE

Published by Kensington Publishing Corp.

Be My Texas Valentine

JODI THOMAS
LINDA BRODAY
PHYLISS MIRANDA
DEWANNA PACE

ZEBRA BOOKS
KENSINGTON PUBLISHING CORP.
http://www.kensingtonbooks.com

ZEBRA BOOKS are published by

Kensington Publishing Corp.
119 West 40th Street
New York, NY 10018

All Kensington titles, imprints, and distributed lines are available
at special quantity discounts for bulk purchases for sales promo-
tion, premiums, fundraising, educational, or institutional use.

Special book excerpts or customized printings can also be created
to fit specific needs. For details, write or phone the office of the
Kensington Special Sales Manager: Attn. Special Sales Depart-
ment. Kensington Publishing Corp., 119 West 40th Street, New
York, NY 10018. Phone: 1-800-221-2647.

Zebra and the Z logo Reg. U.S. Pat. & TM Off.

ISBN-13: 978-1-4201-1967-1
ISBN-10: 1-4201-1967-2

First Printing: January 2012

10 9 8 7 6 5 4 3 2 1

Printed in the United States of America

Contents

The Valentine's Curse

Jodi Thomas

Chapter 1

February 1867

Broderick Monroe shouldered his saddle and moved across the corral toward the barn. He wore a week's worth of trail dirt sweated into his clothes and hadn't slept in three days or eaten in two. All he wanted to do was make sure his horse had plenty of food and fall into his bunk. After about eight hours' sleep, he'd have enough energy to wash and eat whatever the cook had left over on the stove.

"That you, Brody?" someone yelled from just inside the darkened barn. "I thought you'd make it in before dawn and looks like I was right."

Brody, as everyone in this part of the world called him, didn't answer. In the year he'd been at the Double R, he'd learned to keep quiet. Though it had been almost two years since the War Between the States ended, Southerners in Texas still didn't like the sound of a Yankee working among them. Brody had managed to find a pocket in East Texas where every man he worked with had either fought for the South or lost loved ones in the war. He'd thought of moving on, but it had taken him months to find this job and even the cook's leftovers were better than nothing to eat.

Caleb, the broken-down cowhand who took care of the barn and most of the gear, followed him through the darkness to the tack room. "You know, Brody, I'd clean your tack for you and take care of that devil of a horse you ride. It's part of my job."

"I do my own." He'd learned the hard way a month after he'd arrived and his saddle girth had been cut.

The old man leaned against a bench in the tack room. "Truth be told, I'm surprised you made it back this early. I figured you'd try to avoid this evening if you could, what with the dance and all."

"I finished the job. I plan to sleep through the dance. It's none of my concern." Brody knew that half the time the other cowhands made bets on whether he'd make it back alive. He always drew the worst assignments. If an animal was hurt or dying or crazy with loco weed, he rode out alone. Probably the only reason he hadn't been fired was because he kept more cattle from dying than anyone on the place.

"I knew if anyone could get those cattle out of the canyon, you could. Boss told me he'd already written them off for a loss so any you saved was money in the bank."

"I got eleven out and closed the gap that let them into that tiny canyon with enough rocks to stop any more from wandering in. Had to leave one. She was about to calf." Brody thought that if a storm didn't come in the next few weeks, he'd find time to go back and get her and the calf. He didn't like leaving the cow, but at least she could defend herself and there was enough buffalo grass to eat. The calf would be no match for a coyote, though.

Caleb rolled a cigarette with fingers so busted up they looked to have extra knuckles. "You may not care nothing about people, Brody, but you do seem to like animals, and I can't fault a man for that."

Brody didn't need the old man's praise. He didn't need

anyone. He'd learned a long time ago that an animal, any animal, was more predictable than a human. He'd gone through the war sending his money home to buy a farm, only to find that his sweetheart was living on the place his money had bought with her new husband and had been for almost three years while she wrote him loving letters.

When he'd asked why she didn't wait, she'd said simply that she was just holding on to Brody in letters until someone better came along.

"You best get cleaned up." Caleb had been talking, but Brody hadn't been listening.

"Why?"

"You may think you can sleep, but every man's got to attend. Before the sun sets, this place will be all decorated for Mrs. Molly Clair's annual Valentine's Party. Folks will be riding in from any ranch within thirty miles. Red and white ribbons will be on every pole in the place. Every single gal from fourteen to eighty will be here."

"I'm not interested."

Caleb laughed. "Well, you better get interested. Mrs. Molly Clair says every one of the men on the place including me better be dancing ready because she's not having a girl going home without having worn a blister or two."

Brody walked out of the barn as the sun came up. He had no intention of attending a party. With all that was happening, no one would notice if he slept the night away. No one ever noticed him.

Men were leaving the bunkhouse, heading over to breakfast, as he walked in. A few cowhands had warmed up enough to give him a nod now and then, but most ignored him completely. He thought of grabbing a bite before he turned in, but reconsidered. It wasn't worth the hassle. When he tried to eat with the others, he was always reminded that he wasn't one of them.

The bunkhouse cleared as he propped his boots on

the porch and removed his spurs. He walked to the back of the large quarters and found his bunk in the privacy of a little built-on bay that had once stored wood. It was drafty, cold in winter and hot in summer, but it was away from the others.

Brody stripped down to his long johns and crammed his dirty clothes into an already full bag. All he had left was his go-to-town clothes, a white shirt and black wool trousers. He'd have to wear them to work in if he didn't go into town soon.

Unlike the others, he didn't pay the cook to wash his laundry. The first time he had, the shirts had been ripped and the jeans looked like they'd only been dunked in water once then left to dry in a ball. He'd used his entire first month's pay to buy enough clothes to last until he could have the laundry in town do them. Most hands rode into town on Saturday nights, but Brody picked Monday morning. The boss would have probably said something, but his wife, Mrs. Molly Clair, always had a list of things she needed.

After putting his few belongings away, as he'd been taught in the army, Brody finally tumbled into bed, too exhausted to care about anything beyond the plank walls of his little room.

He didn't know if he'd slept an hour or a dozen, but he awoke with a start when someone kicked his bunk.

"Wake up, Yank." Caleb's voice finally reached Brody's brain. "Mrs. Molly Clair sent me to fetch you. The boss says he's serious about firing anyone who doesn't show up to the dance, and Mrs. Molly Clair thinks she's got a job you can handle."

"Why don't you just tell her you couldn't find me?" Brody grumbled.

"I thought about it. Lord knows no one in this place would miss you." Caleb straightened and scratched his head. "Ever since you doctored her horse that the boss was going to put down, she thinks you're needed about the place. Says you're as good a vet as she's ever seen and the only man around the place who can read her writing and bring back what she needs from town."

"I'm not needed at the dance." Brody sat up and ran his hand through hair so dirty it felt stiff.

Caleb grinned, showing both his teeth. "Oh, yes you are. I heard her say she was going to sit you next to Widow Allen. Nobody likes to talk to her, and she never has two words to say to them that tries. So your job tonight might as well be sitting next to a post."

"What's wrong with the widow? Why doesn't she just sit with the other old women?"

"She ain't old and nothing's the matter with her that I can see from a distance. She's right pretty, and as long as she's in black, no man has to ask her to dance, but Mrs. Molly Clair don't like her sitting all alone."

"Why'd she come?" It crossed Brody's mind that the lady might have dropped by just to irritate him. Everyone else for a hundred miles had already had a turn.

Caleb shrugged. "I'm guessing that daddy of hers made her. She's his only chick so he's wanting the best for her even if she is nearly thirty. Her old man don't believe in the curse surrounding her."

Brody came full awake. "Curse. What curse?" For the first time the lady sounded like she might be interesting. He found it hard to believe that there might be another outcast living in the area besides him.

Caleb followed him to the washroom and watched while Brody pumped water for a bath. "Oh, it's nothing to worry about. I don't believe it myself, though I try not to take chances. You got more lives than a cat, near as I can tell. You'll be fine."

"What curse?" Brody repeated as he stripped and stepped into a cold bath.

"Well, they say a man cuts a month off his life if just her shadow falls across him." The old man's eyes opened wide as he settled, seeming in no hurry to go back to the barn dance. "And if a fellow should be dumb enough to touch her, say shake hands, he might as well saddle up for the doctor because he'll be sick, maybe dead by morning. I've heard several say they got to feeling poorly just passing too close to her place."

"I don't believe in curses," Brody mumbled as he scrubbed his head. In truth, he didn't believe in luck either.

He'd never known anything like luck from the point his parents died when he was fifteen to now. He might as well get cleaned up and go over to the dance so he could court a curse.

Chapter 2

Valerie Allen sat alone on a bench near the back of the barn, waiting for the music to stop. She'd been at the dance almost an hour. Every woman in the place had stopped by to say hello in a polite, not too friendly, kind of way. Not one man had come within ten feet of her. If she even wanted to marry a man at the party, she'd have to introduce herself by mail, because none stepped near. She thought them all cowards for believing rumors whispered about her.

"Not that I care," she whispered to herself, thinking the night was offering poor pickings indeed.

She straightened the pleats on her black widow's dress and tried to smile. If she didn't, she knew she'd break her father's heart. He wanted her to be happy, and for him, happy meant married.

Her papa loved her so much, but he couldn't understand why she always stayed out at her husband's old farm. He told her she was still young, but she knew at almost thirty, her life was set. He claimed there was still time for her to find another, but with each year's passing, she believed him less.

Yet she couldn't move back with her papa. If she did, it

would be like giving up any chance of having her own home. If she moved back to town with her father, she'd be his child until he died; then she'd be that sad old lady who lived on among her parents' things. She needed her own place, no matter how small, her own things no matter how few, her own life, no matter how lonely.

Papa never gave up. He kept talking her into socials like this in hopes she'd find another man willing to take a chance on her. Maybe because the doctor said he had a weak heart, Papa wanted her settled again. He undoubtedly feared he wouldn't be around much longer.

She'd tried marriage twice and didn't know if she could live through burying another husband. She had a place where she could grow her food and raise enough chickens and sheep to earn a little extra money. She milked half a dozen cows and sold to several homes in town. She'd never get rich, or probably even comfortable, but she could survive.

A man walked silently in and took the seat next to her on the bench. For a moment, she didn't move. Out of the corner of her vision, she studied the stranger, who didn't seem to notice her a foot away. He was tall and lean like cowboys got when they worked hard and didn't eat regular meals. His hair looked black, and his face and hands were tanned from years in the sun. She couldn't be sure how old he was, maybe as young as twenty-five, maybe closer to thirty. He seemed to be studying the people more than just watching them dance.

She straightened and continued to act like she hadn't noticed him. Even if she never spoke to the man, she knew one thing about him. He was brave.

On the side of his face nearest her, he had a scar along his cheek and another just above his eye, telling her that he, like most men, had seen the war up close. There was a hardness about him as if all kindness had been beaten out of him years ago.

Finally, he took a deep breath and turned toward her. Midnight blue eyes stared at her with the coldness of one who was looking at an object and not a person. "Good evening," he said in little more than a whisper. "May I offer you a drink, Mrs. Allen?"

He'd been polite, but his conversation skills seemed rusty.

"No, thank you," she answered coldly. "Mister . . ."

He nodded as if knowing it was his turn to talk. "My name's Broderick Monroe but here they call me Brody."

"Which do you prefer?"

He eyed her more carefully as if trying to decide if her question was a trick. "I'll answer to either."

"Well, Mr. Monroe, tell me, who asked you to come over to talk to me?" She looked around the barn, but everyone seemed busy having fun. No one had even looked her direction in a long while. "And don't bother to lie, Mr. Monroe."

To her surprise, he answered, "Mrs. Molly Clair, my boss's wife." He raised an eyebrow as if facing her in a duel. "And, Mrs. Allen, I never lie."

"Please tell Mrs. Molly Clair that I'm happy here watching. I don't need to join the group and I don't need anyone sitting with me. I'm quite used to being alone."

Brody nodded his understanding. "She said if I didn't sit with you or dance that I was fired. If you've no objection, I'd rather sit with you."

"Suit yourself."

They watched for a while, and then he rose and disappeared as silently as he'd come. Valerie shrugged. In truth, she kind of missed his company. The strange man seemed a cut above most of the men there. He hadn't flirted or tried to force conversation.

When he returned carrying two plates of sandwiches with desserts piled on top and two coffee cups, she was surprised.

He sat the plates and cups down between them without looking at her.

"Mr. Monroe, I believe I said I didn't want anything." She was always irritated by men who thought they knew what was best for her.

He glanced up from his plate as if just noticing she was still at the other end of the bench. "I know. They're both for me. I've been out on the range and haven't had anything but hardtack for days." He hesitated. "I don't mind getting you something when you decide you're hungry. If you've no objection, I'd like to continue sitting here for a while."

"Don't you want to dance with a pretty young girl?"

"No." His answer came out cold and solid.

Valerie watched as he finished both plates and all the coffee. "Feel better?" She smiled despite her irritation that he'd obviously been sent to baby-sit her.

He stood, lifting both cups as if to say he needed a refill. He circled behind other people sitting around the fringes of the dance floor and headed to the refreshment table.

A few minutes later, Emma Lee Cooper walked by as if on the way to somewhere and just happened to notice Valerie in her path. "Evening," she said, her smile sweet but uncaring. "I noticed you talking to the Yankee. That's mighty broad-minded of you, seeing as how his kind killed both your husbands."

Valerie looked down at her calloused hands, wishing she'd remembered her gloves, as she answered her childhood friend. "He was just sitting on the other half of the bench." She hated herself for even trying to explain. Emma Lee and her friends would say or think anything they liked; they always had. Sitting beside a Yankee couldn't do her reputation any more damage. "The war's over, Emma Lee. It has been for two years."

"I know, but my Earl says that Brody Monroe is a strange one. Says he never talks to anyone, and even when they play little games on him, he won't fight back or even say anything. Maybe he's a coward and that's how he survived the war." She looked out at the dancers as if bored by her own conversation. "He is good-looking, I guess, in a hard kind of way."

"Maybe." Valerie wanted to defend this man she didn't even know, but she didn't dare. "What kind of games do the men play?"

"Oh, you know, the usual. Passing food around and always making sure the empty plate ends up at him. Sliding a burr under his saddle to make the day start with a wild ride. Always forgetting to tell him when the boss says they can sleep past dawn."

"Earl said after a while they quit just because they could never get a rise out of him. He's like a walking dead man, no emotions, no feelings." She waved at one of the men standing by the small band. "You're probably the only woman here who'd let him get close enough to sit down. My Earl and his brother, Montie, told me they'd knock the guy out if he even tried to ask me or my friends to dance. The Timmons boys are the kind who'll take care of a girl."

Valerie almost said she didn't want that kind of man. She'd had two who'd promised and hadn't.

"Earl Timmons is a thoughtful man and handsome, too," Valerie lied. She had nothing against the man other than he probably had to prime his brain to get it working every morning.

"Yeah, I know." Emma Lee grinned. "He or that brother of his is going to marry me. I just haven't figured out which one. Belle Wallace says she'll take whichever Timmons is left over. She's not picky like me."

Emma Lee must have seen Brody coming, because she darted back the same way she'd come. A moment later the tall cowboy sat down.

"I brought you a refill," he said as he set the cups between them.

"I didn't drink the first one."

"I know." He watched Emma Lee rushing into Earl's arms. "That girl tell you not to talk to me?"

"Yes." She watched him take a drink. "Did someone tell you to stay away from me?"

"Yes," he answered without hesitation. "Pretty much everyone who has talked to me tonight. Even one of the ladies cutting pie asked me how I was feeling, then glanced over at you."

She smiled. She wasn't sure who this man was, but she knew two things about him already. He wasn't afraid of her, and she wasn't afraid of him. She lifted the second cup of coffee and took a sip. "To honesty," she whispered. "Thanks for the refill."

"You're welcome."

When she set the cup down, she asked as she fought down a smile, "How are you feeling, Mr. Monroe?"

"Couldn't be better, Mrs. Allen."

She wished she could say they had a long talk, but they did manage to say a few things to each other. Her father stopped by and seemed pleased that at least one man in the room talked to his daughter. He asked Brody where he was from, and when he said Ohio, her papa nodded and commented that he was from Ireland and he guessed that would be a bit farther away.

Papa rested for a few minutes, then headed out on the floor. He reminded her of someone who saw death coming for him and planned to run as long as he could. The doctor had predicted if he retired and stayed home, he might live five or more years. Her papa had laughed and said he'd take his ticket to heaven when it came and there would be no hiding from it. As she watched him dance, Valerie had to smile. He was making the most of the time he had left, and she wouldn't nag him to slow down.

When the band leader announced the last dance, everyone in the barn hurried onto the floor, knowing there would be no more dancing for months.

Everyone except the two people on a bench in the shadows.

Valerie gathered up her shawl. "I think I'll leave before the rush. Thank you, Mr. Monroe, for the coffee." She almost added, "And the company." Though he hadn't talked, there had been a calmness between them, a simple awareness of another person like themselves in the world.

He stood, followed her into the darkness while everyone shouted as the music started. "I'll walk you to your wagon," he said. "If you've no objection."

"I've no objection." She slowed. When he caught up beside her, Valerie linked her hand at his elbow.

She felt him stiffen and wondered how long it had been since anyone had touched him. Or, she smiled, was it possible this hardened cowboy could believe in a curse? She'd heard what they said about her.

A little girl at the door handed each a paper heart as they passed. Valerie put hers in the pocket of her skirt, and Brody folded his into his vest. Neither wanted them, but they didn't want to hurt the little girl's feelings by tossing them away. Valentines were for children and lovers, not for the likes of them.

Awkwardly, he covered her hand with his and moved through the night to the line of wagons near the corral. A few lanterns glowed between them, offering a night light for children already asleep in the wagon beds.

When they reached her father's big box of a wagon, Brody hesitated and Valerie laughed. "My father is the local carpenter. He thinks he has to take his tools with him everywhere he goes, just in case he's needed. You'd be surprised at how many people bring broken furniture for him to haul home and repair. The dance saved them a trip into town."

Brody looked in the back. "Looks like business is good."

He offered his hand to help her up. "How long have you been a widow, Mrs. Allen?"

"A little over three years." She didn't look at him as she gathered her shawl tightly across her shoulders.

"And you still wear black."

She couldn't tell if it was a statement or a question. "I've little hope to marry again. The black serves me well, even though I doubt I'd have a male caller after all the rumors spread about me."

"You have land. There are some who might ignore the rumors and marry you for it."

Valerie shook her head. "Would you?"

She had the feeling she'd embarrassed him and was glad she couldn't see his face. "I'm sorry. Everyone says I speak my mind too quickly for it to be ladylike. I didn't mean—"

"I'm not the kind of man you'd want," he broke in. "I got nothing to offer any woman."

She recognized the hollowness inside him. Like her, he had nothing to give. He just wanted to live out his days. Maybe like her, he was afraid even to dream.

"Thank you for sitting with me, Mr. Monroe."

On impulse she rose to her tiptoes and planted a light kiss on his cheek. "I wish you peace."

"The same to you, Mrs. Allen." Then he took her hand and helped her up into the wagon. While she waited, he checked the harnesses and made sure the wagon would be ready when her father arrived.

She sat in the darkness listening to the last song and

wishing she were already home. As the barn dance broke up, people spilled out into the night. Couples who'd been dancing together were now hugging as they moved through the shadows whispering farewells. A few families had brought bedding to sleep in the loft, and Mrs. Molly Clair told the single girls they were welcome to spend the night at the house.

She hadn't included Valerie in the invitation. Valerie told herself it was simply because Mrs. Molly Clair knew her papa would pass by her place on his way home. He'd see she was safe and Valerie knew she didn't belong with the young women.

She suddenly felt very old.

She wouldn't have stayed even if she'd had to ride home alone. The women who had once been her classmates and friends were now little more than strangers. She feared they avoided her because, for a girl looking for a man, she was a reminder that happily-ever-after existed only in fairy tales.

Valerie looked in the direction Brody had gone toward the corral. She knew, without thinking why, that he was standing in the night watching her.

Most people were driving toward the road when her father appeared at her side of the wagon. "There you are, my Valerie. I was thinking you'd probably sneak out early. If you don't mind waiting, I got to go to the main house and pick up Mrs. Molly Clair's sewing machine. It won't take me but a few minutes and it'll save coming back out to get it." He must have seen her look, for he added, "Now don't you worry, she's already told two of the men they'll be hauling it out and putting it in my wagon."

"I don't mind waiting." The thought of going into a house full of giggly girls, some only a few years younger than her, frightened her. At times the whole world frightened her. For as long as she could remember, all she'd ever wanted was a home and family of her own, but the goal kept slipping through her fingers like sand.

Suddenly sorrow smothered her and all the what-might-have-beens pushed against her lungs like an anvil's weight on her chest.

She swung down from the wagon and ran into the blackness near the corral. Part of her wanted to dive into the shadows and drown. She wasn't ready for all the rest of her life to simply be just a vase for the keeping of a few memories and the shattered fragments of what might have been.

A strong arm caught her suddenly and swung her around.

She jerked, pulling away for a moment from the man who held her. The outline of a fence and the low sounds of horses circling just beyond registered a moment before the man pulled her against him. "Take it easy," Brody whispered. "You'll startle the horses and get hurt."

Valerie gulped for air. She expected him to let her go, but he stood near, not holding or moving away.

Before she let reason rule her life, she whispered, "Hold me. Just for a minute, please would you mind holding me?"

Strong arms came around her and pulled her so tightly against him she could barely breathe. For a while, he just held her; then he leaned down and kissed her forehead.

She felt herself shaking, but she didn't pull away. She needed, more than air, to have someone hold her like he'd never let her go. She wanted to believe in forever between two people if only for one more moment.

Slowly, his hand moved along her spine, pressing her against the length of him. His warm breath moved in her hair as she leaned her cheek against his throat.

She wasn't sure if they held each other for a few minutes or more, but when she heard her father and a few other men coming, she pulled away and he vanished back into the night as if he'd been no more than smoke.

She was beside the wagon by the time her father opened the back and told the men where to put the machine. All the way home Papa talked as she tried to remember every second she'd had in the darkness with a man she barely knew.

People might not want to have much to do with her, but they all loved visiting with her papa. From making cradles to caskets, he was in their lives, and his favorite thing to do when all the others had gone was to repeat to Valerie everything they'd said to him. So he talked and she remembered as they rolled down the road.

When he was within sight of her farm, he finally said something about her. "You know, Boss told me tonight that he'd buy Venny's place if you want to sell. Couldn't pay much, but it would be cash. Then you could move to town and live with me. I'd build you a little house out back with lots of glass so you could grow a garden year-round." He slowed the horses. "I'd enjoy your company, and a woman shouldn't be living alone way out here."

Valerie had lived at the farm since she married Venny eight years ago, but her father still saw the place as her first husband's. When Venny left for the war after the first year they were married, her father wanted her to come to town. When her first husband had been killed six months later, Papa had tried again but without success. She'd lived alone for three years before Samuel, a doctor serving with Terry's Rangers, was home on leave and asked her to marry him. They'd married a day before he'd left to go back, and he'd laughed, trying to sound like her father as he said she'd have to move to town with him as soon as he returned.

Only his body was all that came home months later and her father talked of her moving back even as he built Samuel's coffin.

"I'm not selling, or moving, Papa." She wished she

could add that she was happy where she was, but they both knew that wasn't true. What her father didn't understand was that she would be no happier in town. At least with all the work of the farm, she was usually too tired to even cry herself to sleep most nights, and when she did, there was no one a room away to hear her sorrow.

As she climbed down, she patted her papa's hand and said, "Thanks for making me go. I enjoyed the music."

"Was everyone nice to you tonight, dear? 'Cause if they weren't, they'll be rocking their babies in shoe boxes and be buried in a blanket when they die."

"Everyone was fine."

"And the cowboy who sat down next to you? He didn't say nothing wrong, did he?"

"No." She thought of adding that he didn't say anything much, but then she remembered the way he held her and decided it best not to talk about him at all.

She went inside her little house and crawled into bed trying to remember exactly how it had felt to be held by someone again.

Chapter 3

Brody Monroe stood in the moonless blackness by the corral for over an hour thinking that if he didn't move, maybe, just maybe he could keep the memory of how Widow Allen had felt in his arms. Wind whirled around the barn as if trying to blow any feelings away.

Finally, he turned and headed to the bunkhouse. Within three steps, he tripped over a downed fence post. Like a tumbleweed, he rolled in the dirt until he hit the barn wall.

Brody swore at himself for being so careless. He was still dusting himself off when he stepped into the bunkhouse five minutes later.

Most of the men were still up talking about the dance. Earl Timmons glanced at him. "See you survived meeting the widow."

Brody nodded once and kept walking.

"Lucky you didn't touch her, Yank, or we'd be picking up the pieces of you. I once heard a fellow say he got a blister the size of a silver dollar on his hand from just pointing at her."

"He wouldn't touch her," one of the men behind Brody commented. "He don't even shake hands if he can help it. The Yank don't have a friendly bone in his body."

Brody kept walking. They didn't need him there to continue talking about him. He pulled off his good clothes and crawled into his bunk. For once, it was a long time before sleep found him.

As the days passed, he tried to stop thinking of the woman he'd met at the dance, but she was never far from his thoughts. In a strange kind of way, she pushed away the loneliness he'd grown so accustomed to. She had a pride about her that he admired. What people said about her didn't seem too important.

She wasn't his, she never would be, but a part of her, for a moment in time, had been his, and one memory was enough to build daydreams on even though he knew there would never be more. It probably would have frightened her to know how few times in his life he'd held a woman. Those experiences had been before the war, and they seemed more a dream than real. After the war the only kind of woman who'd pay a drifter any notice wasn't the kind of woman Brody wanted to hold.

Once, months after the war, he'd found a short job that had left him with money in his pocket. He'd thought about buying a three-dollar whore for the night, but he'd elected to build a supply of food instead. Now, thinking about holding Mrs. Allen, he was glad her memory didn't have to blend with one he'd bought.

He'd overheard someone mention the carpenter and his daughter a few times. Brody knew she lived between the ranch and town, but he had no idea which place. Half the farms looked abandoned. The war had added a layer of poverty over almost every part of Texas, and taxes were drawing away any extra money for repairs. The cattle drives last summer had helped, but it would take years before people got back on their feet.

The next Monday, when he went to town, Brody tried to figure out which farm was her place. A wrong guess could end up getting him shot. Finally, two weeks after the party, Earl Timmons gave him the answer.

As usual, the men were playing cards and talking after supper.

Brody climbed into his bunk at the back and pretended to read a book he'd already read five times while he listened to their talk.

Two of the card players began to speculate on how the boss planned to enlarge his ranch. They talked of first one place bordering Double R land and then another with Brody only half listening until Earl said, "I tell you one place that Boss will never buy and that's Widow Allen's land."

Brody closed the book and made no pretense of reading.

"Why wouldn't he take her place on?" a new cowhand asked. "A widow without a man to run her farm would be easy land to pick up, I'd think."

Earl leaned his chair back and stared at his cards. "Oh, it's a good little farm, but a natural wall of rocks separates her land from the Double R."

Montie Timmons nodded. "Boss likes his property to be as flat as possible for moving big herds."

"Don't matter anyway," Caleb said. "Nothin' getting her off her place. Not even her father can talk her into spending a night away. She's tied to it as sure as if she's a ghost haunting Venny's farm."

"You're right, old man," Earl added. "I remember years ago when Venny courted her. He was ten, maybe twelve years older than her and he didn't waste much time courting before he asked her. She was still more kid than woman, as I remember. He promised her all kinds of things, but the minute he slipped the ring on, it might as well have been a yoke. He never let her off the place. Wouldn't even let her go home to see her papa."

"I remember him. Always thought he was a bull of a

man, big and rough," Montie, as always, added to his brother's rambling. "He told me once he didn't have any family and planned to keep her pregnant until she had an even dozen."

Caleb laid down his cards and collected the pot as he continued the conversation, "That plan didn't work. Five years of trying and not one kid. He left when the war started, knowing if he died, so did his family line."

"He must have ordered her to stay on the farm 'cause folks hardly saw her in town all those years he was gone." Earl frowned at Caleb for winning and dealt another hand. "I swear, after her second husband died, I would have offered for her if it hadn't been for the curse on her."

Caleb wiggled his eyebrows. "She's one fine-looking woman, I'll say that, but the risk is too high. I heard a while back a peddler stopped by her place and barely made it to town without bleeding to death. He claimed all he did was talk to her a minute and something flew out of the sky, nearly splitting his head open like a ripe watermelon."

The new cowhand snorted. "The widow must not be a caring person, 'cause I heard that story in town and the peddler claimed she stood on the porch and stared at him as he left. He said she didn't even offer to help."

"That peddler's nothing but trash if you ask me. Him losing his head wouldn't be any great loss. I doubt I'd help him either," Caleb added. "Boss's wife says he gets a little too friendly with the ladies. She won't even have him on the ranch."

The new cowhand asked the question Brody had been hoping to hear. "How's this widow with a curse manage out there all alone?"

Brody leaned forward so he wouldn't miss the answer.

Earl volunteered, "She's got milk cows and chickens or she would have been starved out long ago. I've seen her with her little specially made wagon, hauling milk and eggs to town. Makes bread, too, and sells it at the mercantile."

The men around the table all agreed that the widow was a hard worker and probably a hard woman.

Brody sat waiting, but the conversation never went back to Widow Allen. The woman he'd held for a moment in the shadows hadn't seemed hard, he thought . . . maybe lonely . . . but not hard.

The next time he headed to town, he spotted a little place with a natural fence of rock about twenty feet high on one side, but he couldn't think of a reason to turn onto the land.

On the first Monday in March, Mrs. Molly Clair sent him to the carpenter to see when her sewing machine would be ready. She was wanting to start sewing again and didn't seem to think threatening clouds should slow Brody down on her mission.

When he found the building the boss's wife had described, which looked half shop and half house, he knew he had the right place, but he wasn't expecting Valerie to answer the door.

She looked as surprised to see him. They just stood staring at each other for a moment, neither having any idea what to say.

"I'm here about Mrs. Molly Clair's machine," he finally got out.

She waved him into the parlor. "My father's had a cold, but he's on the mend."

"I'm glad to hear that," Brody said without really caring. All he wanted to do was stare at her. She was still dressed in black, this dress with far fewer frills than the one she'd had on at the dance. In the shadows of the barn he hadn't noticed that her hair was so light or her eyes were so green.

He'd spent most of that night trying not to look at her for fear she'd tell him to leave.

"If you'll follow me . . ." She turned and moved down a corridor that he guessed led to the living quarters.

"Papa," she called as she stepped into a wide kitchen. "You have a customer."

She looked back at Brody and their gazes met. Neither said a word as they waited. Brody balled his hands into fists, fighting the need to touch her. He'd been thinking about her so much, he didn't care about a curse, even if it was real. He'd risk death if he could just move his fingers down her slim back and pull her close again.

When the carpenter walked in, he apologized for keeping them waiting.

"It's early," was Brody's only answer. "I'm just here about the sewing machine. Mrs. Molly thought I'd have plenty of time to pick it up, if it's ready, and get back before the storm hits."

"I'm not moving as fast as I used to but it's on my next-to-do list." He waved Brody to the table. "Let me offer you some coffee at least for making you wait."

Brody would have turned it down, but he was in no hurry to leave. The idea of being able to look at the widow seemed promising. He nodded and took the chair against the window so he could see Valerie moving about the kitchen.

She had a grace about her and Brody couldn't turn away.

Papa Riley appeared hungry for company. He asked his daughter to get out some of the bread she'd brought him and offered it to Brody.

"My daughter's a fine cook and a hard worker, too," he bragged as if trying to sell her talents.

The loaf could have been made of sand and Brody wouldn't have noticed. He watched her slice off a piece and hand it to him while Papa talked about how he hated getting a cold in early spring when all the weather did was rain.

Brody's fingers covered hers for a moment when he took the bread, and she glanced at him without a smile.

A bell rang from beyond the corridor, and Papa shoved himself up. "I'll get this one, Valerie." He looked at his daughter. "Offer the man more coffee and try not to talk his ear off." He disappeared, laughing at his own joke.

She lifted the pot and refilled Brody's cup without saying a word. The hem of her skirt brushed against his leg. Brody didn't move. He wasn't sure he would have if he'd heard a shot.

He knew this might be his only chance to say anything to her, but he couldn't think of a way to start. Finally, he cleared his throat, fully aware that something might come flying and hit him on the head at any minute. "I pass by your place a few times a week. I could stop by and see if you need anything the next time I make the trip to and from the Double R."

"No, thank you for your kind offer." She said the right words, but they sounded hard somehow as if he'd made her mad by asking.

She moved away as her father entered talking. "Josh Minor's porch blew down last night in the storm. He wants me to get over there and help him shore it up before the whole side of the house collapses. I told him three years ago he should have had me put it up, but he gave that cousin of his the job."

"Why doesn't the cousin come fix it now?" Valerie asked. "You're not over your cold, and it looks like it could start raining at any moment."

"The cousin's too drunk to stand, and stop fretting over me, dear. I'll be fine." He turned to Brody. "Tell Mrs. Molly Clair I'll get her machine out to her the first sunny day."

While the man she called Papa pulled on his coat, Valerie did the same. "I might as well get back, too. If it starts raining, the road will be muddy." A loud clap of thunder rattled the house as if warning her.

Brody followed them out the back door and across to a little barn as drops began to fall. Without a word he helped Papa load enough lumber to do the job, then turned and lifted Valerie into her little buggy made to get milk and eggs to town. It was well built and would keep out most of the rain on her ride home, but he took the time to check the harnesses and found one of the lines twisted. When he handed her the reins, her fingers were freezing, but she didn't look like she wanted to be lectured about wearing gloves. He touched two fingers to his hat in farewell as she hurried away.

After he closed the barn door, Brody circled round the house and collected his mount. From the look of the clouds, he'd be soaked to the bone by the time he got home.

When he saw Valerie's buggy ahead of him on the road, he followed, telling himself they were going the same direction. He could have moved faster and been home in half the time, but he wanted to keep her in sight. If she didn't like it, she could just ignore him, as she'd done most of the time he'd been in her father's kitchen.

By the time they reached open country, her mare acted up every time lightning flashed. Brody caught up to the widow the third time she pulled the buggy to a stop.

"Will you let me help you?" he yelled over the thunder.

She nodded. He didn't miss the fear in her eyes.

Without another word, he tied his horse to the back of the buggy and climbed in beside her.

When she handed him the reins, her palm was bleeding. He frowned at her and took control of the horse. With a strong hand he kept the poorly trained animal in tow while being very much aware of how close the widow sat next to him in the buggy. She was shaking, but he had no idea if it was from fear or the sudden north wind.

Twenty minutes later they were at her place. From the road the house looked plain, almost abandoned, huddled into a rise of rocks, but up close he could tell it was well built and organized. A square house with a wraparound porch and a low roof stood solid against the storm.

He drove the buggy straight into open barn doors and helped her down before taking care of the horse. She just stood, cradling her hand and watching the rain. He thought she might be crying, but somehow she didn't seem like the sort to cry over a cut. She was afraid, he realized.

When he finished, he closed one barn door and latched it against the storm, then lifted her up and ran for the wide back porch. The need to protect her, to shelter her, surprised him as he set her out of the rain.

"I don't need your help." She pushed away and he was almost glad to see anger overrule fear.

"You're hurt."

"I can manage."

He didn't want to fight with her. Just holding her for a few minutes while he ran to the house felt great, but the lady glared at him as if the storm in her gypsy green eyes might be bigger than the one outside. "How about you take care of that hand? I'll close the barn door and see to my mount. I'll be out of your way as soon as the storm breaks."

She didn't look as if she liked being ordered around, so he took the coward's way out and ran. By the time he got back from the barn, he was dripping wet. He hesitated only a moment before opening the back door. If she planned to shoot him, he might as well get it over with.

A fire was raging in an old potbellied stove. She stood, her hair still dripping, at the sink.

He knew he was tracking in mud, but he'd apologize later. Right now he needed to have a look at her cut. When he held out his hand, she laid her palm in his and he felt her tremble.

"It'll be all right, Mrs. Allen."

She shook her head. "I know. It's not the cut, it's the storm. I don't mind the lightning, but I've always hated the sound of thunder."

As he opened her hand, he smiled, thinking she sounded more like a little girl than a full-grown woman. "The cut's long," he said more to himself than her, "but not deep."

She was so still as another roll of thunder rattled the house, it almost frightened him. "You have a medicine box, Mrs. Allen?" he said, hoping to distract her.

She pointed to a box already on the tiny kitchen table.

He led her over to the table and sat down across from her, then opened the box without letting go of her hand. The kit was well supplied with everything he'd need. "If I wrap it correctly, and you don't try to use it much for a few days, I think it'll heal without needing to be stitched up."

"You a doctor?" She sounded more in control now.

"No, my dad was a vet. I followed him around for years, then went one year to college before the war. You're my first human."

She smiled and her whole face lit up for a moment. "How about I moo now and then to make you feel more comfortable?"

"That might help." He looked up, glad to see that her eyes were no longer angry or frightened. Being as gentle as he could, he cleaned the wound and applied salve to keep infection out, then wrapped the hand carefully so the bandage wouldn't wear against her palm.

After a long silence, she asked, "Were you a vet in the war?"

"No." He didn't want to talk about the war. He didn't want to think about what he'd done to stay alive. "They needed soldiers more than they needed vets."

"You shouldn't be here," she said as she pulled her hand away. "It's not proper."

He closed up the medicine and put it back into the box. "I know. I'll wait out the storm in the barn and be gone as soon as it lets up."

She thought for a moment and seemed to change her mind. "I guess you could wait in the kitchen, if you like. I'll get you a towel, and if you stand by the stove, you'll be dry in no time. It is the least I can do to repay you for the doctoring."

He moved to the stove. She brought him a towel and left. Brody wasn't sure what he should do. She offered him the comfort of the kitchen, but she hadn't told him to make himself at home. They both knew how it would look if someone found out that he was in her house, but no one was likely to drop by in the storm.

When she returned, she'd changed into a dry gray dress. Over it she wore a pale gray apron and she'd pulled her hair back with a black piece of ribbon. It occurred to him that she might be trying to hide her beauty and he couldn't help wondering why.

"I forgot to thank you for helping me. My horse often gets—"

"The horse needs training."

"I know." She smiled. "So does the driver. For years I had an old mare who knew the way back and forth to town. All I had to do was ride along."

"I could teach you. It's not hard. You could come over to the Double R some Sunday and I could show you how to work with the horse."

She looked down and he feared he'd been too bold.

He didn't feel right being alone in her house with her, and he guessed she felt the same. "I'm about dry," he lied. "I thought I'd sit on the porch and watch the storm die. Sometimes it's a beautiful sight."

She seemed to like the idea. "I'll get a couple of quilts and join you."

It wasn't all that cold to Brody, but he thanked her for the quilt and held the door as she stepped onto the porch. The western sky put on a show as they watched, and he couldn't help wondering what it would be like to sit there and watch the sunset some night.

They didn't talk as they watched the thunderstorm play itself out. He felt her jump a few times when the thunder rolled, and he wished they'd been close enough that she'd let him put his arm around her.

When the first touch of blue sky showed through, Brody knew it was time for him to go.

He moved to the steps and turned. She was so close behind him he almost bumped into her. "Thanks for letting me stay awhile." He watched her, trying to memorize exactly what she looked like. "I know you don't want a man around and I'm not anyone a woman would consider seeing. I understand that, but if you're agreeable, I'd like to hug you good-bye. Then I promise I'll never bother you again."

He thought she was going to turn away, but she finally took a step toward him and he closed the rest of the distance between them. He held her as he had that night after the dance and she felt so good in his arms. She was a woman he could dream about, but someone like her would never belong to him.

Without a word, he turned to leave.

"Mr. Monroe," she stopped him. "How do you like working for Boss Ramsey?"

The question surprised him, but he answered, "It's a job. I figure in five, maybe six years I'll have enough saved to buy a place. Somewhere like this away from people, where I can live in peace. As long as there is hope of that, I can put up with anything."

She looked up at him as if weighing his worth by the pound. "Mrs. Molly Clair says you're a good hand. Maybe one of the best Boss has ever hired, but you don't mix with people. That true?"

He nodded. "I don't know about the first part, but she's right about me being a loner."

"If you had my place, what would you do with it?"

He thought she must be as starved for conversation as he, so he answered, "I'd farm that spot by the road. If you planted grain, you could harvest enough to have a good cash crop by fall. Along the back, where it looks rocky, you could run a few head of cattle, or sheep."

"Which would you run?"

"Cattle probably. There looks like enough grass to fatten them up then mix them in with a passing trail drive. With the price of beef, you could double your money in a year."

"How many could you keep up with and still farm the front?" She stared at him directly as if truly needing to know.

"You want me to work for you?" Brody raised an eyebrow. No one since the war had offered him work he hadn't had to fight to get. Working for her would mean long days, but it just might bring him a bit of the peace he'd been longing for since the war.

"No." She held herself very still. "I'm offering you a partnership that would include marriage. We'll live together here for a year. After that, if we don't get along, I'll move to town. I will remain your wife if you've no objections, but we'll live our lives out just as we'd both planned to, alone. I'll ask nothing from you but your name and expect nothing in return except for a share of the profits from this place if there ever are any."

"But I have nothing to offer in this deal. In a year I've only managed to save a couple hundred dollars."

"Of course you do, Mr. Monroe. You offer your work,

your knowledge, and we may need that money you've saved to buy the cows." She pressed her lips together and added, "If you live, you'll offer me acceptance in the community, and if you don't, I doubt I could be much worse off."

"You want to marry me to get rid of some stupid curse?"

"No, I want to marry you because you, not me, might make this farm pay. All I want to do is be able to live without people staring at me."

He still didn't believe her. "Why me?"

"You're smart. You're a hard worker. You treat me with respect, and you're not afraid of me. In other words, you'll do." She offered her unbandaged hand. "Do we have a deal, Mr. Monroe?"

She had no idea how badly she'd hurt him by saying *he'd do,* but she was offering him a chance at a dream and he'd be a fool if he didn't take it. "It's a deal."

They stood for a few minutes, each lost in their own thoughts. Brody looked out over the land and thought half of this spread was more than he'd ever hoped for. Since he'd been a kid and lost his home when his parents died, all he'd ever hoped to have was a piece of land. She was offering him so much more. A year. She said she'd stay with him a year. And for that time he'd have the closest thing to a home and family that he'd had in almost fifteen years.

She moved to the back door of her place. "You might as well come in, Mr. Monroe. I'll fix you some lunch while we talk. We've a great many plans to make before this deal is done."

He followed her in, looking at everything in a different light. She made him a simple meal that beat anything he'd had at the Double R. He made a list of all that needed doing. Now that they'd made up their minds, there was no sense in waiting. It was already time to get the ground ready to plant.

When she saw his empty plate, she laughed.

"I'll be fatter than the cows by fall if you always cook like that, Mrs. Allen."

"You could carry a little more weight. Once I know what you like, I'll adjust my baking schedule."

"I like everything," he answered, "except grits. That's all that was usually left over in the main kitchen."

"I'll never cook grits."

As simple as that, they began a pact. When the sun came out, Brody walked the land making notes of all he'd have to do to make this a productive farm. The buildings were in good shape, but the fences had been neglected. He'd use some of his money to buy supplies for fencing first, before he bought cattle.

As he walked around, he slipped twice on the muddy ground and knew he'd be sore for a few days but that didn't matter. By taking the bargain the widow offered, he'd be working his own land.

When he finally made it back to the house, she was waiting on the porch. They rode into town and were married by the preacher with her papa and the preacher's wife as the only wedding guests.

When the preacher told Brody to kiss the bride, he kissed her as he had the first night in the darkness. Only this time, his lips brushed over her lips as lightly as they'd touched her forehead before.

She smiled up at him, looking as unsure about this rash thing they'd just done as he felt.

At the bank she had his name put on the deed to her land as well as all her accounts in town, and he deposited his money into what had been her account. Most of the people were speechless to see the widow with a third husband. A few even mumbled that they'd be attending a funeral soon.

"Promise me you'll try your best to stay around," she whispered.

"I'll do my best," he said as he tried his best not to limp from the fall he'd suffered a few hours before. If he could make it through the war, surely he could survive marriage.

The sun was touching the horizon when he headed over to the Double R to pick up his gear. Boss and Mrs. Molly Clair were eating supper when he knocked. The boss looked angry to be bothered, and when Brody explained that he was leaving, Boss Ramsey looked downright mad.

Mrs. Molly Clair seemed pleased and promised them a wedding gift.

Brody collected his things and rode out. He'd planned to say good-bye to Caleb, but all the men were eating, so he just loaded all he owned on the back of his saddle and rode away. So few of the cowboys ever talked to him, he didn't figure they'd miss him much.

For the first time in years he couldn't wait to see what the next day brought. It didn't matter that Valerie thought he was just a *you'll do* husband; he planned to do his best to make the place something they'd both be proud of.

Chapter 4

When he rode in, Brody saw his new wife in the kitchen window. They might have signed the papers, but he didn't feel an ounce's worth of married. She was still very much a stranger to him.

He put his horse in the barn and spent an hour putting all the tools in order and adding things that needed doing to his now long list. She might keep a good house but it was obvious she spent only minimum time in the barn. The milk cows' stalls were clean but most of the leather gear in the place looked like it had never been cleaned or oiled. That might explain why the reins had cut her hand.

When he stepped on a shovel and hit himself in the knee with the handle, he thought the blade rusty until he turned it to the light and saw what looked like dried blood. Some animal, or someone, had been hit hard, and whoever swung the shovel hadn't bothered to clean the blade. If the tool had been used by his wife, he decided she probably had good reason.

Brody blew out the lantern and stood at the barn door looking toward the house. He realized he knew few facts about this woman he now shared half of everything with. One thing he was sure of, she needed him. If she could have done it on her own, he knew she would have, but she'd been just surviving. Without help, ten years from now she'd still be delivering milk and eggs in town to try to make a living. By marrying him, she was giving herself a chance for more. And, he decided, she was giving him a chance at life, maybe the first one he'd ever really had. No matter what happened, for that he'd be grateful.

He'd do his best to always be kind to her. It didn't matter how hard the work was, this place, this life promised to be better than any he'd had. Just watching her move, he decided, gave him more pleasure than he'd had in years.

When he walked into the kitchen, everything was in order as if closed up for the night. Brody wasn't sure what to do. He'd never gone deeper into the house, and he wasn't certain he should without an invitation.

"Valerie?" he said her name for the first time.

"Yes," she answered as she appeared in the doorway.

He stared at her. She had on a long midnight blue robe over a white nightgown, and her hair was down, touching just past her waist. He finally said the first thing that seemed reasonable. "Where do I put my things?"

She moved across the kitchen and picked up the lantern. "Follow me."

They crossed through a parlor, well organized and clean. He looked to his left and saw a small study with a desk and one chair. Behind the desk was a whole wall of books. He couldn't help stopping and staring.

She waited. "You like to read?"

"I do." He took a step in, wanting to make sure all the books were real.

"My father never knew what to buy me for Christmas or my birthday after my mother died when I was eight, so he always bought me books. They've become my treasures. This winter, when there's not much to do, you're welcome to read any you like."

"Thanks."

"In fact, please consider this little study yours. I've noticed you writing things down. If you like, I'll get you more paper and a ledger to keep here on your desk."

"I'd like that." He brushed his hand over what she'd called *his desk.*

He would have said more, but she moved on as she said, "Now, as to where to put your things."

She led him to a bedroom with a double bed, a wardrobe, and a dresser. This room, like the parlor, looked almost too bare to be lived in. No pictures or needlework on the walls. No keepsakes sitting on the dresser. Every surface had lace across it, but the room seemed colorless. It reminded him of her dressed in black, very proper but without warmth.

"There's a washroom just beyond with a few pegs if you want to use them. I cleaned out half the dresser and half the wardrobe for your things, but if you need more, we could put more shelves in the washroom."

He could see a basket of what looked like her things by the door. "I only need a few drawers of the dresser and none of the wardrobe. The laundry in town always folds all my clothes."

"If that's the way you like them, I'm fine with it." She pulled out her brush from the top drawer and walked to the window as if she could see something out in the night. "There is no lock on the washroom door. I hope we can both respect each other's privacy. It wouldn't be proper to ever see one's spouse undressed. Since we've only one bedroom, I think we should both use the washroom for changing."

"Agreed."

Brody realized he'd have to cross her bedroom to get to the washroom. "Where do I sleep?" He'd seen all the rooms, and none looked big enough to add another bed.

"With me," she answered without looking at him. "You are my husband." She began braiding her hair without facing him.

About ten thousand questions popped in his thoughts, but he decided it might be wise to keep quiet. He moved to the washroom and closed the door. This had all happened so fast he hadn't had time to think about more than the farm. Not that he hadn't thought of sleeping with her someday, but she seemed to think they could sleep together without ever seeing each other. All he could figure out was maybe she meant just sleep.

When he washed and stripped down to his long johns, he opened the door to the bedroom to find her already in bed.

"You don't wear a nightshirt?" she whispered as she turned toward him.

"No," he answered, wondering if he should offer to start.

He slowly moved to the other side and slipped beneath the covers, and then he lay on his back and tried to think of something to say. He felt like he'd stepped into a game of chess covered in black velvet. He not only didn't know where to move, he didn't even know where the pieces were on the board.

Finally, she said in little more than a whisper, "I've been a wife twice before. I know what to expect and I understand men have needs. I ask that you never embarrass me by going to another woman's bed."

"I wouldn't do that," he answered. "No matter what is or isn't between us, I swear I'd never do that."

He saw her nod. After a long pause, she added, "All you have to do is tell me to lift my gown and I will without protest, but try not to touch me any more than necessary and please move away so I can lower my gown when you are finished. I'll try not to make a sound and I ask that you do the same."

Turning slightly, he looked at her outline beside him.

He'd never been married, but he had a feeling this wasn't quite right. Maybe it was because they hadn't taken the time to court. He thought of following orders, but Brody had spent his life following orders. If he was going to be an equal partner, it was time to start. He might as well know all her rules tonight. "If I touch you like that, Valerie, there is the possibility of children."

"I think not. I've been through mating several times. My first husband insisted on it once a week and he would tolerate no protest. The second husband did it to me both nights after we were married. I think the chances are good I'll never have children. My mother was forty before she had me." He could tell she was nervous, and he thought he heard a touch of fear in her voice.

She'd always been honest with him, and he hoped she would be now. "Did you love your husbands?"

"That didn't seem important, but no." She was silent for a moment, then added, "Have you ever loved anyone?"

"I thought I did once." He rolled on his side toward her. "Why don't we start the partnership out by being friends? Real friends. The kind of friends who trust one another."

She turned her face and he saw her smile in the moonlight. He lifted his arm. "How about hugging me? After having a couple of your hugs, lady, I find I've grown accustomed to them."

Slowly, she came up against him.

"Is that so bad?"

He felt her shake her head. "No," she answered. "It's nice, I think."

"Now," he said as he moved his fingers over her hair. "Go to sleep. We've got a full day tomorrow."

She let out a long breath, but he knew she took a long time relaxing against him. When she finally did, he tugged her closer and smiled, liking the feel of her so near more than he'd liked anything in a long time.

Chapter 5

Just before dawn Valerie woke and cuddled against the warmth of a man's body beside her. For a moment she didn't want to wake; then she realized she was in bed with Brody Monroe. Yesterday the rain must have made her crazy. Somehow the heavens' opening up washed out all the emotion she'd been banking for years and all she wanted was someone to be with, someone to count on, someone to trust.

Holding her breath, she climbed out of bed and tiptoed to the kitchen, carrying her robe and slippers with her. As she dressed and started the fire, she thought of how insane she'd been yesterday to offer him marriage. He would have come to work for her if she'd asked; maybe he would have even waited to be paid until fall. She had nothing against the man, he seemed polite and strong, but she couldn't believe she'd married him.

Maybe she was just tired of being out here alone, or maybe she hated seeing every man in town cross the street when they saw her coming. When she'd seen him being treated pretty much the same way by everyone, she felt somehow kin to him. Or, she reconsidered, maybe she was just tired of talking to herself and the cows.

As she started breakfast, the realization that she'd slept with him settled into her mind. She'd slept with him and he hadn't lifted her gown like the other two husbands had. Maybe there was something wrong with him.

As she pulled the biscuits out of the oven, she looked up and saw him standing, fully dressed, in the doorway. This new husband of hers wasn't handsome, not with his sharp features and hauntingly dark eyes. There seemed nothing soft about him, nothing flexible. Yet he'd held her gently last night, almost as if he could protect her from the world.

"Morning." He smiled slightly. "Did you sleep all right?"

"Fine." She blushed, remembering the feel of his body next to hers. "Have a seat. Breakfast is almost ready."

He sat watching her as she brought everything to the table, and then he stood halfway up as she took her seat. They ate in silence, neither seeming to feel any need to force conversation.

He stood and reached for his hat. "That was a grand breakfast. You're a good cook, Valerie."

"Thank you," she said, following him to the door. She couldn't help wondering how bad the cooks he knew in the past were if he considered her good.

He turned toward her as he took one step onto the porch. "There's a few things you need to know. I'll work until the sun's straight up, then I'll come in if I've time. I don't expect a meal on the table, but would appreciate it if you'd leave bread where I can find it. That and buttermilk is more than I usually have at midday. Or I like coffee if it's cold. I will come in by dark and I'll be hungry. If I'm later than you like to eat, just leave the food on the stove. I'll find it."

"Fair enough." She smiled. "Only supper will always be when you get in. No matter how late, I'll wait and eat when you do."

"And one more thing," he added slowly. "I expect to kiss my wife before I leave every morning, so if you've any objections, you should voice them now."

She didn't say a word as they stepped out on the porch. After putting on his hat, Brody leaned over and touched his lips to hers. Valerie told herself a kiss from a man she barely knew was not something she welcomed yet, but if it was important enough for him to mention, she would tolerate it without complaint.

To her surprise, Brody's kiss was more than tolerable.

Laughter sounded from several feet away, making them both jump. She took a step back and Brody moved in front of her. Protecting her again, she thought. The morning sun was in her eyes, but she saw two men on horseback coming toward them.

"Hell, Montie," one said, "I told you it was true. The widow married and looks like husband number three survived the night."

Earl Timmons's brother shook his head and added, "I was betting we'd find him dead."

She backed away, not wanting to hear what the Timmons brothers had to say. Emma Lee Cooper might want to marry one of the cowboys, but Valerie didn't even want to talk to them, much less have them on her land. They'd always treated her like a thing and not a person, even talking about her as if she couldn't hear them.

Glancing at Brody, she saw the fire in his eyes, but his voice was calm. "Other than to check on my health, what are you two doing off Double R land?" He didn't sound angry, but she noticed he'd moved his right hand to the butt of his Colt.

She didn't think he'd draw on them, but for the first time she saw the soldier he'd been, always on the ready, and wondered if the Timmons boys were smart enough to be aware.

The brothers urged their horses closer. "Boss told us to bring those half-dozen mavericks you've been taking care of over here. He says they'll just die if he turns them out, and maybe you'd take them off his hands."

Valerie looked past the man to six calves between her place and the road. The cowboys hadn't been wrong; the cattle already looked near death. Not one had enough meat on its body to make a stew.

"I'll take care of them," Brody said. "Thanks for bringing them over." He reached behind him and took Valerie's hand, tugging her forward with a firm grip. "And when you see my wife again, call her Mrs. Monroe, not the widow."

Valerie expected the cowboys to argue, but they didn't. They might not like Brody, but it was obvious they respected him. Both touched their hats and rode away.

"What are you going to do with them?" She pointed at the calves.

"Those cows you milk have extra every morning?"

"They usually do. The barn cats are getting so fat they can barely walk."

"Well, it's past dawn, we need to start milking." He held her hand all the way to the barn as he explained how he planned to get the six mavericks healthy enough to be feeding off the grass along the rocky side of her land before summer.

As they worked, she learned a great deal about her new husband. He knew little about milking a cow, but he tried.

Almost finished, she heard a noise and turned to see him spread out on the barn floor a few feet behind one of the cows. "Brody?"

He didn't move.

"Brody? Brody!" She was up and running. He looked like he'd been struck dead on the spot.

Picking up his head, she shook him. "If you die on me, Broderick, I swear I'll never, ever forgive you."

To her relief, he groaned and moved his head. When he pushed his hair off his forehead, she saw the beginning of a huge bruise.

"I'm all right." He sat up. "I didn't know milk cows kicked so hard."

She didn't know whether to hit him for being so careless or hug him. Anger took over as she stood. "How dare you scare me like that! Can't you be more careful?" She put her fists on her hips and glared at him. "If you die on me, I swear I'll haunt you into the next life and make your eternal days miserable."

He broke out laughing. When he folded over still laughing, she couldn't stay mad at him. Dropping to her knees, she joined him.

When they both lay on the barn floor exhausted, he smiled at her. "Even with the kick in the head, it's a good day to be alive, wife."

She agreed and they helped each other up.

When she carried the last of the milk to the house, she saw him moving the calves one by one into a small corral beside the barn.

All morning, she watched him working, first with the calves, then cleaning the barn and repairing the corral. When he didn't stop at noon, she carried bread and buttermilk out to him. He thanked her but barely took time to eat.

That evening he looked tired as he washed at the sink in the kitchen, then sat down to eat.

"I washed your clothes," she said halfway through the meal when he hadn't said a word.

"Thank you."

"You don't have to keep thanking me for doing things," she said. "I'm just doing my part. Tomorrow I'll go into town with my milk and eggs. Do you need me to pick up anything for you?"

He shook his head. When he'd finished eating, he helped her do the dishes, then brought in firewood as she went to dress for bed. She returned to bank the fire and it was his turn to change.

She stayed in the kitchen for as long as she could, not wanting to interrupt him. When she finally blew out the light and moved through the dark house to the bedroom, she was surprised to find him standing in the dark staring out the window.

"Are you all right?" She moved to his side and brushed her fingers over the knot on his forehead.

He caught her hand and held it for a moment before letting her go. "I was just thinking of all that needs to be done. I'll ride in with you in the morning and pick up seed. It may be a week before I'll have the field ready, but I'll want the seeds when I do."

"Stop thinking about work, husband, and come to bed." He'd worked twice as hard as she had today and she was exhausted. She moved to her side of the bed and climbed in. He did the same.

He lifted his arm and she lay an inch away from him. After a few minutes he shifted to face her and touched her cheek with his hand. "It was a good day, Valerie," he said so low she wondered if he knew he'd said the words aloud. "The best I've had in longer than I remember."

"I'm glad," she added. "I feel like we've got a strong plan, and for the first time in years, I seemed to be working toward a goal of more than just existing."

His hand traced her jaw and moved to the lace at her throat, then slowly trailed down the front of her gown, touching the tiny pearl buttons that ran from just below her chin to her waist. There had to be thirty buttons. It might as well have been thirty locks between the two of them.

"What are you doing?" she asked, afraid he'd tell her to lift her gown.

"I'm getting my mind off work by thinking you have way too many buttons to unbutton," he said as his hand stopped moving just between her breasts. "I feel your heart pounding, Valerie. Tell me to stop if you don't want this, but I find I do like touching you."

"No."

He straightened and moved his hand away. "No, you don't want this, or no, don't stop?"

"No, I won't tell you to stop. You have a right."

He sat up. "What are you afraid of? That I'll hurt you? That I'll force you? I don't want to do something just because you think I have a right to. All day I thought about being here with you and if it was possible that you might just want to be here with me."

She didn't answer for a long time and he remained stone. Finally, she spoke her mind. "I'm afraid if I'm not the proper wife, you'll leave me."

Brody fell back on the bed so fast he bumped his head, almost cracking the headboard. After a few swear words, he sat back up again. "Let's get something straight. I'm not going to hurt you or force you or leave you. I would like to sleep next to you, but if it bothers you, I'll be fine in the barn."

She nodded and wondered if he could see her in the dark. "All right. I'd like you to stay here, with me, and if you want to touch me now and then, I wouldn't mind." She knew she didn't sound sure of anything, but it was the best she could offer.

After a while, he slid back down beside her. "Why on earth would you think I'd leave? Being here, working for myself, makes me feel alive, and touching you just now and then is more than I'd ever dreamed of asking for. But much as I like it, I don't want you letting me if you're just doing it because you think it's your duty."

She wanted to ask Brody a dozen whys, but she didn't.

The memory of her first husband came to mind. This had been his place, and he'd been fifteen years older than her when they married. He'd always made her feel like she was visiting in his house, even yelling if she moved anything. He'd made her feel like she'd married up when she'd found him and she should always be grateful. With each month's passing he seemed angrier at her because she didn't get pregnant. By the end of their first year they were no longer talking. He just gave orders and yelled complaints while she grew silent.

When he left for the war, the last thing he'd said to her was not to change anything on his farm. She'd waited a year after they notified her he'd died before she even put away his clothes. She'd never cried for Venny or for Samuel five years later.

Yet a tear rolled down her cheek at the possibility that she might have been treating Brody as a visitor in what was now half his house. He hadn't started this, and he hadn't asked for much.

Silently, she moved until they touched. As always, she felt him stiffen at the contact for that first moment. "Hold me," she whispered, "until I fall asleep. Not because you should, but only if you want to."

His arm tightened around her. "I'm not leaving," he answered and kissed the top of her head. "We'll figure this out somehow." His hand moved comfortingly along her shoulder.

She didn't answer, but ten minutes later when she knew he was asleep, she reached up and unbuttoned a few buttons at her neck.

Chapter 6

The next morning Brody woke Valerie up after he'd dressed. Dawn was just coming into their room as he stood over her. Strands of her braid had come free, and as he moved her hair from her face, she opened sleepy eyes.

"Morning, beautiful," he said.

"Morning." She stretched.

He fought the urge to trace his hand over the outline of her body as the cotton molded against her skin. Several times in the night he'd reached to touch her lightly, tucking her arm under the cover, shifting her against his shoulder, and one time letting his hand rest atop her hip. Once, she'd rolled slightly toward him, pressing her breast against his side. He'd kissed her lightly on her sleeping mouth, and he swore she'd made a little sound of pleasure.

"I'll milk the cows while you get dressed and fix breakfast. Then we'll be ready to leave for town." He noticed that the collar of her nightgown was open and wished he'd been brave enough to talk about how it had felt to have her beside him all night.

"Be careful," she ordered, cuddling back into the covers. "Watch out for the cows."

He laughed. "If you hear a shot, you'll know you have one less cow."

An hour later, as he helped her into the buggy, he kissed her lightly on the mouth and said, "You taste like pancakes."

She straightened to her very proper self. "I don't know why. You're the one who ate them all."

He climbed in beside her, patting her leg resting next to his as though he'd touched her there a hundred times. When she didn't move away, he flicked the reins to start the buggy moving and let his hand rest on her knee. The feel of her, the knowledge that she didn't mind, made him half drunk with need. "How's your hand?"

"The cut closed fast. Only the puffiness remains. How's your head?"

"Nothing but a blue mark." He settled, letting his leg press against hers. They might not talk, but in a strange way, they were communicating.

They were almost to the trading post when he broke the silence. "I want you to buy yourself a good pair of gloves."

"I don't—"

"You need them." He could tell she was planning to argue, so he added, "End of discussion."

"All right, but while you go to the grain store, I'd like to visit with my father."

"We need to get back as soon as possible. It's only been two days since—"

"I'm stopping by his place." She met his gaze. "End of discussion."

They both laughed as they pulled to a stop, drawing the attention of several people. Brody was used to people frowning and looking away when he scanned a crowd, but today a few met his stare and one lady he remembered seeing at the dance even smiled at him.

In the trading post, most of the talk was about rustlers

moving into the territory. Times were hard and there were those who took what they wanted. The war had left too many men wounded in more than just body; some seemed stained all the way to their souls. After five years of fighting they didn't much care about anything but themselves and staying alive. To add trouble, the Indian Wars were raging to the north and rustlers were running the border.

Brody had a pair of Colts and a rifle, but he hadn't noticed any weapons at the farm. While Valerie was busy picking up supplies, he slid in ammunition and another rifle to the pile she was collecting.

The store owner noticed and gave a slight nod. "Better safe than sorry," he mumbled and moved around next to Brody. "I've been meaning to ask you, Yank, how have you been feeling lately?"

Brody thought for a moment that maybe the bump on his forehead, or the one in back from hitting the headboard, might be showing. "I'm fine," he answered a bit too quickly.

"No fever. Not feeling sickly?" The store owner pushed. "Folks been asking. After all, you've been married going on three days."

Brody knew people were waiting for the widow's curse to kick in. "No, I've never been better." Despite the bruises over a few falls lately, he'd answered honestly.

The store owner looked like he believed him. "Well, I'm glad to hear it, but if you do get to feeling bad, you get right to a doc, you hear."

Half an hour later, Brody was still thinking about how folks were just waiting for him to pass away any moment when the blacksmith asked him how he was doing.

"Fine, Parker," Brody answered. He'd known the big man for over a year, but Parker had never asked about his health.

"Here you go." The blacksmith passed him an old horseshoe. "You might hang this over the barn door. They say it's good luck. Might keep away a curse. Make sure you turn it upward to catch the luck."

"I'll do that." Brody frowned. "What's the odds on me over at the saloon?"

The blacksmith shrugged, seeing no problem in telling the truth. "Two to one you'll be dead in a week."

Brody pulled out a twenty-dollar gold piece he'd been keeping for emergencies. "Place a bet for me, would you?"

"Which way?" Parker grinned.

Brody smiled. "That I'll make the week. If I don't, I won't need the money, and if I do, I'll have tripled my investment."

The blacksmith smiled. "I like your way of thinking, Yank. You know, if you limped when you walked back to your buggy, you might get better odds."

Brody didn't know whether to laugh or get worried. There was something unsettling about people betting on when he'd die and he'd been concentrating on not limping all morning thanks to yesterday's fall. Everything from the cow kicking him in the head to him slipping on the muddy ground when he walked the land could all be just accidents.

By the time he picked up grain and drove over to get Valerie, two more people had stopped to ask how he was feeling.

He said hello to her father, but couldn't think of much to add. The old guy wanted to see her married, but Brody had a feeling Papa thought he'd be involved in the husband picking.

As soon as Brody walked with Valerie off the porch, he slipped his arm around her waist. "I missed you," he said and was surprised at how much he meant it.

He would have kissed her when he lifted her into the buggy, but several people were standing on the road looking like they were waiting for a parade.

Brody growled low in his throat and moved in beside his wife.

"What's wrong?" she whispered as she waved at a few of the small groups out walking.

"I wanted to kiss you," he answered.

"Of course, dear," she answered with a pat of her hand. "As soon as we're alone. It wouldn't be proper in public."

He slapped the reins and moved through town at what some were probably predicting was a reckless speed. There would be bets at the saloon tonight on how he'd die.

Valerie talked about a book her father told her he was reading, but Brody barely listened.

As soon as the town disappeared from view, Brody pulled the buggy to a stop. "How about now?" His words were not as forceful as they should have been.

"How about what?"

He looped the reins. "How about you kissing me? We're alone." He cleared his throat, forcing back what sounded like an order. "I mean, if you've no objection."

She hesitated, then lifted that perfect chin of hers. "Well, all right, though I don't think the middle of a road is the place for such things."

"I don't care," he whispered as she put her gloved hands on his shoulders and leaned forward.

When her lips touched his, everything else vanished. Her mouth was soft and hesitant. He felt laughter against his lips as if she thought herself wicked for giving in to such things in broad daylight.

He circled her with one arm and pulled her against him, loving the feel of her next to him. When she didn't pull away, he opened his mouth and took control of the kiss. He felt her shiver as his hand moved up and held her head just right so that he could take his time tasting her lips.

He never dreamed a woman could taste so good. He was becoming addicted to his wife. He told himself it was just all the years of being alone, but he knew it was more, far more. He didn't just want a woman; he wanted her. Just her, like this in his arms, kissing him back.

When she broke the kiss, she leaned against his chest, breathing rapidly. He held her gently, brushing his hand slowly over her back.

"That was . . ." she whispered, then took several breaths.

"I know," he answered, cupping her face in his hands. The hunger to taste her again was already building in him. "I could get used to kissing you."

She smiled shyly and stretched toward him.

A wagon rattled along the road in front of them. For a moment they both just watched it grow near.

When she finally pulled away and straightened her clothes, he whispered, "I wouldn't mind if you want to kiss me again like that sometime in the near future."

"I'll remember that," she answered.

The couple in the wagon waved as they passed, and Brody took the reins. He didn't say anything the rest of the way home, but he thought he was going to have a heart attack when Valerie's hand reached over and patted his leg.

This woman who wanted as little contact as possible was changing, and he wasn't sure he'd be man enough to handle her soon.

All day, as he worked, he thought about her. She'd had so much sadness in her life, maybe she thought she had to ration feelings. She might never love him, but he believed he could make her want him, and if she wanted him, that would be enough. He was just the first man who came along she thought would risk stepping over the curse to be with her, and in truth, he wasn't really living anyway before he sat down on that bench at the dance.

He finished up work an hour before sunset. They ate supper and sat out on the porch as night came on. Their nearest neighbor rode past and yelled hello. To Brody's surprise, he turned in and asked how they were doing. He said his wife had made a pie and told him to take it over to the newlyweds.

Brody had seen the man several times, but had never spoken to him. Suddenly, the farmer was talkative. When Valerie went in to get plates and forks, the farmer asked how Brody was feeling.

"Fine."

The farmer offered him a two-headed coin. "Keep this in your pocket at all times. It'll bring you luck."

Brody didn't want to go into the fact that he didn't believe in luck or curses. He just thanked the man. When Valerie returned, they ate the pie on the steps; then she said good night to the gentlemen as if she thought they'd want to discuss important matters.

All Brody wanted to do was go to bed with his wife.

The farmer sat around talking about crops and tricks he used when planting for another half hour before climbing on his horse and heading back across the road.

Brody knew Valerie would be in bed, probably already asleep by the time he cleaned up and joined her. It didn't matter; as long as he could hold her, it would be a perfect ending to the day. All the years of having no one to hold drifted away at just the thought of her. He'd never known himself to miss such a thing, but now, he knew he'd miss her beside him the rest of his life if they separated.

She rolled toward him as he stretched his arm out. "You asleep?" he whispered.

"No," she answered.

"Mind if I kiss you good night?"

"No." She sounded sleepy.

He rolled toward her, pressing her lightly into the pillows as his mouth found hers. He'd meant to kiss her softly, but when he tasted her, he couldn't hold back. Her mouth opened, and he was lost in one wonderful kiss. The feel of her breathing beneath him almost drove him mad. He pressed just a little more, letting her take some of his weight.

When he finally pulled an inch away, he whispered against her cheek, "You weren't asleep at all." She'd been fully awake and waiting for him. The knowledge made him proud.

"I'd like another kiss, please," she whispered. "If you've no objection to losing a few moments' sleep. I find I rather enjoy the feel of your lips on mine."

"You can have the night, if you want it." His hand slid along her throat as he kissed her tenderly. The collar of her gown fell away and he kissed down her neck, loving the softness of her skin and knowing the open buttons were her silent gift to him. He wanted more, much more. He wanted his wife, but reason told him to move slowly. After one more kiss, he lay on his back and settled her head on his chest.

His finger moved down the vee of her gown. "Thank you but there are still far too many buttons. Unbutton another, love."

He felt her stop breathing for a moment, and then her hand slipped between his and the cotton of her dress. She pulled one more pearl free.

She didn't move as he tugged the material back and kissed the hollow of her throat. Then, with every ounce of effort he could muster, he leaned back as she rested on his chest.

For a while they were both still, but he knew she wasn't asleep.

Finally, she put her chin on his chest and asked, "What do you want of me? If I can't have children, will you still want me near?"

"Yes," he answered against her ear. "I don't think I'll ever stop wanting you, Valerie. Right now I want to brush my hand over you with only the gown between us but I fear I might frighten you."

She lay back. "All right, if that is what you want. I like that I can make you happy. I'm not afraid of you, you know, and so far everything you've done has been quite nice, but you have to promise to kiss me before and after. That way, if I don't like it, I'll at least have the kisses."

He touched his lips to hers briefly, then moved his hand down her arm. "You're going to like this," he whispered against her cheek. "And I promise I'll kiss you before and after and in between." When she didn't protest, he spread his fingers at her waist and moved upward. She made a little sound when his fingers slid over her breasts.

"They're fuller than I thought," he said more to himself than her as he cupped one lightly. "And much softer."

Her entire body seemed to warm, but she didn't make a move as he gently circled his hand over her again and again, learning the feel of this woman. When he brushed her cheek, he felt a tear.

"Are you all right?"

She began to nod, then answered, "I've never been touched like that."

"Like what?"

"Like I am cherished."

He kissed her again and said simply, "It's time we got some sleep."

As she cuddled against him, his arm bent and rested lightly over her breast. She didn't move away.

"You are cherished," he whispered as he kissed the top of her head. "You always will be."

He lay thinking of the wonder of this woman and pushing sleep aside for as long as possible. He'd been trying to breathe easy for a while when he felt her raise one hand and unbutton another pearl button of her gown.

Someday, he decided, he'd make her scream with passion, but for now, this was enough. This was Heaven.

Chapter 7

The next morning Valerie kissed Brody once on the cheek to say good-bye.

He laughed, grabbed her waist, and pulled her solidly against him. "We'll have no light kisses between us. If I'm to be without you until sundown, I'll taste you fully."

He bent over her and opened her mouth with his hunger. She could feel the solidity of his body pressed against her as she wrapped her arms around his neck and held to him.

When he pulled away and set her on her feet, she laughed. Never in her dreams had she thought a man would want her so. She'd always thought of herself as serviceable to a man. She tried to be a good wife, but neither of her husbands had shown such passion. Venny had thought of her only as someone to bear his children and keep his house. Samuel only wanted someone to come home to. But this one, this husband of convenience, seemed to want her.

He kissed her nose. "You're an easy woman to love," he said. "Any chance you'd be willing to let me touch you like I did last night?"

She blushed. "We shouldn't talk of such things."

"Fair enough," he answered as he put on his hat and held the door for her as they walked to the porch. "I should be back by supper."

She watched him swing into the saddle. He'd said he had to go over to Boss Ramsey's ranch and take care of a cow he'd left in a canyon almost a month ago. He wanted to get an early start.

As she watched him go, she wished she'd said something about how glad she was she'd asked him to marry her or even about how she'd let him touch her again, but she hadn't. She'd let him go without knowing how she felt about him. Fear had kept her silent. Fear, not of him, but of caring too much.

She hated to admit it, but he'd lied to her. He'd said she was an easy woman to love, but she knew that couldn't be true for he was the first man who'd ever even tried.

An hour later when she went into town to make her deliveries, she wore her gloves. Brody had been working with the horse and the animal seemed to have the concept that he should go in one direction.

At one house the woman followed her out to her wagon and handed her a ball of blue twine. "Tie it in a bow on each bedpost and you'll sleep many years with this one."

Valerie took the yarn guessing Brody would laugh at her if she tried such a thing.

When she stopped to have an early lunch with her father, he commented that people were leaving good luck charms with him.

"How you getting on with this one?" he asked.

She remembered a week after she'd married the first husband, she'd been too proud to beg to come home, but her father must have seen her sorrow. With the second husband, Samuel, it was more a long shot from the beginning. They barely knew each other and the mating between them had been fast and mechanical.

She hadn't loved either of them, but she'd done her duty and mourned them both.

"He's a hard worker," Valerie said to her father when she realized she hadn't answered. She wanted someone to talk to. "He cares about me, Papa. Little things, like he doesn't start eating until I sit down, and he's kind. He worries about me. He even made me buy gloves. And he kisses me, not because he thinks he should or out of duty, but just because he wants to."

Valerie knew she was rambling, but she had to get all that was Brody Monroe put together in her mind. One thing he was not. He was not going to be just a partner she could walk away from after a year. He'd proved that this morning when he'd kissed her good-bye.

Her father nodded his head as if he were reading his daughter's mind. "I saw that, even from the first. Men like him, they've been damaged by the war. Hurt bad in more ways than just the body. They may never say the words, but I think he loves you or, at the least, he's willing to try his best."

She shook her head. "Four days married and he left me to go finish a job for Boss."

"When it's done, he'll stay around. If you want him?"

She smiled. "I want him, Papa."

An hour later when she got home, she was a little surprised Brody wasn't waiting for her. She spent the day cleaning house and planning a garden. By nightfall, when he wasn't home, she grew worried.

Finally, after midnight, she went to bed alone. She spent the night worrying about what might have happened to him, and by dawn, she had the buggy ready at first light. She didn't know where he was, but she knew two things. He didn't stay away of his own will, and she didn't plan to sleep until she found him.

Dead or alive, she'd bring Brody Monroe home, where he belonged.

Chapter 8

Brody spent the night leaning against a huge rock that had wedged his leg so completely against the solid wall of the canyon he couldn't move. Hours ago, he'd climbed over the barricade he'd built to check on the cow and her calf before spending a few hours moving rock so he could get them out. Only, when he was almost all the way down, he slipped, causing an avalanche tumbling after him. His right leg slipped between two rocks and others piled down on top, bruising him all over and making it impossible to move enough even to get a grip on any rock so he might try to free himself.

He spent a few hours yelling for help, then trying to reach his Colt, but it was no use. His voice grew hoarse and the back of his hands were scraped and bleeding. As nightfall came, he tried to sleep, conserving his energy so he could fight to get free at first light. He knew no one would be coming for him. No one on the Double R knew where he was, and if they did, he doubted any of the cowboys would search. He'd always been invisible to them.

If he was lucky, his horse might go back to the barn. It had been her home for over a year. If she was hungry enough, she might wander back. Then at least Caleb would know he'd been on the ranch. He might come looking, but with all the miles of open range, he wouldn't have much luck at finding one man hidden behind a wall of rock.

Luck, Brody thought. For the first time in his life he'd found something worth keeping, someone worth loving, and right now she was sitting at their little place probably crying her eyes out because she thought he'd left her.

He wanted to scream to high heaven that he'd never leave her. His proper little wife with her firm belief in what was right and wrong to do in the daylight. His wife who thought she could survive out on a farm alone, but was afraid of thunder. His wife who felt like heaven to touch, and when she smiled, he swore he could feel his heart start beating.

He'd been cold inside for so long he'd forgotten how it felt to care, but he cared for her more than he'd probably ever be able to explain. He wanted to build the farm with her at his side. He wanted to watch storms and sunsets from the porch and sleep the rest of his life with her cuddled against his side.

An hour before dawn he finally passed out from the pain. For a while he felt like he was home with her. He could feel her breathing next to him. How could there be any luck left in the world if fate let him find her and lose her so fast?

When he woke, he screamed again and shoved at the hundreds of pounds of rock holding him in place. For a while, he lay back, giving up to the pain he felt inside his heart and all along his leg. The memories of the war came to visit like old relatives he'd hated. Memories of being hurt and lying among the bodies one night when the air seemed too cold to even breathe in. He'd been sure he would die before morning. All seemed dead around him. Memories of being lost in the night, cold and hungry. He'd walked toward a fire knowing there was a fifty-fifty chance it would be the enemy and he'd be dead before he could feel the fire.

It occurred to him that he was already dead, maybe had been for years, and God was playing a joke on him, letting him see a window of what his life could have been like.

"No!" he yelled. He wouldn't give up. Valerie was real. If he closed his eyes, he could see her face. He could feel her breath.

He could curl his hand to the exact size of her breast. Valerie was real and she was his wife. He'd promised not to leave. He'd promised he'd never lie to her.

Brody pulled his wits together and began to plan. He'd yell as loud and as long as he could every thirty minutes. If he heard anything, he'd throw handfuls of rocks as high as he could and maybe a few would reach the surface. He'd keep trying to get his Colt free.

An hour later, he budged the Colt an inch, then another. The sun was at midmorning when he pulled the gun out, relieving an ounce of the pressure. He tried to move his leg, but it wouldn't respond. He checked the gun. Six bullets. Six chances.

He fired off the first shot.

No answer.

Brody knew it was important to wait. If no one heard the first shot, it would be unlikely anyone would hear one ten minutes later. He had to wait.

At noon, he fired the second shot.

No answer.

At about one he tried again and again at two.

No answer.

He guessed it to be three when he fired off the next to last shot.

He thought he heard a gunshot echo thirty seconds later, then another closer to him. Brody yelled and kept yelling until he heard horses.

A few minutes later, Earl Timmons looked over the ledge above him and shouted, "That you, Yank?"

"It's me! I'm wedged into the rocks!" Brody saw Montie's red head lean over the top. He'd never been so glad to see the two worthless cowboys in his life.

They didn't waste time talking. In a few minutes, both were heading toward him with ropes looped about their waists.

"We'll get you out," Earl said as he hit ground and started moving rocks bigger than his head. "If we get a few of these out of the way, Montie and me should be able to shove one enough to get you free."

Montie worked as hard as his brother, but complained the entire time about how they'd better hurry. "That wife of yours arrived banging on the boss's door this morning with the sun. She was so sure something had happened to you the boss told us all to get to searching."

"Valerie came here?"

Earl laughed as he paused long enough to wipe off sweat. "She claimed she wasn't going to tolerate another husband just riding off and dying on her. She said she wanted you back even if it was in pieces."

Montie agreed. "We thought about heading back, but we didn't even dare go back for lunch. Between her and the boss, they'd chicken-fry us up for supper if we didn't come back with you."

Brody groaned as they pulled one of the rocks away from his leg.

Earl knelt down and moved the next rock away carefully. Brody saw his blood-soaked right leg for the first time.

"It's broke, Yank."

Brody didn't argue. The rocks had kept pressure on the wound, but now blood flooded over the rocks like a thin stream.

The brothers wrapped the leg as fast as they could and

carried Brody over the rocks. As they lifted him onto Earl's horse, Brody asked between clenched teeth, "Why didn't you just leave me, Reb? I know you've always hated me because I'm a Yankee."

"Yeah," Earl agreed as he tied Brody into the saddle, "but you see, Yank, you're *our* Yank and we don't want to lose you."

Montie laughed. "And as long as her curse is directed at you . . ." He couldn't help giggling as he tried to talk. "The rest of us feel pretty safe."

Brody would have laughed if he'd had the energy left. He felt Earl swing up behind him as he passed out.

An hour later, he clenched his teeth around a washcloth as the doctor set his leg just below the knee. It hurt like hell, but he was alive, and for that, Brody could only be thankful. He'd made Valerie leave the room and she hadn't been happy about it, but he'd seen her eyes when she'd stepped aside as the men brought him in. She'd been crying. *No,* he thought anew, *she'd been crying for him.*

The doc cleaned away the blood and told Earl to let the widow in.

"She's not a widow," Brody said. "I'm here, and unless you're not telling me something, I think I'm going to live."

The doc smiled. "That you will. Looks like the boys found you right in time. Another hour or two and I'm not sure you would have had enough blood left in you to make it."

The doctor talked to her in a low voice as he insisted she help. "I don't want his leg moved any more than absolutely necessary for three days. I'll be by to help you with the first cleaning. After that he'll be in a brace for a month. Don't let him take it off, period."

She nodded, listening to every word and not even looking at Brody.

When the doctor stepped away to mix up some medicine, Valerie moved to Brody's side. She reminded him of a little soldier, and he had the feeling there would be no bending the doc's rules once he got home.

"He's fine," the doc said one more time to calm her. "When you get him home, keep him there. If you feed him, he'll heal, Mrs. Monroe. I'll come by and add a proper splint when the swelling goes down. Then he should be able to hobble around until it heals. He was lucky, it was a clean break."

"Lucky," Brody mumbled as the medicine the doc had given him and the lack of blood and sleep finally caught up to him.

When he woke, it was almost dawn the next day. Valerie was sleeping in one of Boss Ramsey's office chairs beside his bed. She almost took his breath away with her beauty, all curled up in the boss's chair with her hair a mess around her.

He reached for her hand and woke her.

"Are you all right?" she leaned close and whispered.

"I'm fine," he lied. "You should be in bed sleeping."

She shook her head. "Not without you."

He smiled, guessing every part of his body ached except his heart. "I want to go home," he managed before drifting back to sleep.

When the doctor came in, he sent Valerie off to eat breakfast while he checked Brody's leg.

"Looks like the bleeding has finally stopped." Doc Hollis was a plain man who never wasted words.

As he wrapped the wound and tied Brody's leg to a splint to prevent any movement while they got him home, the doc said, "You know, there's a rumor that your wife has a curse on her. Seems every man she marries dies. You almost had it come true."

"I don't believe in curses." Brody wanted to add that he was tired of hearing about the widow's curse, but he didn't figure it would be wise to argue with the man trying to fix him up.

The doc nodded and asked, "Tell me, Yank, what would you do if you knew the curse was true? What if you knew that you only had a day to live if you don't get away from her?"

Brody smiled. "Well, then I'd go home and spend one last wonderful day with my wife."

The doctor laughed. "Spoken like a man who loves his wife."

Brody saw no use in denying it. "I do love her and you can tell all in town to stop worrying about me because I'd come back from hell itself to be with that woman."

He heard a tiny scream and turned to see Valerie in the doorway. Her eyes were huge, and she looked like she might bolt at any moment.

He couldn't chase her but he couldn't turn away either. Sometime in the hell of being trapped between the rocks, he'd made up his mind and he wasn't a man who changed it easily.

The doc bumped his way past them, suddenly in a hurry to leave the two of them alone.

She walked slowly into the room carrying a bowl of warm water in front of her. Without a word she knelt beside the bed and began cleaning the dried blood off his hand.

He watched her, wishing she'd look up at him. She was so beautiful. He had no idea if his statement to the doctor had frightened her or pleased her. He didn't care. The truth needed to be said between them.

"I'm all right," Brody finally said in a far more angry tone than he'd meant to use. "I'm not going to die on you."

She looked up at him, tears in her eyes. "I know. You promised you wouldn't leave me and I'm trying to believe you, but you never promised to love me. That wasn't part of the partnership between us."

"I hadn't planned on it," he admitted. "But you seemed in need of loving and I couldn't stop myself. Damned if you're not the most lovable woman I've ever met."

She frowned and stopped cleaning his hand.

"I didn't mean to say it like that. I don't have the words to say how I feel about you, and saying I'm not leaving doesn't seem enough."

"It's enough," she answered so low he barely heard.

He'd expected her to kiss him, but his wife was very proper. They were in someone else's home. She bandaged his hands and had the men carefully load him into the buggy. All the way home, she didn't touch him or say a word. Brody didn't feel like talking. He'd downed half a bottle of the doctor's pain medicine, which tasted a lot like whiskey, and sleeping seemed the only thing worth doing.

She helped him into bed and he passed out.

It was dark outside when he finally woke. She was sitting beside him in the little rocker he'd noticed in the parlor. He didn't miss the dark circles beneath her eyes.

"You were mumbling in your sleep." She set her knitting aside. "I think you were dreaming about being back in the war."

"I often do." He realized that since he'd been here with her, the dreams hadn't made their nightly visits. "Sleep with me," he whispered. "There have been no nightmares when you were by my side."

"No. I might hurt your leg."

"If we both remain very still, it'll work." He didn't like the idea of her spending another night in a chair. "Valerie, sleep with me."

"All right," she gave in, "but all we do is sleep."

That worked the first night, but the second he insisted on holding her hand. All he could think about was touching her, but if he did, Brody wasn't sure he could stop with one touch.

After three nights, the doctor dropped by and cleaned the leg, then wrapped it tightly in a splint that barred both sides. When he belted it together, he told Brody that come morning he could try walking with a cane.

"I need to get my field plowed," Brody said, knowing it was already late.

"If you're talking about that field between here and the road, it was plowed yesterday."

"By who? No man could plow that hard land in less than a week."

"I don't know. I passed by on my way back from a call and saw a dozen men working horses pulling plows."

Brody wasn't sure he believed the doctor. The first thing he planned to do when he got back on his feet was to check the land.

That night Brody insisted on getting up to sit at the table for supper. Then, he sat on the porch and looked out at the plowed field. Valerie was worse than a one-year-old's mother following him around. If she thought he'd let her, she probably would have put pillows in front and behind him just in case he stumbled.

"Who do you think did such a thing?" He stared out at the field.

"The neighbors," Valerie answered. "They knew you were hurt and it needed doing. You would have done the same for them."

Brody leaned back, ignoring the pain in his leg. He wasn't sure he would have until now. It was getting harder and harder to ignore these slow-talking Southern people. They had a way about them. He thought about it until she told him that it was time for him to come to bed.

He let her help him undress. When they reached the bedroom, he kissed her for the first time since the accident. "I love you, Valerie, and I want you to be my wife in every way."

He saw the panic in her eyes. All the progress he thought they'd made seemed to have vanished. He didn't want their loving to only be in the darkness with neither one of them speaking of it in day, but he didn't know where to start. Somehow the accident had made her believe in the curse. She'd barely let him out of her sight for three days. She wouldn't love him, couldn't love him, as long as she believed he might die at any moment.

"How long do I have to stay around before you know I'm not going to die on you? A week, a month, a lifetime?"

"You don't think I really believe what people say, do you?"

He wasn't getting into that argument with her. "How long until we start being man and wife? I don't want to tell you to raise your gown. I want to make love to you. I love you, and I want to show you just how much. If you tell me I have to wait a year or ten, I will, but one day you'll have to know that I'm here and I'm your husband."

One tear slid down her cheek.

"Prove to me you don't believe in curses. Prove to me that you accept my love even if you never plan to return it." He watched her, knowing his need to love her would still be there no matter what she said or how she felt about him.

"One month," she whispered. "I need one month to think about it."

He swallowed and made up his mind. "If at the end of a month, the answer is no, I want you to understand that I'll still stay, but I don't think I can sleep with you in the same bed without being your true husband."

She nodded as he traced the buttons along her gown. Thirty buttons.

He let her help him in bed. When his covers were tucked in, he caught her hand and tugged her close. "How about we count the days in buttons. Thirty days until I get the cast off. Thirty days until you decide to love me."

She moved onto her side of the bed, careful not to touch him. "All right."

Her answer left him speechless.

Chapter 9

Each night, Valerie counted a day's passing by leaving one more button unfastened. She guessed Brody didn't trust love any more than she did, but she was willing to give it a try.

As the days passed, he grew stronger, being able to do more and more with first a cane and then without. She knew his leg hurt, but he never complained. At the end of each day, he'd sit on the bed with her standing in front of him and watch one more button fall open.

By the second week he began touching her, first lightly, hesitantly, then more boldly. He was a hard man trying to be tender, and his efforts affected her so deeply she had to remember to breathe.

On the third week he shoved the vee of her gown open and kissed her breast before he turned off the light. She felt her cheeks burn, but she didn't stop him. The next night when he did the same, he looked up at her and said simply, "Would you like me to do that again?"

Though it was most improper, she answered politely, "Yes, please."

All night, as she slept next to him, their kisses grew longer. Once she woke to him kissing her and reality seemed to slip into her dreams. The surprise midnight kisses were always deep and passionate as his hands roamed over her body. When she didn't comment on his action, he repeated it the next night and the next.

Valerie caught herself thinking of his touch during the day and looking forward to each night. He always insisted on her standing before him in the light as she unbuttoned her gown; then he'd pull her into bed, turn out the light, and begin driving her mad with need for him. He handled her gently, but he handled her all night. Just before dawn, he'd pull her close and move his hands one more time over her body as if he was trying to memorize every curve.

At the beginning of the fourth week, she wanted to tell him that she'd made up her mind. She could think of nothing better than loving him, but Brody wouldn't let her. Only one button, he'd say. Only one each night.

She'd wake to his kisses, or the feel of his hand gripping her breast or bottom all through the night, but when she offered more, he always pulled away. Slowly she grew used to him watching her undress and even smiled knowing he was holding his breath each night until she reached the new button to fall.

She could have managed with the nights if it hadn't been for the days. He wanted a kiss each morning, and not a light one. Some mornings breakfast was cold by the time he pulled away and laughingly told her that was enough as if she'd been the one insisting on more.

During the day, if he passed her, he always stopped to touch her. Maybe he'd play with her hair, or brush against her. Once he even kissed her hand before whispering what he planned to kiss once they were in bed.

There was no doubt about it. Her husband was driving her mad. Three days before the month was over, he watched her unbutton, kissed her lightly, and said he had some paperwork to do. To her shock, he left her in the bedroom.

He didn't come to bed until very late, and when he did, he didn't touch her. She felt the cold and cuddled against him, but he was asleep and didn't gather her in his arms as he always had.

The next night, he did the same. After she unbuttoned all but one button, he ran his finger down the open front of her gown and told her how beautiful she was, then went back to the tiny study.

She found him at dawn asleep in the chair with his head on an open book as if he'd read all night.

The last night. The last button. She waited forever for him to take a bath. When he walked out of the washroom, he no longer had wrappings on his leg. He didn't limp as he walked to her and kissed her lightly.

"The month's over," he whispered. "Have you made up your mind?"

"I want you as my husband in every way." She almost added that every part of her body ached from the need to feel his touch.

"Then we begin tonight. There is no past. No curse. No scars. No war between us. It's just you and me, in love for the first time in our lives." He took her hand and slipped a plain gold band on her finger. "I came into some extra money from a bet and I wanted you to wear my ring."

"I've never had one," she whispered.

"I noticed. It's time you did and this one you'll never take off."

She stared at the ring. "I promise."

He reached down her gown to her waist to the last button and slowly unbuttoned it. Then, he slipped his hands beneath the cotton and pushed the gown off her shoulders.

Valerie closed her eyes. He was seeing all of her and somehow it felt right. She felt his hand brush lightly over her skin. "My valentine," he said laughing. "My love. My wife."

She couldn't put into words how she felt, but she knew he was right. She was in love for the first time in her life and nothing else mattered.

"Come to bed, my love," he whispered against her hair. "From this night we start, not a partnership, but a marriage."

She smiled as he lifted her up and carried her to bed. There was no curse between them. There was only love and she knew no matter how long they lived, there always would be.

Epilogue

Brody and Valerie Monroe lived together for fifty-three years. They raised eight children, and when she died, she counted over sixty grandchildren. Old-timers in town still called Brody the Yank, but they all knew the man would do anything for any one of them.

Their farm was productive, but they never grew rich. Not in money anyway. The legend of the widow's curse was broken completely. Until the day Brody died of a heart attack a year after he buried Valerie, the Yank never suffered a single injury. Some claim he never even had a cold.

Cupid's Arrow

LINDA BRODAY

Chapter 1

Rue Ann Spencer stepped from Mrs. Fitzhugh's Dress Shop, where she was being fitted for her wedding gown, into the blinding afternoon sunlight.

She quickly raised her hand to shield her eyes, but it wasn't soon enough to keep her from plowing into the solid wall of a man's body.

His quick grasp kept her on her feet.

"Pardon me. I didn't see . . ." She stared up into the liquid brown eyes of none other than Logan Cutter. Her words trailed off as she suddenly lost the ability to form coherent thought. Her heart raced. Why did she have to run into the one person who still had the ability to drive a knife straight into her heart?

That's why she'd stayed far away from Texas and Shiloh for three years. She'd never forgive him for what he'd done.

"I heard you were back in town, Rue Ann." Logan's deep growl indicated he wasn't thrilled with the encounter either. "And I also hear congratulations are in order on your upcoming nuptials."

"Thank you, Mr. Cutter," she replied stiffly. "Now if you'll excuse me, I have a million things to do to prepare for my wedding. Valentine's Day will be here—"

"In exactly two weeks and five days," he finished for her.

Shocked that he knew to the day how long before she'd become someone else's wife, she gathered her shredded composure and turned in the direction of Whipple's Dry Goods. Refusing to give Cutter the satisfaction of knowing how deeply he'd affected her, she moved on, keeping her gaze glued to the sidewalk, never once glancing back.

The truth of the matter was that Logan Cutter *had* jarred her. She had tried to prepare herself for the inevitable crossing of their paths, but seeing him today had been a shock.

Trembling, Rue Ann opened the door of the dry goods store and hurried inside. Thankfully, Mr. Whipple had his hands full with the spinster Barlow sisters.

Rue Ann headed for a dark corner, and sagging there against a shelf of men's hats, she blinked back sudden tears and gave herself a stern talking-to.

She would not shed one more tear over that man.

Logan Cutter wasn't worth it.

Before her world had come crashing down around her, she'd lived and breathed the knowledge that one day they'd share the rest of their lives together.

But Logan had betrayed her.

The bitter truth lodged in the center of her heart like a double dose of Hostetter's Celebrated Stomach Tonic.

A stillness washed over Rue Ann as seething anger replaced the pain. He'd never get another chance to hurt her. She was older now and far wiser. Life had been a strict taskmaster, but she'd learned her lesson well.

Soon she would be Mrs. Theodore Greely.

And life would go on. One day she might even be able

to think of Logan without pain welling up from the deep wound inside.

"Are you okay, dear?" A woman's quiet voice broke into her thoughts.

Startled, Rue Ann hastily forced a smile for Miss Emily Barlow. "I'm fine. I was just looking at the men's hats, thinking I might get one for my father," she fibbed, running a finger along the brim of a fine Stetson. "His birthday isn't far off. But I haven't a clue about his size so I suppose I'd best wait until my mother can come with me."

Miss Emily patted her arm. "It's so nice to see you back in town, dear. Some people around here have missed you."

Rue Ann wasn't sure who the *some people* were. It was best to let sleeping dogs lie where that was concerned. Instead she hugged the woman who dressed in black from head to toe and had done so as far back as Rue Ann could remember. If Miss Emily had worn any other color today, it would've been another shock. Her mother had told her that Miss Emily's fiancé had died a week before they were to wed. It had so devastated the sweet lady that she remained locked forever in the moment of her grief. Sadness of it all swept through Rue Ann. She wouldn't want that to happen to her.

"It's nice to be missed." She kissed Miss Emily's pale, wrinkled cheek that was so thin the skin seemed scarcely able to cover her bones without tearing.

"How are you doing, dear? I've been quite worried about you." Again, more of the tender patting.

Now why would Miss Emily worry? Studying at a women's finishing school shouldn't cause anyone to fret.

"I'm in the best of health, thank you."

"There you are, Sister," exclaimed Miss Charlotte, the other half of the matching Barlow set. Only this sister dressed all in white. They were salt and pepper. "Oh, Rue Ann. It's been ages since we've seen you, hasn't it, Sister?"

Miss Emily nodded in agreement, setting the black hat with yards of netting bobbing on her silver hair.

"Didn't I see you talking with Mr. Cutter a few minutes ago?" Miss Charlotte continued without pausing for air, "I daresay he found the sight of you breathtaking. He's been quite lonely, you know. That is, until he began courting Celeste Wiggins. Now the two are inseparable." Miss Charlotte leaned close and whispered loudly in Rue Ann's ear, "It's rumored the two will wed soon."

Pain once again rose swift and without warning. Rue Ann forced air past the huge lump in her throat.

So Logan Cutter was stepping out with Celeste.

Rue Ann had no idea how she'd handle this unpleasant situation. The fact that Logan and Celeste were keeping company drove the dagger deeper. She struggled to find a reply.

"Miss Charlotte, it's no business of mine who Mr. Cutter chooses to spend his time with," she finally managed quietly. "Lord knows he's a free man."

But why did he have to be involved with Celeste? The woman had spurned Rue Ann's overtures of friendship at every turn.

Rue Ann had always felt like an ugly stepsister next to Celeste. Her mass of red curls was impossible to tame, and the row of freckles marching across her nose like so many foot soldiers gave her a childish air. Rue Ann had accepted long ago that she'd never be a raving beauty. Nor did she want to, she sternly reminded herself.

Logan Cutter had traded his relationship with Rue Ann for a thousand dollars. That was what she'd been worth to him. He was nothing but a Judas, and she was better off without him.

If only she could convince her heart of that.

* * *

Logan Cutter stared after Rue Ann until she vanished into Whipple's Dry Goods Store. His mouth had gone dry. She was every bit as desirable as she was three years ago.

He thought he'd been prepared for the inevitable meeting after hearing that she'd returned to Shiloh. He'd tried to steel himself against the power of those jade green eyes and auburn hair that reminded him of beautiful autumn leaves.

But the minute she'd met his gaze, he was lost, thrown back to an innocent time when they'd lived and breathed each other's presence.

If only he knew what had happened, he might make some sense of her sudden disappearance from town.

Logan gave himself a hard mental shake. Why dwell on has-beens? He needed to forget the taste of her lips and move on with his life. As indeed he was trying. Celeste Wiggins was everything a man desired in a wife. The woman was quite something with her silky golden hair and expressive lavender eyes. But for some reason he couldn't bring himself to ask her to marry him. Why he held back, he couldn't say exactly.

He only knew one thing—she wasn't Rue Ann.

Someone touched his shoulder. "There you are, Logan. What size nails did you say you needed to pick up?"

The voice belonged to his older brother, Matthew Cutter, who had ridden into town with him to pick up some supplies. Matt and his wife lived on a small fifty-acre spread next to Logan and were trying to make a go of farming. Although it pretty much looked like all they'd succeeded in raising was a bumper crop of kids. Six of them so far.

"Gathering wool, little brother?" Matthew prodded, leaning against the hitching rail in front of the store.

"Of course not, why?"

"I asked what size nails you needed and you paid me

no mind. You were a million miles away. What's going on with you?"

"Just have my thoughts somewhere else." His thoughts certainly weren't on ranch repair. "I need a sack of ten-penny nails."

"Do you want me to get them? I need to get back home as quick as possible. Lucy needs a sack of flour. She said if I dawdle, I won't get that loaf of fresh bread or the apple pie I've had a hankering for." Matthew pushed back the brim of his hat and scratched his forehead. "I saw you talking with Rue Ann."

That figured. Probably half the town saw them. Just what he needed. He'd have to tell Celeste before someone else did.

"There wasn't much talking going on. She was coming out of this dress shop here the very moment I was walking by and we collided. That's all there was to it."

"I can't believe she threw you over for Theodore Greely."

Logan was stumped as well. Rue Ann could choose from a dozen or so men who were far better suited than Greely. So why take up with a man of that ilk? He wished he knew.

"Yeah, well, she did and that's that." Logan tried to tear his gaze away from the door of Whipple's Dry Goods. It seemed a lost cause, though. He wanted one more glimpse of Rue Ann.

"The shyster is nothing but a little beady-eyed stuffed shirt. Struts around town like he owns Shiloh and half of Texas. I still don't know why Rue Ann's father took the man into business with him. Typical lawyer, I reckon, but Greely sure rubs me the wrong way."

Logan would gladly pay a fine if he could set the man back on his heels just once. He sighed. "Do you think your Lucy would fix me a pie if I asked her real nice-like?"

Nothing could improve his spirits like a homemade pie.

Matthew snorted. "If you'd quit mooning after Rue Ann and marry Celeste, you'd have all the fruit pies and whatnot you could eat. What's the holdup?"

"That's none of your business, big brother," Logan snapped.

"You ask me, Celeste would make some man a mighty good wife. Might as well be you."

"I didn't ask you, though, did I?"

"You're grouchier than a grizzly with a toothache. I wash my hands of the matter." Matthew pushed away from the hitching rail. "You want to waste your time waiting for Rue Ann to come to her right mind, it's no skin off my nose."

"Keep your horseback opinions to yourself."

"Fine. I'm heading to the mercantile. You coming?"

Just then Rue Ann emerged empty-handed from Whipple's. Logan's eyes narrowed. "You go on. I'll catch up."

This was as good a time as any to get some answers.

With long strides, Logan headed toward the woman who'd spurned his love. A look of surprise crossed her pretty features when she saw him coming. She whirled on her heels, lifted her heavy skirts, and in a near all-out sprint, aimed for her father's law office.

"Oh no, you don't," Logan muttered under his breath, increasing his pace.

He caught up with her between the telegraph office and Doc Pritchard's. Planting himself in her path, he grabbed her arm.

"Please unhand me this instant," she demanded icily.

People had begun to stare, but Logan didn't pay them any mind. "I will if you'll tell me why you didn't have enough gumption to come to me before you just packed up and left town."

She hadn't even bothered to trouble herself with a note to tell him where she was going. He'd spent the better part of two years trying to locate her but to no avail. He would've done the right thing and married her. He'd have done anything for her, gone to any lengths, swum any ocean, fought any dragon.

If only she'd trusted, loved him, enough to have come to him when her back was against the wall.

Instead she'd simply vanished. A wealthy state senator for a father had made that happen.

Deep, heavy sadness washed over him, so powerful it nearly dropped him to his knees.

Rue Ann gasped. "Me? Gumption? Of all the nerve!"

Whatever she was trying to pull wouldn't work.

"Yes, you. You were the one who didn't trust me to take care of you, who didn't give me so much as a fare-thee-well." Logan hardened his heart against the effects of her nearness, which lured him like a prideful she-wolf to a steel trap.

Fire flashed from the green depths of her eyes. And then strangely he thought he saw tears gathering, but decided it was a figment of his imagination because they vanished as soon as they formed.

"I said let me go," she ordered from between clenched teeth. "You're not going to get your pound of flesh today or any other."

Logan believed there was a golden hour in every relationship where problems could be fixed. This was theirs. Even if they couldn't return things to the way they were before, at least maybe they'd pass on the street without crossing to the other side. That would be a good start.

"I'm not after a pound of flesh. I simply want to know what happened. That too much to hope for?" Cutter asked.

"I know what you did," she whispered angrily.

The anguish in her tone, the hurt in her eyes, bruised something deep inside him.

"What are you talking about?" He searched his mind for

a hint of whatever he'd done. For the life of him, he couldn't remember. Had the months erased his memory?

Rue Ann looked over his shoulder. Her green eyes widened as she jerked her arm from his grasp. "Now is not a good time."

A stern male voice came from behind. "Sweetling, did you forget that I told you to meet me at three-thirty? You're four and a half minutes late."

Logan turned and stared into Theodore Greely's hard, granite eyes. The man reeked with disapproval as he returned his ornate watch to his vest pocket. Logan had never wanted to hit anyone as much as he wanted to now. The two men sized each other up like two curs who couldn't stand the scent of the other.

Forcing himself to unclench his fists, Logan smiled frostily. "It's my fault. Miss Spencer and I were talking."

"I'm sure you have nothing to say that would be relevant to anything." Greely jerked Rue Ann's arm. "Come along, sweetling."

Rue Ann lowered her gaze as Greely propelled her, with force it seemed, toward her father's law office.

Logan watched, powerless to intervene. Until the lady wanted and asked for his help, his hands were tied. Things were in a sorry state, and his confrontation with her hadn't accomplished a thing except to raise Greely's dander.

It wasn't over yet, though. He still wanted an answer to his burning question.

And he meant to get it one way or another.

Chapter 2

The last thing Rue Ann wanted was to risk running into Logan Cutter again. But she had little choice in the matter.

Their nearest neighbors, the Williamsons, invited her and Theodore to the betrothal party for their daughter. And since Bethany had managed to snag one of the town's most eligible bachelors, they'd spared no expense. The Williamsons were beyond delighted for a chance to crow a little.

The end of January wasn't the most ideal time for such a social affair, but the crisp weather was clear and beautiful, especially on this night.

Buggies and buckboards packed every square inch around the barn. Seemed people from most all of the ranches had come.

Inside the Williamsons' barn, Rue Ann cast a glance around the gathering, tapping her foot nervously. Feeling like a spring that'd been wound too tight and was about to come undone, she hugged the hostess. Pressing close beside her, Theodore Greely must've felt some anxiousness himself because he was clingier than usual. His cloying scent circled around her head.

For the umpteenth time, Rue Ann asked herself why she was marrying the man. She didn't love him, would never love him. But her father had handpicked Theodore to be her mate, and no one ever dared cross the powerful Devlin Spencer, who ruled the Texas Senate and his family with an iron fist.

No one crossed him without serious repercussions anyway.

Besides, weren't security and comfort good enough reasons to marry? Some people had tied the knot for less. All she had to do was smile and pretend. She could do that. Except for the months she'd known Logan Cutter, she'd done that most of her life.

Failing to see the man in question, she relaxed. With a bit of luck, he wouldn't show up.

Maybe he'd stayed at his ranch, the one bought and paid for with her father's money, and would pass on this social affair. Though, given Celeste's penchant for parties and the like, Rue Ann couldn't see the woman missing an opportunity to gloat.

And maybe Logan had given up trying to talk to her. They really had nothing to say to each other. He'd made his choice. He could offer no excuse that would undo the moment of his betrayal.

The musicians had finished warming up and launched into a waltz. The beautiful strains of the fiddle reached into that quiet place in her soul and calmed her jitters. She swayed to the rhythm, enjoying the feel of her ruffled satin skirt swishing around her ankles.

She didn't object when Theodore swung her out into the midst of dancing couples.

For once she didn't have to pretend. She loved waltzing. And good fiddle music just added the icing on the cake. The only problem was her partner. Theodore was cold, stiff, and unyielding. It was like dancing with a fence post bound with leather that had been left out in the elements until it was dry and cracked and beyond hope.

She closed her eyes. If she tried really hard, she could imagine the arms around her were the kind that could heat a woman's blood. Strong and caring, they could easily carry the burdens of the world.

For a second she allowed herself to feel cherished.

These arms should belong to—

"I can't believe this," Theodore spat angrily, interrupting her daydream. "He has a lot of gall showing up here."

Rue Ann's eyes flew open. "Who?"

She followed his gaze to the barn entrance, and her heart dropped into the pit of her stomach.

Logan Cutter stood with his feet apart as though bracing himself for trouble. His dark hair, shining with a deep luster in the lamplight, brushed the collar of his coat, which had seen plenty of wear. And his defiant, stormy gaze met hers across the crowded floor.

Rue Ann sucked in her breath as doom settled over her.

Then her gaze lit on Celeste Wiggins, gorgeous in the latest fashion, a formfitting gown that seemed designed from nothing more substantial than moonbeams and starlight. The satiny folds sparkled and shimmered with each movement. The woman clutched Logan's arm as though she feared he'd take off, running straight for Rue Ann.

"Did you know he was coming?" Theodore's punishing grip on her wrist left her wincing.

"You're hurting me." Rue Ann struggled, breaking free. She drew herself up and shot her intended a glare. "Believe it or not, I'm not privy to Mr. Cutter's comings and goings. I'm the last one he'd share his plans with."

"He has no business here," Theodore snapped. "I'll wager he's only interested in spying on you."

"What a foolish statement. It's no surprise that he'd come. You know how Celeste thrives on social occasions, no matter the circumstances." Although she strongly suspected Logan would've preferred to stay far removed from the festivities if the black scowl was any indication.

"Your father will be furious. There's no love lost between them. It's high time Cutter got it through his head that you belong to me," Theodore snarled, again grasping her wrist. Wrenching her to him, he set off across the dance floor to another waltz.

Rue Ann struggled to keep her feet under her. When at last she gained her footing, she ordered, "Stop this instant. Get it straight right now. I'm not your or anyone else's property."

She was so busy trying to make her point that she didn't see the dark-haired figure until he politely tapped Theodore's shoulder.

"The lady isn't a sack of potatoes to be manhandled." The low timbre of Logan's voice held warning.

Theodore drew himself up and glared. "This is a private matter and I'll thank you to keep out of it. You forget that Rue Ann is engaged to me, not you, Cutter."

"The only thing I'm forgetting is how good it would feel to knock you from here to Galveston and back, and that's because I haven't done it yet. I can rectify that situation in about two seconds . . . Teddy."

Theodore's face turned a ruddy color at Logan's derisive tone.

"I can't believe this—" Rue Ann began, only to be interrupted by her father.

"Gentlemen, take it outside. This isn't the time or place." Devlin Spencer glared his disapproval.

"With pleasure," Logan directed his wintry smile at Theodore. "After you . . . Teddy."

Rue Ann died with mortification. Two grown men were fighting over her as if she were some kind of prize they gave out at the county fair. She looked for a hole to crawl into. But she saw nothing except some bales of hay scattered around the barn for guests to sit on. Not exactly a place to hide.

Just then Celeste swept regally into their midst and fixed a cold stare on Rue Ann. "I hope you're satisfied now. See what you caused?" Then she turned to her escort. "Logan dearest, can you please get me a cup of punch? I'm ever so parched."

For a second Rue Ann thought Logan would refuse Celeste. At last he sighed and addressed Theodore. "This isn't over. We'll meet again. In the meantime you'd best watch yourself. You're too dumb to know how to treat the best thing you'll ever have." Then he swung to Rue Ann. "Miss Spencer, it's good seeing you again."

Rue Ann's heart broke into a million pieces as she watched him walk away with Celeste clutching his arm.

Conflicting emotions consumed Logan as he moved toward the refreshment table with Celeste stalking ahead as though to blaze a trail. The way she kept glancing over her shoulder to make sure he was following made him feel like an obedient dog. Celeste's rigid spine told of her anger.

Logan couldn't help it. He couldn't have lived with himself if he'd turned his back on Theodore Greely's mistreatment of Rue Ann.

He itched for a chance to pummel the obnoxious man. Someone needed to teach Teddy how to treat a lady. But on the other hand, Rue Ann had chosen, albeit not wisely, the man whom she wanted to marry. He needed to drop the matter and let fate chart her course.

But could he do that?

The churning in his gut said that would be about as possible as lassoing the moon.

"What was the meaning of that little display?" Celeste demanded in an icy tone when they reached the refreshment table. "Rue Ann Spencer is not your problem. I'll not have you chasing after her like some buck in rutting season."

Logan planted his heels. "You can find someone else to court you if you want. You should've learned by now I'll be no lapdog for you or anyone."

Celeste faced him, placed her hands on his chest, and wheedled, "Now, Logan, you know I didn't mean to criticize you. I was merely trying to bring your attention to the fact that you humiliated me back there in front of the entire town." She puffed out her bottom lip. "I don't know how I'll hold my head up. Surely you care about my reputation?"

"Of course I care. It wasn't my intention to bring you pain and humiliation. But you should understand what kind of man I am. I can't, I won't, sit idly by and watch someone mistreating a woman."

"Rue Ann Spencer, you mean," she uttered stiffly.

"Don't put words in my mouth, Celeste."

"Let's just drop the whole thing, shall we?"

"Suits me fine." He grabbed a glass of punch and thrust it into her hands. As much as he hated to admit it, Celeste was right and he knew it. He couldn't go around making sure Rue Ann received the respect and care she deserved. The woman made it perfectly clear that she wanted nothing to do with him. The more he tried, the more he'd look like a fool.

But he found himself searching for her across the crowded dance floor and wishing for things long past.

Their golden hour had come and gone and not a blamed thing had changed.

Chapter 3

Two days after the Williamsons' party, Logan Cutter rode into Shiloh to pick up some books he'd ordered from back East and get more materials for his fence. Seemed there was no shortage of things needing fixing on his place, which he'd named The High Lonesome. It seemed an apt name to call it.

His lack of funds to keep things in working order wore on him. It was nothing new, though. He'd had a rough go all his life, the least of which was monetary. Those kinds of struggles were small in comparison to the pain lodged inside that ate at him.

Even after twenty-eight years, he could still hear his father deriding and taunting him. Zachary Cutter would sneer and say, "Prove you're a man. Prove you have my blood in you."

To this day when Logan looked in a mirror, he saw a scrawny kid still trying to prove he was good enough.

Maybe by the time he got to be an old man, he'd have nothing left to prove. He hoped so. But for now he had to show the world, more importantly the town of Shiloh, that he was made of the right stuff.

The wide expanse of blue Texas sky overhead and a

gentle breeze seemed to hold promise. It was the kind of day that had fat, lazy cats curling up in the sun on windowsills and purring. Although the February day held a nip in the air, the sunshine reminded him spring was around the corner and none too soon. He'd had enough of winter. The cold months had seemed to drag on forever.

He drove his wagon onto Hayes Street and pulled up in front of the mercantile. Setting the brake, he was about to climb from the wagon box when he spied Theodore Greely emerging from Lady Alexandra's establishment adjacent to the Red Slipper Saloon.

Logan's eyes narrowed. Plainly, Teddy had passed the night in the company of a soiled dove. The man had draped his coat over his arm. His shirt was untucked and his vest unbuttoned.

Lady Alexandra had formed a very exclusive male establishment that catered to a man's every need. He wondered what Rue Ann would say if she knew how Teddy spent his time. Doubtless, it would devastate her.

Should he try to warn her before she learned the hard way?

Every part of him yearned to protect the woman who'd spurned his love. But she'd made it crystal clear she wanted nothing more to do with him.

Logan released a deep sigh and climbed down from the wagon, tied the horses to the hitching post, and entered Shiloh's only mercantile.

An hour later he emerged and loaded the fencing supplies in the wagon. Finished with that, he decided to pay a visit to the sheriff and let him know about a pack of wolves he'd seen that morning on the ridge overlooking his ranch. They'd been too far away to get a shot off. But Logan was sure they were the ones responsible for killing three of his cows.

He'd just passed Maggie's Confectionery Shop when

angry shouts on the other side of the street drew his attention.

Theodore was yelling at a scraggly mutt that had half an ear gone and an injured hind leg. From the way the poor dog's ribs stuck out, it hadn't eaten in a month of Sundays.

Before Logan could cross the street, Theodore delivered a hard kick to the animal. The blow sent the yelping dog into the street into the path of a horse and wagon, which had to quickly veer to miss it.

Long, purposeful strides carried Logan to the dog's side. He lifted the animal in his arms and carried it to the sidewalk. A quick glance told him it was a female . . . and she'd be having pups before too long.

After making sure the dog was out of harm's way, he rose and settled his attention on his adversary. Without a word of warning, he drew back and slammed a fist into Theodore's face. The man's head snapped back.

When Theodore could speak, he bellowed, "Cutter, you've done it this time. I'm filing charges against you for assault." He fumbled in his vest pocket for a handkerchief.

Logan's silky reply held more than a measure of challenge. "I catch you laying a hand on this animal or any other again, I won't stop with one blow. You'll be a bloody pulp when I get through with you . . . Teddy boy."

Theodore dabbed his split lip with the monogrammed handkerchief and shrugged. "It's just a no-account mutt. Besides, it was blocking the sidewalk."

"You'd best heed my words if you want to keep drawing breath." He turned his back on the man, effectively dismissing him.

Logan squatted down and ran his hands over the dog's legs but didn't detect any broken bones. However, a long, jagged cut ran the length of a hind leg and needed some attention. When he felt her ribs, the animal released a low whine.

"Sorry, little lady. Just be patient. I'm going to get you seen to." Logan needed a good dog. She'd fit in well at The High Lonesome, seeing as how they were both misfits looking for someone to care just a little bit about them.

"What happened?" The woman's voice belonged to Rue Ann. He glanced up and slammed into her vivid green eyes. She was breathless from hurrying.

He jerked his head toward Teddy. "Ask your intended."

"I'm asking you, Mr. Cutter," she said, putting her hands on her hips.

Rubbing his sore jaw, Theodore spoke up. "He hit me for no good reason, Rue. He's a menace to law-abiding people. It's time someone locked him up."

"Is that true?" she asked.

If she meant he needed to be locked up, Logan probably wouldn't argue with her. But he took exception to the menacing part.

Logan didn't bother to reply. He gathered up the pregnant dog and carried her to his wagon. He needed to get far away from Rue Ann before he said something he'd regret. But she followed, nipping on his heels, her boots striking the packed dirt of the street. He found it telling that she left Teddy alone to nurse his wounded feelings.

"I want to know why you persist in tormenting Theodore."

He gently laid the wounded dog on an old burlap bag in the back of the wagon. "Rue Ann, think long and hard about the kind of man Greely is. You're about to get your heart broken."

"You've never liked him."

"Could be there's a reason for that."

"I don't think you can stand to see me happy." Green sparks flew from Rue Ann's eyes, and the sun shot streaks of gold through her crimson curls, turning them into a breathtaking mass that stole his breath. She'd never looked more desirable.

Or more out of reach.

"Are you truly happy, Rue Ann? The woman I knew wouldn't settle for second rate. The woman I knew would fight tooth and nail for what she wanted, excepting me, of course." That she'd thrown him away faster than a pair of old shoes smarted. She'd tossed him right onto the dung heap all right and lit a match. Now he had nothing left besides a handful of ashes to show for the months of pure happiness.

"You'd do anything to ruin my relationship with Theodore just to spite me."

The accusation stung, penetrating the vulnerable part of his heart. Memories of their time together shriveled up like a sun-dried piece of fruit that had once been so succulent. He ached to see the bit of hope he had die.

"Then you don't know me at all. You probably never did. Now you'll have to excuse me. I have a dog to take care of." Logan untied the horses, climbed into the wagon box, and released the brake. "Take care of yourself, Rue Ann. Your fiancé is keeping secrets from you. You'd best find out what they are before you hitch yourself to him."

Logan turned the wagon around and didn't look back. From experience, he knew how painful looking back could be.

Rue Ann watched Cutter's wagon disappear out of sight before she joined Theodore. "Did you see what happened to that dog? I never got a chance to ask Cutter."

He shrugged. "The mutt was lying in the street and barely escaped getting run over. That's all I know."

Why would Cutter say Theodore was hiding secrets? Was it merely to get under her skin?

. Nettled that the man lay bare the growing list of doubts she had about her upcoming marriage, she slipped her hand through Theodore's arm. "Where were you headed?"

"No place in particular, sweetling. Your father gave me the day off."

"Excellent. Then how about a ride out to Bent Tree? We can have some lunch and plan our life together. In less than two weeks we'll be man and wife. We have lots to discuss."

"Can't come too soon for me. Yes, I think I'd enjoy spending the day in your company. As long as Logan Cutter's name doesn't come up," he warned.

Rue Ann cast him a sideways glance. "Whyever should it?"

"The man seems obsessed with you despite the fact that soon you'll belong to me."

She frowned. She didn't like people treating her like a piece of property. "I don't *belong* to anyone. I'm my own person, not a possession."

Theodore paused in front of the window of Whipple's Dry Goods Store and cocked his head this way and that. She found his practice of admiring himself very irritating. "You know what I mean. I'll be your husband and you'll have to understand that I'm the boss. That's the way it's done. Ask your father. I know he'll agree with me."

"My father is no expert on marital matters, believe you me." Indeed he and her mother hadn't seen eye to eye on several issues; the most serious was her father's involvement with the sensuous Lady Alexandra. Her mother, Jenny, had been furious when she found out where Devlin Spencer had been spending his Thursday nights when he'd claimed to be working late at his office. It had been the only time Rue Ann had ever heard Jenny Spencer raise her voice. And now a chilly freeze had developed between her parents. It wasn't how Rue Ann envisioned wedded bliss. She wanted more than that for herself.

Her marriage would be built on love and mutual respect . . . but most of all, trust.

She thought she'd chosen the perfect partner in Logan until he'd betrayed her love. Was Theodore any more trustworthy? She didn't know if Logan had warned her about her husband to be because of valid concerns or if he was simply trying to sabotage what she had.

Rue Ann and Theodore walked on toward the stables, exchanging pleasantries with several of the townsfolk.

"Do you have secrets, Theodore?" It was a question that had been on Rue Ann's tongue since leaving Logan. She knew it was far too blunt, but she couldn't think of a good way to ask without seeming to pry.

He stopped abruptly in his tracks. His eyes widened. "What kind of fool question is that?"

Maybe Cutter was wrong. The coiled tension inside eased.

"Let's just forget it and enjoy the day." She smiled and waved to the Barlow sisters, who had exited the milliner shop.

"No, I want to know what brought this on. What did you and Cutter talk about while I was busy taking care of my bloodied lip? Do you even care that he darn near broke my jaw?"

A heated flush rose to her cheeks. "Of course I care. I'm not callous. We talked about the dog. It was perfectly innocent."

"Nothing about Cutter is innocent. I don't trust him."

Then again maybe Cutter had something after all. Theodore seemed to be awfully defensive for someone who had nothing to hide.

"Everyone has their secrets," he snapped, continuing. "I'm sure you have some, too, but I don't go around pestering you about them."

So it was true. She wondered what Theodore had kept from her.

And curiosity about what Cutter knew got the best of her. If she wasn't so afraid of falling into his arms, she'd ride out to his ranch and ask him.

But she knew she couldn't do that. She wouldn't open herself up for more heartache and disappointment.

Besides, Logan Cutter wasn't the sort of man to tell on another. Whatever, whoever, else he might be, he wasn't one to dish dirt or spread gossip.

Chapter 4

Rue Ann's day wasn't going well at all. First, the run-in with the infuriating Logan Cutter and his cryptic warning, then discovering that Theodore did, in fact, harbor secrets from her.

And now her day seemed to be taking yet another turn.

Through narrowed eyes she watched Celeste stalking toward her with a set mouth and outrage in her measured strides.

Celeste was huffing by the time she drew to a stop in front of Rue Ann outside the livery, where Theodore had left her while he rented a horse and buggy. The woman's mouth was drawn in a perfectly tight line. "I will have a word with you, Rue Ann."

"I don't know that we have anything to discuss, and Theodore will return any minute."

Celeste grabbed her arm and yanked her to the side, away from the comings and goings of patrons. "I demand that you leave Logan alone."

"Is that so? And Mr. Cutter can't tell me this himself? The man I knew didn't need any female to speak for him."

"He's much too busy to concern himself with such

matters. You had your chance with him and now it's my turn. You stay far away from him. He cares about me now."

Rue Ann jerked her arm from Celeste's clutches and drew herself up. "Sounds like you're none too sure of your relationship with Logan," she pointed out. "What are you afraid of? That he'll remember the wonderful times we had together and try to rekindle our love?"

Celeste's reddened face gave her away. "Heed my warning. Go near him again and you'll regret it."

"Are you threatening me?" Rue Ann's voice hardened.

"Take it however you wish. You might be a senator's daughter and have money to burn, but I'm much prettier than you." Celeste twisted a curl around her finger.

"And what will you do if I refuse?"

"You'll force me to take the matter up with your intended."

Rue Ann had no idea what that meant. It seemed an empty threat because Theodore didn't own her, couldn't tell her whom to speak with, and darn sure didn't pick her friends. At least not yet. Still, she knew that given Theodore's overwhelming dislike of Logan, it would be easy for Celeste to plant seeds of discord even if they were sown from lies. The situation vexed her, to say the least.

"I know you find this hard to believe but my relationship with Logan Cutter is over. I wouldn't have him back on a dare. We're through. Understand? I've moved on and so has he. So you see, you have nothing to worry about." Rue Ann gently laid a hand on the other woman's arm. She truly felt sorry for the jealousy that consumed Celeste.

They'd been rivals since as far back as she could remember. Even farther back than the time in the one-room schoolhouse when Jack Blackmon had kissed Rue Ann behind the woodshed. Celeste had found them and yanked out a good chunk of Rue Ann's hair. She wondered if the woman would resort again to physical attack.

Celeste jerked away. "I'm not stupid, Rue Ann."

Just then Theodore led a handsome horse and buggy from the livery.

With nothing else to say, Celeste Wiggins whirled and marched toward the town square with her nose high in the air and her back as stiff and straight as a fireplace poker.

Theodore helped Rue Ann into the buggy. "Was that Miss Wiggins you were talking to?"

"Mainly I just listened to a list of demands. Seems Celeste had a fight to pick with me. For some reason she thinks I stand between her and happiness with Logan. It's hogwash pure and simple."

"I happen to agree with her. I've been trying to tell you but you won't listen. Where there's smoke, there's fire."

"Oh, for pity's sake! You've picked all the meat off that bone, Theodore. The subject is growing tiresome." She cast Theodore a sideways glance and noted the disapproving line of his rigid mouth. It suddenly occurred to her that it'd been well over a week since Theodore had kissed her. "Let's talk about something else."

"Like what?"

She captured her bottom lip between her teeth. "Why haven't you kissed me lately?"

He shrugged. "Just haven't been in the mood, that's all. It's difficult to find passion when your thoughts have been on someone else."

It didn't take a mind reader to figure out to whom he was referring. Reluctant to start a new round of ranting, she left the bait untouched.

Theodore put an arm around Rue Ann's shoulder. "Besides, a man doesn't have to go around kissing all the time for a woman to know how he feels about her. I know lots of couples who rarely kiss or only on occasion. Once we're married, I'm sure we'll have no need to kiss."

Rue Ann gave a shocked gasp and pulled away. "I will not have a loveless marriage, Theodore Greely."

"There are other ways to show love besides kissing."

"Am I repugnant to you?"

"Certainly not. You're a beautiful woman. I'm proud to be seen with you."

He definitely didn't show it. They were nearing the turn in the road that led to Dutchman Creek and the pretty little valley she'd fallen in love with. She'd been trying to think of how best to tell Theodore about the property and this seemed as good a time as any.

"Could we take a detour?" she asked.

"Sure. Where would you like to go?"

"Dutchman Creek would be nice."

"Why there of all places?"

"I've always loved the countryside around it. And I have something to show you."

Theodore turned the horse in the direction of the creek. They navigated a sharp bend in the road, and the rich, fertile valley lay in front of them. The lush vegetation and fresh cool water made it a prime piece of real estate.

"Stop the buggy here, please. Do you see how special this land is?"

"It's nice, I suppose. Why?"

Rue Ann held her breath, hoping he'd be pleased. "It's mine . . . ours. A wedding gift from my father. Can't you just picture a house here overlooking the winding creek?"

She crossed her arms, hugging herself. It was the perfect place to start married life and raise some children. She wanted three boys and two girls. She'd already chosen their names. The first would be a boy, of course, and she'd name him Spencer, which was her maiden name. A little girl would come next. She'd be the spitting image of Rue Ann and have so much life in her it would be difficult for the child to sit still. She'd name her Jenny, after her mother. It was perfect for such a special child. Theodore could—

"I'm not living out here." Theodore burst her daydream.

"What?" She struggled to understand the words that seemed to come through a thick fog.

"I said I want no part of this. I'm no country hayseed."

Rue Ann had trouble breathing. It felt as though hands were around her throat squeezing the life from her.

"Then where will we live?" she asked quietly.

"In town, of course."

"Where in town?"

"The hotel, I suppose. I already have a perfectly good room at the Ambassador."

"The Ambassador Hotel?" she asked weakly. "We can't raise children in a place like that." Where had this side of Theodore been? And why was it just now coming out? She couldn't imagine anything as ridiculous as living in a hotel, much less rearing children there. Her mouth gaped open. She struggled to close it.

"Who said anything about children? I certainly didn't."

Quiet unease swept over her. "Everyone looks forward to starting a family when they get married. I just assumed you felt the same as I do."

"I don't want any snot-nosed brats running around."

Anger surged. The buggy seat suddenly shifted as Rue Ann straightened. "You don't have to be so hateful about it. What's wrong with having children?"

"They mess everything up. They demand all the attention. There's no sense being married if children take all my wife's time and energy. A wife should devote herself solely to her husband."

Something must've happened to Theodore to cause such a narrow view of marriage and family. He'd never told her anything about his parents or his life before he arrived in Shiloh while she was away at finishing school.

"Theodore, why don't you talk about your mother and father? I don't even know where you came from."

He shrugged. "Not much to tell."

"What were your parents' names?"

"You're getting awfully personal, Rue Ann," he said stiffly.

"I just want to know something about you."

He sighed. "I don't know how this is going to change anything. My father is Ebenezer Greely. He was never married to Sally Stone although they lived together as man and wife for thirty years and bore fifteen children. We all lived in a two-room dugout ten miles from Fredericksburg. There was never enough of anything—enough food, enough clothes, enough love. We lived like a bunch of dirty cockroaches, always scurrying around looking for a measly bite of anything to put in our bellies. Many were the times we wrestled each other for a morsel of food."

Rue Ann's heart broke. She couldn't imagine the type of life he'd had. "I'm sorry. That must've been so hard."

"Hard doesn't describe it." He rubbed his eyes as though to rid himself of the images. "It was impossible. When my mother died, I left there and never looked back. I made a good life for myself working in your father's law office. He told me I have a bright future."

"I'm sure you do. Thank you for sharing your past. I can now understand the reasons behind some of the things you said."

But Rue Ann couldn't give up her dream of having three boys and two girls. God in heaven, she wanted children more than anything in this world! She just hoped that Theodore would change his mind once they'd married and settled down.

"Theodore, could you possibly reconsider living in the hotel? Could we at least have a house? Please?"

He leaned to place a peck on her cheek. "We'll see. It's difficult to deny you, sweetling."

She raised her hand to touch her cheek. Though she better understood why Theodore was the way he was, she didn't know how long or if she could live without physical affection.

It sounded like he didn't intend to show her much attention once they tied the knot.

Her heart sank like a rock.

If she couldn't bear children or engage in marital bliss, why was she marrying Theodore? He seemed to want nothing more than a cook and maid. And if they had to live in the hotel, he must not want a cook either, for they'd take their meals in the dining room.

How long could she survive without touching, kissing, and intimate conversation? How could anyone?

Her mouth couldn't have dried more if she'd rinsed it with alum.

Chapter 5

Logan didn't know how he'd manage to live without Rue Ann.

A lifetime was awfully long. His would indeed be lacking excitement and passion without her in it.

But it was apparent that he'd better start learning to cope fast, for the lady had shunned him.

Dust rising from the road caught his attention. The injured dog that he'd named Sheba rose to sit on her haunches and perked up her ears. Ever since he'd rescued and brought her to the ranch, she'd remained close to his side. She'd proven an excellent companion.

He squinted into the sun, trying to see the buggy that had turned onto his property. It wasn't his brother or sister-in-law. In fact he couldn't imagine who was coming to call in the middle of the afternoon.

He laid down the string of barbed wire that he was using to repair a fence. Tugging off his thick leather gloves, he went to meet the visitors.

As they came closer, he could see bonnets and skirts flying in the breeze created by the fast-moving buggy. Then through the cloud of dust he made out the gray hair and wrinkled faces of the spinster Barlow sisters.

"Now what on earth are Miss Emily and Miss Charlotte doing out here?" he muttered. They could be lost, he supposed. Older folks seemed prone to forgetfulness and were easily turned around. He covered the last few feet between him and the buggy and offered a hand to the two women.

When their feet were safely on the ground and he'd waited for the sisters to set their hats to rights, he asked, "To what do I owe the pleasure of having such a charming pair of visitors?"

"Mr. Cutter, how lovely to see you," trilled Miss Emily, who was outfitted as usual in her legendary funeral weeds.

Miss Charlotte, in her big white hat, which on a man would be called a ten-gallon variety, and yards of ivory and yellowed fragile lace, piped up, "Sister and I have a matter of the utmost importance to discuss, Mr. Cutter."

"Then please come into the house, ladies, and make yourselves comfortable."

Sheba trotted along beside Logan and took her normal place on the rug in front of the stone hearth in the small parlor.

Once seated, Miss Charlotte retrieved the ivory fan dangling by a string on her arm, flipped it open, and began to stir the air. "I told Sister that we'd interrupt your work and I saw that was the case when we rode up. She never listens to a word I say."

"You're not always right." Miss Emily shot her sister a warning glare. "Many's the time you had to eat a mess of crow. I recall in the afternoon on June twenty-fifth, 1841, that you were most certainly wrong when you said Mr. Ashton Tidewater would not ask me to marry him. But he did for a fact."

Miss Charlotte perched on the edge of her chair like a fidgety bird that didn't know whether it wanted to take flight or sit on its nest. Her back was as stiff as a whalebone corset. The woman sniffed and fanned harder. "And then he got in that dreadful duel and couldn't outshoot that blowhard Marvin Gatsby." Miss Charlotte turned to Logan. "Papa always said Sister could do better than Mr. Tidewater. We had to bury the man on what would've been his and Sister's wedding day. And—"

Logan took advantage of Miss Charlotte's pause for a quick intake of air. "Can I get you ladies some refreshment? I can heat you some mulled cider."

"That's mighty nice of you to offer, Mr. Cutter, but we really won't be here that long. We must get back to town as soon as we have that word with you that we came for."

Logan hid his agitation and eased back into his seat. He desperately needed to get that barbed wire strung. "Then please let's get to it."

Miss Emily smoothed her black crepe skirt. "It's about our dear beloved friend Rue Ann Spencer."

A jolt ran through him at the mention of the lady who'd occupied his thoughts ever since she'd come back to Shiloh. "What about her?"

If the Barlow sisters asked him to shoot the little weasel Teddy Greely, he'd gladly do so in a heartbeat. Nothing would please him more than giving the pip-squeak his just deserts.

Miss Emily's hat bobbed when she leaned closer and patted his hand. "Mr. Cutter, I'll be perfectly frank here. We don't like Theodore Greely. He's all wrong for our lovely Rue Ann. She deserves to be happy. She deserves someone like you."

Logan raised his hand to stop the woman. "Ladies, you're wasting your time and energy here. Miss Spencer has made it abundantly clear that she wants nothing more to do with me. I have no choice but to respect her wishes."

"Oh posh! The woman is only trying to see how hard you'll work to get her back. Haven't you heard that things that come easy are rarely appreciated?" Miss Emily's hat slipped at an angle over one ear. She pushed it back in place.

Charlotte Barlow nodded in agreement. "We have it on good authority that Rue Ann still carries feelings in her heart for you."

Was that true or only wishful thinking? He'd gladly walk through fire if only Rue Ann waited at the end of the pit for him.

"Did Rue Ann send you out here?"

Miss Emily's eyes widened. "Absolutely not. We came of our own volition because we can't bear to see you and Rue Ann marry the wrong people. Nothing causes us more pain. We want to see you two back together, like you should be."

Logan stood. "I've done all I can concerning this matter, ladies. Now, I really have to get back to work. That fence won't repair itself, and I have a herd of cattle arriving tomorrow."

Charlotte Barlow rose also. "Trust us, Mr. Cutter. We know about affairs of the heart. Just don't give up on Rue Ann. She's a fine woman and you shouldn't let her get away."

Didn't the two sisters understand? *Rue Ann didn't want him.* There, he'd said it to himself, and the truth hurt.

"I appreciate the advice, honestly I do. But even if I'm inclined to take your words to heart, I have Celeste to consider. I can't, I won't, hurt another."

Miss Emily pushed herself from her chair in the small parlor. "Miss Wiggins will find another who's more suited to her. Such as Mr. Greely. Now, he'd make a fine match for the woman."

Logan helped the sisters to their buggy and watched them until they careened around the bend in the road. Though it touched him that the two meddling women wanted to fix the problem between Rue Ann and him, it wasn't possible. They might as well be content to go home and tend to their own knitting and forget the impossible.

On the way back to town, Charlotte Barlow kept a firm hold on the reins and addressed her younger sibling. "Sister, I think that went well. Do you think we put a bee in his bonnet?"

"I do indeed. We've set the ball rolling in the right direction. Our plan might need a little more tweaking, though, in order to succeed." Emily giggled and rubbed her hands together. "This is going to be such fun."

Rue Ann rode down Shiloh's Hayes Street and stopped in front of Mrs. Fitzhugh's Dress Shop. She dismounted and tied her horse to the hitching rail.

She had no idea why she'd come to check on her wedding dress when her heart wasn't in a wedding. After yesterday's eye-opening conversation with Teddy, as Logan insisted on calling him, marriage was the farthest thing from her mind.

But her father insisted, as he had from the beginning, that she go through with the sham or else he'd cut her out of his will. Her brother would inherit Bent Tree and everything else.

No one loved the ranch more than she. The land was in her blood. She breathed the same air as her ancestors who settled Shiloh and Hays County when Texas was fighting for independence. This was her birthright. She'd not give it up.

Rue Ann's boots struck the wooden sidewalk as she strode to the door. She paused with her hand on the doorknob. An awful racket came from the back of the dress shop.

Curious, she moved in the direction of the sound. When

she cleared the corner, she saw that the noise originated from the outhouse. Someone was bellowing like a stuck pig and banging on the door for all they were worth.

Moving closer, she could see a board had lodged against the door, trapping the person inside.

A crowd had gathered, drawn by the commotion.

Rue Ann was the first to reach the necessary and wrenched the board free. A woman burst from the structure with a sudden lunge. But as she cleared the door, a bucket fell from the roof onto her head and thick, gooey molasses oozed down her face and covered a fancy dress that most likely cost a pretty penny.

The throng of people laughed. Two of the people with front-row seats were Miss Emily and Miss Charlotte Barlow. They tittered and whispered to each other.

The victim of the prank yanked the bucket off her head and slung it.

With the woman's head unencumbered, Rue Ann recognized Celeste as the outhouse occupant, and to say that the woman was livid was an understatement.

She looked like a soggy pancake with her prized hair plastered to her scalp and her dress hanging limp on her voluptuous frame.

Celeste caught sight of Rue Ann through the mess. "You! You did this!"

Rue Ann turned to go but Celeste grabbed her arm. "Oh no you don't, I'm going to make you pay for this, senator's daughter or not."

"I didn't do this. I just rode into town and heard the commotion and came around the dress shop."

Celeste Wiggins used her fingers and both palms to dig some of the molasses from her eyes. "I'm sure Theodore would like to know the kind of woman he's marrying. And Logan needs to find out what he escaped by the skin of his teeth," she snapped.

"If it'll make you feel better, go ahead and spread your venom. Do what you need to do. You'll be telling lies, though."

Just then Mrs. Fitzhugh appeared on the scene. "I watched Rue Ann ride up and hitch her horse to the rail in front of my dress shop. She couldn't have played the prank on you."

Celeste sputtered like a candle that had burned all the wax and left nothing but the charred wick. "Well, she would've if she'd thought of it. She delights in making me a laughingstock."

The way Celeste acted, Rue Ann had ruined her every chance she got, which couldn't be farther from the truth. Rue Ann had never done anything to the woman.

Miss Charlotte stepped forward and handed Celeste a wet towel. "Better watch what you say about Rue Ann, missy. She's our friend. You're not fit for her to wipe her feet on."

Without another word, Celeste snatched the towel and stomped toward her home.

Lured by the sweet molasses, a swarm of bees circled her head. Celeste finally threw the towel over her head and took off running with a pack of dogs giving chase, barking and growling around her feet.

Miss Emily put her arms around Rue Ann and hugged her. "That hussy doesn't need to be running loose. She's crazier than a Bessie bug. Try not to let her upset you."

"I learned a long time ago that I can't control what others do or say. The episode embarrassed her dreadfully, though."

Miss Charlotte sniffed. "It's good for that one to be taken down a notch. Celeste is too prissified for my tastes."

Rue Ann returned to the dress shop for another fitting of her wedding dress. Within minutes she stood in front of the mirror admiring the silk and satin emerald creation. It was the most beautiful dress she'd ever seen. But then it should be, seeing the amount of money her father had forked over for it.

Her stomach was a mass of nerves as she fingered the rows of seed pearls and ruffles. This was all wrong. She couldn't go through with the arranged marriage.

She got back into her riding skirt and jacket and left the little shop.

It was time she talked to her father. It was time she told him he couldn't run her life. And it was past time she took charge of her own destiny.

The house was quiet when she entered through the kitchen. She wondered if anyone was home. But as she neared her father's study, she heard low voices. She recognized her father's gruff baritone. And the other voice belonged to Theodore.

"I'll get my daughter in line. You just stick to our plan," Devlin Spencer urged. "Rue Ann will come around."

"And what if she doesn't?" Theodore asked.

"She will. I know how to handle her."

Rue Ann stopped dead in her tracks. What bargain were they talking about? It sounded like Theodore had an arrangement of some sort with her father and it involved marrying her.

The knots in her stomach tightened.

"You just go back to town and take care of things there, Greely. And for the love of Pete, quit fighting with my daughter. Marry her first before you lay down the law and tell her how things are going to be. That's how men handle these things."

Theodore murmured something Rue Ann couldn't hear. Not wanting to face him, she backed away from the study door and returned to the kitchen. A few minutes later she heard the front door open and close.

She waited until she deemed it safe to venture out before

she headed back to the study for the intended talk with her father. After what she'd overheard, it was more imperative than ever.

Again she heard voices as she neared the room. Her mother's sharp tone reeked of disapproval. "Have you lost your mind? Rue Ann will find out what you did, make no mistake about it. One of us needs to tell her before she finds out from someone else."

Devlin Spencer scoffed. "No one else knows besides the two of us and Cutter. And Cutter will keep his mouth shut if he knows what's good for him."

"Are you so sure?"

"Of Cutter or of you, Jenny? Are you threatening to cross me and go to Rue Ann with the truth? I'll make you regret it if you do. Just remember who you're dealing with."

"As though I could ever forget." Deep sadness laced Jenny Spencer's brittle words. Rue Ann ached for the woman who'd given her life. She heard her mother's misery and wished she could change it somehow. "I won't be the one to break our daughter's heart. But just remember this . . . the truth always finds a way to rise to the surface. I'd have thought you'd learned that from your years in the Texas Senate."

"In politics, a man has to do what he thinks best. As a father, I do what I must no matter how ugly the chore."

Tears sprang to Rue Ann's eyes. That her father could be so ruthless concerning his own flesh and blood drove an arrow into her chest.

She clenched her jaw and vowed to find out what secrets Devlin Spencer kept from her.

Chapter 6

On the first Saturday of February, Logan sauntered through the center of Shiloh on his horse with Sheba walking alongside. He was extremely pleased with his morning.

He now belonged to the Texas Cattle Raiser's Association. His chest swelled.

With the recent purchase of a sizable herd of longhorn, he'd gone a long way in proving he was a man. His father's words didn't sting as much as they once had. Logan just wished his father could've lived to see what he'd done with his life. His father probably wouldn't have actually said he was proud of his son, but maybe the harsh lines of his face would've softened some. The senior Mr. Cutter had been as hard-nosed as they came, though.

Logan couldn't ever remember getting a kind word or as much as a pat on the back from his strict father. He wouldn't have minded it as much if Zachary Cutter had treated Logan's mother with the love and respect she richly deserved. His mother was a saint for putting up with Zachary's mean streak.

A lump as big as a tree stump blocked Logan's windpipe. He missed his mother's sweet smile and gentle voice. He sighed and shook himself. The past was over and done

˙ with. Wishing things could've been different or easier would change nothing.

Life was what you made it. A man did the best he could.

He pulled his hat low on his forehead and straightened in the saddle.

He belonged to the Texas Cattle Raiser's Association. A big grin formed. He kept telling himself it wasn't a dream.

When Logan drew even with Widow Simpson's laundry, Theodore stormed out, his face mottled with anger. Sheba growled deep in her throat. The dog sure didn't like Teddy. And for good reason.

A dozen or so pink shirts filled Theodore Greely's arms.

"Just see if I bring you any more laundry!" he yelled at Mrs. Simpson, who stood in the doorway. "You ruined them, ruined them all. What am I supposed to do with pink shirts?"

"I don't know what happened, Mr. Greely," Mrs. Simpson said. "I don't know how that pair of red long johns got in with your white shirts. I've always been so careful. Please tell me what I can do to keep your business."

"I won't be back. And I'm telling all my friends—"

What friends? Logan wondered. And besides, this was the only laundry in town. Teddy had no choice except to return or clean his own clothes.

Just then Theodore spied Logan. "You did this! I don't know how but you did," he accused.

Sheba would've lunged for the weasel if Logan hadn't calmed the dog down with firm orders.

Logan pulled back on the reins and slowly dismounted. "What's the matter, Teddy? Someone make you look like the fool you are? If you're accusing me of something, don't hold back, spit it out. Before you do, though, just know that I've been out at the ranch until I had to come to town for a Texas Cattle Raiser's Association meeting."

"You try every way in the world to belittle me not only in front of Rue Ann but the whole blamed town. The only white shirt I own is the old one I'm wearing, and it's destined for a rag bin. And then I found out the mercantile is sold out and won't get in another shipment until next month." The man threw his pink shirts on the ground and stomped them. "I refuse to get married in a pink shirt."

Mrs. Simpson ran from the laundry. "Mr. Greely, get a hold of yourself. Throwing a temper fit won't do a lick of good."

Just then Logan saw the Barlow sisters sneaking around the building into the alley. He smothered a laugh before it could escape.

Those sly sisters! Suddenly he knew exactly what was afoot. The two spinsters had spoken frankly about their dislike for the pair, and they were trying to see how far they could push them. Especially Greely. Making him call off the wedding had to be their ultimate goal. What with Celeste's episode in the outhouse a few days ago and now Greely's unfortunate mishap, it seemed their plan might be working. One thing Logan was sure of—no part of it was accidental.

He wondered what the Misses Emily and Charlotte's next move would be.

On Sunday, Rue Ann was on her way home from church in the buggy. She was busy mulling over what her mother and father were keeping from her. She hadn't yet found an opportunity to confront them. Each time she tried, something always interfered, much to her frustration.

All of a sudden she came upon an animal sitting in the middle of the road with a red ribbon around its neck. The long-haired reddish pooch, of the retriever variety unless she missed her guess, seemed lost.

She quickly pulled back on the reins and climbed from the buggy. Reaching the animal, she knelt down. Surprise rippled through her. She recognized it as being the dog Logan had rescued from town and taken to his ranch. But the red ribbon stumped her. It didn't sound like the Logan she once loved with all her heart to go around tying ribbons to animals' necks.

"How did you get here, girl?" She glanced around for Logan but failed to see him.

What she did notice were the heavy gray clouds and a smell of rain in the air. She prayed the storm held off until she got safely indoors.

Just then another buggy barreled around the bend and slid to an abrupt stop. How unlike the spry Barlow spinsters to be so far from town. But remembering back to the church service, she couldn't recall seeing them. That had been rather odd also. The sisters rarely missed a Sunday.

"Hello, ladies. Taking a leisurely Sunday drive?"

"Oh goodness no," answered Charlotte. "The Williamsons invited us to lunch, so that's where we're headed."

"What do you suppose Mr. Cutter's dog is doing out here?" asked Miss Emily.

It vaguely occurred to Rue Ann how the two women knew the dog belonged to Logan. Strange to say the least.

"The poor thing seems lost." Rue Ann couldn't resist the pitiful whine and the luminous brown eyes that seemed to look right into the depths of her soul. She lifted the dog into her arms and stood. "Someone will have to take her back to her owner. I don't suppose you ladies would volunteer?"

Rue Ann had worked so hard to avoid Logan. If she were to ride to his ranch, she'd have to speak to him, and that would lead to him grilling her on matters she'd put behind her. Or else he'd try to convince her that marrying

Theodore was all wrong. She preferred not having to defend herself.

Miss Charlotte patted a stray wisp of silver hair back into place. "We'd love to, dear, but we're late. We're afraid we'll have to dump the chore in your lap."

Rats! Well, maybe she could just let the dog out at Logan's gate and leave without seeing him.

"You ladies enjoy your lunch." She put the dog in her buggy and waved good-bye.

About a mile from the Cutter ranch the skies opened and a regular old gullywasher commenced. Though the rig had a top over it, it was small and the wind blew sheets of rain right up underneath, drenching Rue Ann.

Everything appeared quiet as she turned onto the property. Maybe Logan wasn't home. Maybe he'd gone to town. She looked at the pretty dog that would soon be a mother. Maybe he'd gone out looking for the dog. He cared so deeply about all living things.

Except her.

Why had he decided that money was more important than their love? Tears lurked behind her eyes.

Through the rain, she noticed the fenced pasture that held over a hundred head of longhorn unless she missed her guess. An ache formed in her chest and grew until she could no longer breathe. It seemed Mr. Logan Cutter had done quite well for himself . . . all with her daddy's money, most likely.

Her father must still be paying him to stay away from her. In the conversation she'd overheard, he'd told her mother that only three people knew the truth.

What truth?

It didn't pertain to the money her father had given Logan not to marry her because she knew about that. No, it was something different. But it involved Cutter.

She couldn't get the conversation out of her head. Her

mother had warned Devlin that the truth always rose to the top despite efforts to keep it suppressed. She wearily wiped the rain from her face, which did no good in the downpour. Life used to be so simple.

Those days were gone, quite possibly for good.

Rue Ann set the brake and was about to climb down when a horse came alongside. The dog yipped and leaped from the seat. Rue Ann looked up.

Logan.

Her heart sank. Fate had played a dirty trick on her.

"I see you found Sheba." He dismounted and greeted the happy dog.

"She was about a half mile from Bent Tree. I have no idea how she got so far from your ranch. Has she run off before?"

Water poured from his hat in rivulets. "She usually stays close by since she'll have her pups any minute now. Thank you for rescuing her. Come into the house and dry off."

Rue Ann looked longingly at the sturdy shelter he offered. "I really must be going."

"Don't be foolish, Rue Ann. Looks like this storm has settled down on top of us. You're soaked." A smile deepened the creases at the corners of his mouth. "It's the least I can do to properly thank you for bringing my dog home."

Just then a jagged lightning bolt split the sky. Seconds later a huge clap of thunder vibrated the air and shook the ground. That settled it. She had no choice. She'd have to accept his hospitality.

"I can't leave my horse out here in the storm," she finally replied.

"Pull the buggy into the barn around back. I'll open the doors for you." He mounted his horse and motioned her to follow him. Shivering, Sheba ran to the overhang on the porch of the house.

Ten minutes later, Rue Ann made a dash for the kitchen

door. Her teeth were chattering and she couldn't seem to control the quivers that swept through her.

Both she and Logan more resembled drowned rats than people. He removed his hat and hung it beside the door. Water dripped onto the clean plank floor. If she could've spoken, she'd have warned him that it would ruin the nice wood. But she couldn't stop her teeth from striking together.

"Wait here." He disappeared for a moment and returned with two towels. Laying one aside, he proceeded to dry the rain from her face with feather-soft dabs. "I wonder . . . do you still kiss the way you used to?"

"Stop, Logan." Her voice was but a whisper. "This will accomplish nothing."

"I think we should find out if your marriage to Teddy is a mistake or not before you actually go through with it." His mouth was so close she could feel his breath on her lips.

"Don't start this or I'm walking out the door right now, storming or not." She snatched the towel from him. "I can dry myself."

Logan shrugged, got the other towel, and dried himself off.

When he'd finished, he wiped up the water from the floor. "Come into the parlor, Rue Ann. I'll have a roaring fire going as soon as I let Sheba inside."

That must have been what he'd named his new pet. Nice name.

Water squished in her shoes as she let him lead the way, lured by the promise of blazing warmth. After Logan let the dog in and dried her off, he lit the fire. Rue Ann stood as close to it as she could get, conscious of water pooling around her feet.

"Do you have something I can use to mop up this water?" she asked awkwardly.

"You get warm. I'll take care of it in a minute. First I'm going to make a pot of coffee. I seem to recall how much you value your hot tea but unfortunately I don't keep any."

"I'll drink anything that's steaming."

After circling around a couple of times, Sheba lay down on the hooked rug and curled into a ball. Rue Ann could hear Logan rumbling around in the kitchen. She should probably offer to help. But that would be dangerous. The close confines of the kitchen would offer no escape should she need it.

Sitting on a chair, she pulled off her wet shoes and dried her feet with the towel. She stretched her icy toes toward the fire. When she got some feeling back in them, she knelt and mopped up the water from the floor.

She glanced around the small but tidy house. Logan had made a nice home for himself. Rue Ann wondered who had created the homey touches. Hooked rugs and curtains gave the room an inviting air. Tintype photos of his brother Matthew's family were scattered around the room.

Celeste Wiggins?

No doubt the woman wielded quite a bit of influence. Rue Ann didn't know why that particular thought sat on her chest like a wagonload of rocks. It didn't bother her whom Logan courted. Or married, for that matter.

"Liar, liar, pants on fire," a mischievous imp in her head chanted.

She guessed the deep sadness filling her came from the fact that what she had with Logan had ended a long time ago. And in a crazy way it was as if he'd died and she'd buried him.

Maybe he had died. And most certainly part of her had also.

Rue Ann rose and stood in the parlor doorway, listening to Logan in the kitchen. She could see his bedroom through an open door across a small hallway. Like the rest of the house, everything was in its place. No clothes littered the floor, and a framed painting of a Texas landscape portraying masses of bluebonnets in all their splendor hung on the wall. She smiled. He'd always loved the Hill Country with its gently rolling landscape, lush trees, and abundant wildlife. They had that in common.

Logan would truly appreciate the rare beauty of the parcel of land her father had given her in the lush valley. Logan wouldn't scoff as Theodore had and refuse to live there.

The bed drew her gaze and a lump formed in her throat.

She recognized the beautiful quilt in the Lone Star design that covered it as one she'd given him. He'd lived in the boardinghouse back then and she'd wanted to make his sparse room more comfortable.

Panic swept through her. She shouldn't be here.

What was she thinking?

Sheba raised her head and gave a pitiful whimper as though she was in pain.

"Join the crowd," Rue Ann murmured.

She grabbed her shoes and strode to the door, her courage in tatters. She had to get away before Logan returned.

Chapter 7

"Where are you going, Rue Ann? You can't leave after I made coffee." Logan held out a cup to her, wishing he could draw her into his arms and hold her until she quit shivering. Wishing she'd come willingly. And wishing she didn't have that look of distrust in her pretty green eyes.

He took a few more steps toward her. "Besides, the storm is still too fierce. Even if you want to risk your life, you can't risk your horse's."

Rue Ann finally released the doorknob. "I realized I shouldn't be here. It's too much."

"I won't hurt you. Please trust me. You can't go home in the middle of a raging storm. That lightning could kill you."

"As well it might if I stay."

Logan wondered what that meant as he covered the space between them. Once she'd reluctantly taken the cup of coffee, he urged her toward the fire. "You need to get out of those wet clothes. I should've insisted on that when I first got you safely inside."

But he was having a hard time thinking straight. After all, he'd received quite a jolt when he found her on his premises with Sheba in tow.

Rue Ann quickly raised her hand to stop him. "Oh, no you don't, mister. You're not getting these clothes off me."

Logan quirked an eyebrow. He found the wild pulse in her throat very intriguing. "Not even to keep you from catching your death? What I propose is perfectly innocent. I can find you something to wear while yours dry."

He noticed her indecision. She still didn't trust him enough to lower her defenses. Shoot, at this point he didn't know if he trusted himself either.

To be frank, he wanted her. Every fiber of his being, every single part of him, cried out for her.

Yes, he most definitely wanted her.

On her terms or his. Didn't matter. The love he had for her was all-encompassing. It was the kind that wouldn't fade, the kind that weathered any storm and only got better with age like a fine French wine. Without her, he was nothing but a shell.

"I won't wear any of Celeste's," she managed stiffly.

Logan took a sip of coffee before he troubled himself to reply. "I hate to break it to you, but Celeste has no clothes here."

"I just assumed—"

"Then don't. Celeste hates it out here. In fact, she's only been here once." And only for a few minutes at that, but he had a hard time admitting it even to himself.

Strange how he never noticed Celeste's shortcomings except when Rue Ann was near.

And yet sometimes in the dark of night when only the sound of his beating heart broke the silence, when only God could hear his thoughts, he knew Celeste and he were very ill suited.

Rue Ann gripped the coffee cup with both hands. Probably so she wouldn't wallop him, he surmised.

"Well . . ." Her voice trailed off.

Would wonders never cease? He grinned. "Finish your

coffee and you can change in the bedroom. Just don't expect the clothes to fit. You're much smaller than I am." Not to mention having soft curves in all the right places.

"Your clothes?" she asked. "They'll swallow me."

"Don't look a gift horse in the mouth," he growled.

While she sat in front of the fire and enjoyed the rest of her coffee, he rummaged through his belongings and came up with some things she could wear. Then he hurriedly exchanged his wet clothes for dry ones before he turned over his bedroom to Rue Ann.

Logan felt like a new man. That rain had near frozen him. He picked up his wet clothes and went to get Rue Ann. Leaving her to some privacy, he stretched his clothes before the fire to dry, leaving plenty of room for hers.

Rue Ann wasted no time in getting out of her limp dress, chemise, and petticoats. She dried herself off and looked at the pair of faded long johns, trousers, a shirt, and a length of rope to cinch it all with that Logan had laid out. They wouldn't come close to fitting, but maybe she could make do.

At least they'd be dry. She thanked God for that.

She held up the long johns and thought about leaving them off. But considering the chill bumps that were almost as big as goose eggs on her skin, they'd feel mighty good.

"Pride can't keep you warm, you silly girl," she whispered.

Minutes later, she looked at herself in the mirror, feeling like she'd been swallowed whole. With Logan considerably taller than her, she'd had to roll up the legs of the long johns and trousers by more than a foot. Thank goodness for the rope that kept the pants from falling down around her ankles. And the shirt must've been sewn for a giant.

She bent to gather up her wet clothes, but as she did so, she knocked off a book that she'd noticed on a little table beside the bed.

It was *Treasure Island* by Robert Louis Stevenson. She found it a little odd that he'd chosen a book about pirates. But then he'd always loved escaping into his imagination. And he'd always been a ferocious reader when he could afford books.

The leather-bound book had come open when she'd knocked it off, and something had flown out.

Rue Ann picked everything up and her breath caught when she saw the valentine and silhouette of herself she'd given Logan several years ago. When they were still sweethearts.

Tears filled her eyes as she ran her fingers across the words she'd scrawled: "I'll love you forever."

Funny how forever lasted only until he'd traded a future with her for her father's money.

That knowledge brought waves of pain that made it difficult to draw in air.

Angrily wiping away her tears, she wondered why Logan had kept the token of her love. Why hadn't he gotten rid of the items since she evidently meant so little to him?

All of a sudden the dog's cries of distress penetrated the closed door. After putting the valentine and silhouette carefully inside the book and replacing all on the small table, she clutched her wet clothes and returned to the parlor.

She found Logan sitting on the floor beside Sheba. He looked up when she entered. Was that a look of expectation on his face? Mirth danced in his smoky gray eyes. "I was about to knock on the door and ask if you needed my help."

"You know better than that." But the thought of his big hands touching her bare skin brought hotness to her cheeks. She had to stop this nonsense here and now. The safest thing was to change the subject. "I heard the dog."

He gently caressed Sheba's head while the dog looked up at him adoringly. "Her pups have decided they want to make an appearance and meet the mother who nurtures them."

"The poor dear." Rue Ann laid her clothes down and joined Logan at the dog's side. "What can we do? I've had pets for years at Bent Tree but never assisted in any births."

"Nothing much to do except make her comfortable and let nature take its course."

"Seems like we should—"

"Make tea or tat some lace for her?" Logan chuckled and gave her a lopsided grin.

Rue Ann hit him lightly on the upper arm. "Don't be silly. Of course I know better than that."

She'd noticed the solid feel of his muscled arm. And the way the firelight played with his hair, which was the color of dark, rich earth. If only . . .

He grabbed his arm and feigned an injury. "You wound me."

"I will for real if you don't quit making fun of me." She hoped the scowl hid the traitorous efforts of her mouth to smile. "I was about to say that we should make a warm nest, get her comfortable."

"I think I have a box in the barn." He got to his feet. "And I have plenty of old flannel to line it with. I'll be right back."

The storm chose that moment to intensify. Sheets of rain pounded on the tin roof, drowning out the sound of the kitchen door closing.

While she waited for him to return, Rue Ann stood and spread out her clothes to dry in front of the fire. The faster they dried, the faster she'd be able to leave when the storm moved out. She certainly wouldn't dawdle. Her parents would be worried about her. If they—or Theodore—caught her here, it would be disastrous.

The dry clothes Logan had just put on were plastered to him by the time he hurried back in with the box. His breath came hard. He must've run every step of the way. He put the box down, then went into the bedroom and came back with a length of an old soft flannel blanket. After arranging it inside the box to suit him, he carefully lifted Sheba into the warm bed. The dog chuffed softly as though to thank him.

Unshed tears stung Rue Ann's eyes.

He'd braved the storm for a scared dog that no one else wanted. His unselfish caring touched something deep inside her.

"I'll get more coffee," she said, blinking hard. "You need some dry clothes before you get lung fever."

Shivering, he handed his empty cup to her. "Sounds good."

She padded to the kitchen. The bedroom door was still shut when she returned with two cups of Arbuckle.

At the rate they were going, he'd soon run out of clothes.

The clock on the mantel ticked off the minutes until he emerged. He thanked her, taking the hot brew she offered. Their hands touched and it was as though a bolt of lightning from outside ran up her arm.

Rue Ann jerked back and took a chair, as did Logan. He sipped on the coffee, his smoldering eyes never once leaving her face.

She fidgeted when he set his cup down and rose. He moved slowly toward her.

When he reached her, he placed a hand on either side of her and bent over until he was inches from her face. He'd trapped her. The panic that had been present from the moment she'd set foot in his house blossomed into full-fledged alarm. She cleared her throat awkwardly.

"Now that I have you where you can't escape, lady, we need to talk." Logan's voice was as soft as velvet.

Chapter 8

Theodore Greely looked at the note in his hand. He was at a loss to explain why Celeste Wiggins had sent it.

Please come to my house immediately. We have things to talk about. It's quite urgent.

The note had arrived in the hands of a small boy a few minutes ago. Theodore had asked no questions.

Though he'd long admired the lovely Miss Wiggins, he'd never done more than exchange pleasantries. Now he found his pulse quickening in anticipation. Celeste was the most vivacious, most exciting woman he'd ever seen.

And she'd requested that he come to her home.

It was quite urgent, she said.

If he could steal her from under Cutter's nose, he would in a heartbeat. It would serve the arrogant man right. To be able to shake Cutter's confidence would bring him a great measure of satisfaction.

Theodore closed his eyes for a moment, imagining holding Celeste in his arms, his mouth leaving a trail of kisses down her long slender throat and across her generous bosom.

Oh, the joy!

Anticipation tingled in his stomach.

Sunday had never been his favorite day of the week . . . until now.

He stopped in front of the watchmaker's window to take stock of his appearance. His lip was still cut and a bit swollen from the uppercut Logan had given him the day that mangy cur had blocked his path. He wiggled his nose. It was sore. He didn't suppose that would matter to Celeste, though, since she'd requested his company.

All of a sudden dark clouds blocked the sun and drew his attention to the skies. The air was thick with the smell of rain.

Theodore decided he'd better hurry before the deluge hit.

He lengthened his steps, attempting to whistle a jaunty tune. Except the notes came out all garbled because of his split lip.

"We have something else to settle between us, Cutter."

Rue Ann moistened her dry lips. Logan was much too close. Her heart pounded like a thundering herd of spooked longhorn. "We have nothing at all to discuss, Cutter."

"Oh, darlin', you're so mistaken." His silky voice set pricklies bumping along her spine.

"What good is it going to do? How can it possibly change anything?"

"We'll soon find out. You're not leaving here, though, until you answer some questions."

"You have things to answer for yourself," she replied hotly, clinging to her anger. It would help her resist the magnetism that made her want to forget everything.

"What things? What have I done?"

"Quit pretending, Cutter." She shoved him out of the way and jumped to her feet. "It's a little late for pretense."

"I'm guilty of nothing but loving you."

How could he possibly love her after all that was said and done? Did he think she'd just forgive and forget?

"What I want to know is why your greed for money out-weighed that love you so profess now."

"Greed?" Logan shoved his hands through his damp hair. "What money?"

For a moment she almost believed his denial. His fore-head wrinkled in thought, and the piercing gaze that never left her face seemed to back up his claim.

Rue Ann put her hands on her trousered hips. "Like you don't know. I'm talking about the thousand dollars you took from my father. Money he paid you to walk away from me." Her voice sounded hoarse to her own ears, the words bruised. "You can't deny it. My father told me all about it."

"Darlin', you'd better get your facts straight. I didn't take Devlin's money. Sure, he offered it, but I told him what he could do with his money in no uncertain terms."

"That's what you expect me to believe?"

"Either you will or you won't, but it's the truth. I told him my love for you wasn't for sale. Not for all the money and power your father has at his disposal." He drew her into his arms and rested his chin on the top of her head. The smell of wild Texas sage enveloped her. "I loved you then and I still love you now."

She closed her eyes for a moment, enjoying the familiar sound of his heartbeat, which she'd missed.

Logan felt so good, so right.

And she was so very tired of carrying her grudge.

Could he possibly be telling the truth?

Rue Ann wavered and she hated that he could make her doubt her father's word. And she had overheard her father saying that Logan would never reveal whatever secret the two men kept.

She pushed out of his arms. "It's all a little too convenient.

I'm not the naïve girl you used to know. The hard lessons of life have taught me well. Tell me this . . . how did you get the money to buy this ranch?"

Sudden anger swept Logan's face. His smoky eyes became hard granite and as dark and dangerous as the storm clouds outside. He added another log to the fire. "I was in an awful state when you left without so much as a word. I didn't care where I went or what I did. So after a couple of weeks passed, I saddled up and rode out."

Logan checked on Sheba before he continued. "I ran across an old U.S. marshal friend of mine out on the trail. He was after a man who'd just murdered a family of six outside San Antone. Marshal Baker had taken ill and couldn't continue the chase so he asked me if I would, said there was a sizable bounty on the murdering scoundrel's head if I'd bring him in. I knew it'd be more than enough to buy this ranch, which I'd had my eye on for years. So I accepted the job and tracked down the jackal. I bought this ranch, end of story."

Rue Ann stilled. He made it sound like nothing. A man who'd murdered six people must've fought with everything he had to stay free of the law. Logan could've been killed.

And if that had happened, they wouldn't be having this conversation.

She believed his story. Her father had been the one who lied, not Logan. Devlin had come to her that night and told her Cutter had snapped up the money to walk away and not look back. Her father had laughed and said he'd been right about Cutter all along. He'd told her to pack her things because she'd leave for Chicago at daybreak in his private train car.

A groan escaped her lips. She'd been so gullible. Devlin Spencer had manipulated her every step of the way.

"I feel so stupid. But why didn't you come to me and tell me what happened?"

Logan's gray eyes turned to shades of charcoal in the dim light. "I tried. I went to Bent Tree and your mother met me at the door. She told me I'd just missed you, said you'd left town and I shouldn't bother to come back."

"My mother?" Devlin must've repeated to her mother what he'd told Rue Ann. Rue Ann couldn't imagine any other scenario. Jenny would never be involved in her husband's lies.

"Yes. Your mother was the only person I saw at the ranch."

Just then Sheba let out a sharp yelp. Rue Ann and Logan hurried to her. One of the puppies had entered the world. Over the next hour five more had joined their brother. Only one of the six puppies didn't live.

Logan's jaw tightened. The dead pup was most likely the result of the kick Teddy had delivered to Sheba's side.

"It's all right, girl." He patted the dog's head. "I'm so proud of you. You did real good."

Sheba whimpered and licked his hand. Then she cleaned each of her babies and lay there patiently while the pups rooted for the teats. When the runt of the litter couldn't locate one, Sheba nudged it into an empty spot.

Logan gently lifted the dead pup and wrapped it in one of the wet towels to bury later after the rain stopped.

"She's going to be an excellent mother." Rue Ann's thick voice told him she was fighting emotion. Most likely she was thinking about losing her baby. He reached out a hand toward her but let it drop instead. He wouldn't push her.

"Yes, she will," Logan agreed. "Remember when we stretched out in a field of wildflowers and planned our future? We were going to have five kids if memory serves. Three boys and two girls."

Wetness sparkled in Rue Ann's emerald eyes. "We were

going to name the first boy Spencer. Then would come Jenny, named after my mother."

"Rue Ann, why didn't you tell me you were in the family way when you left Shiloh? Did you think I wouldn't have been a good father? Was that why you left?"

Pure shock crossed her beautiful features. "What are you talking about? Me? In the family way?"

"That's what your father told me a few days after you disappeared. He said he'd sent you away to have the baby. He laughed and told me I'd never find you." He rubbed the nightmare from his eyes. "The good Lord knows I tried, though. I traveled from town to town searching."

"Then why did you return my letters?"

"You wrote me?"

"More times than I can count. Each one came back unopened."

"I promise I never saw any letters."

"And I promise I was never pregnant."

"Wait just a minute. I have something to show you." Logan strode to the bedroom and found what he was looking for in the bottom of his trunk. He went back into the parlor and held it out to Rue Ann. "Read this. It's from your father when he was in Austin."

She took the yellowed envelope and removed the letter inside. Her face darkened as she read it.

Dear Cutter,
    I thought you should know that Rue Ann had her baby. It was a boy. Unfortunately, he didn't live to see his mother's face. We take comfort, her mother and I, in knowing the trying ordeal is over with and that Rue Ann is beyond your reach. Never try to contact her or you'll live to regret it.

                    Senator Devlin Spencer

Rue Ann looked up. Anger shone in her eyes. "That's what my father was talking about. That's the secret he kept."

She told Logan about the conversation she'd overheard that day outside her father's study. "It all makes sense now. And also why he forced me into an engagement with Theodore. My father manipulated and lied to me every step of the way."

Most likely the man had intercepted Rue Ann's letters and returned them. Easy enough to do with Logan being out of town chasing a murderer.

"Seems he lied to us both. He was bent on keeping us apart. Too bad his ploy didn't work."

"Like my mother said, the truth always rises to the top. Fortunately for us, secrets don't stay buried." Rue Ann handed the letter back to Logan. "I'm sorry I've made such a mess of things."

"It wasn't you, it was your father." Logan brushed her cheek with his palm. He leaned closer, hoping Rue Ann wouldn't pull away.

His heart beat wildly when she didn't.

He nibbled on her mouth before covering her lips with his in a searing kiss that curled his toes. She tasted just the way he remembered.

"Do you think we can start over?" Rue Ann asked in a whisper when he finally let her come up for air.

Those words were music to Logan's ears. "Most definitely."

Rue Ann wiggled until she got comfortable in the crook of his arm. "Logan, why did you put a red ribbon around Sheba's neck?"

"Me? I thought you did that." He kissed her neck. Now that things had sorted themselves out, he couldn't stop kissing her. They had to make up for lost time.

"When I found Sheba in the road, the ribbon was already on her. I wonder who tied it there."

"And you noticed no one else around?"

"Not at the time. Although the Barlow sisters rode up in a buggy a few seconds later."

Mystery solved. It was clear to him exactly who bore responsibility for the ribbon. Miss Charlotte and Miss Emily must've taken Sheba out off his property and driven the dog close to Bent Tree, where they knew Rue Ann would be going. He told her what he knew of the two matchmakers. Her eyes widened in disbelief.

"Good heavens! Why didn't I see what they were up to?"

"They're too clever. And not only did they play a part in getting us together, I believe they're also to blame for the pranks on Celeste and Teddy."

"Now that you mention it, the sisters were standing close to the outhouse when I got Celeste out. I never suspected them at all. They've been quite devious, it appears."

"I doubt I'd have put the facts together if the sisters hadn't visited me here at the ranch a few days back. They were very forceful in their opinions. They insisted you told them you still cared for me."

"I never said such a thing. Just wait until I see them."

Contentment washed over Logan. His world had righted itself. He had everything he always wanted—the woman he loved, land of his own, and a sizable herd of cattle. His future looked bright. He reckoned he'd finally proven he was a man his father would've been proud of.

Logan tucked a strand of silky hair behind Rue Ann's delicate ear. "So you continue to deny that you care for me?"

She caught her bottom lip between her teeth. "Not exactly. But I have lots of things to sort out." She cupped his jaw. "And I have to break off my engagement to Theodore before I can entertain any notions of a future with you."

Logan sighed heavily. "We've lost so much precious time. I don't want to lose any more."

Rue Ann snuggled against him. "I've made more mistakes than a body allows. I want to make sure this is right. Besides, you still haven't answered one question."

"Shoot, darlin'. Spit it out and I will."

His slow Texas drawl and mischievous grin set Rue Ann's blood pumping through her veins. She wished she didn't have to ask any more questions. She wished she could forget everything except how very much she wanted to be in Logan's arms and never have to leave.

But she had to know how dangerous his life was. If she contemplated a future with him, she had to know if he'd be around to help raise their three boys and two girls.

"Are you through chasing bad men?"

Chapter 9

There really wasn't any other way to explain how he filled his pastures with cattle. Was there? After all, he'd just admitted he hunted outlaws and murderers for money. Rue Ann didn't shrink from his penetrating gaze.

"Of all the harebrained things to ask." The muscles in his jaw bunched.

Rue Ann sat up straighter in her chair. "I think I have a right to know."

He got to his feet in one sudden fluid motion. "I suppose you do at that. I gave up bounty hunting. Not because of the danger. That part I loved. I also liked the feeling of bringing desperate criminals to justice. And you know what? I discovered I was rather good at it. I gave it up because I didn't want to be away from Shiloh in case you returned. Which you did. I have no reason to go back to it now."

Thank goodness for that.

"I'm a poor man, Rue Ann Spencer. And I have some debt. You should know I took out a loan at the bank to buy my herd. I figure I can sell off enough periodically to keep afloat. I don't want you worrying your pretty head."

So that explained how he bought his herd. "I can't

promise to never fret about things, but I'll always trust you to do what's best for us."

Logan pulled her from the chair and into his arms. A delightful shiver of longing ran through her. Her knees grew weak as her mouth eagerly met his in the kind of kiss that promised more things to come. A slow, delicious sizzle crawled through her body just under her skin. It teased and caressed each nerve ending, making her feel treasured and more alive than she could ever remember being.

This was true, absolute love. She had no doubts.

She thanked her lucky stars that he'd never be the kind of man who would, or could, live without affection. Like her, he needed physical contact to survive.

A contented sigh came from the tips of her toes.

The rain began the moment Theodore lifted the heavy brass knocker on Celeste's door. He adjusted his vest and frock coat so that it hid the greater portion of the pink shirt he'd been forced to wear and stared out at the heavy deluge. He was glad he hadn't gotten caught in it.

Celeste opened the door, looking resplendent in a dress the color of ripe peaches. The shade brought out her rosy cheeks and luscious mouth.

"Please come in," she said, ushering him inside.

She offered to take his frock coat but he quickly refused, not wanting her to see what he'd been forced to wear. Leading him to a large, tastefully decorated sitting room, she motioned him to the plush velvet settee.

"Would you like some refreshment now or after we've concluded our business?" she asked.

"I prefer to wait." Theodore leaned back and crossed his legs. "What is this about?"

She dropped beside him with a confused look on her

face. "I could ask you the same thing. Your note only mentioned urgent things to discuss."

"I fear someone has played a joke at our expense, Miss Wiggins."

"Celeste, please. It does seem we've been duped."

Over the course of the next fifteen or twenty minutes they discussed which party was at the bottom of it and arrived at the same consensus.

Rue Ann.

"We simply must take her to task," Celeste said heatedly.

"I agree, Miss Wig . . . Celeste. Rue Ann has developed this obsession with Cutter." Theodore wasn't all that upset, though. Celeste was much more enticing than Rue Ann. "What do you suppose is her reason behind getting us together?"

Celeste pursed her mouth adoringly. "It's plain she wanted us out of the way so she could spend time with Logan. She could be at his home now."

"What do you propose we do about it?"

She scooted closer to him on the settee and ran a fingernail up his arm. "She needs to get a taste of her own medicine. Let's show her two can play this game."

Theodore's breath came in big gulps when she nibbled on his ear. Providence had smiled down on him. "Yes. Oh yes."

Seizing the open invitation, he cupped her breast. Celeste's bosom reminded him of mounds of soft bread dough. He stretched her out on the settee and lay on top of her.

"Mr. Greely, it appears you might have to spend the night."

"Yes. Oh yes."

Darkness had fallen. Logan lit the oil lamps scattered around the parlor. He still couldn't believe his good fortune. Rue Ann was in his house, and she wanted a future with him.

Furthermore, it appeared she'd not be able to leave until tomorrow. The rain showed definite signs of sticking around.

Devlin would be fit to be tied. Logan's smile stretched. He prayed the man would come looking for his daughter. He had a thing or two to discuss with Senator Spencer. And he had a sneaking suspicion that Rue Ann had some things to say as well. It was time. Devlin had wielded too much control over his daughter.

Logan sank into his chair in front of the fireplace and listened to her humming a tune as she rumbled around in his tiny kitchen preparing supper. He'd offered to help but she'd insisted she wanted to do it.

He seemed to breathe a whole lot easier since they'd gotten all the misunderstandings and lies that had stood between them out of the way. He was glad that Rue Ann hadn't given birth to his child—yet. That was something he wanted to be there for. He wanted to hear the baby's cry for the first time. And he wanted to hold Rue Ann in his arms and tell her how very much he loved her every day for the rest of their lives.

The back of his throat burned with the need to take care of her.

Ever since she'd walked out of the rain into his house, his body had no trouble remembering the silky feel of her skin that was hidden underneath her clothing. Heat rose and made his trousers tighter.

An idea hit him. He rose from the chair and quietly stole into the kitchen. Walking up behind her, he put his arms around her and nuzzled the nape of her neck.

"May I have this dance, Miss Spencer?"

She turned to face him. "There's no music."

"I distinctly heard some a minute ago." He slowly kissed

each eyelid and the tip of her pert nose before he reached her mouth. "Besides, we have the raindrops on the roof and I have a song in my heart that's playing the most beautiful music you ever heard this side of heaven."

"In that case, we can't let all that go to waste."

Rue Ann slipped her arms around his neck and leaned into him. They waltzed around and around the small house until the ham in the skillet started to burn.

It was the best meal he'd ever tasted. His eyes never left her as he satisfied his hunger.

When they'd finished, he set their dishes aside and knelt in front of her. His heart hammered loudly in his ears. He took her hands in his.

"Rue Ann Spencer, will you do me the honor of marrying me?" The words came out hoarse and raw.

Tears glistened in her eyes. "I know I told you I didn't want to move fast, that I had to break off my engagement with Theodore before I could plan a future with you. But I don't want to wait. I know what I want and I want you. Yes, I'll marry you. I'll be your wife and have your babies."

He pulled her into his lap, nestling her against his chest. If he could've somehow opened up the skin, bone, and muscle, he'd have tucked her inside him, where it was safe and nothing could hurt her.

His breath was ragged. "Darlin', I'll make sure you won't regret the decision."

The kiss was long and deep. He loved her more than he ever thought he'd love another person. She consumed him. And that was the way he wanted it.

Pounding on the door awoke Theodore. He jerked upright, not exactly sure where he was. Celeste was curled up beside him. Early morning light streamed in the window.

"Who on earth?" Celeste murmured, rubbing sleep from her eyes.

The pounding continued. Whoever stood on the other side of the door was god-awful insistent.

Theodore jumped up and, dancing around, thrust his legs into his pants. "I don't know but it's time I got out of here before someone sees me."

Celeste quickly pulled on a dressing gown while he finished donning his clothes. Panic swept through him as she went downstairs. He threw back the curtains on the window, desperate to escape this situation. But the window wouldn't budge. It seemed someone had nailed it shut.

He looked around for a hiding place and had just slipped behind Celeste's dressing screen a second before the bedroom door opened.

"Honestly! For the umpteenth time I told you Mr. Greely is not here. Why you would even think that, I have no idea." Celeste's voice was raised in anger.

"I have my sources and they don't lie." The booming voice belonged to Devlin Spencer. "I know he spent the night."

Theodore's heart pounded. If Devlin found him, the promising life he'd built would be over. The career he wanted more than anything would go up in smoke.

"That's preposterous, sir."

"Then tell me, dear lady, whose feet are behind that screen?"

"You can't barge into my house and insult me this way."

Shaking like a sapling in a heavy gale, Theodore gathered his courage and went to meet his fate. "You wanted to see me, sir? I just dropped by to help Miss Wiggins with some legal advice. How you can think I spent the night here is beyond me. I love your daughter and I'm going to marry her."

The senator's icy blue gaze pierced him. Theodore

wanted to duck behind something. "Our deal is off. There'll be no marriage. I didn't care who you bedded as long as you did it discreetly. But you've flaunted this in Rue Ann's face. It might surprise you to know that half the town has gathered on Miss Wiggins's lawn. Even if you could escape my scorn, you can't dodge theirs."

"Then I'm not going to be in politics, take a place in the Senate, like you promised?" Theodore hated the whine that colored his question but he couldn't help it.

"I don't know how much plainer I can be. The deal is off. I groomed you for nothing."

The words struck Theodore in the heart. Everything he'd worked for, everything he'd wanted, had vanished, gone as quickly as a bird taking flight. Unsteady on his feet, he drew in a shaky breath. "I didn't want to marry your daughter anyway. You'll have a hard time getting someone to take her off your hands."

"Be that as it may, I want you to clean out your desk before noon. I'm through wasting time on you. You've done nothing but embarrass me."

Walking in a daze, Theodore made it to the front door. True to Devlin's words, half the town waited to witness his disgrace.

"What're you gonna do now, Greely?" the mercantile owner asked.

"How does it feel to account for your sins, Mr. Greely?"

He shot Charlotte Barlow, the speaker of the question, and her meddlesome sister a hard stare. He'd have no choice but to leave town. No one would enlist his services. He was a laughingstock. He'd worked so hard to overcome that cold, smelly dugout and days without food.

Devlin Spencer had followed him out the door. "There's a train leaving town at one o'clock. I suggest you be on it."

* * *

Rue Ann awoke to thin glimmers of golden light, turning Logan's bedroom into a beautiful haven in which she'd taken refuge.

Logan lay beside her, his legs entwined in hers. She lifted her head from his shoulder and marveled at the power of the man she loved.

Every time she thought of what her father had done, she seethed with anger. The lies, the manipulation by her father, had come close to destroying everything precious and good.

She tenderly cupped Logan's jaw. "I almost lost you."

He nipped playfully at her fingers. "But you didn't."

"I have to confront my father, you know."

"I know." He lowered his head. The kiss sent spirals of ecstasy through her. And when his hands moved to caress her bosom and down to her belly, she shivered with pleasure.

"I'm not sure I have strength to look him in the eye and condemn him for what he's done. He's a master at intimidation." Tears lurked behind her eyes. "Sometimes he frightens me."

Logan outlined her lips with the pad of his thumb. "Darlin', you don't have to face him alone. I'll stand beside you. Lean on me whenever you need to."

A tear slipped from the corner of her eye. "I don't know what I ever did to deserve you, Logan Cutter."

He took her face between his hands and gently kissed her.

"I thank God that He brought you into my life. Here's a promise I'm making to you. I'll not only be your strength today but every day for the rest of our lives. I will fight your fight. I'll dry your tears, my love. And if you think I'll throw you to the wolves you have another thing coming. We belong together for the rest of eternity."

Chapter 10

Breaking off her engagement with Theodore occupied all of Rue Ann's thoughts on the ride into town. This would be the first order of business before she and Logan confronted her father.

Seated beside her in the buggy, Logan drove. He'd tied his horse onto the back so they'd have transportation after she left the buggy at Bent Tree. Doubtless her father would insist on that. She cast him a sideways glance, admiring the firm set of his chin and the broad shoulders that would hold her up when she didn't have strength.

She loved this man.

Devlin Spencer had a lot to answer for. She and Logan could never get back the time they'd lost.

Pulling to a stop in front of the Ambassador Hotel, Logan took her hand. "Are you sure you don't want me to go with you?"

Rue Ann shook her head. "This is something I need to do alone."

"If you're sure." He stepped from the buggy and went around to help her down.

When his hands lingered on her waist, she very nearly

changed her mind. The heat of his nearness banished the chill of the rain-cooled breeze.

"I'll wait for you," he murmured in her ear.

She had almost made it to the hotel door when the Barlow sisters called from across the street. They seemed in a hurry to talk to her. Logan joined her on the sidewalk, his hand resting on the small of her back.

The sisters were quite out of breath by the time they reached them. First one sister then the other related the sordid events that'd taken place between Theodore and Celeste.

"He's at the train depot now about to leave town," Miss Emily finished.

"Good riddance, I say," spouted Miss Charlotte.

Remembering what Logan had told her concerning the Barlow sisters' cunning, Rue Ann smiled. "I don't suppose you ladies had anything to do with Theodore getting caught."

Miss Charlotte blushed. "Well, we might've had a little something. But that's just between you, me, and the fence post."

"You and that weasel really weren't suited, dear," Miss Emily chimed in. "I take it everything worked out with you and Mr. Cutter?"

Rue Ann met Logan's gray eyes and her heart beat wildly. "It did indeed. The wedding will be on Valentine's Day only with a different groom. To delay it would waste a perfectly good dress."

And there was no reason left to talk to Theodore. They really had nothing to say to each other. She felt lighter than air as Logan helped her back into the buggy.

The care he took of her made her feel very cherished.

Devlin seemed to have been expecting them when Rue Ann and Logan reached Bent Tree. Her mother was

waiting also. From all appearances, Devlin and Jenny
had been arguing.

Rue Ann clutched Logan's hand tightly as she entered
the luxurious sitting room. She wished she weren't so nervous but she was all the same. Her father always had this
effect on her.

When she wanted to sprint for the door, she met Logan's
clear gaze and saw him mouth the words "I'm right here."
That calmed her. No matter what transpired, no matter
what anger Devlin heaped on her head, no matter what he
threatened, she'd still have Logan's love.

"You have a lot of explaining, young lady," Devlin
started in. "I take it you spent the night in Cutter's company.
How you can disrespect me—"

"Hold it right there, Father. I won't have you belittling
or intimidating me." Rue Ann took a deep breath. Her
voice was strong when she continued. "I wouldn't show
my face if I'd done what you did. You're a cruel, spiteful
man. I didn't know how much until yesterday. I know
about your lies and manipulation. Yes, I spent the night at
Logan's and I'm proud to say I enjoyed it, but I'm not here
to explain. I'm here to give you the conditions under which
you'll abide or—"

"Who are you to lay down the law to me, little girl?"

Logan wouldn't keep silent any longer. His deep timbre
held warning as though he spoke to a snake about to strike.
"She's your daughter and she deserves to be treated with
love and respect. I'll not have you speaking to her as if
she's a bug under your foot waiting to be squashed."

Fire shot from Devlin's eyes as he addressed Rue Ann.
"You'll give up this ranch and everything you have for
him?"

She met Logan's eyes. "Yes. I figure that'll be a good
trade-off. I've found something far better than a piece of
land. If you can't respect our decision, so be it."

Rue Ann's mother turned to her husband. Her voice shook with anger. "I told you there would be consequences for what you did. You wouldn't listen. You never do. You think you can do whatever you wish and no one will say a word to the powerful Devlin Spencer."

"Mother, did you know?" Rue Ann prayed she'd say no. She needed her mother to be innocent.

Tears filled Jenny's eyes when she answered. "I didn't know everything until recently. And your father threatened me; said I'd regret it if I told you. Please forgive me. I'm so sorry. I should've stood up to him years ago. If I had, things would've been different."

Rue Ann went to her mother and folded her arms around the woman who'd brought her into the world. "There's nothing to forgive. You didn't deliberately set out to ruin my life."

She swung to face her father. "Logan and I are going to marry day after tomorrow on Valentine's Day. We'd love to have your blessing, but understand this, we're tying the knot no matter what you do or say. We've wasted far too much time being apart, miserable and alone."

"And that's the way it is?" Devlin asked stiffly. "I get no say in the matter?"

"No, sir. None at all." Logan drew Rue Ann into the circle of his arms and pulled her close. They presented a united front. Nothing could destroy them now. "This is our decision and you'll have to honor that."

"I see."

"Stop being so god-awful stubborn, Devlin," Jenny admonished. "Tell them you give your blessing."

"It appears you've left me no choice. In that case, Cutter, welcome to the family." Devlin stretched out a hand to Logan and the men shook.

Rue Ann let out the breath she'd been holding. Everything was going to be all right.

* * *

Valentine's Day dawned fresh and clear. She felt like a newborn babe seeing the world for the first time.

Rue Ann stretched. This was her wedding day. In a matter of hours she'd be Mrs. Logan Cutter.

They had so much in common. After confronting her father, they'd ridden out to her property on Dutchman Creek. As expected, Logan took it all in with awe and reverence. He'd proclaimed it to be a piece of heaven on earth. They'd decided to build a house there in the little valley. But while they erected the house, they'd live on the ranch he'd bought and maintained with his own hands and the sweat of his brow.

How could she ever have thought him capable of taking her father's bribe to stay away from her?

Logan had more honor and more strength than anyone she'd ever known. Oh, how she loved that man!

The bedroom door opened and her mother entered. "Rise and shine, lazybones." She pulled back the curtains. "You have some visitors."

Rue Ann threw back the quilt. "This early?"

Her mother smiled. "The Barlow sisters pay no attention to time. They live by their own special clock."

After hurriedly dressing, Rue Ann went downstairs to the sitting room and greeted her callers. Shock rippled through her to see Miss Charlotte in a lovely royal blue dress. "Ladies, how nice to see you."

Miss Charlotte smoothed the skirt of her new frock. "We hope you'll forgive us for the early morning call, but we wanted to catch you before you headed into town."

"What a beautiful dress. It's quite stunning on you."

"Sister decided to give up her white wardrobe in favor of something with more color," Miss Emily explained, still outfitted in her funeral garb. "She had her heart set on being a nun, you see. Charlotte wanted to remind herself to stay pure for her calling."

"But I decided that I was being foolish. I believe the good Lord put all the colors of the rainbow on earth for us to find enjoyment." The older Barlow sister's voice lowered to a whisper. "I saw this dress in Mrs. Fitzhugh's shop and it took my breath away. I wanted it right then and there."

"Well, it's quite lovely."

"You're probably wondering what we're doing here." Miss Emily handed a brightly wrapped gift to her. "A little something *old* for your wedding."

Rue Ann opened it and lifted up the most exquisite pearl necklace. "This is . . . this is too much."

"Nonsense. It belonged to our mother. We want you to have it. We insist." Miss Charlotte stood as if to signal the end of the discussion. "Come along, Sister."

Rue Ann put her arm around each of the sweet ladies and kissed their wrinkled cheeks. "I'll wear it with pride. I wouldn't be marrying Logan if not for the two of you. Thank you for all your help."

Three hours later, just as the clock on the town square struck eleven, Logan stood at the front of the church waiting for his bride. His chest swelled. He didn't think he'd ever been so happy in his life.

Rue Ann would soon be his wife and they'd begin their journey side by side, through thick and thin, rain or shine, hay or grass.

He allowed it wouldn't be easy. They'd encounter bumps in the road and maybe have to go around some of the wallowed-out parts. But they'd make it. He had no doubt about that.

Another thing he harbored no question about—he'd finally put the ghost of his father to rest.

He'd proven he was a man.

Come to find out, he'd been one all along. It had just taken a while to know it.

Matthew Cutter slapped him on the shoulder. "Are you ready to do this, little brother?"

Logan returned Matthew's grin. "More than anyone knows. I waited a long time for this moment. Thought it would never happen for a while there."

"Just shows it pays to never give up." Matthew's wife, Lucy, straightened his jacket and brushed off some lint. "You make a fine-looking groom. Remember now, anytime you want some lessons on rearing children, we'll be glad to loan some of ours out for you to practice on."

He laughed. "That's mighty generous, Lucy."

All of sudden a luxurious carriage with the Bent Tree brand emblazoned on the side pulled to a stop in front of the church. Logan couldn't think of a more fitting mode of transportation for the most beautiful woman in the world. "Excuse me. My bride is here." He strode confidently forward to help Rue Ann alight.

The sight of her made it hard to draw in air. She was the reason he'd been born.

He tucked her arm around his. "Darlin', we're going to make some good-looking children. They can't help but be the spitting image of their mother."

A blush rose to Rue Ann's face and spread across her cheeks. "Flattery will get you everywhere, my soon-to-be husband."

Logan's breath ruffled the silky hair at her temples when he leaned close and whispered, "I can't wait to get you alone."

"And what do you have planned, pray tell?" Her teasing grin made his stomach turn somersaults.

"I'm better at showing things than talking about them."

"You wicked, wicked man. I love you, Logan."

"All right, that's enough." Rue Ann's father gruffly broke into their private moment. "Make an honest woman of my daughter, Cutter, before you bed her right here on the church steps."

Rue Ann gasped. "Father!"

"It's all right, darlin', I'm a patient man," Logan assured her.

Several times during the ceremony, Logan's throat closed with overwhelming emotion. He took his vows very seriously. This was one thing he meant to get right.

He couldn't take his eyes off his bewitching bride. He was without doubt the luckiest man alive.

When it came time to seal their vows, he swept Rue Ann into his arms. His lips covered hers hungrily.

"Happy Valentine's Day, darlin'," he murmured against her mouth. "I'll love you forever, and then I'll love you some more."

Loving Miss Laurel

PHYLISS MIRANDA

Loving Miss Laurel *is dedicated to my sisters,*
Mary Kathleen and Martha Ann, who are very special
and mean more to me than they'll ever know.
I love you both.

In memory of:

Our sister, Clara Paulette Pannier Duncan,
March 8, 1948 to May 8, 2001.

Rest in peace, precious sister.

Chapter 1

Texas Panhandle
February 1887

Hunter Campbell entered the Sundance Saloon with an attractive darlin' hanging on his arm, as well as his every word. He looked forward to this afternoon's meeting about as much as trying to keep a pack of wild dogs away from a newborn calf.

He nodded to one of the two bartenders, who came from behind the bar and headed his way with glasses and a bottle of whiskey.

The cuddly thing on Hunter's arm leaned into him, pressing her ample, overly exposed breasts against his bicep and spoke only loud enough for him to hear. "Good luck. Not that you ever need it."

Before he could reply, she gave him another press of her breasts, ran her palms up the front of his brocade vest, over his starched shirt, and straightened his tie. She whispered, "I'll be over at the Coyote Bluff waitin' on every handsome inch of you."

"I'll be there as quick as I can, darlin'." He returned her kiss on the cheek with a light pat on her rear.

Adjusting the gawd-awful hat perched on her head, she turned and sashayed out the door, as if to say to the other women, "I've just marked my territory, so stay away from my man."

The bartender, a short, seasoned man with curly black hair, set the Black Jack and glasses on the table, before settling in the chair across from Hunter.

"You still going through with your plans to convince the knuckleheads of this one-horse town that we need that confounded railroad, so we can become a big citified railhead?" With bony, weather-worn fingers, Stubby poured drinks, and slid one over to Hunter. "You know our womenfolk are wantin' a library pretty damn bad. It'll be a tough sale, Hunter, even if we're made the county seat."

"I'm plannin' on doing everything I can to make sure it happens. It's been a goal of mine for as far back as I can remember." Hunter surveyed the room. "We need it. As mayor, it's my obligation to do everything I can to improve the town. If the railroad bypasses us and goes over to Panhandle City, or that new town Berry platted this side of the Frying Pan Ranch, Farley Springs will dry up and blow away like tumbleweeds on a windy day. We gotta make this town attractive to the merchants who will want to set up shop here." Hunter took out his gold pocket watch and checked the time.

"And you think paving Main Street will do the job?" Stubby took a sip. "Ever since I've known you, Hunter, and that's comin' up onto what—nearly thirty years now—you've always been a dreamer. Just like your paw, you see everything bigger than life."

"You know my life's complicated—"

"Of your own makin'." Stubby laughed. "But I guess following in your paw's footsteps as a cowman hasn't been easy. You know he'd really be proud of what you've done to that spread of yours." Stubby leaned forward and stared straight into Hunter's eyes. "The Triple C wouldn't be what it is today if it hadn't been for you, son—always lookin' into the future."

"I may be an idealist, but I promised Paw on his death-bed that I'd see that our family was never poor again, and I plan on keeping that promise."

Stubby leaned back in his chair. "Why didn't you have this shindig over at your saloon across the street any-ways?" he asked, then added, "As if I don't already know the answer." He let out a low laugh. "Keep the money flowing into the Coyote Bluff. Right?"

"Don't forget that I'm part owner of the Sundance and guess I can hold a meeting here if I want."

"You better not let your mama hear you say that. She'll tell you damn straight that you might be but the mice have more ownership than you."

They both laughed.

"You know me pretty damn well, Stubby."

"Yep, I sure do." Stubby lowered his voice, then contin-ued, "Heard a bit of news that I reckon you'll be interested in. Laurel Dean Womack's back in town."

"Why do you think that'd be of any interest to me? I care about what's going on with her about as much as I care how many trips to the outhouse you make a day."

"Humm," Stubby guffawed. "You sure as hell have a strange way of showing it by the way you look at her. You might be able to fool some of 'um around here, but not me."

"Her aunt and uncle sent her off to some floozy school back East after her parents died and before Paw passed, and I haven't heard hide nor hair from her since, not that I care," he half-lied.

Stubby pushed his chair back and pulled to his full five-foot-height by five-foot-width stature. "Gotta get busy. Got a lot goin' on this afternoon with this blasted meetin', plus your mama gave me Cal as a backup and you know how patient he is." He headed toward the bar, but before he got out of earshot, he spouted, "Maybe with your luck, you'll run into Miss Laurel."

"Don't bet your best redheaded heifer on that."

Hellfire and brimstone, bring on the matches . . . why had Stubby mentioned Laurel Dean Womack? Hunter hadn't seen her in years.

One thing for sure, since he had beaten her uncle in the mayoral race, Hunter doubted she'd even bother to say hello if they did run into one another. When she left town, whatever they had in the way of a friendship disappeared about as fast as raindrops on a hot afternoon. She was there one day and gone the next, without even a good-bye to any of her friends.

Thinking of her brought back memories of his youth.

When Hunter began to notice girls, he was taken with Laurel. She was a pretty little thing, but not like some of the other girls who took two days to get ready for a barn dance. Although most of the boys saw her as plain and quiet, Hunter didn't. He saw her as refreshing as the first wildflower of spring.

Back in those days, no matter how many shenanigans he pulled trying to catch her eye, she never paid him any mind. He just blended in with the other tall, lanky cowboys around.

Even today he could still recall feeling that maybe she ignored him because he was too poor for her liking . . . or more not to the liking of her aunt and uncle because he was unfit for their niece's station in life.

By now, the gossipmongers, led by Laurel's cousin, had made sure she knew that he'd become a successful gambler, even owning his own establishment catawampus from the Sundance, where he'd spend most evenings with a pretty woman on his lap, a cigar between his teeth, and a bottle of whiskey within reach.

The truth . . . he considered gambling little more than a hobby and had always kept his focus unyielding and clear on what was important to him—cattle and ranching, a lifestyle he had cut his teeth on.

But right now, Hunter Campbell had to be the town's leader and get the men packed into the Sundance Saloon to commit to raising the money needed to gravel the dusty, muddy streets. It had to be accomplished before the women in the community convinced their men that any funds raised could be better spent building a library.

And his only true supporter was none other than Gideon Duncan, the man Hunter had beat in the mayoral race . . . Laurel Dean Womack's uncle.

Chapter 2

Hunter checked the time again, took a hefty swig of whiskey, and sorted his thoughts. If he wanted a positive outcome, he needed to present his ideas in a cohesive way.

As he watched the gathering crowd, from both sides he was engulfed in lace and feathers hanging off two of the saloon's working girls, each carrying a shot of whiskey. Miss Marla spoke softly, "Darling, if you need anything else, just give me a nod." She set down her glass, smiled, and didn't make a move until the other woman presented him with another drink. She pushed back his Stetson a bit and ran her fingers through his sandy-colored hair before she reset his hat and gave him a peck on the cheek.

Together the women flounced off, whispering to one another.

It was time to convene the meeting, make a decision, and hopefully, in short order he'd be back at his own saloon taking care of business.

Hunter removed his Colt and tapped the table with the butt to quiet the crowd. "As president of the Farley Springs Men's Club, I call this meeting to order—"

Andy Baker, the robust stubble-bearded blacksmith, interrupted, "Where in the hell did we get such a sissified name anyway?"

"If we are gonna be taken seriously, we need an official name, so that's what I came up with." Hunter clinched his jaw, anticipating nobody else would question his choice. The afternoon was going to be a whole lot more challenging than he'd expected. "Ladies and gentlemen, if you don't mind, we have grave business that needs attention, so the Sundance will be closed for an hour to tend to it."

"We ain't havin' one of them there secretfied meetin's where we have to promise never to tell anything we talk about, are we?" Andy hollered from the corner table. Not waiting for a reply, he continued, "Get them gals outta here. We cain't have no spies goin' back and blabbing to them womenfolk what our plans are."

A concerto of voices agreed.

Talking over everyone else, Duncan said, "I agree. The women have no say-so and have no business here, so get 'um out."

Hunter nodded to the piano player, who stopped playing, leaving a noticeable void in the air.

Adjusting one then the other of the cuffs on his tailored white shirt, Hunter touched his gold cuff links to make sure they were secure. As if his gestures were an order, the working girls gathered their belongings and headed upstairs, followed by more than one man, whom Hunter presumed were among the soiled doves' belongings for the time being.

Chairs creaked, spurs jingled, and glasses clanged together as the men moved closer to where Hunter stood.

"Make this short, Campbell," snorted a bone-thin man with a few sprigs of hair on the crown of his head. "I've got my own dealings to take care of, plus it shouldn't take no hour to hear what you and Gideon say we're gonna do anyhow." He leaned back in his chair and crossed his arms over his chest.

"Hell yeah, Campbell, quit beatin' the devil around the stump, we know what we've got to do," spouted Cal the bartender. "You can save us a lot of time by callin' for a vote. No way in hell are we givin' our hard-earned money to the women for any library we don't even need. Your mama won't like us losin' so much business, so get to it."

Before Hunter could answer, Gideon Duncan pulled his tall, potbellied frame to his feet and faced the crowd. "If you all will hold your horses, we can get this over with and be on our way in short order." Duncan, who looked like a buffalo stuffed into a suit and tie, rubbed his beard. "Cal, you're right, we've beaten this horse to death, so we need to come to an understanding."

Hunter tolerantly waited for Duncan to speak his mind. The mayor felt it was important that each man have his say, and as a longtime businessman, Gideon Duncan had plenty to say on the subject.

Duncan continued, without even giving Hunter a glance, "Once the streets are paved, the supply wagons can move easier and quicker, stirring up a lot less dust. We'll use soil and stones from the riverbed and the canyons nearby, and when it rains, there'll be better drainage and less mud to deal with. Plus, it'll keep down any loose dust from coming into all of the shops. We don't want Farley Springs bypassed by the railroad and left to wither and die, do we?"

Voices bounced off every wall, mostly in agreement.

Duncan turned to Hunter. "Mr. Campbell and I share the same views. Right?"

"We certainly do." Hunter took over. "If we plan to make certain the railroad comes through Farley Springs, we've got to entice the merchants to realize our town is a place they want to conduct business; otherwise, they'll move on down the line."

"So we gotta make sure the womenfolk see that the money we collect will be best spent on paving the streets, not building any dern library," Stubby said. "Besides, not many of us can even cipher books. The womenfolk are already throwing a conniption fit about us even thinkin' about graveling Main Street."

"And I've already got my woman's back up by trying to tell her how paved streets will benefit her 'cause it'll keep the mud off her pretty little shoes and the hem of her dresses when it rains," said the man with three hairs on his head. "I'm gonna get my plow cleaned for sure and be roostin' with the chickens if I keep it up."

Hunter patiently listened to every man who had something to say, but he couldn't afford for them to give in to the female persuasion that he feared was building.

Possibly feeling the same way, Duncan said, "We have an obligation to make the women see the benefits our town will receive from the railroad. The men are here to do what is best for Farley Springs. We leave the cookin' and housekeepin' to the women, so they need to let us do our job. There's a place for them and it's at home tending the children." Gideon Duncan spouted off as if nothing of what he said was thought through.

His tirade set off a full-fledged prairie fire.

Dozens of voices chimed in, giving their own opinions. Some agreed. Some did not. Some straddled the fence.

Hunter felt ill at ease with the man's personal rant. He'd known the banker forever and didn't always agree with his approach, especially about the place of women in society. If Duncan's support for the railroad wasn't needed so badly, Hunter would do the town a favor and kick the pompous ass to Georgia and back.

By inserting his personal belief, Duncan had succeeded in complicating the issue at hand.

Now Hunter had to try to calm the situation. He couldn't afford to have the men lose their objectiveness; but the thought of any woman being browbeaten into accepting the opinions of her husband simply because she was his wife was unacceptable to him.

"Gentlemen, that's one person's opinion. I'd like to hear others before we put this to a vote," Hunter said.

Joseph Dobson took the floor and rambled on about how the men could reason with their little women and compromise, thus doing both projects, making everyone happy.

While the owner of the hotel tossed around his ideas on how to accomplish the deal, none of which were of any real value, Hunter kept a watchful eye on the crowd.

Hunter didn't recognize the guy unloading whiskey behind the bar. He observed Cal lifting the heavy crates to the counter for the young man, which was odd behavior for the bigheaded bartender. The kid couldn't be much over fourteen by his size and lack of a muscle larger than the one under his cheekbone. Hunter guessed that his mama felt sorry for the lad and gave him a job.

Another strange new face caught Hunter's eye. A man dressed as if he'd stolen his odd assortment of clothes off various clotheslines while nobody was looking squatted near the end of the bar. Hunter wasn't sure whether the person was dressed as a cowboy or a drummer, but an aura of bizarreness surrounded him.

As the gentlemen hashed and rehashed their options about how to raise money for their project, Hunter couldn't keep his eyes off this strange assortment of new faces working in the saloon.

Although he was part owner, his mother never bothered him with the day-to-day operations. She managed just fine without his advice. But one thing for sure, his mama never allowed the cuspidors to be cleaned or whiskey stocked in the middle of the afternoon. Those tasks were reserved for early morning while business was at its slowest.

Hunter wasn't sure what instructions the spittoon cleaner

had been given, but he was pretty sure it didn't include taking the rags hanging from the brass rails beneath the bar and turning them into makeshift gloves. Even with the cloths on his hands, he held the brass receptacles as far away from him as possible, as if they were something he was unfamiliar with. At that rate, he'd never get all of the spittoons cleaned by daybreak.

Movement outside the swinging doors to the saloon reflected off the mirror above the bar and caught Hunter's eye.

At first he thought a late arrival was about to enter, but he never did. The good thing about the half doors was simply to be able to see whether friend or foe was approaching. Anyone inside could generally tell whether trouble was about to visit by a man's boots and hat; however, this guy had a unique and very strange appearance.

Shorter than the average man, he wore a brand spankin' new dove gray Stetson that must have cost at least two months' wages even without the ornate hat band, complete with some type of feather Hunter couldn't even begin to identify. It didn't come from a pheasant or turkey, but some strange bird with blue and purple in it. No working cowboy or even an outlaw would be caught dead in the contraption.

Whoever was there spent a lot of time squatting down and then rising on his tiptoes, which only added to the mystery. The man's boots were fancy, shiny with little wear on them, no spurs, and were probably bought back East. Like the hat, no man in this neck of the woods would wear such girlie-lookin' footwear.

With a punch in the gut much like being gored by a bull, Hunter realized what was happening.

Spies! Probably sent in by his own mama.

Now he was smack dab in the middle of a predicament—whether to feed them information, be it half-truths or total falsehoods.

Over the years, Hunter had faced bigger challenges, and compared to some, this should be a cakewalk. He shuddered at the thought of having to resort to a frilly event to raise money, but it gave him an idea.

Hunter addressed the crowd of men, who were spending more time drinking than anything else. "Gentlemen, we have to come to a final decision. Since I'm the town's mayor and have been given the authority to decide if we don't have a general consensus, and it's obvious that we don't, I know exactly how we will handle the whole situation." As he spoke, he walked toward the doorway.

Raising his voice, he continued, "In order to raise money to gravel the streets, we will challenge the women and whoever gets the most money by—let's say Valentine's Day—gets their project done."

Gasps came from every corner.

"The little women are pretty damn good at doing bazaars and such to raise money, so how do you plan to outdo the womenfolk?" Stubby seemed to play along with Hunter's game.

Hunter surveyed the room before answering. The lad stocking liquor stopped in his tracks, as did the spittoon washer. The visitor standing outside the saloon doors stood on tiptoes, probably to be able to hear above the noise.

"We'll hold a box supper and Valentine's dance." Hunter almost chuckled out loud at the whole idea but contained himself.

"What in damnation are you trying to pull, Campbell!" Gideon Duncan exploded. "We had an understanding, and now you want us to just lie down in the middle of Main and let the women build their damn library right over us?"

"A girlie thing won't bring us in no money. We need something fittin' for a rough, tough bunch of cowpokes. We gotta have the hired men from the surroundin' ranches to make it work," proclaimed the three-sprigs-of-hair man.

"None of 'um will come to a dern dance in the middle of the month. Not even the men ridin' for your brand, Campbell."

"I can handle my hands. You all just worry about your own," Hunter said.

In a flash both the whiskey stocker and the spittoon cleaner left their tasks unfinished and charged out the back door like they were being chased by an irritated rooster. That only confirmed Hunter's suspicion they were probably two of the ladies on the side of building a library. If they were who he thought they might be, Pearl and Ruby Wilson, they were hoofin' their way back to the other women to give them a heads-up on what the men planned.

But that still left the flamboyant one standing outside.

Speaking loud enough that the intruder wouldn't have any problem hearing, Hunter chuckled to himself and then said, "We don't want any of this information to get out to anyone because I'm afraid the women will try to outdo us, even undermine our endeavors. That's why we've gotta keep everything under our hats even from our womenfolk until they accept our challenge and announce their own fundraiser."

Suddenly, Hunter grabbed both of the batwing doors and pulled them toward him, coming face-to-face with Miss Laurel Womack, complete with her expensive hat and boots. She had a scowl of surprise on her face that would make a totem pole drop over dead.

Hunter's heart pounded against his ribs. He was certain everyone heard it as loudly as he did. Quickly recovering, he reminded himself that she meant nothing to him.

"Do we have an understanding, Miss Womack?" Hunter said with a deceptive calm.

Miss Laurel Dean Womack only shot him another look that left no doubt which end of a bull she thought he was acting like. She turned and strolled off.

Over her shoulder, she said in the finest boarding school English that Hunter had ever heard, "Go to hell, Mr. Campbell. I'm not one of the *little women* in town whom you can call darlin' and think you can bowl over with your charm and a flashy smile."

With his thumb, Hunter tipped up the brim of his black Stetson a bit to get a better look at the backside of the spitfire sashaying down the boardwalk.

Leaning against the building, he pulled out his gold-encrusted cigar case and removed a cheroot. Rolling it between his finger and thumb under his nose, he took in the sweet smell of the tobacco as well as Laurel's perfectly proportioned hips swaying to and fro in riding britches that hugged every curve known to man. Her hair, the color of wheat, swung in the wild West Texas wind. He stood in place, taking in the pleasing view until he lost sight of the intriguing woman near the mercantile.

Hunter broke into a leisurely smile and mentally added one more thing to his list of goals to accomplish before he turned thirty . . . Miss Laurel Dean Womack.

Chapter 3

As soon as Laurel Dean was far enough away where Hunter probably couldn't see her, she shifted into a not-so-ladylike stomp down the street. With every step, she got madder. She was about as angry as she'd ever been in her life and it wasn't at the charismatic rancher either . . . it was at herself for getting caught up in her own trap of being too curious for her own good.

She knew nothing about a fundraiser, and certainly had no reason to support the paving of Main Street. But if she had to select one project to support, which she had no intention of doing, without fail, it'd be the library.

In the distance she saw the livery. Once she got there, she'd check on her bay, and let them know she wouldn't be taking him out again this evening. She'd then head for her aunt and uncle's house. A perfectly nice day of riding had been ruined when she decided to stop by the Sundance to see Hunter's mother. She hadn't expected Hunter to be there, much less her uncle and almost every rancher and merchant in the area.

What in heaven's name had she been thinking sneaking around and eavesdropping like a teenage girl trying to see if another girl was swooning over her beau?

Laurel could still see Hunter's face, as if he were standing right in front of her. She hadn't seen him since she had left town nearly eight years prior. She had been told he was a different man than the youth she'd admired from a distance. She had just wanted to see it for herself.

Not wanting to admit it, she quickly noticed he was certainly more muscular than she remembered. Strong and powerful, he stood tall and straight like a towering spruce. One thing that would never change was his dark blue eyes, which would make any woman want to invite him into her private chambers.

She had managed to embarrass herself beyond belief; not to mention she could barely hear what was said. She'd let her curiosity override her sensibility. Why hadn't she just walked away when she discovered he was in the Sundance? She should have never tried to catch a peep of him to see if the rumors about him were true. Now she was caught up in a mess of her own making.

As she approached the area between Campbell's Millinery Shop and the stage line, two people stepped from the shadows. Each grabbed an arm and pulled her into the alley.

"Shush, don't make a fuss."

Laurel recognized the voice belonging to Ruby Wilson, but she wouldn't have recognized her if she hadn't spoken, because she was dressed like a delivery boy. Ruby released Laurel's arm.

"What in Hades is going on, Ruby?"

The person holding her other arm let go. Laurel jerked her head in that direction and came face-to-face with the second Wilson sister, Pearl, who looked like an urchin directly off the street.

"What are you two up to?" Laurel straightened her leather vest and rubbed one arm, then the other. "Unless things have changed since I left town, Halloween's over and it's nearly Valentine's Day, so what are you dressed up for? And you didn't have to scare the dawdling out of me either. We've been friends for as long as I can remember."

Ruby spoke first. "We need to talk to you before you go home and blab everything you heard at the Sundance to your aunt and uncle."

"First off, I don't blab! Both of you should know that. I might be a little more frank than most, but I certainly do not tell tales out of school, plus I couldn't hear much of anything to go *blab* about anyway." Frustrated, she stirred up a tiny cloud of dust with the toe of her boot.

"Okay, so you don't blab, but since you haven't been back in town but a few days, there are a lot of things you don't know." Pearl took a step forward and looked up and down the street. "We gotta talk, Laurel."

"It's obvious there's a lot of things around here that I didn't know about." One thing that crossed her mind was the realization that her uncle and Hunter were in cahoots over the need for a railroad. "So let's talk, but not in an alley. I have to go over to the livery first." Her wish to take her bay out again for a leisurely outing had turned to a need for a long, hard ride with nobody but her horse and the sunset to keep her company. "Then we can meet anywhere you want. By the costumes you two are wearing, I'm sure you want to go to your house to change."

"Well, that getup you're wearing doesn't look that much better," said Ruby.

Pearl looked up and down the street again. "Wearing all that citified garb."

"It's the latest fashion from back East," Laurel said much more proudly than she felt.

Both Wilson girls cackled. "And we're wearing the latest fashions from back here," Ruby said.

All three joined in on a good-natured laugh. The Wilson

sisters had no idea just how badly Laurel needed to share a little bit of merriment with friends.

"We aren't going to our house; we're going out to the Triple C to talk to Mrs. Campbell."

"Melba Ruth Campbell?"

Both sisters nodded.

Ruby plastered a mischievous smile on her face. "You didn't think I was meanin' that Hunter had gotten hitched, did you?"

"Well, as I already said, I have been gone a long time, so anything could have happened. But I had planned on seeing Mrs. Campbell today anyway." What she wanted to say was simply that there was no way in hell she wanted to take a chance on having another confrontation with the devilishly handsome rogue rancher today . . . or any other day, for that matter.

"He won't be there. Didn't you see Greta Garrett panting after him? She, along with about every woman under the age of forty who can still breathe, has been swooning over him for as long as we can remember. He'll be over at his saloon most of the night, probably with her hangin' on to him like he might slip into one of the spittoons or something worse." The sisters looked at each other and burst into laughter.

"You remember her, don't you?" Pearl asked.

"Yes. I just found out, if you can imagine it, she's my cousin's best friend." Cold chills ran through Laurel at the thought because she hadn't figured out yet whether she had been told of the friendship as a warning or if it was her cousin being such a braggadocio. "I walked up about the time she waltzed out of the Sundance. I'm sure she didn't see me because her nose was turned up like she smelled animal excrement in the air."

"You mean bull crap." Ruby laughed at Laurel's boarding-house verbiage.

"Exactly. She has not changed an iota, just gotten bigger, hum—you know, her ta-tas . . ." She trailed off, knowing they knew exactly what part of Greta she was referring to. "I presume she is as much of a femme fatale as we all expected she'd turn out to be."

"Well, if that means a woman of ill repute—"

"Plain ol' whore to me." Ruby corrected her sister. "Our buggy is over at the livery. So let's get a wiggle on. We don't have long before sunset to get out to the Triple C and get back to town." Ruby took off her hat and unpinned her hair, letting it fall over her shoulders before resetting her dirty, battered hat in place. "That feels better."

"Ruby," said Pearl, "Laurel can tie her horse on the back of our buggy and ride with us, can't she?"

In short order the bay trotted behind the Wilson sisters' buggy, and the three women were on their way to the Campbell place, no more than a good forty-minute ride from town.

Laurel listened to the sisters' attempts to fill her in on everything that had happened in Farley Springs over the last six years when in truth, more than anything else, she wanted to know about Hunter Campbell and his enormous success. Finishing school had exposed her to the finer parts of being a lady, but hadn't corralled her curiosity.

That same inquisitiveness got the best of Laurel. "The first thing I noticed when I walked down Main Street is that every other building has the name *Campbell* on it. When I left, Hunter and his parents were barely making payroll running cattle on their ranch and helping out at the Sundance."

Ruby held a firm grip on the ribbons. "Hunter nearly killed himself working days at the ranch growing the herd and then at the Sundance at night helping out his ma—"

"And she worked for your uncle, too." Pearl squirmed in her seat. "But you knew that, of course."

"No, I didn't." Laurel wondered how many more things she didn't know. "What did she do?"

Ruby answered, "She kept house for your aunt for a while, and once your uncle found out she knew numbers, he hired her at the bank. She wasn't there long, as I recall. Something happened, I think, because she left suddenly—"

"It was right after Mr. Campbell died," Pearl interjected.

"I didn't realize he had passed." Strange, disquieting thoughts began racing through Laurel's mind.

"Back to your question about Hunter's success . . ." Ruby seemed to be deliberately changing the subject. "You know Hunter could make a coyote roll over and let him scratch his tummy with nothing but a smile and a wink. I guess that charm is what made him into the businessman he is today. A very successful one, too. One thing for sure, he doesn't mix gambling and ranching. When he plays poker, he takes no prisoners. If anyone bellies up to his table, they'd better be a good player because he'll take 'um for every penny they have plus some. And when he's out on the ranch, it's all about winning, too, but in a different sort of way. You should know that since he kicked your uncle's butt from here to the Rio Grande and back when he ran for mayor—"

"Of course she knows it." Ruby frowned at her sibling.

"I didn't, but that explains a few things," said Laurel.

"Didn't your aunt and uncle keep in touch with you while you were up in New York at that highfalutin' college? Heard you got some kind of degree as good as any man." Ruby sounded impressed.

"No on the first matter. And yes on the second." Laurel took a deep breath and tried to chase away the not-too-fond memories of her life in New York.

After finishing school, with grand flare her aunt and uncle had escorted her to the dean of the elite, private Elmira College. Before leaving town, they had introduced her to the higher echelon of influential people to make certain she would receive invitations to the finest social events where the privileged attended. She'd never heard from either of them directly since they'd walked out of her life.

She shuddered, remembering how month after month she'd receive an envelope at her boardinghouse from her Uncle Gideon. Inside was always a draft for the same measly amount that constituted her monthly allowance from her parents' estate. After a couple of months, she became accustomed to expecting not a single word of affection written on the parchment inside.

All of her educational expenses were paid directly to the college by the trustee of her parents' estate—her Uncle Gideon Duncan. She had never gotten over the feeling that she'd been sent away for an education and her only family had forgotten she existed.

That was why, after Christmas, she was taken by surprise when she received a letter from her uncle stating how much she was missed and wanting her to return home. He even promised her a job at the bank, which so far had not come up in conversation. A ticket to Farley Springs had been enclosed.

"Laurel," Ruby almost shouted. "Hello, Laurel . . . I think we lost you."

"No, I just got lost in the beauty of the countryside. I'd forgotten how blue the Texas sky is." She changed the subject back to Hunter as quickly as possible. "I understand how Hunter did well with the ranch, but how did he acquire all of the other businesses? Two saloons, the millinery shop, the mercantile, and I bet there are others that don't have the Campbell name on them."

"It shouldn't take a girl with some big-fandangled college degree to figure that one out," Ruby quipped. "He won them gambling."

Pearl, who hadn't said a lot so far, chimed in, "But it isn't like you think. He did win most of them in high-stakes games of chance, but then handed over most of them to either one of the Campbells or he turned them back to the poor, losing poker player with the understanding that he would keep a small interest in the business."

"I see." Laurel smiled. "Things haven't changed very much since I left town after all."

All three ladies seemed to lapse into their own thoughts.

With the abundance of moisture over the winter and the early spring, as Laurel was told by the sisters, the prairie was carpeted with red-orange Indian paintbrush and spotted with waist-high yucca plants, promising the most beautiful springtime yet.

In the distance, the main house of the Campbell Ranch came into sight, a huge two-story plantation-style house with a wraparound veranda. So different from the long, low prairie-style homestead where Hunter's parents had raised him and his sister.

When the Wilson buggy pulled up in front of the main house, a lanky, toothless ranch hand met them and helped them down from their carriage, then untied Laurel's horse. "Mrs. Campbell is waitin' for you all in the parlor." He turned to Laurel and said, "Good to see you again, Miss Womack. I'll see to your bay. He sure has a good-lookin' black mane and tail."

"I think so, too. His name is Buckey."

Laurel followed Ruby and Pearl up the stairs.

When she reached the front porch, she stopped. Taking a lace hankie from her pocket, she dabbed away some of the perspiration from her forehead. She didn't want to look all hot and sticky for Mrs. Campbell.

For early spring, it was certainly a warm day.

A rich, deep-timbered voice she'd know anywhere called from somewhere off to the right of the door.

Laurel whirled in its direction.

Hunter leaned against the porch railing and shot her his familiar, charismatic smile that would set any woman's heart to racing.

Dressed in a black Stetson that had seen a lot of seasons, a chambray shirt, and tight-fittin' work pants, with a gun belt holstering a single Colt hanging over slim hips, he looked nothing of the suave, debonair businessman she'd seen earlier in the day.

Tipping his hat, he said, "Nice to see you again, Miss Laurel. Welcome to the Triple C . . . but only if you don't tell me to go to hell for saying so."

Chapter 4

Laurel and Hunter stood on the porch only inches apart, but it could have been miles between them from the way they reacted to each other. She deliberately set her chin in defiance. He stood with his arms folded across his chest.

A blue jay hovered low over the ground and made his presence known with his distinct, harsh call, which seemed to mimic the screams of a hawk.

"I apologize," Laurel and Hunter said in unison.

"Ladies first." He successfully disarmed her with his open, friendly smile.

"I shouldn't have said what I did in town. I was, uh . . ." She wasn't sure exactly how to explain away her frustrations without admitting that what happened was her fault. She took a deep breath to scrounge up enough courage to offer an acceptable explanation. "I stopped by to see your mother. But when I realized a meeting was taking place, I was hesitant to come in. I simply should have left, so I owe you an apology." She swallowed hard, finding it more difficult than it should be to say, "I'm sorry."

"Apology accepted. I should have been more cordial a minute ago myself."

Laurel met his smile, and the hand that was offered. "Friends?"

"Friends." He tipped his hat. "Have a great day, Laurel Dean."

Slipping back into the shadows of the porch, she watched Hunter swagger his way toward the cowboy who was untying her horse from the buggy.

"I'm on my way to the barn, Slim," Hunter said as he came up even with the lanky ranch hand. "I'll see to Miss Womack's gelding."

"I figured you'd be at the Coyote Bluff this afternoon." Slim handed over the reins.

"Nope. Got troubles up near the river, and I need to go out there and see to them. Part of the fence is down and there's a heifer having problems birthing. Don't have much time before dark, so I'm headin' that way right now."

"You got good hands out there that are capable of handling it," said Slim.

"Yep, but can't take a chance on losing the calf and certainly not the heifer. Every head is money in the bank."

The pair, leading Buckey, sauntered in the direction of the corral and out of earshot.

The front screen door opened, startling Laurel.

Ruby stepped out. "What's keeping you?" She raised an eyebrow and nodded in the direction of Hunter. "Oh, I see what, or I should say who, caught your attention. I didn't think Hunter would be here, but it makes it convenient for you, just in case you wanna eavesdrop on him some more." Amused at her own humor, Ruby smiled with an air of pleasure.

Not finding anything funny about her friend's comment, Laurel straightened her shoulders and took a couple of steps toward the entryway. When she was even with Ruby, Laurel leaned over and whispered, "For your information,

I couldn't care less about that man. I was wiping perspiration from my forehead."

"You mean sweat?" Ruby corrected.

Laurel shot her a benign smile as if dealing with an impolite child, then walked past her.

Heavy oak French doors led into the well-furnished parlor. Ceiling-to-floor bookcases filled with leather-bound volumes covered one wall. The rest of the room was papered in shades of blue and white, reminding Laurel of the bluebonnet fields of the Hill Country.

"There you are, Laurel Dean." Mrs. Campbell appeared, carrying a silver tray with a porcelain tea set and a plate of tiny fried pies.

After setting the refreshments on the low table in front of the settee, she gathered Laurel into her arms and they exchanged hugs. Apparently not satisfied, the older woman set Laurel out at arm's length and looked her up and down, stopping at her gawd-awful boots. Mrs. Campbell raised an eyebrow. As she released Laurel, her smile widened in approval. "You look well, dear."

"As do you, Mrs. Campbell." Laurel reached out and took the hand of the youthful-looking woman who was tastefully dressed and nearly as tall as her son.

Laurel offered condolences at the loss of Mr. Campbell, then said, "I've really missed you."

The only thing that had changed since Laurel had last seen the older woman was her hair, which looked like a beautiful snowdrift.

"We've all grown up, Laurel Dean, so call me Melba Ruth." A flash of humor crossed her face. "Makes me feel younger. Ladies, we don't stand on formalities in this house, so please make yourself at home." She sat on one end of the settee and patted the empty space next to her. "Laurel Dean, have a seat."

Melba Ruth served tea to first Ruby then Pearl, who settled in chairs on each side of a small parlor table covered with a finely crocheted doily.

To Laurel's plate she added an extra fried pie. "I made these when I knew you were coming out."

"Apple?" Laurel smiled. "I remember making them with you when I lived here before. You always said the little ones taste better than the bigger ones."

"You thought so, too." While taking care of her hostess duties, Melba Ruth chatted like a magpie, asking one question and barely waiting for an answer before posing another one.

"Thank you, girls, for coming all the way out here. I didn't want to meet in town, for all the reasons you know." She took a sip of her tea. "So tell me what the men's meeting was all about. I asked Hunter, but of course, he dodged my question and ducked out without giving me an answer." She looked at Ruby, then over to her sister. "Cute disguises, girls."

Neither of the women breathed a word, but each gave her a knowing look that made Laurel realize Melba Ruth knew exactly why they were dressed the way they were.

Although Laurel had caught only a couple of glimpses of the inside of the Sundance, she had seen both of them plain as day, but of course, she didn't recognize them until they had met in the alley.

"I know it was about the railroad." Melba Ruth took a sip of tea. "Hunter has always been driven, and for a kid born and raised in this simple part of the country, he's a visionary and has always been."

She kept talking, barely taking a breath in between sentences. "I remember when he was just a little boy, he'd help me gather eggs and I'd sell them in town. Times were tough. We were so poor we couldn't even get a charge account at the mercantile. Eventually, I realized that either our chickens were gettin' lazy or someone was stealing eggs. As it ended up, Hunter was beatin' me to the chicken coops and was gathering a dozen or so eggs each morning. He'd then take them to town and sell the dern things to his schoolteacher."

Melba Ruth laughed with sheer joy at her memories.

"It's funny now, but it wasn't then. He was undercutting me and I lost a customer, and didn't know why for a long time." Melba Ruth's expression stilled and grew serious, but quickly relaxed into a smile. "He didn't realize how much we counted on those eggs to put food on the table."

"What did he do with what he made, buy candy at the mercantile?" Laurel attempted to lighten the mood.

"No. He saved every penny and bought his sister a doll for her birthday. It was endearing, but it was just the first of many times we had a discussion with him about how the end doesn't necessarily justify the means." Melba Ruth giggled softly under her breath. "That's when I knew he had a special gift and someday would be a good businessman." She set her teacup on the table. "And he didn't disappoint me either."

"I bet you kept count on your chickens from then on to make sure he didn't sell them next?" Pearl said.

Laurel couldn't control her burst of merriment at Pearl's observation. The others joined in. It felt good to laugh, something Laurel hadn't done for a long time.

"Okay, enough of what was, we need to talk about what can be," said Mrs. Campbell. "What did you all find out at the meeting?"

Laurel sat back and sipped her tea and listened while absorbing everything being said. She wasn't sure exactly what the problem was, so she'd best save her opinions until she knew more.

Ruby led the conversation, and filled not only Mrs. Campbell but Laurel in on every detail of the meeting. She didn't miss the opportunity to discuss Greta Garrett at length, then went on to tell just how happy she was that Pearl had drawn the short straw and had to clean the spittoons instead of her.

Melba Ruth listened patiently, while making sure the teacups were filled. "I want to make this very clear. I totally support my son and know why he's so passionate about the railroad coming to Farley Springs. Frankly, I can see some validity to it, but this time I think his vision of how it would impact our community is more of an obsession than good logic. It could be his undoing, and I can't stand by and let that happen."

"Why do you think so?" Ruby set her cup and saucer on the parlor table.

"This town was little more than a Comanchero trading post not too many years ago. The original town was platted in a buffalo wallow. It isn't ready for what the railroad will bring. The stage line that Hunter has an interest in would be shut down, leaving a lot of people without jobs. It'd change his whole life, as well as the lives of others."

"But it'd bring in new people, new jobs," observed Ruby.

"Riffraff and shady characters galore. Our town is simply not ready to be that big . . . not yet. Only a handful of people think we're prepared to become a railhead, much less the county seat. Most are just happy that we have a schoolhouse and would settle for a library."

Melba Ruth's eyes were sharp and assessing, as she spoke. "Hunter is very passionate about whatever he is doing, and is driven, but he *needs* something else . . ." She stopped and focused squarely on Laurel. "Or *somebody* to love more than his work."

Laurel stirred uneasily in her seat and deliberately smiled, smoothly betraying nothing of her annoyance at the older woman for her underlying message.

Deep inside, Laurel's soul screamed, *Not me! I don't need anyone to need me for anything!*

Melba Ruth continued, "But that will come in time. He's wrong about what's best for our town right now." She hesitated and looked straight into Laurel's eyes. "And so is your uncle. To be fair, I think those of us who feel we need a library should stick together. I know the railroad would be nice, and frankly, I wouldn't miss the dirty drovers and dusty cattle drives, but we can't afford to have a train here."

"But he said the railroad will bring a lot of new merchants. Isn't that good?" Pearl asked.

"Not if nobody in town can read the signs they put up. We have everything we need now, and my son knows exactly how I feel. We don't need any more merchants butting into our business, taking away customers, making more competition for all of us. My mama always said, 'Don't trouble trouble until trouble troubles you.' More competition will mean less income for our existing merchants. Few women are convinced that the men's way is the best."

Ruby sat back in her chair, then said, "We can get anything we want here in town, and if we can't, we can order it out of the Sears, Roebuck or Montgomery Ward catalogs and get them shipped to us direct from Chicago. It looks like it'd be just a waste of money to pave the streets, hoping the railroad *might* come someday."

Melba Ruth took up where Ruby left off on a grocery list of reasons a library would be better than paved streets.

A picture of young Melba Ruth and Hunter, at the age of about thirteen or fourteen, hanging on the wall caught Laurel's eye. Memories flooded her mind, reminding her of the first time she met Melba Ruth Campbell. A day still vivid in her mind.

At the tender age of thirteen, Laurel had stepped off the stage originating in San Antonio, feeling as though the whole world were spinning inside her. She felt strange and so out of place, but stood outside the stage line office as she'd been told to do by her uncle, waiting for him to return with his carriage.

The month prior to her arrival had been horrendously heartbreaking for her; first with the untimely death of her parents, then being snatched up by her mother's brother from the only life she had ever known in the Hill Country and shipped off to the Panhandle.

She was too immature to understand her parents' deaths, much less what was happening around her. It was as if she'd been awakened from a beautiful dream and dropped into a nightmare.

Laurel recalled standing there surrounded by total strangers, scared out of her wits.

That was the moment she had made the decision to always stand alone and never allow anyone into her heart again. She didn't want anyone to need her and she didn't want to need anyone but herself. It hurt too much when they had to leave.

Laurel watched a tall, motherly-looking woman waiting on the porch in front of the stage line fussing at her son, who Laurel later learned was Hunter Campbell. She wore a faded, threadbare calico day dress with a nondescript bonnet that had seen better days.

The woman introduced herself as Melba Ruth Campbell and obviously felt sorry for the frightened teenager because she struck up a conversation with her. Later, the lady gave Laurel a big hug and told her that she was welcome to their little homestead outside of town any time.

Even today, Laurel's heart filled with affection when she thought about how the stranger had turned to walk away, but returned to give Laurel another hug. The woman used the excuse that if Laurel had any problem with her son, Hunter, just to let her know.

In no more than a flash in Laurel's life, Melba Ruth Campbell had given her a gift that could never be taken away . . . a gift of time. Every day since then, Laurel had thanked the good Lord that he'd given her a living, breathing angel on this earth.

That saintly voice disturbed Laurel's daydreaming. "Laurel Dean, since you've been living back East and have been involved with all kinds of social organizations, what is your opinion?"

"I was so young when I lived here before and don't feel right expressing my beliefs in regards to something I know little about, so I'd much prefer to stay neutral."

"Just give me some idea how you'd handle a quandary when two groups don't see eye to eye."

Laurel took a deep breath but decided she felt comfortable enough to give them a fairly basic observation that could apply to most any situation. "The local women's organization should take a stance and stick together. I'll give you an example. Think about a play with only one actor. The story wouldn't be very interesting or even make much sense, but when you add a cast of characters, it comes to life. It's a cohesive play, not one lone actor attempting to fill an entire stage by himself."

"We've never thought about having a women's group." Melba Ruth tapped her index finger on her lip several times, as if a plan was coming together. "What'd Hunter call his men's assembly?"

"Farley Springs Men's Club," Ruby answered.

"Then we'll be the Farley Springs Women's Society. That sounds more like something, uh, more political, not an ol' boys' social club. What do you think, Laurel?"

Laurel had already lent some of her opinion, so what difference did more make? Against her better judgment, she asked, "Then why don't the folks who are as passionate about the library as Hunter is about the railroad stick together? Your women's organization could do a lot to accomplish that."

"That's exactly how I see it. We think so much alike. You'll be our new president . . . problem solved!" Melba Ruth blurted out.

"No. I can't. I haven't been back in town long enough to even know which way the wind blows, and I'm not sure how my aunt and uncle might feel about it."

"You're a grown woman and there's no reason you can't have your own views whether they are along the same lines as others' or not." Melba Ruth looked her straight in the eye. "Look at Hunter and me. We have totally opposite opinions but respect the other's right to believe the way we do. I still think you're the perfect person for the job. You'd be impartial, are well educated, and have been living in a big city, so you'd know more than anyone how to run a women's group."

"I can *not* do it," Laurel said softly but sternly.

"Well, we'll see about that." Melba Ruth smiled confidentially.

Chapter 5

Laurel twisted uncomfortably in her chair, absolutely flabbergasted at Melba Ruth's statement, which appeared more of a promise than a passing remark. Setting her chin in a stubborn line, Laurel took a deep breath and adjusted her smile, hoping that her friend would realize that she was as determined not to be a part of the women's social club as Melba Ruth seemed to think she would.

For a two-cent piece, if it wouldn't be rude, Laurel would say her farewells and head back to town.

Laurel would not—absolutely would not—get involved regardless of how much respect and love she had for the older woman.

Melba Ruth settled back in her chair, picked up her teacup, and took a sip. As if reading Laurel's mind, she looked over the lip of her cup and raised a questioning eyebrow. She shifted her gaze to the Wilson sisters. "Then what did the men decide to do to raise money?"

The Wilson sisters looked at one another as though if they stared long enough one would give in and answer the question.

"A Valentine's Day box supper and dance," said Pearl.

Melba Ruth almost choked on her drink. "A what?"

"A Valentine's Day—" Pearl repeated, but was interrupted by her sister.

"She heard you the first time, Pearl."

"There's no way for the love of Jesus my son would ever go for such an idiotic idea. He'd pay for it out of his own pocket before he'd get involved with a girlie thing like that." The lines of concentration deepened along her brows. "There's just no way."

"There was a lot of talk about how much money the women could make if they held one, so I think he was sincere," said Pearl, although her sister gave her a look that questioned her sanity.

The women batted the notion around. Suddenly, Laurel had an overwhelming desire to contribute her own observations. Surely it wouldn't be a sign of her willingness to become permanently involved in their mission . . . surely!

"I don't think he was serious at all," she said as the others stared at her. "I agree with you, Melba Ruth, there's no way he'd go along with something like that. I couldn't hear very much, but by the time he got around to making that part of the announcement, he'd stepped near me at the front door and made it very loud and clear that since he was president of the men's organization and there was no clear consensus as to what should be done, he'd make the decision. It came straight from the mayor's mouth. I believe he wants us to *think* he's going through with the plans he announced."

"That makes sense." Melba Ruth pursed her lips, seemingly in deep thought. "He's trying to sell us a pile of cow patties and make us think they're flapjacks. He might be my boy, but he's as sly as a fox when he wants to be."

"You mean he knew that we'd come report back to you, and then we'd all jump onto their idea. Then it'd look like we were being underhanded and stole their project. That'd make it seem that we forced them to change projects, making us look bad." Pearl smiled and looked at the other women as if she was really proud of herself.

"That's right, Pearl." Melba Ruth rubbed the palms of her hands together. "But we'll turn the tables on them. We need everyone's ideas on what their real plans might be."

"First off, they are going to challenge us to see who can raise the most money. No doubt they won't do bake sales or bazaars. Might be a rodeo of some sorts."

"I don't think that's it. Maybe horse races like on the Fourth of July. If it were cutting season, it'd definitely be a calf fry, but it's too early," Melba Ruth said confidentially.

The women tossed around a number of ideas. Laurel added a few, but remained determined that once the meeting was over, she'd go back home, settle in for the night, and wouldn't be involved in whatever was decided. One thing was for certain—she wanted to see the town have a library, but she had to admit that not getting mud on her shoes when it rained sounded good, too.

"I know what it is." Melba Ruth jumped to her feet. "It has to be something that would only appeal to a man."

"Taking a donation from the soiled doves' earnings one night," said Pearl.

Everyone shook their heads in amusement.

"No. They'd get the men into the saloon, get 'um drunk, and get donations of some sort. Maybe put a beef on the spit, something that would draw in the men, and a boxed supper and dance wouldn't do it."

Ruby said, "I'd say it isn't a secret, since Hunter announced it in a public meeting—"

"Except he told the men to keep it quiet," said Pearl.

"Which only proves it's a ruse," said Melba Ruth. "How long do you think it'd take your ink jockey friend to print us up some posters to place all around town?" She looked squarely at Ruby. "I know he's a little sweet on you, so maybe . . ."

"He's probably puttin' the weekly newspaper to bed, and if so, he might have time once he's finished." A wicked smile crossed Ruby's face. "I'll drop by and see if I can entice him to get some printed as soon as possible."

"Have him send me his bill, regardless of the cost. Here's the deal. We'll beat Hunter and the men at their own game, something he isn't accustomed to." Melba Ruth continued to rub her palms together, as if it helped her think. "We'll lend a hand to the men. We'll prepare flyers announcing both events on Valentine's Day and plaster them all over town. If you're successful . . ." She raised a knowing eyebrow at Ruby, then continued, "We can have the posters out before anybody even realizes what is going on. The men, as a matter of pride, will have to go through with a boxed supper and dance, while we'll roast a beef and give away beer."

"Give away beer!" Ruby sounded astonished. "I figured you'd do something like donating a percentage of the proceeds or something on that line, but never free beer."

"Well, it's my saloon and I can do anything I damn well please. For every glass of beer sold, I'll give them a free one and donate the money to the library fund."

Laurel could see by the expression on Melba Ruth's face that her mind was made up. "We'll need a lot of help, so I'll expect you girls to be my extra eyes and ears."

Everyone nodded, except for Laurel. Mentally she had to stay strong and true to her convictions, while her heart screamed that she could do something that would make a difference in people's lives by helping the town raise money for a library.

"Okay, ladies. Just like Hunter told the men, keep this under your bonnets." Melba Ruth looked at each woman as if appraising their surprised looks. "We're gonna give the men one hell of a run for their money, ladies!"

Melba Ruth pointed a bony finger at Laurel Dean. "And you, my dear, will be our president."

"I've already said, I can't. I don't even have a job yet."

"That makes it easy then. I have a need for a bookkeeper and someone to help me with my businesses, and you're the perfect person." Melba Ruth stood up, smiled at each lady, and focused on Laurel's eyes. "My dear, you said you didn't have a job yet, so I'll see you at nine o'clock in the morning."

"I haven't said I'm taking the job, Melba Ruth."

"But you will, my dear."

Hunter wandered around outside the ranch house, feeling like he was standing guard at his own fort. With the big windows on two sides of the parlor, he couldn't help getting a good view of what was going on inside.

Although his mother and her friends drank a lot of tea, they sure talked a lot, too. Not much of a surprise, but he was pretty dern sure what they were talking about without hearing a single word. Their body language spoke volumes.

His mother rubbed her palms together from time to time, so he knew she was in her "organizing the whole state of Texas" mode.

Ruby was about to wear out the parlor table picking up and putting down her cup and saucer, while her sister sat quietly, wringing her hands in her lap.

He took out a cigar and lit it. Smiling to himself, Hunter couldn't help thinking about what was really going on inside. No doubt they were figuring out how to finagle things in order to hold a Valentine's box supper and dance and spoil the men's plans for their fundraiser. Part of him felt ashamed at being deceitful, yet he wanted to laugh aloud about what he'd pulled off. All in the name of betterment for Farley Springs.

He really wanted to go inside to change into fresh clothes, but couldn't take a chance on getting caught. He'd hedged enough questions for one day.

Although he had stopped and washed up as best he could, with the humidity it hadn't done a lot of good. He was muddy and his shirt probably smelled like the south end of a northbound bull.

Hunter felt pretty satisfied with himself for what he'd accomplished since returning to the ranch.

With Slim's help, they had saved both the mama cow and her calf, although it had been a long, hard, laborious effort. By the time they finished, the cowboys had repaired the downed fence and were already at the bunkhouse enjoying an evening meal. He'd grabbed a bite with them before the cards came out.

Hunter had one hard, fast rule: he never played games of chance with his employees. Made for bad relations.

He finished his cheroot and ground it out in the dirt. His original plan had been to go back to town and enjoy a little poker and a bit of pleasure with Greta Garrett. As the evening wore on, he saw no signs that any of the three visitors chatting in his parlor seemed to have any intentions of leaving to return to town anytime soon, so he got less interested in making the ride back to Farley Springs.

One thing was certain—he didn't have to feel bad about leaving Greta high and dry because she never stayed lonely long.

Maybe the real reason he wasn't all that disappointed about not going back to town was because of Laurel. One look at the strength and stubbornness in Laurel's dark, fiery green eyes set off a stampede of emotions. And one thing for sure, he was certainly not a weak-in-the-knees type of man. He swallowed hard and wondered if she even recognized her own charm and beauty.

Laurel's gelding snorted and restlessly pawed the ground, drawing Hunter's attention away from Laurel Dean.

His big sorrel stud stood hitched beside Laurel's horse, ready to make the trip back to Farley Springs . . . sooner or later. Now both of their mounts, as well as the Wilson sisters' team, were rested and impatiently waiting to get on the road . . . much like Hunter.

Thinking the women might never leave, Hunter gave up and strolled to the rear of the house and came in through the back porch. He unbuckled his gun belt and hung it, along with his Stetson, by the door. Surely he'd have no need to have his Colt on in his own house . . . unless the women figured out what he and the other men in town had pulled on them. By now, the Wilson sisters, and of course Laurel Dean, however she fit in, had given his mother every detail of the meeting.

By morning, with Stubby's help, Hunter would have everything in place and be prepared to make the big announcement that since the women had decided on a box supper and dance, then the men would fall back on another plan—a big cookout at the Coyote Bluff Saloon.

Thinking how it would play out, he took a deep breath and couldn't stop the smiles from coming. It'd be hard not to say anything until the women made a big deal out of their own shindig. Then the poor men, being the gentlemen they were, would let the ladies have the men's idea and then they'd be forced to have a regular ol' barbeque to raise money.

Maybe Hunter should practice at being mad or upset over being outdone by the women.

By morning, Gideon Duncan would be thanking him for

what he'd done for the town. After all, it was his idea to throw the women off with his little ruse.

But Laurel Dean's participation still troubled Hunter. She was a total mystery to him. He wasn't exactly sure how she fit into the women's plan, but obviously, like the Wilson sisters, she must have been part of the spy brigade sent into the Sundance.

Or could she be a snitch for her Uncle Gideon? A double agent like in the War Between the States?

One moment she was a Johnny Reb and the next a Billy Yank.

The only way to find out was to get next to her and feel out the opponent.

Chapter 6

Hunter left the mudroom and entered the kitchen. He was shocked to find his mother standing at the sideboard, writing on a plain piece of stationery, while she had guests in the house. The moment she saw him, she quickly folded the paper in quarters. "You startled me, Hunter," she said before straightening up to her full height. "I'm glad you got back before my guests left."

Although she was almost as tall as him, she had to look up at her son. An impish smile he'd seen too many times crept across her lips, and he would bet a week's profit at the Coyote Bluff it had something to do with Laurel Dean.

"I was finishing my grocery order," she said with obvious deception. She slipped the paper in her pocket before continuing, "I need a word with you—privately." Her tone grew serious and she motioned him farther away from the door that led to the parlor.

"Will you please do me a favor, and keep careful watch over Laurel Dean?" She lowered her voice even more. "Something is bothering her. I think she's smack dab in the middle of some type of situation she might not be equipped to handle. It could well concern her uncle and aunt."

"What makes you think that?" he asked.

"I sense it in her whole demeanor. She's not the same person she was when she left here."

"Of course, Mother, she isn't. Laurel was only a girl when she left for boarding school. She's accustomed to the big-city life with all of its fancy theaters, the opera, and shopping for the finest clothes in the world. She's about my age, so she's a fully grown woman now."

Oh, how had the shy teenager grown into a sexy, appealing woman! he thought.

"No. It's something else. She's plenty mature, knows her mind, and doesn't act like she misses New York an iota. Just trust me, son. Please help me by keeping an eye on her."

He nodded. He'd oblige his mama because he'd do anything she asked if it was in his power—and she knew it. An additional incentive, it'd give him a legitimate reason to stay close to Laurel Dean.

Melba Ruth placed her pen in the sideboard and closed the drawer. "The ladies have been waiting to see you, so please go in and say hello."

Hunter shook his head dubiously and could only smile down at her. His mama had a way with words and he knew exactly what she meant with her last statement. It was his signal to interrupt the gathering, so the visitors would say their good-byes without making his mother appear to be an unappreciative hostess.

With grace and purpose, she escorted him into the parlor.

"Look who I found in the kitchen," she announced as if he were a cookie thief she'd caught red-handed. "Hunter insisted that he come in and give his regards before he heads back to Farley Springs."

"Good evening, ladies." He smiled at each woman, letting his gaze linger on Laurel a little longer than was appropriate.

After brief pleasantries were exchanged, Ruby said, "We were just about to leave. It's getting late, and I've got something to take care of in town." She took her sister's arm and almost pulled her out of her chair.

Pearl looked baffled. "But we could stay a little bit—"

"*I* have to return right away because *I* have someone to see this evening."

"Yes, oh yes, I almost forgot." Pearl fiddled with her hat and stood. "We've got to run. So nice to see you again, Hunter."

"I'm sorry you have to leave so soon," he lied. "Slim has your carriage waiting out front."

The Wilson sisters thanked him and chatted for a few more minutes about a variety of things. Noticeably the subject of the library or the railroad didn't come up. Not particularly odd either, if you were to ask him.

From the corner of his eye, he observed his mother slyly removing the sheet of paper she'd written on out of her pocket. She then slid next to Ruby and handed her the paper.

Perplexed, he turned his attention to Laurel and eased into a friendly smile. "That little bay of yours is getting testy. I think he really needs to be ridden. He's a feisty one for sure. All the horses have been watered and given some oats."

Laurel looked up, flashing a smile of thanks.

Staring into her warm, enchanting face, he had a hard time ungluing his tongue from the roof of his mouth, but he finally did. "The horses are refreshed and rarin' to go. If you'll give me a couple of minutes to change shirts, I'll be pleased to escort you all back to town."

"That's so kind of you," Pearl gushed.

"While I thank you kindly, I've driven the road from here to town in the late evening before, so no need for us to take up your valuable time." It was as if Ruby didn't particularly want him to ride with them.

"It won't be necessary," Laurel sternly added. "Like Ruby said, we've ridden this trail many times."

His mother smiled sweetly. "Pish posh! Hunter was going back to town anyway . . . weren't you, darlin'?"

"Yes, ma'am." He wanted so badly to give her a frown for calling him darlin', but knew it'd be pointless.

There was a side benefit. An evening ride with Laurel would give him an opportunity to talk, although he figured it wouldn't be all that productive with the Wilson sisters being nearby. He could certainly wish they'd ride ahead, but knew it wasn't about to happen. The Wilson girls were sweet, but nosy.

Taking the change of events in stride, Hunter said, "Ladies, I'll meet you out front in two minutes." Without waiting for their response, he hurried out of the parlor and headed to his room on the second floor two steps at a time.

Within moments he'd changed shirts and thrown on a coat. After strapping on his Colt, he added his Stetson and walked down the steps to the hitching rail out front.

Laurel Dean had already mounted. She impatiently tapped her boot in the stirrup. His mother was nowhere in sight. Nor did he see the Wilson sisters' carriage.

Wishes do come true!

In one fluid movement, he stepped in his stirrup and swung his long leg over his saddle, then said, "Ready?"

"Hunter, you really don't have to ride back with me."

"I don't mind a bit, plus when my mama tells me to jump, I ask how high." He laughed and she joined him.

Before he could ask, she volunteered, "Ruby and Pearl drove on out."

"What was so important they couldn't wait?" He figured he wouldn't get a straight answer out of her but tried anyway.

"Uh, Ruby had to, uh, to join a friend for dinner."

Most likely that wasn't the truth, but he was less interested in Ruby than Laurel Dean. He was deeply bothered by how much Laurel's welfare troubled his mother. There had to be more to it than just being a worrisome friend.

"Let's head out. I think your Buckey's really hankering for a long, hard ride."

With only a slight movement of the reins, Hunter's horse trotted toward the trail, joined by Laurel's bay.

"Your new ranch headquarters are beautiful," Laurel said as soon as they'd cleared the ranch gate.

"Thanks." He didn't know whether to say more or just be glad she was still speaking to him, after he'd been such a jackass earlier in the day.

"It's really nice. You've done so much with the ranch since I was last there, but that was a while ago." She spoke in such a soft voice that he could barely hear her over the wind.

"When the ol' homestead burned, after Paw died, I wanted to give Mother a place like she'd always dreamed about having. When we didn't have two bits to rub together, she'd clean houses for folks in town. Even your aunt's place for a while. In the evenings, over supper, she'd tell me all about each house. How they were decorated. She'd describe every picture on the wall, talk about colors, and mention fabrics I'd never heard of. I just called them frilly girlie things and it'd make her laugh." Hunter found himself watching Laurel as she turned her head from side to side.

About as much as he took pleasure in Laurel's affection for his mother, he also liked sharing his memories with a woman who truly cared for others.

To his recollection, Greta Garrett had never seemed the least bit concerned about what made him the man he was today. She seemed more interested in a romp in the hay and lookin' good on his arm. Suddenly, hot nights, warm whiskey, and Greta didn't seem as important as they once did.

As he and Laurel rode along, crimson hues of sunset swallowed up by purple shadows of early evening mellowed the western horizon. *One of the purest of pleasures in Texas is our beautiful sunsets.*

So far, he hadn't seen even so much as a dust trail from the Wilson carriage. What was so important that they would push their team so dern hard?

Possibly being alone with Laurel, he could find out what was bothering her. Maybe even how she felt about paving Main Street. There were so many questions he had but couldn't just blurt them out. It'd take time. A slow nurturing of their relationship would be a test for a man who had little, if any, patience.

Out of the corner of his eye, two jackrabbits appeared chasing a prairie dog . . . heading directly in the path of his and Laurel's horses.

In a split second, Buckey stumbled, then reared back and pawed the air, sending Laurel Dean backward, head over teakettle. She landed on her side, cushioned by a thick bed of early spring wildflowers.

Hunter dismounted in a flash. Grabbing Laurel, he pulled her into his arms. "Are you hurt?" With trembling hands, he pushed back flaxen tendrils of hair from her forehead and brushed dirt from her face. She rolled farther into his arms, and looked up at him with a glazed expression. He could feel her quickened pulse. Again, he asked, "Are you okay?"

"Yes. I'm fine. Just a bit shaken is all," she said through winded words. "Uncle Gideon warned me that Buckey could be a little skittish."

"He's more than a little skittish." Under his breath Hunter muttered, "And the bastard shouldn't have allowed you on him."

With assistance, she stood and brushed away the grass and dirt from her vest and pants.

In the distance, Hunter saw a billow of dust as Buckey galloped toward town.

"Did you see what scared him?" Laurel asked.

"A couple of jackrabbits chasing what could've been a prairie dog or a ferret. I couldn't tell for sure, it happened too quick."

Hunter wasn't sure whether his heart or hers was beating faster. Color had returned to Laurel's pale face, and he heard an audible intake of breath.

Once he was satisfied she wasn't hurt and had given her time to compose herself, he asked, "Want a ride?"

She shot him a childlike grin, raising a questioning eyebrow, and said in a calm, silky voice, "Only if you're going my way."

"Sure am." Hunter wondered if she realized she had such a sensual smile. He mounted his horse and gave her a hand, easing her in the saddle in front of him. His knees settled comfortably against her thighs. "I can guarantee you'll ache in muscles you've forgotten you had."

"I'm sure so, but right now I'm okay." Then she added, "I think."

It took her a minute to situate herself. By the time she was settled in, her continuous squirming around had caused him a really big problem. He mentally groaned in agony, because she had succeeded in setting off a prairie fire of flames within him. With nothing but a couple of layers of denim separating them, there was no way she didn't feel it, too.

Hunter would have been a fool not to have enjoyed her nearness—her warm, sensual body pressed against him. He tried everything he could to put as much distance between them as possible, but sharing a saddle didn't allow much room for negotiation.

"I think I'd be more comfortable riding behind you," she said.

"Considering what happened, I don't think it's a good idea. I need to be able to catch you if you go off to sleep and try to fall off." Hunter tried to make light of the situation.

"You think I can't ride a horse?" Her words were laced with steel.

"No, I didn't say that. You might be injured more than you think, and I don't want to take the chance."

"You're too bossy. I'm just fine," Laurel fired back.

"It's my horse. My rules, so sit back and enjoy the ride," he said, trying to make his words sound friendly yet leaving no room for compromise.

The sun dipped deeper into the horizon, shrouded by a wash of ocher and cornflower blue. The evening breeze grew cooler, and Laurel shivered. He halted his horse long enough to remove his coat and put it around her shoulders. The chill helped to cool his fiery response to her nearness, but it did nothing to alleviate the heat still kindled in his blood.

"Thanks. I've forgotten how fast the temperature drops at sunset in the Panhandle." She snuggled deeper into the jacket. "Tell me more about the ranch house."

"Well, by the time we got ready to rebuild after the fire, I'd become a damn good poker player thanks to Paw. I decided I'd stay in the game, as long as I kept winnin', so I could have enough money to build the house exactly the way Mama wanted. We had a very good year with our herd of cattle and turned a profit, so with that added to my winnin's, we built it, one stone at a time. I'm kinda embarrassed sometimes because I think of it as my house, when it's really Mama's, and always will be."

Her body had lost some of its stiffness and he found his legs clamped alongside her hips, as she moved a little in the saddle. Hunter's left hand settled on her thigh, but he quickly jerked it away.

"That's very admirable of you to do something so

special for your mother. She's one in a million, and you know how much she means to me." She rested her hand on his knee to leverage herself, as she shifted her weight once again. "It has to be hard on you."

It took everything in him not to say, "If you want to know hard . . ." As difficult as it was, he forced himself not to think about how much just being near her aroused him.

He gathered his thoughts and focused on her words, not the way his body was reacting to hers. He felt like he did as a teenager when he first discovered the difference between a man and a woman.

"I was young, healthy, and invincible. Sure didn't mind the work. Mama and Paw raised me that if I wanted anything, I had to work for it. I've never considered my gambling anything but a hobby, maybe a bad one. I learned from my paw to never put anything on the table, be it money or property, unless you can afford to lose it. That philosophy worked for me. I still play that way today."

"Maybe you should teach me the game." Laurel laughed full-heartedly.

"Well, I could but you don't need the money and it's hard to stop once you begin. Pretty addictive, unless you play smart. If you play dumb, you lose everything, but if you play smart, you can have the world."

"Maybe we could play for sticks of Arbuckle's peppermints," she said, then added, "I presume they still give you one in every bag."

"They do," he said.

"I just have one question. How would we determine the winner? The one with the hardest stick wins . . . or maybe the longest?"

He could imagine the playful smile she had on her face, as she settled back against his chest. She knew exactly what her words inferred. The wind tossed her hair around, and he smelled the scent of honeysuckle and lilacs, only increasing his awareness of Laurel.

Hunter smiled to himself. She had no idea just how much he'd like to play some high-stakes poker with the woman molded against his body.

As if she read his mind, she changed subjects. "Hunter, I apologize for taking so long to tell you how sorry I was to learn of your father's passing." With warmth and caring, she lightly patted his knee. "I didn't know about it until today."

"Thanks. Everyone had money on him gettin' shot in a bar fight, not trampled by a bull." He shook off the horrific memories of finding his father's body and said, "Never a day goes by that I don't miss him."

It seemed only right that he mention the loss of her own parents, although it'd been years before. "I'm sorry that I never had the opportunity to express my sympathy to you for your loss, too. How did they die?" He stopped and took a breath before he went on, "That is, if you want to talk about it."

Laurel's back stiffened and he felt her arms shaking. Even after all the years, it was obvious talking about their deaths was still too painful for her to handle. He quickly said, "I'm sorry. I shouldn't have brought it up."

Only the rustle of the wind on the mesquite and yucca answered.

Hunter felt about as low as a slithering rattler for even bringing up the subject. He was enjoying how Laurel felt in his arms—all grown up—and he tried to avoid the awkwardness by stating, "We're not too far from town, and we haven't seen hide nor hair of that hammerhead you call a horse."

"He isn't mine. He belongs to my uncle," she corrected him.

"I wouldn't ride that snake-eyed snorter again, if you

ask me." Another stiffening of her shoulders told him she didn't appreciate his warning. "Do you want to go to the stables first, or should I take you to your uncle's house?"

"No! Not Uncle Gideon's house!" she exclaimed much too quickly. "The stables will be just fine. I can walk from there. It's only less than a block."

The fear in her voice was tangible, setting Hunter's jaw into stone. He would find out what had caused such terror in her if it meant giving up everything he'd ever acquired on this earth.

Chapter 7

Laurel was glad Hunter couldn't see her face. He would have seen right through her, and she didn't want to have to explain why she wasn't looking forward to going home tonight . . . or any night, for that matter.

She was relieved when he said, "I bet you loved New York. Had a lot of fun and made plenty of friends, I suspect. That's probably what I should have done. Gone to school and taken the test to be a lawyer like your uncle. I would have become rich drawing up people's wills and resolving business disputes. Much easier than breaking up bar room fights. I could have then started up a bank like he did."

"I figured you, as well as everyone in town, knew that the original bank was in East Texas. He inherited it from my grandfather. Uncle Gideon and my mother were the only heirs, so when Grandfather Duncan died, my uncle took over the bank. Eventually, he closed that one and moved to the Panhandle. Since we lived in San Antonio, Mother was happy to let him handle the business. I presume she received her share of the profits in some form or fashion. I was too young to know anything about their affairs."

"So those investments paid for your education?" Hunter asked.

She stopped and took a deep breath. It was about time to set things straight about some of the speculation she knew had been floating around for years; yet she didn't want to expose any family skeletons.

"Unfortunately, that isn't how it played out. I was told that my parents had made some bad business choices and ended up losing everything right before their deaths." She paused and forced her mind not to think about their horrific deaths. Steeling herself, she said, "As trustee of their estate, my uncle had to sell off what assets there were to pay off debtors. They took everything, leaving me a little for my education. So if it hadn't been for Uncle Gideon and Aunt Elizabeth taking me in, I wouldn't have had a place to live or food to eat."

"Sorry, I shouldn't have pried into your private matters, I didn't mean to insult you or your uncle, I've just never figured out how he raised the money to buy the bank here, but this explains it. He's always been secretive about his business, and I respect a man for keeping the affairs of his family to himself."

"It feels strange to see him in any other profession than a lawyer because he wasn't involved with banking until my grandfather passed, which wasn't very long before my parents' deaths."

Hunter pulled her closer to him, and she rested her head on his chest.

Unchecked raw emotion stretched even tighter around her heart. She couldn't control the trembling within her. A warning voice whispered in her head that she'd already told him too much. She was thankful when the conversation took another direction.

"I guess being a lawyer and then a banker is the perfect combination. Very lucrative," Hunter said, "or at least profitable enough to end up with several parcels of land near the river not far from where the railroad could pass through."

Laurel had found her bearings and realized that if the nice folks of Farley Springs knew the secrets that were buried with her parents, the only family she had would be totally ostracized by the community. She deliberately turned to more pleasant thoughts. Memories hurt too much.

"If you'd taken the test to be a lawyer and were nearly as good at law as you say you are at gambling, you would be home planting rosebushes for your mama and holding private, high-stakes games at the ranch." She shifted and elbowed him lightly, in a gesture of friendliness. She wasn't the least bit surprised at how rock solid his stomach felt. Her fingers ached to touch him and her heart was hammering foolishly.

"With Mother!" His heartfelt laugh rippled through the air. "If it's not too bold to ask, what did you do between the time you got out of college and returned home?"

"I was a journalist for a women's magazine. *Lippincott's.* I wrote literary criticism, book reviews, and even a short story or two. Not much demand for that in Farley Springs, huh?"

"You could write for the newspaper. Do you plan on sticking around here or going back East?"

"It depends. Uncle Gideon offered me a job at the bank, so if he comes through on his promise, I'll work there." She probably emphasized the word *if* too much, but that was the way she felt. So far, he'd avoided the issue.

In the distance, the lights of the town came in sight. Deep inside she was a little sad that their evening was drawing to a conclusion. With her riding in front of him for all those miles, leaning back against his rock-hard body, enjoying whiffs of leather and the outdoorsy smell of work, not to mention his arms holding her, he'd ignited feelings she'd kept hidden for too many years. He'd stoked a gently growing fire within her like no man had ever done.

Although Buckey had acted up, it turned out to be a delightful ride. Frankly, she should give the dang, unruly nag an extra bucket of oats. If it hadn't been for his misbehaving, she wouldn't have ridden double with Hunter. She didn't want the night to end but knew it would shortly.

Laurel couldn't allow something like tonight to happen again. She was already finding herself too comfortable with the rugged strong-willed, cowboy.

With all the distractions, Hunter still hadn't asked the question he wanted the answer to the most: Where did her allegiance lie with the town's two projects? Toward his mother as her friend or her uncle as family?

He wasn't so dumb that he thought Laurel had kept him distracted by talking about an array of subjects because she thought he'd be interested in them. More that she did it to make sure he didn't ask any questions about her visit to the Sundance or the Triple C. He had to handle his questioning gingerly because no doubt she'd see right through him. *Slow and easy*, he reminded himself.

Typically, Hunter liked to think things through and know how deep the water was before jumping off the bank, but for some reason she kept him leaping into the unknown.

Against his better judgment, he found himself just saying what was on his mind. She'd gotten into his mind and he couldn't think straight.

"I know Mother called you to the ranch to get your help on raising money for the library," he said in an all-business fashion. "But considering your uncle's wishes to make sure the railroad comes to town, I guess it put you in an awkward position."

She squared her shoulders and stiffened in his arms, not

saying anything for a second. "It's not awkward at all. I'm staying neutral. My uncle hasn't mentioned the railroad." She pulled her hand away from his leg and shifted uncomfortably.

"Laurel, at least be honest with me. I know Mother wants your help by influencing your uncle and probably sent you to town to find out what the men had decided. You've always been close to the Wilson sisters, so if it wasn't her, then it was them."

"I can't believe you said that. I only saw Pearl and Ruby for the first time today. I find it offensive and you're really making me angry." The veins in her neck tightened. "I said I was staying neutral and made that very clear. I love Melba Ruth, but this is one time I will not take a side." She twisted in her seat and looked him squarely in the eyes. "If you've ever believed anything I've said to you, Hunter Campbell, it should be now."

For some odd reason, he almost accepted her explanation, but not quite. For every question she answered, a dozen new ones surfaced.

He leaned into her until his lips were only inches away from her ear. "I'm sorry. I didn't mean to upset you." He really didn't like hurting her feelings and he knew he had, but there was too much at stake for him not to have asked.

"I'm still madder than Hades at you. It's none of your business but I'll tell you why your mother wanted to see me."

Laurel turned her head farther toward him, making her cheek almost touch his lips.

"Temper, temper, Laurel Dean," he said. *Now wasn't that a dumb approach?* he thought.

Not too surprising, she suddenly jerked forward and looked ahead, but not before he saw the ire on her face. "She offered me employment."

"And you took it?"

"No. I turned her down. Since my uncle wants me to

go to work for him, I couldn't accept her offer without consulting him first." With a silken thread of warning in her voice, she added, "So now that you know, you can relax because I don't give a tinker's damn about you or your precious railroad."

He leaned back in the saddle and enjoyed the remaining five minutes of their ride. As they neared the stables, Buckey stood proudly outside waiting for them.

After reining his stud to a halt, Hunter dismounted and helped her down.

She planted her feet firmly on the ground and looked up at him with eyes that glowed with a savage inner fire. "Thank you for letting me ride with you back to town. It would've been a long walk otherwise."

"Much obliged, ma'am." He tipped his hat. It took everything in him to resist taking her into his arms and kissing the daylights out of her.

But the sun always rose on another day!

Hunter watched as she took Buckey's reins and led him into the shadows of the livery. He tied his horse to the hitching post. As much as he didn't want to leave her, he knew the blacksmith would take care of her dumbnuts of a horse, and she'd be safe walking the short distance home.

Stepping deeper into the shadows and farther away from the corrals, he pulled out a cheroot and settled against the railing. He kept a watch out until Laurel left the livery and continued keeping an eye on her until she opened the gate and walked up to the Duncan house.

Once he knew she was safely home, he headed in the direction of the Coyote Bluff. Some urgent business waited for him, and he planned to take care of it tonight.

He hoped and prayed Greta Garrett still waited for him, too.

Chapter 8

With a sundry of bewildering thoughts attacking her from all sides, Laurel unlatched the gate to her aunt and uncle's massive house, which looked like it belonged on a Southern plantation. Taking two steps inside, she glanced back toward the livery.

Once she had turned her back on Hunter and led Buckey inside the blacksmith's shop, she hadn't seen the gambling rancher again. All the way home, however, she kept looking back over her shoulder feeling she was being watched. Maybe she was just hoping he'd follow her and ask her to supper or something . . . anything to keep her from having to go home. If one could call the cold, unwelcoming structure the Duncans lived in a home.

Soft light filtered through the lace curtains in the study, so she knew her uncle was home and probably still up working.

Instead of entering from the front of the house, she walked to the back and came in through the servants' entrance. She climbed the stairs with a mixture of emotions at odds with one another. While some demanded that she stay as far away from Hunter as possible, others pled with her to run back and throw herself into his arms. He was certainly a multifaceted man who created complex emotions within her. In a very physical way, he had definitely led her to believe he enjoyed her company. Yet at the same time, he sent her another set of confusing signals.

Her heart recognized they shared an undeniable bond, and had for a lot of years. Her conscience screamed for her to be cautious. Things were not as they seemed.

For the most part, she felt satisfied with how the evening had gone, although it had started out rocky, to say the least. She'd told him the truth about the job offer from his mother, although she'd failed to mention anything about the pressure put upon her to lead the women's group. Since that was a moot issue, she saw no reason to bring it up. She could have warned him about the posters, but that would be taking sides . . . the one thing she was determined not to do. She couldn't have made it any clearer to Melba Ruth and the Wilson sisters, although she wasn't certain Pearl had gotten the point, that she refused to take any part in their scheme.

Besides, she had all she could handle with her family.

She pushed open the door to her tiny, airless room with little more than a featherbed, a highboy, and a washstand. A small rocker took up one corner, next to an aged rickety wardrobe, which held all of her belongings.

As late as it was, she'd missed supper—not that it mattered. Maybe the cook had found it in her heart to save Laurel a plate of leftovers, and if so, she'd eat alone in a silent kitchen. She couldn't afford to purchase another meal out. Her savings were down to very little, since her monthly allowance stopped the moment she graduated. She was fortunate to have made good grades and obtained an internship with the magazine during her final three months of school. It brought in money, although not much.

Right now, getting a job had to be her priority. So far, every time the subject of her going to work at the bank came up, her uncle sloughed it off as being unimportant.

The position Mrs. Campbell offered might well be her only choice, becoming more appealing by the second. She'd have a steady income, it'd be interesting, and she could find a place of her own to live, even if it meant getting a room in a boardinghouse. Ever since she'd been back, she'd been concerned for her aunt's health, and the thought of moving out and leaving her alone left a taste in her mouth somewhere between rancid lard and sorghum syrup.

If she took the position, she'd have regular run-ins with Hunter. Only a fool would believe she could maintain a relationship with Melba Ruth and not have to do the same with her son. Something that couldn't be avoided and she'd have to take under careful consideration before making her decision.

Laurel took off the silly hat she'd been wearing all day, and considered tossing it across the room just to see if she could hang it on the coat hook on her first try. What had possessed her to wear it in the first place?

After walking across the tattered rug, which provided little more than faded color in the room, she eased down on the side of the bed. The mattress sank dangerously low beneath her weight. She pulled off the gaudy boots. Again, she wondered why she had gone ahead and worn the stupid-lookin' things, but then she'd had little choice if she wanted to go riding. Without her knowledge, her cousin had taken Laurel's only decent pair of boots and hat, leaving the gawd-awful ones for her. She almost smiled thinking how they looked like something a rodeo clown might wear.

She was washing her face with a bar of soap that stung like lye when her bedroom door swung open.

Unceremoniously, her cousin, Victoria, stomped in. A

couple of years younger than Laurel, the dumpy, bloodless-looking girl who hadn't spent more than two hours out-doors in months began bellowing at the top of her lungs.

"Where are my boots and hat?" Her shrill voice sent chills up and down Laurel's spine.

Taken aback, Laurel whirled toward her cousin. "I, uh, they are right by the bed."

Victoria rushed over and snatched up the boots and began examining them. "You're lucky. You didn't scuff them up any." She looked around. "And my hat better not have so much as a smudge of dust on it." She put her hands on her plump hips. "So where did you get the idea you could wear them without asking permission?"

Her cousin had always acted like a spoiled brat, and age had only encouraged the entitlement she seemed to think was rightfully hers.

As angry as Laurel was, she chose her words carefully, knowing whatever she said would be twisted around to benefit Victoria. "I didn't borrow them. You knew I was going riding and took mine, so I presumed you had left yours for me to wear. You left me with little choice." Laurel tried to depict a calm she didn't necessarily feel. "Besides, I bought them in New York—"

"With my father's money!" Sarcasm laced Victoria's shrill screech.

"No, with what I earned at the magazine," Laurel said with deceptive calmness.

"Oh yes, you saved *your* money, but continued to take what Father sent you." Victoria hurled out the words as if they were stones.

"I'll have a regular payday soon when I go to work at the bank."

"You think Father is going to hire you? Maybe to clean the floors or empty the trash, just like your mother used to do, but not anything where the public can see you. You know nothing about fashion, and would probably scare customers away." Her dark eyes narrowed and she let out an evil, haunting laugh meant to humiliate. "You should hear what others say about you. Why don't you take better care of yourself? You're too plain, almost ugly, and wearing riding pants doesn't help. And Father wants to find you a fitting beau to get you off his hands . . . and out of our house as soon as possible." Every word was calculated and meant to hurt.

Old fears and uncertainties rose within Laurel. A flicker of dread coursed through her.

As if she hadn't said enough hurtful words, Victoria continued in a chiding tone that angered Laurel beyond belief. "Just so we're clear, don't ever touch anything that belongs to me again or you'll be sorry." She stalked toward the door, then whirled back. "I can make your life a living hell. Oh, by the way, Father wants to see you immediately." A twisted, cynical smile spread across Victoria's plump lips. "And I wouldn't make him wait, if I were you. He's not in a good mood, and it's all because of you."

She slammed the door behind her, then opened it again to say, "And be quiet. Mother has taken to bed as she's feeling poorly today."

Victoria deliberately closed the door louder than before.

Laurel sat back down on the side of the bed. Leaning forward, she propped her elbows on her knees and rested her face in her hands. She fought back the few tears that she'd not already shed. She doubted there were any left in her soul.

Why was everything that went wrong in life always her fault? She'd been a good girl, or tried to, but no matter how hard she worked at doing the right thing, something went awry.

For over fifteen years, she'd carried the burden of being the cause of her parents' death. If only she could express her concerns. Her anger. Her doubts. But then who would believe her?

Why had she come up with the stupid idea to take a ride today anyway? If she'd stayed home like she should have, then she wouldn't have run into Hunter. Now she was not only caught up in old feelings about the crafty cowman, but had a dilemma with his mother. An issue that seemed to have ripped the town apart. The last thing she needed was to divide what little family she had left.

Now her uncle was angry with her or at least that's what Victoria wanted her to think.

Laurel walked to the washstand and rinsed her face with cold water. She tied her hair back with a ribbon and changed into a plain brown calico dress.

With as much resolve as she possibly could scurry up, she descended the stairs to the study, being careful to be quiet. She didn't want to upset her frail Aunt Elizabeth.

Uncle Gideon sat behind his massive oak desk in his well-appointed study fit for a banker. Even as big as the desk was, he dominated every inch of it. Tall, potbellied, with a full beard and sideburns, he looked to some people like a big, wild woolly stuffed into a suit and tie. She couldn't have described him better herself.

"Shut the door," he bellowed, without looking up. "So you finally decided to come home."

Laurel did as she was told, easing the door closed, but took a stance in front of the desk. Determined not to be browbeaten, she folded her arms across her chest. "I've been out riding—"

He interrupted, "And sneaking around the Sundance Saloon with those no-good Wilson sisters." He turned the paper he was writing on face down on the desk. "You were also out at the Campbell place."

"Yes, sir."

"I want you to get this straight." He leaned back in his

chair and gave her a cold, nasty look of displeasure. "As long as you're living in my house, you will have nothing to do with that woman or her son."

Fury rocked her. "With all due respect, I'm old enough to decide who I will and won't be friends with."

"If you want a place to live, you'd best not let me find out you're consorting with any of them, especially Melba Ruth Campbell. She's a troublemaker, and is doing everything she can to ruin our town." His face was marked with loathing, unnerving Laurel. "She's little more than a tramp, owning a saloon, cleaning houses for people, and then she thinks she's good enough to lead a rebellion against the men. I will not allow anyone in my family, or my employment, to associate with rubbish like her. She's determined to undermine the railroad. I don't trust that son of hers either."

"Mrs. Campbell befriended me when nobody else did, and I made it clear that I'm not taking sides on what is best for Farley Springs."

"Oh, but you are. As long as you're in my house, eating my food, and wearing the clothes I bought for you, you will do what you're told, and that includes making certain the railroad comes to town. It's in your best interest." His mouth took an unpleasant twist. "This is your one and only warning, so listen up, girl." His eyes darkened dangerously. "I'm a man of little patience. You'll do as I say or you will be sorry. Very sorry."

Laurel had no intentions of being dictated to, and girded herself with resolve, praying for self-control. "I can't understand how you can have such disdain for Melba Ruth, while supporting her son's stance on the need for the railroad."

"That's the men's affairs. Good business makes for strange bedfellows. You need to learn your place as a woman. Apparently, all the money I spent on giving you an education went to waste. The only thing you'll be any good at is staying home, having babies, and trying to make your man happy." He took a long look at her. "Without a dowry, and with a lot of work, you might find a man who will have you."

Reality of what the future held sank deep into her stomach. "And the job in the bank you said I could have?"

"I never promised you anything. I simply wrote that there might be something available, but after I've seen what tramps you like to associate with, there's no job for you. Just learn to do women's things. That's all you're fit for," he replied with contempt that forbade any further argument.

"I am certainly capable of making something of myself and doing a lot of good things with my life."

"There's one more thing. I cannot overstate how you must not associate with that rogue gambler who calls himself a businessman and beds any woman who bats her eyes at him. That is, of course, if you haven't already fallen under his spell and into his bed. We have certain allegiances for business' sake, but as for you . . . you will not so much as speak to him."

Laurel seethed in her soul, and she wondered how much of his anger was with Hunter as a businessman and how much was because he beat him in the mayoral race. She had to work hard to contain her words. "I am not thirteen years old. I'm an adult. I have my own values, and can assure you that I do not fall into bed with any man. I believe I'm capable of cultivating my own friendships. I will talk to whomever I so desire." She wanted so badly to add, "And neither you nor anybody else will intimidate me into doing something I don't want to do," but she held her tongue.

She stepped backward and opened the study door.

"As long as you live in *my* house, you'll follow *my* rules.

If you walk out of that door without heeding my warnings, you'll never be welcomed back again . . . I promise you."

Gideon Duncan picked up the glass of whiskey sitting on the desk, but never took a drink, just glared at her in a cynical, frightening way she'd never seen before.

Lifting her chin, she replied, "You've dictated to me in some form or fashion since I was barely a teenager. I've done exactly what you wanted me to do all of my life, and asked few questions. I gave up my twenties and have no intention of doing the same for my thirties. I will find a job and move elsewhere, if that's what it takes, but I'll no longer be dictated to." She wished that she could have added the words "as much as I respect and love you," but not only would they not come out, they weren't in her heart.

"You can't find a job, and without money, there's no place for you to live. You can't make it on your own, and I can promise you if you move out of my house, you'll never see your next birthday," he said with contempt that forbade any further argument.

The dull ache of foreboding seeped into every crevice of her soul, but with it brought a determination she'd never felt before.

"I don't need your damnable job. I already have an offer and it comes with a place to live." She squared her shoulders, turned, and walked out, praying that Melba Ruth Campbell was as true to her word as she'd always been.

"In a room above a saloon, no doubt!" His words echoed off the walls as if they were spoken in an empty tomb.

Glass shattered against the study door, which she'd barely closed behind her.

Fear tightened in her stomach, yet she felt liberated. Although it scared her to death, she was on her own for the first time in her life.

One big problem existed: Did she really have someone to turn to and a place to lay her head?

Chapter 9

Anger dripped from every pore of Laurel's body as she bounded up the stairs to her bedroom. It took less than five minutes to gather her belongings and pack them in her dilapidated valise. After taking a long, thoughtful look at the garments hanging in the wardrobe, she shut it. She wanted nothing that her uncle had given her.

She closed the door behind her, then walked down the backstairs from the servants' quarters. Stepping out into the cool spring evening air, she relished its freshness, representing the first real sense of freedom she'd felt in many years.

As she walked away from the cold, heartless house, she let her thoughts wander like a maverick calf looking for his mama.

From the moment her uncle rushed her away from her parents' graves until a few minutes ago, she had been like a marionette, with her uncle pulling the strings. Even before she was whisked off to boarding school, he'd tried to keep her segregated from people, as if she were some kind of nasty secret not to be revealed.

She had no idea what the townfolks had been told about why she had come to live with her relatives. But by the way they shunned her, it must have been that she was an escapee from a leper colony. The only kids brave enough to stand up for her were the Wilson sisters and Hunter Campbell. Even her own cousin would walk on the other side of the street just to taunt her.

The only normalcy she felt during that time was when she worked very hard in her studies and made good grades, even though she did so more out of fear than her own desire to excel. Her fun times existed when she sneaked away and spent time with Melba Ruth Campbell and her family or the Wilson sisters.

They all treated her like somebody, not a servant.

Only too vividly she was reminded of how Aunt Elizabeth would punish her for the tiniest infraction by having her polish all the silver in the house, although she had servants. It would take hours, and when she'd finally finish, her aunt would always find fault with the job she'd done. It took Laurel years to realize that her aunt was too scared to think for herself, and did as her husband dictated.

Laurel ended up following suit. It was better to do what she was told and ask no questions than to take the verbal abuse. Her uncle knew how to leave scars that could not be seen.

As Laurel walked along Main Street, she wanted to put her hands over her ears to quiet her thoughts.

She took a deep breath. *That was then and this is now.* She promised herself she'd never speak of the past and look only to the future.

Wrapped in new resolve, she continued along the darkened storefronts. The wind moaned and whispered between the buildings, and the only movement, other than a stray dog, was an occasional cowboy staggering out of one of the saloons either at the insistence of the barkeep or with the assistance of the toe of his boot.

Reality set in. She needed a place to spend the night and

be safe at the same time. Running through a limited list, one by one she eliminated each of them.

The Wilson sisters were nowhere to be found, most likely working on their secret project for the library committee. Not to mention their place was much too cramped for another living creature.

It was too dark and dangerous to make her way back to the Triple C all alone. She quickly discounted trying to find Hunter and ask to sleep in one of the rooms above his saloon. Of course, the Sundance was out of the question.

At such a late hour, the only logical place for her to go and not be seen was the stables. The blacksmith would be settled in for the night and he'd never know she was there. She could sleep in one of the wagons, or if worst came to worst, Buckey's stall. She'd rest until sunup, saddle the gelding, and head out to the Triple C to accept Melba Ruth's offer of employment.

Her reflection caught her eye in the glass window of the unoccupied Campbell's Millinery storefront. She pushed her hair back from around her face. An odd, yet warm feeling coursed through her as more memories of better times washed over her. Yet at the same time, a chill ran down her spine.

An idea flittered around in her head. Since Hunter's sister had married and moved away, the town no longer had a hat shop. Laurel was well versed on headwear, and had written several articles on the fashion of hats. Why couldn't she open a shop? Once she got settled in and saved every possible penny, maybe she'd do just that. No doubt she couldn't afford to purchase the building, but surely she could negotiate a monthly rental fee that would be reasonable.

At least now she had a goal for the future. Of course, she'd have to change the name. Staring at the sign above the door, she envisioned WOMACK MILLINERY written across it.

Laurel saw Greta Garrett's reflection in the window before she got within an arm's length of her, so she was able to turn around to face the woman as she approached. The look on Greta's face made it clear that she wasn't there to invite Laurel to Sunday dinner.

"I want to talk to you," Greta said in the same hasty, demanding tone of voice she'd had since grade school.

"I don't have time," Laurel replied just as Greta grabbed her by the arm.

"Then take time." Greta stood so close to her that Laurel could smell her breath, which reeked of cheap whiskey. "Hunter Campbell is my man, and if you don't leave him alone, you'll regret it." Her eyebrows narrowed, and she said, "So stay away from him!"

Laurel jerked her arm away from Greta but chose to say nothing, because anything she said would only accelerate the argument. *Be the bigger person*, Laurel reminded herself.

Obviously thinking Laurel's lack of response was an indication of compliance, Greta whirled and strolled toward the center of town as if she'd just finished a pleasant conversation with a friend.

Why were so many people intent on her keeping her distance from Hunter Campbell and his family? Jealousy fueled Greta's insecurities, but what were the real reasons behind Uncle Gideon's demands?

They will not frighten me away! Laurel said over and over in her mind as she continued down Main Street. If anything, it only solidified her resolve.

As expected when she reached the blacksmith's shop, there were no lights on, so she came through the wagon yard and found Buckey's stall near the back door. He might well be a stupid hammerhead, as Hunter called him, but the bay was the only friend she had . . . and he didn't judge her.

She rubbed him down and brushed his black mane and tail. When she was finished, she pulled his saddle blanket from the rails separating him from the horse in the next stall, and headed for the nearest supply wagon, which was somewhat sheltered by a big cottonwood tree. The night weather was perfect. Although the Panhandle was known to have beautiful days and frigid nights during early spring, Mother Nature had smiled down on the town and shrouded it in a warmer-than-usual night.

After tossing her bag into the bed of the wagon, it took two tries for her to lift herself up. The wagon was loaded with lumber and supplies, but several bags of chicken feed and seeds of some sort lay end to end, making a perfect bed. She lay down, and frankly it wasn't that much more uncomfortable than the bed she'd been sleeping in. She pulled a rough horse blanket over her, removed her Derringer from her bag and put the weapon under the covers but within reach, then tucked the satchel beneath her head for a pillow.

Lying awake, Laurel looked up at the black ceiling of sky strewn with thousands of glittery stars. An unbelievably full moon sent a cascade of silver light down upon the earth.

Tears welled in her eyes and rolled down her cheeks.

Tomorrow would bring the first sunrise of the rest of her life, and she'd never look behind her again . . . only forward to the future. One as bright with promise as the stars overhead.

Satisfied that Laurel was safely at home, and he'd done what his mother requested, Hunter headed to the Coyote Bluff Saloon. Like any other night, it was filled to the brim with customers. The piano player, complete with a crimson armband on his right sleeve, played as loud as he could but still his tune could barely be recognized over the racket. Thunderous noise meant lots of activity, translating into good profits for the saloon.

The stubble-bearded blacksmith yelled at Hunter the moment he walked through the swinging doors. "Got a serious poker game going over here. Saved a chair for you, Campbell."

"Andy, you know I rarely pass up an opportunity like that, but tonight I've got business to tend to." He shot the blacksmith an apologetic grin.

Typically, the poker players knew that if he passed up a game, it was only because he had a better offer and that generally included a woman and a warm bed. But tonight was different. The business that he couldn't get out of his system was the memory of Laurel's body against his.

Hunter strolled directly to the bar, stopping to shake hands and acknowledge customers along the way. He spoke briefly to the bartender to make sure things were running smoothly, then took a bottle of Jack Daniel's and a glass from behind the bar and headed toward a corner table, where his old friend Stubby Johnson sat nursing a drink.

"Look like you're fresh off a cattle drive," Stubby said.

"Should've seen me before I changed clothes." Hunter opened the bottle of whiskey and poured two fingers in each glass, before asking, "Have you seen Greta?"

"Last time I saw her, she was over at the Sundance flirtin' with any cowboy who'd buy her a drink." Stubby picked up his glass and took a slug. "You know her, always wantin' to make a feller happy. Gonna break it off with her?"

"Nothing to break off."

"Cain't tell me she means more to you than a good romp in the hay. I've known you too long."

"That's all it's been for both of us. Greta's told that to plenty of studs no matter what she tells the fillies." After gulping down his whiskey, Hunter refilled his glass.

"Might've had something if we'd tried harder, but neither of us was much into trying that hard."

"And I can bet my last eagle that the trying stopped altogether when Laurel Dean Womack got back into town?"

"She has nothing to do with it," Hunter lied, not only to his friend but to himself, then changed the subject. "Everything ready for tomorrow?"

"Yep. All the men know we're meetin' at two and will finalize our plans. Got a couple of volunteers to build the pit, and so far have three cowmen who have donated beeves to put on the spit when it's finished. Still plannin' on Valentine's Day?"

"Don't see any reason not to. All the women from the ladies' group were out at the ranch with their heads together, so I have little doubt that my plan worked and they are preparing for a boxed supper and dance."

"You're sure of that? You know you scared the pee diddlin' out of us when you changed plans at the last minute." Stubby ran his hands through his curly black hair and plopped his Stetson back on. "I thought you'd been nipping on loco weed for a bit, but then when I saw the womenfolk skedaddlin' outta the Sundance like their bloomers were on fire, I knew what you were doing. All we have to do now is to get the word out to the cowboys and they'll all be bitin' at the bit to come to town for beer and barbeque and won't mind leaving a donation to help pave Main Street. They do like their beer."

Hunter couldn't help smiling. "And then they can stay for the girlie festivities if they want. They probably won't sell many boxed suppers, but the men will want to dance, if they get tanked up enough."

"Yep, we got our share of pretty calicos here," Stubby said with a twinkle in his eye.

After Stubby made sure Hunter was going back to the ranch early the next morning, he reminded him that there was a wagonload of supplies over at the wagon yard that needed to be taken back to the Triple C.

"What did Mother order that takes a wagon to haul out there?" Hunter asked.

"Mainly lumber, wire, and nails. Chicken feed and some sort of seeds."

"She's bound and determined to build a vegetable garden and flower bed, so guess it's the stuff she ordered from Fort Worth." Hunter shook his head, realizing that once his mother made up her mind to do something, there was no changing it.

"Yep, and two or three rosebushes."

Hunter rolled his eyes and almost laughed out loud, thinking back to Laurel's comments about him planting rosebushes for his mama. Did she know something he didn't?

"Mrs. Kruger brought over a sack of burox for your mama, and said to make sure she got 'um and for us to keep our muddle-grubbing mitts off of 'um." Stubby smiled. "So don't touch 'um."

"Yes, sir. Mama sure does like Mrs. Kruger's German burox."

"Got one question," Stubby remarked, but didn't wait for a reply. "How did Laurel Dean get hornswoggled into helping out your mama and the women's committee?"

"She didn't. Swears she's not taking sides, and that makes sense, because Gideon would probably disown her if she went against his wishes. He really wants to see the railroad here, and will do just about anything to make it happen." Hunter felt uneasy with the thought. "Mother offered Laurel a job?"

"She's been thinkin' about gettin' someone to do her books, since her eyesight isn't what it used to be, but don't tell her I said that or I'll be the one on the barbeque spit."

They threw back their heads and shared a gut-splitting laugh.

"Then you are totally convinced that the women are plannin' on the boxed supper?" asked Stubby.

"One hundred and fifty percent sure. I saw Mother pass off a list of things to do to Ruby Wilson, and nobody has seen either of the Wilson women anywhere, so they are on a mission no doubt." Hunter chuckled. "They wouldn't even ride back to town with us, they were so excited about getting on with what they had planned."

Hunter surveyed the room. "I think we've got the women exactly where we want them. We'll just let them announce their benefit to raise money for the library, and we'll act like we're sorta upset they stole our idea, but we'll figure out something else, which will make three times the money for the paving of Main Street."

"Speaking of Main Street, you know that building that your sister had her hat shop in would make a good library," Stubby chuckled to himself.

"So you're workin' on the women's committee now, Stub?"

Before his friend could respond, he switched his attention from his whiskey glass to the front door. "Trouble. Trouble. Trouble."

Hunter looked up and saw Greta flouncing his way.

"There you are," she said long before she reached his table.

Stubby excused himself and went back to the bar and ordered another drink.

Damn it to hell! Hunter wasn't up to dealing with her tonight. Earlier in the evening he'd wanted to talk to her, but now he was too tired and frustrated. Besides, he was having trouble sorting out his feelings about their relationship except for the realization that whatever they had was over. Taking her into his bed again wasn't about to happen and he knew that was her intent.

For the first time since laying eyes on her, at least two decades before, instead of seeing a sexy, alluring woman with plenty of mouthwatering assets to offer him, he saw a shallow female filled with nothing but fluff. He could be assured any thoughts that came through her insensitive brain contained the words *me* or *I*.

"I need to talk to you, Hunter." She latched on to his arm and leaned into him. "I'll be waiting in your room." She lowered her voice but it was still cold and challenging. She added, "Now!"

Before Hunter could respond, she stood straight up, thrust out her best assets, and sauntered toward the staircase.

Annoyance flowed through him at her demanding demeanor, and Hunter almost tipped over the table when he rose to his feet.

From the bar, Stubby caught his eye and lifted a questioning eyebrow.

Feeling she deserved at least a private breakup of their relationship, Hunter followed Greta up the stairs and into his room. The second the door closed, she whirled on him. At first he thought she was lifting her arms up around his neck, but in a flash he saw an open hand.

He caught her by the wrist just before her palm met his flesh. "I'd suggest you never try that again," he warned. Letting go of her, he added, "You'll only get the chance to slap me once."

Hunter had never touched a woman in anger and didn't have any plans on doing so now; however, Greta made him irate enough for him to consider going against his principles.

"What were you doing with that piece of rubbish, Laurel Womack?" Her voice dripped with sarcasm. "I saw her waiting for you outside the Sundance. I almost laughed at the getup she had on, and she's supposed to have been in New York at finishing school." She laughed in a cynical, uncaring fashion. "Victoria told me that you were with her most of the day. Why would you spend a second more than necessary with a dim-witted twit like her when you have a woman like me waiting for you?" She ran her hand up his chest and tried to unbutton his shirt.

More gingerly than he wanted, he grabbed her hand. "What I do is none of your business." Her arm dropped to her side. "Our time together wore thin long ago, Greta. I believe it's best for both of us to admit it and quit seeing one another."

"You're rejecting me!" She snarled satirically, and then her voice hardened into clay. "You can't do that to me!"

"It has nothing to do with rejection. I'm just through with us using one another." He looked her straight in the eyes. "I'm a man with feelings, not a plaything to satisfy your whim-whams. And you deserve something I've never been able to give you."

She stared in his direction. "But you've enjoyed every minute of me, and you know it." Suddenly she brought her hand up, but apparently thought twice before she slapped him. "You're making the biggest mistake of your life."

"No, ma'am. I'm trying to keep us both from making the biggest mistakes of our lives."

Five minutes later Hunter stood beside Stubby at the bar and took another slug of Black Jack.

"I guess that didn't go as well as you expected, from the way Greta came down the stairs. I wasn't sure if she was moving on her own or had the toe of your boot up her fanny, but she didn't lollygag."

"Went about like I expected, but I don't want to talk about it," he said to his friend. "See you tomorrow." Hunter addressed the bartender. "I'll be in before noon, if you need anything."

Stubby caught him just as he turned to leave. "Don't forget your mama's wagon or she'll skin your hide and mine, too, for not reminding you." Stubby laughed and went back to drinking. "And you dang sure better make certain everything is there before you head out."

"Don't worry, I will." Hunter grabbed the half-filled bottle of Jack Daniel's and stuck it in his jacket pocket, then picked up the wrapped burox.

Having no desire to stay in town and plenty of reasons to get back to the ranch, Hunter headed for the livery. He probably looked like a fool with a bottle of whiskey in one pocket and German stuffed bread in the other.

In the mood he was in, he might well drink the whole damn bottle of whiskey, eat every bite of the bread, and deal with his mama tomorrow.

Within minutes, Hunter stood with his feet apart and arms folded across his chest staring at the sleeping angel curled up in the back of his wagon.

What in the hell had happened to cause Laurel Dean to leave home in the middle of the night and wind up sleeping in a bed of supplies?

Chapter 10

A cloud quickly cloaked the full moon, shadowing Laurel. Before Hunter could speak, she sat straight up. With a steady hand, she aimed a Derringer right between his eyes.

"Put the damn gun down, Laurel," Hunter bellowed. He resisted adding, "If you call that thing a gun," because he was pretty certain she'd fire at him just to prove him wrong. At least, he knew she wasn't hurt.

Slowly he held up his hands as a sign he wasn't holding a sidearm.

"Hunter?" She lowered the pearl-handled woman's weapon. "You shouldn't have sneaked up on me."

"What in the hell are you doing sleeping in the wagon yard?" He knew his voice was more confrontational than he would have liked.

"I came here to check on Buckey. I brushed him down, and was enjoying just looking at the full moon and guess I fell asleep," she said with a firm, yet gentle softness in her voice. She looked up at him as if she really thought he believed her explanation.

A cloud quickly scurried away from the face of the moon, allowing moonlight to once again flood the wagon yard.

Laurel slid the gun in her bag and pushed it behind her.

"So you brought a carpetbag with you to groom a horse?"

"It's a valise!"

"Valise, carpetbag, it doesn't matter what it's called, I just want to know why you're hiding out here and not home in bed, where you belong?" Hunter impatiently ripped out his words.

The look on her face told him she wasn't all that happy being questioned by him.

"I'm not hiding. I simply fell asleep."

Although she looked him straight in the face, he knew a lie when he heard one. Why wasn't she telling him the truth? Her safety was more important to him than any reason she could give. But something strange and unsettling filled the air.

"Get down from there right now." A tightening came to his chest. "It's obvious you need to talk to someone, so it might as well be me."

Laurel physically drew back from him. Tears welled in her eyes. She was frightened, truly frightened, and he was pretty sure it had nothing to do with him.

She finally whispered, "Hunter, I'm not coming down. All I'm doing is sleeping. I'm not hurting anything, so please leave me alone." In a soft voice, she continued, "Thank you, but I don't need to talk to anyone."

"You picked the wrong wagon, Laurel. This one belongs to the Triple C, so if I say you can't sleep in it, you can't."

"Go get the sheriff and have me arrested, but I'm not leaving." She crossed her wrists as if prepared to be handcuffed.

"At least you'd be safe in the hoosegow," he said under his breath, but felt sure in the stillness of the night she heard his every word. "If you won't come down here for us to talk, I'm coming up there."

Laurel seized her valise and scooted back into the far corner of the wagon.

"You can make it either easy or hard on yourself, it's your choice." Receiving no response, Hunter heaved himself into the back of the wagon and maneuvered his big frame around until he was seated next to Laurel. He stretched his long legs out in front of him, trying to make himself comfortable.

He didn't want to frighten her more by pressuring her for a better explanation, so they sat in silence for a long time, just staring at the stars.

"I'm not going to ask you any questions about what sent you out here to sleep, but I'm not fool enough to believe your story that you just fell asleep."

"Thanks," she stalled, then said, "My uncle and I had a disagreement. I just needed some fresh air."

"Did he hurt you?" Hunter quickly asked.

She shook her head. "Not physically."

"Your uncle can be an arrogant, insensitive sonofabitch." Hunter almost bit his tongue to keep from saying what he really thought about Gideon Duncan, knowing he probably wouldn't tell her anything she didn't already know. "Then why didn't you go to the hotel for the night?"

"I don't have any money . . ." She stopped, as if she had to think up something else to say before adding, "I mean, I have no money with me."

He believed her about as much as a cattle rustler just happening to have wire cutters in his pocket to pick his teeth with. She had the wherewithal to pack some of her things in a bag, take a pistol with her, but didn't think about money. Not a likely story; but right now, he felt in his soul that she needed a friend.

"I'm sure Gideon has an account at the hotel, but if you don't want to go there, how about coming to my saloon? I have an extra room on the second floor you're welcome to use."

Way too fast she responded, "No, thank you."

"Then let me take you out to the ranch—"

She vehemently shook her head.

"Bobbie Ray's room is empty. You can stay there. Mama will probably insist you stay in my sister's old room, if you decide to go to work for her."

"We can decide that *if* I get the job."

Catching a whiff of the meat and bread pies in his pocket, Hunter asked, "Are you hungry?"

She hesitated, but by the way she licked her lower lip, he knew she hadn't eaten.

"Come on." He pulled the sack of burox from his pocket. "Mrs. Kruger sent these," he said as he began unwrapping one and offered it to her. "They're delicious."

She eagerly accepted the beef and cabbage–stuffed roll and began eating it like she was starving. "Thanks," she said between mouthfuls. "I was hungrier than I thought." She took another bite and smiled over at him.

Hunter took the whiskey from his other pocket. "Don't have anything to offer you to drink other than this." He held out the bottle. "It's either drink direct from the bottle or I guess I could go find a dipper in one of the horse stalls."

"It wouldn't be the first time I've had whiskey straight from the bottle." She raised an eyebrow mischievously, and he heard a little bit of playfulness in her voice.

"I'm not asking any questions." He was just glad she was distracted for even a few minutes from what was bothering her. "Remember, this isn't just plain ol' rotgut, it's Jack Daniel's, Tennessee's finest."

Laurel barely took a sip. The smile she shot him carried a tad of amusement, and for the first time she seemed to relax. "Thanks." She handed him the bottle and wiped her mouth. "Do you still own the building where your sister had her millinery shop?"

"Yes. Guess you want to sleep in it?" he teased, thinking a little off-the-cuff humor might keep the mood light, but she just shot him a withering glance.

She didn't waste any time getting right to explaining why she'd asked about the shop, including her plans to open another millinery shop and provide the ladies of Farley Springs the newest in fashion.

Hunter sat there for a minute or two taking everything in, then said, "Tell you what, I won't rent it, but when you're ready, I'll lease it to you for one dollar a year." He looked in her face, and laid a hand on her arm. "Cash in advance, please."

For the first time a true smile crossed her lips. He wondered if she had any idea how sexy she looked. Her moon-kissed hair glittered. Her skin was smooth and velvety.

"Thank you," she whispered. Leaning into him, she kissed him on the cheek.

The woman disturbed him in ways he didn't think possible. Without thinking, he slipped his arm around her and pulled her to him. A lurch of excitement exploded within him as he tipped up her chin and brushed his thumb along her jaw. Emerald green eyes smoldered with fire.

"You have beautiful eyes," he whispered.

"And you've got . . ." She ran her fingertips along his unshaven jawline. "A perfect chin even with that little scar where your sister used a cottonwood limb for a saber," she said softly. "You didn't think I'd remember, huh?"

"You don't forget anything." The undeniable magnetism they shared boiled over between them. He took her hand and pressed it against his cheek and they locked gazes. Courage and fear shone from the depths of her green eyes.

Her skin was even softer than he'd imagined, her scent more alluring. Honeysuckle and ivory. A heady combination in any woman. A man could live forever and never find a more perfect woman. She had a way of touching him that made him burn with wanting.

Desire fisted in his gut, heating his blood as he continued to study her. He needed to taste her full lips, to see if she was everything he thought she'd be. And because he wanted her so badly, wanted her kiss, her touch like some men need to ride the wind, he dropped his hand and fought against the ache inside him.

Hunter knew she needed him, but not in a physical way. When the time was right, they'd both know it and nothing would make him stop. Right now he'd settle for a kiss.

Slowly they slipped down as one and lay with their bodies meshed with one another.

Hunter couldn't resist touching her again. Dipping his head, he brushed his mouth across hers so gently it was barely a whisper. He parted her lips and his tongue slipped inside to dance with hers. He savored the taste of whiskey and sweetness, loneliness and longing, and knew he'd never be able to get the taste of the kiss off his lips. His heart thundered out of control, and an overwhelming hunger set off a blaze in his gut.

He locked Laurel in an embrace. Devoured by his kisses, she allowed him to caress her. Their ragged breathing echoed in the silence of the night. Slowly, she opened her eyes.

Hunter felt the thudding of her heart beneath his fingertips as he touched her breasts, and he knew she felt his show of how much he wanted her pressed hard and heavy against her. Dangerous! She was much too dangerous. A gentleman would never take advantage of a venerable lady, and no doubt Laurel certainly fell into that category.

It took everything in him for Hunter to pull himself away from Laurel, if only an inch, but he knew it was the right thing to do.

Neither spoke, just embraced one another, enjoying what might have been.

"Good night," he whispered as he pulled her tighter against him. "If you won't go with me, then I'll stay with you." He kissed her on the forehead and closed his eyes, taking in the smell of fresh hay, a spring night, and moonlight.

Hunter's soul told him he needed to protect Laurel, but how could he protect someone who didn't want to be protected?

Chapter 11

Hunter opened his eyes and stretched. A thin seam of orange and red peeked over the eastern horizon, and he knew the sun would follow in only minutes. He rolled to his side and watched Laurel as she slept. Amazed that he'd gotten such a good night's sleep in the bed of a supply wagon, he needed only one glance at Laurel Dean to remind himself how easy it was to rest when he held a beauty like her in his arms. He kissed her on the forehead.

Laurel stirred and opened her eyes. "Good morning," she said as she wiggled a little, resting her hand on his shoulder. "Thanks for staying with me."

"You're welcome," he said as if he'd spent the night in her chambers and was waking up to a cup of hot coffee handed him by a butler.

"I need to go over to the Coyote Bluff and check on things before we leave for the ranch." The truth, although he did need to check in at the saloon, he planned to get some cash to loan Laurel until she got her first paycheck. He knew she'd fight him tooth and toenail if he tried to give it to her. He'd make it plain that it was only a loan, because he knew she was too proud to take it otherwise.

Laurel pulled herself up to a sitting position and he followed.

"I need to freshen up and I'll be ready to go." She touched his cheek with her fingertips, something he had quickly become accustomed to. "Take your time. I have everything I need here in my bag and I bet Andy won't mind if I borrow a bit of water." She broke into a radiant, leisurely smile.

"We'll have breakfast at the ranch, if that's okay with you." He combed his hair with his fingers and rubbed his scrubby day-old whiskers. "Then you and Mama can get together on your new job responsibilities." He picked up his Stetson, brushed off some of the dust, and put it on. "You are taking the job, aren't you?"

"Yes," she said in an assertive, confident, yet sensual-as-hell voice.

Jumping from the wagon, he reassured her that he wouldn't be gone long. He made a mental note to freshen up a bit and shave while he was at the saloon, if time allowed. He wanted to get Laurel away from town and out at his ranch as quickly as possible. No doubt whatever had sent her to the wagon yard wouldn't waste time finding her as soon as the sun was up.

Hunter sought out the blacksmith, who was busy with the morning chores. The smithy looked like he'd been ridden hard and put away wet, so no doubt last night's poker game had lasted into the wee hours of the morning.

"You're up early, Campbell," Andy said as he threw a blanket over the horse he was saddling. "Gotta get him ready bright and early."

"Gonna be a busy one, so gotta make hay while the sun shines." Hunter leaned against the gate.

Andy asked, "Heard the meetin' for the men to decide exactly what we're doing to raise money is supposed to be at two o'clock."

Hunter shook his head, and tried to keep the smirk off his face. "Yep, two o'clock, and it'll be full of surprises, so I've gotta get back to town as soon as I take the supply wagon out to the ranch. Can you have the horses ready in about thirty minutes? I'll saddle my horse when I'm ready to leave."

"Sure. Will have your team hitched and waitin'," said Andy.

"Uh . . ." Hunter wasn't exactly sure how to tell the smithy about Laurel, but straight and to the point was probably the best. He could make his own assumptions if he so desired. "Laurel Womack is out there right now and will be going back with me."

"She's just sittin' out there?"

"No . . . well, yes. She'll freshen up a little before we leave, so if you could afford her some courtesies, I'd appreciate it."

"Reckon I have some of them hangin' around." Andy stopped and gave him a look that reeked of "I'll ask you no questions, and you'll tell me no lies." He just smiled and went back to work.

Although the sun was barely up, the town seemed as busy as a beehive on honey day. Hunter didn't get half a block before he came face-to-face with the owner of the hotel, who swished the weekly newspaper in front of him as though it were a weapon. "So this is what you had in mind. Sell us all down the river for a calico!" Dobson was anything but calm. "I thought we were meetin' today to come up with a plan, but you in your holier than thou ways decided on your own—"

Hunter cut him off. "Wait a damn minute, Dobson. I don't know what in the hell you're talking about."

"This." The hotel owner wielded the paper in front of Hunter. "*Your* announcement about the moneymaking project to pave Main Street." Ire rose in his voice. "The damn street you're standing on right now. The one that won't get paved, so the railroad will be certain *not* to come to our fair town."

Hunter snatched the paper from Dobson and began to read the headlines of *The Springs Gazette*:

1ST ANNUAL VALENTINE'S DAY CELEBRATION

At a meeting of a number of representative men of Farley Springs held yesterday at the Sundance Saloon, belonging to the mayor's mother, in answer to a previous call for the purpose of considering means of providing an interest to pave Main Street, Mayor Campbell announced that the Farley Springs Men's Club will hold a Boxed Supper and Dance on the Saturday before Valentine's Day. Benefits to be derived from the festivities will go to the project.

Laurel Dean Womack, niece of banker Gideon Duncan and the newly elected President of the Farley Springs Women's Society, also announced that in conjunction with the men's benefit, the newly formed women's benevolent group will hold a barbeque and free beer. Donations will be accepted and directed to building a library to be erected in a structure in a radius of one mile of the town of Farley Springs. The necessity of the distance is apparent. Come one, come all . . . free beer, dance, and fun!

A second article below caught Hunter's attention.

Banker Gideon Duncan, a known advocate of the coming of the railroad to our fine community, told the Gazette, "Laying aside all discussion as to the advantages or disadvantages of a railroad coming through Farley Springs, it is almost an indisputable fact that not another twelve months will have passed until the shrill cry of the whistle and the roar of the iron horse will be heard in the land. Farley Springs will do everything possible to have railroad facilities in that length of time, but if we fail, we can rest assured some part of the Panhandle will succeed. We base our predictions on the fact that, according to late reports, work will commence soon."

Hunter didn't even have time to absorb the implications of what he'd just read before half a dozen men surrounded him and the hotel owner.

A variety of accusations were thrust around and tempers flared about how the men's plans had been sabotaged and speculations on how it'd gotten into the paper.

"This has to be the doing of Gideon Duncan," said one man, while another accused the owner of the newspaper of trying to interfere with everything they'd done to get the attention of the railroad.

An anger like Hunter had never felt before coursed through him as more allegations whirled around him like dust devils on a windy day.

Had he been duped by Laurel Dean? Even his own mother? Had Laurel lied directly to his face? She had assured him that she was not involved with the women's group, yet it was plain by the newspaper article that she not only was involved but was its leader.

Had she deliberately distracted him and made him feel sorry for her just so the women could undermine the men's group?

But what he couldn't understand was the second article quoting her uncle about the railroad coming to Farley Springs.

Had Laurel turned his head and tricked him? Did her uncle instigate it? After all, she'd offered no reason for the argument between her and her uncle.

Hunter had just been used by a woman and was stupid

enough to let it happen. He wouldn't blame the men if they decided to tar and feather him. If he could, he'd do it to himself.

"There's a note on the *Gazette*'s door that the printer has gone fishin' and there won't be another weekly newspaper out for two weeks," said Cal, who appeared from the Sundance, along with another group of men. "The coward. He's the only one who knows who wrote the article."

Furor engulfed Hunter. Not only was Laurel seemingly in cahoots with the Wilson sisters and his own mother, not to mention lying to him, but they had printed what he said at the men's meeting, but changed the date from the fourteenth to the Saturday before, knowing every cowboy who owned a horse would ride to town for barbeque and free beer.

Now the men were stuck with a boxed supper and dance, which wouldn't bring in enough money to pave the floor of the Coyote Bluff Saloon with sawdust.

Hunter turned his back on the grumbling crowd and stalked toward the livery, gripping the newspaper for dear life.

Stubby came abreast of him. "How can you let a calico catch you so off guard?"

"I don't know how she pulled it off, but I'm fixin' to find out." Hunter continued on, leaving Stubby standing alone in the middle of Main Street.

The one thing that bothered Hunter more than being made a fool of was . . . how did she pull this off when he was with her almost continually the last twenty-four hours?

Reaching the wagon yard, Hunter stopped in front of the Triple C wagon. No Laurel in sight. The horse blanket was gone, but her bag was exactly where she'd put it last night.

Andy came up behind him. "Lookin' for Miss Womack?"

"I certainly am." Hunter didn't even try to cover the contempt in his voice. "Do you know where she is?"

"Wish I did, but I don't. Buckey's gone, too." Andy shook his head. "I sure don't think much of her being out on him alone, but the good thing about the buzzard is that he's like an old whore at a barn dance—he'll roam all day long but always comes back with the one who brung him." He laughed, then grew serious. "I'm not certain who rode him out of here because there was so much commotion around here."

"What do you mean?" Hunter's heart jumped. "Who all was here?"

"Might ask me who wasn't. Greta Garrett and that wacky Victoria Duncan was here flappin' their gums and raising all kinds of hell with Laurel."

Hunter's misgivings increased by the minute. He paused to catch his breath, his fears stronger than ever.

"Do you know what it was about?"

"Mainly the two were yammering at Laurel, and she was doing the listening, but I didn't hear anything in particular except Greta telling her that she'd warned her once and guessed she needed a lesson on leaving another woman's man alone, but I'm pretty sure she was here when they left, but I'm not certain." He spit tobacco in the dirt. "Figured it was just gals gettin' into a catfight, so I didn't pay much attention to them."

"You said there was a lot of commotion. What else was going on?"

"Mind you, I was mucking the stalls pert near the wagon yard, so that's why I could hear what I did."

"Who else was here?" Hunter grew impatient.

"Laurel's uncle showed up about that time." Andy spit out another stream of tobacco juice. "I was close enough to hear them. Gideon and her were going at it. She was givin' as good as she was gettin', but I thought a couple of times I might have to go out there and break it up. Mind you, if he'd laid a hand on her, I'da been there for sure."

"So how did it end up?" Hunter asked, becoming more uncomfortable with the situation by the second.

"Gideon said something about how he'd changed his mind and he wanted her to come to work for him at the bank but she'd have to move back home first. She told him something about opening a shop or something. He was really loud and obnoxious, then they seemed to settle down. Or at least I didn't hear him yelling as much as before, but about that time the Wilson sisters came to get their carriage, so I had to go back out front to meet them."

"So you never saw who Laurel left with?"

"Nope. Now that I think about it, I never saw any of them leave. Once the Wilson girls got on the road, headed towards your place, I suspect, it was all quiet and nobody was in sight. Not even Buckey. Still can't imagine Gideon letting her ride him. Like I said, he's skittish as hell, and if he gets a chance to get away and run off, he'll do it. Almost gotta hobble the hammerhead, if you want to keep him around."

Andy and Hunter walked back toward the wagon, and Hunter heaved himself inside. Grabbing Laurel's bag, he felt around inside until he came across her Derringer.

No way in hell had she left her bag and her gun behind if she had willingly gone with anyone!

Laurel Dean was missing, and Hunter planned to go to hell and back if need be to find her and get some answers.

Chapter 12

Hunter believed the ride from town to the Triple C was the longest he'd ever made in his life except for the one following the funeral of his father. He wiped those horrific memories from his mind. The early spring made the prairie colorful but he didn't enjoy a second of it. All he had on his mind was being betrayed by Laurel, yet at the same time a serious need to find her and hear her explanations overwhelmed him. Something deep inside was keeping him from crucifying her until he'd heard all of the story. A nagging sensation made him think she was in danger.

When he reached the ranch, he quickly tied his sorrel to the hitching post outside of the main house and stomped up the stairs, not giving a rip whether he dirtied the floors or not.

"Mother!" he bellowed and walked into the dining room, where she sat eating breakfast.

"I know my hearing isn't what it used to be, darlin', but you don't have to holler," she said lovingly.

Setting her coffee cup down, she looked up and Hunter could see by the look on her face she knew trouble had arrived and all hell was about to break loose . . . especially if she was instrumental in any of the problems that had led to Laurel's seeming disappearance.

"What's wrong, Hunter?" Her tone turned serious.

"Have you seen Laurel Womack?"

"Not since yesterday afternoon." Melba Ruth bit at her lip. "Something's wrong, isn't it? She's in danger."

"How do you know?"

"Sit down, and have some breakfast. We need to talk."

"Thanks, but I'm not hungry." Hunter's stomach was tied in knots, but he took a seat and let his mother pour him a cup of coffee.

"I'll tell you the honest truth, son. You know we've always been competitive and that's been the fun part of raising a son like you, but I'd never do anything to ruin the trust we have." She reached over and touched his hand.

"I know, Mama. Tell me what went on yesterday out here with Laurel and the Wilson sisters." He took a sip of tasteless coffee. "And what do you know about the article in the newspaper?"

It was obvious by his mother's expression that she knew nothing about what had been published.

Hunter shoved the paper across the table, and waited while she read the article. She laid it down when she was finished and exhaled deeply. Concern creased her forehead.

"Son, all Ruby and Pearl were supposed to do was have the owner of the newspaper print up some flyers to put all over town announcing the men's project, as we understood it from the meeting . . ."

Hunter wanted to rip into her about having spies at the meeting, but now wasn't the time. He'd save that for another discussion. "So they were supposed to do flyers?"

"Yes, and if I had to venture a guess, Pearl got all excited and got the facts bassackwards. She could have easily confused the printer," she said.

Over two cups of coffee and dry toast, Hunter's mother

filled him in on everything that had gone on the day before among the women, ending with, "Laurel absolutely, un-equivocally turned down my request to head up the library committee. The note I gave Ruby had the instructions for the flyers and said nothing at all about you or Laurel." Tears welled in her eyes. "I'd do nothing to hurt that girl. She means as much to me as if she were my own daughter."

"I know, but there's something going on with her uncle." Hunter told her about spending the night with Laurel in the wagon yard and that she and her uncle apparently had had words. "The thing that keeps gnawing at me is why didn't she have money to stay at the hotel? You told me once that her uncle was the trustee of her parents' estate and there was a substantial amount of money. I hadn't thought of that until now. She acts like she's a pauper." Hunter dropped an uneaten piece of toast on his plate.

"That's the reason her uncle fired me." Melba Ruth took a deep breath. "I came across her parents' will and trust agreement one day when I was cleaning his study. I know I shouldn't have, but I read it." Another tear cropped up in her eye. "It was wrong of me to invade anyone's privacy, but I was much less mature and a whole lot more nosy then than I am today." She gave him a pleading look to please believe her.

Before he could say anything, she continued, "There's something else you need to know." She took a deep breath and it was obvious what she had to say next hurt deeply. "I was sworn to secrecy, but it's apparent to me that Laurel means more to you than anyone ever has, so you need to know."

"What, Mother?" He almost lashed out at her, then soft-ened his voice. "What do I need to know?"

"Elizabeth Duncan confided in me that Laurel's parents committed suicide. I was employed by the Duncans at the time, and I overheard her uncle telling Laurel on more than one occasion that it was her fault because of all of the luxuries she had become accustomed to. There was nothing her parents wouldn't give their only child. If it hadn't been for her, she'd still have her parents." Color was beginning to come back to Melba Ruth's face. "I never believed it for a minute."

"Neither do I," Hunter said. "I guess that's why she didn't want to talk about their deaths."

"Suicide brings with it a certain amount of social and religious stigma, and her uncle pounded that into her head. It wasn't to be spoken of."

"Do you think Gideon had anything to do with her parents' deaths?"

Hunter's mother sat silently for a long time, obviously mulling over things in her mind, while Hunter worried about how he was going to go about finding Laurel Dean. Who had taken her and for what reason?

"I'm not sure. I know he went down to San Antonio to help them out with their finances. Elizabeth told me that much. They owned cotton gins, I believe, and weren't doing as well as they should. Nobody would loan them money, and they couldn't take the embarrassment, so they took their own lives. That's what Elizabeth was told by her husband.

"At Laurel's tender age, she was lucky that her uncle had come to town to take care of business," she said, then stopped and stared ahead. "I remember thinking when I saw the will and trust that it was signed the day before their deaths." She got back on her original line of thought. "So if it hadn't been for her uncle, Laurel would have ended up in an orphanage. I remember Elizabeth Duncan saying one time that Laurel's parents couldn't handle their business failures compared to Gideon's successes. He was a lawyer long before he was a banker," Melba Ruth pointed out.

Hunter nodded. "How'd they commit suicide?"

"I don't know, I just heard rumors that it was arsenic." She rubbed her forehead. "I wish I could remember all of it, but it's been so long ago. Laurel's mother and Gideon had just inherited the bank in East Texas from their father shortly before this happened. I think Victoria was the one who told me that. Can't count the times I heard her braggin' about how rich they were but resented every penny they had to spend on Laurel's schooling. I just can't remember it all." A frightened look came over her face but it took her a while to put her thoughts into words. "Something just hit me. Laurel might be in more trouble than either of us realizes."

Hunter's chest grew tight and he couldn't breathe. How much worse could this get? "What is it, Mother?"

"I remember distinctly reading that Laurel is to get her inheritance when she turns twenty-five and that's—"

"Valentine's Day!"

Hunter almost tipped his chair over when he rose to his feet.

Melba Ruth physically began to shake, but her son rounded the table and put his arm around her. "It's okay, Mama. I'll find her." He kissed her lightly on the forehead.

From the distance, the neigh of a horse mixed with Hunter's sorrel's response filled the air. Help had arrived . . . Buckey had come to bring Laurel Dean home.

Hunter grabbed his Winchester from above the fireplace in the study and hit the front door, just in time to see Stubby Johnson reign in his horse, and say, "You ain't goin' nowhere without me, son. I followed that stupid hammerhead from hell and back, and ain't about to stop now." He wiped the sweat from his forehead. "He'll lead us to Miss Laurel."

Chapter 13

The stifling dust, dirt, and mold in the old abandoned wooden line shack where Laurel was being held captive choked her. The smell of burnt wood still lingered in the air. Although she'd pled for some water to stop her coughing, Gideon Duncan had only wielded his pistol in the air and demanded she hush up.

Shivers ran up and down her spine, and she felt about as cold as if she had been tossed into an icy stream in the dead of winter.

Laurel kept a watchful eye on Gideon, whom she had stopped thinking of as her uncle hours before.

"What did I do to make you hate me so much?" Laurel asked.

She received the same answer she'd been getting to any of her questions.

"Shut up!" Gideon wiped sweat from his forehead and lumbered along in front of her, pacing. His huge body filled the room with the smell of sweat and musk, enough to gag most people.

Unbearable anger rose within Laurel for allowing Gideon to trick her into going with him instead of waiting for Hunter at the livery. She wasn't sure what Gideon was capable of although she'd witnessed his temper many times over the years. She tried to understand why the deception, but couldn't.

She should have known that he didn't just come to his senses and change his mind about her. He hadn't suddenly decided to ignore the things he'd said the day before and welcome her back into the fold. But she had wanted so badly to hold on to the little bit of a family she had left that she allowed herself to be taken in by him. He had convinced her that he was remorseful for having made demands on her. He'd said he was wrong for trying to rule her life and wanted to make amends. He even went so far as to tell her that he had a building the bank owned that would make a good place for a hat shop. If she liked it, he'd give it to her.

To celebrate their new beginnings, he asked her to take a ride with him, just to enjoy the morning air and to reinforce their renewed respect for each other. He had promised she'd be back in time to meet Hunter.

Now her world was being torn apart, yet an overwhelming determination filled her soul. She would not allow him to hurt her. She tried to get her bearings. Although she wasn't exactly sure where he'd taken her, she was fairly certain it was Triple C land.

The longer Gideon paced the dirt floor, the more agitated he became, kicking up dust and charred timbers as he walked.

Had he gone mad?

As he'd done for the last two hours, he haphazardly wielded a pistol like a crazed animal. Laurel was more concerned that the weapon would discharge accidentally than him actually killing her. She knew her uncle was a lot of things, but a murderer he was not . . . or at least she prayed that was the case.

Think, Laurel, think! Laurel said over and over to herself.

As much as she disliked giving Gideon the honor of having "Uncle" in front of his name, she didn't want to antagonize him, and said, "Uncle Gideon, what did I ever do to you for you to hate me as much as you do?"

He pulled the weekly newspaper from inside his coat and laid it down on the ground. She had to crane her neck quite a bit but read the article.

Laurel didn't want to believe what she read. "I am not the president of the women's group and had nothing to do with this article," she said softly, perplexed as to where the newspaper had gotten the erroneous information, but she wouldn't be surprised if Pearl had gotten confused, since she fairly well lived in a world of her own.

"You ruined it all by working with those women to get things all stirred up about the railroad, when I've got to have it to survive. Without it, I'll lose everything."

Why did the railroad mean so much to him except for what it'd bring him as a businessman? How could he lose everything if the railroad bypassed Farley Springs?

"You made it so easy for me when you walked out last night and ran into the arms of Hunter Campbell," Gideon said. "I hadn't planned on your accidental demise until just before your birthday, but you gave me the perfect opportunity. Everyone knows we fought and you ran off."

Like an explosion, true fear like none she'd ever experienced in her life ramrodded her body. The words *accidental demise* bounced off every part of her mind.

What had she ever done to him to make him want to hurt her?

"I know you've always felt you were saddled with me and put upon because you just happened to be there when my parents died and ended up having to bring me back to Farley Springs, but why do you want me dead? Surely you're not that insecure that you think my relationship with Hunter would affect you in the least."

He took a step toward her and slapped her across the mouth with the back of his free hand, forcing her head to snap backward. "Shut up. Just shut up." Anger blazed in his eyes. "I'm not insecure!"

She raised her hands up enough to use her sleeve to wipe the blood from her mouth. "At least, I deserve to know why you want me dead. I know it isn't because of whatever you think my involvement with the women's group might be." The salty taste of blood assaulted her mouth. "And it has nothing to do with Hunter, so tell me the truth." She looked him straight in the eye, not backing down in the least. "If you're going to kill me, you owe me that much. I've lived with the guilt and unknown too many years to carry it with me to the grave."

"You really don't know, do you!" He eyed her like a caged animal. "All that money spent on schooling and you didn't get anything but book learning. They didn't teach you enough to be able to see the truth when it hit you in the face."

Pools of sweat collected on Gideon's forehead, although the air was cold. His breathing became more labored and his chest heaved when he spoke.

Deep inside, Laurel had known for a long time that not everything added up with the story she'd always been told about the events surrounding the deaths of her parents, but she had nowhere to turn and no one to ask to find out the truth.

For months after they died, she lived in a haze, going to school and not really caring one way or another about much of anything. She'd even learned to accept the ugliness of her resentful, bratty cousin.

Gideon Duncan continued his pacing, as if not knowing what his next move would be, while keeping a gun on his captive. It was becoming more obvious that the man who normally calculated his every move was becoming more confused and agitated.

If Laurel could stay calm and not say anything to set him off, maybe she'd best him and survive. Unless she played his game against him, she was a dead woman and she knew it.

Hunter's advice from his father raced through her mind: never put anything on the table, be it money or property, unless you can afford to lose it.

Laurel made a crucial decision. If she could keep him talking about the past, it'd keep his mind off the present.

The one question she wanted answered the most was the hardest to ask, but she couldn't leave this world without knowing. It was the core to everything that had ever happened to her. "How did Mama and Daddy die?"

He let out a nervous sigh and his expression clouded in anger. "You haven't figured that out." His nostrils flared in fury. "Then you're more stupid than I thought." Like the trained lawyer he was, he avoided her question while erecting smoke screens for distraction.

A shadow beyond Gideon caught her eye, but she quickly lowered her gaze, not sure if it was a tree limb blowing in the wind or maybe a tumbleweed. But she prayed it was help. Surely someone had seen them leave the livery and thought it odd.

Tiring, Gideon leaned against one of the two walls that could hold his weight, wiped his forehead, but kept his pistol aimed on her. Possibly he'd seen the same movement as she had, because he alternated his gaze between the opening and her.

He steadily slid down the wall as slow as molasses running uphill until he reached the floor, while keeping an eye peeled on her.

Afraid to say much, Laurel tried to untie her hands, but he'd bound the leather strips too tight. A burst of cold air came through the opening that was once a door. Cold shivers ran over Laurel. Thoughts of Hunter's coat around her to keep her warm made the waiting bearable.

She racked her brain trying to figure out why Gideon wanted her dead; other than she'd become an albatross around his neck.

"If you won't tell me about my parents' death, then I deserve knowing why you want me dead," she demanded, trying not to aggravate him more than he already was.

"You don't need to know anything." His lips thinned with anger. "If you'd just done what I told you to do and not got involved with the Campbell bunch."

"I don't understand how being friends with them caused a problem for you."

"You wouldn't. You twit."

"But you and Hunter are working together to bring the railroad to town."

"And it would have happened except you decided to get all high and mighty on us and sabotage the whole thing."

Laurel wanted so badly to argue with him, but decided the best approach would be to patronize him. "I'm not the president. That article is misleading. I only made Melba Ruth Campbell believe that I wanted to help. I can see now that paving the streets would be more beneficial. She offered me a job, but I didn't take it, because I knew you'd come through at the bank."

Think, Laurel! Stay calm and cool. Don't let him get under your skin.

"I want to know what I ever did to you . . . so I can change it." She once again found herself playing coy with him.

"I never planned on having to deal with you for the rest of my life." A sudden thick chill hung on the edge of his words. "The last thing I needed was another brat to deal with."

"What are you going to do with me?"

"I haven't decided. There's an abandoned well out there.

Nobody has been here at this line shack for years, not since it burned down when the prairie fire got most of the Campbell land, including their house. Nobody would ever look for you here."

She tried to keep calm, and use her good senses. That was the only thing that would keep her alive.

A partial shadow crossed in front of the opening. This time she knew it wasn't a branch or a tumbleweed. Hope washed over her. She needed to keep Gideon distracted, so he wouldn't notice what she thought she saw. "I deserve knowing why," she pressured him, recognizing he was getting more confused by the minute.

"Just shut up." He rubbed his forehead.

"Tell me and I'll never say another word."

"If it'll shut you up, I guess it won't hurt. As soon as I figure out the best way to dispose of you, you'll be dead anyway."

"Did my parents really commit suicide?" Laurel asked, choking on the question.

"I said shut up, I'll do the talking!" Gideon bellowed. "My sister married way below her station in life. Your dad took her right after the wedding back to San Antonio to take care of his precious cotton gins. When Father died, your mother and I jointly inherited the family bank but she didn't want anything to do with it. Just wanted me to send her share of the profits to her every now and again, and she was happy. So that left me to do all of the grunt work, spending sleepless nights, while she reaped the profits without lifting a finger."

Laurel refused to accept what she was hearing, but had to stay alert to watch for any movement and noise coming from outside. Her uncle rambled on about how poorly her father had managed the cotton gins, while Gideon was working to buy up land around Farley Springs in anticipation of the railroad coming through town without asking Laurel's mother's permission.

His world was about to come to an end when Laurel's mother asked to liquidate her shares in the bank. He didn't have the money any longer because it was all invested in land in his own name and she didn't know it. He'd had her parents prepare a new will and trust, naming him as a trustee, thus giving him adequate time to rebuild the trust account at the bank. But that never happened.

"So you see, you are supposed to inherit your trust on your birthday, but the money is all invested in land . . . so you have nothing. Everything you might have had now belongs to me."

Laurel took a deep breath and tried to understand the awful truth, but had trouble absorbing what was being thrust at her so quickly.

"But that doesn't tell me anything about my parents' deaths," Laurel said.

Hunter stepped through the opening, backed up by Stubby. Two Winchesters were leveled at Gideon Duncan.

"Go ahead and answer her question, you bastard," Hunter demanded. "Tell her who killed her parents."

The reality of what Hunter was implying turned Laurel's stomach. She'd never heard anything about someone killing her parents.

"Two against one." Gideon kept his pistol aimed at Laurel from his sitting position on the floor. "I can have her brains all over this shack before either of you can get off a shot."

Hunter stepped between Gideon and Laurel, shielding her with his body. "Stubby or me, if not both of us, will have you down before your bullet clears the barrel. To get her, you've got to kill me first. That's two shots." Hunter kept a steady aim on the overstuffed man trying to bring himself to his feet while keeping aim on his captive.

Hunter continued, "Why don't you go ahead and tell her the rest of the story? How you put arsenic in her parents' coffee to make it look like they'd committed suicide because you needed control of her mother's inheritance to keep the bank solvent. They didn't have any financial problems; you just made it look like they did. You don't have the guts it takes to kill anyone."

Suddenly, Hunter rushed Gideon, knocking him back to the ground, and snatching the pistol out of his hand, while Stubby pointed his Winchester right at the old man's head.

"For two cents, I'd tie your flabby ass to Buckey and let him take you anywhere in hell he wants, but the ol' bushwhacker doesn't deserve someone like you on his back. Besides, I'd much prefer to see you hang for killin' Laurel's parents and doing everything you can to destroy her."

Hunter tied Gideon's hands behind his back and, with Stubby's help, pulled the banker to his feet.

"You're the sorriest sonofabitch I've ever met," said Hunter.

With a smile on his face, Stubby kept the nose of his Winchester pointed directly at Gideon's heart.

After untying Laurel, Hunter took her into his arms and wiped away her tears. "And you're the bravest woman I've ever known." He kissed her forehead.

"I'm sorry that you had to learn the truth about your parents in such a horrible way," he said. "I'm truly sorry."

"I think deep inside I've known for a while, but wouldn't admit it because it was sure to open up too many old wounds that I wasn't sure I could face. I never believed Mama and Daddy killed themselves, although Gideon pounded it into my head that it was all my fault. For years, I've carried the guilt that maybe, just maybe, it was."

"Hush," Hunter said tenderly. "It wasn't your fault." He kissed her fully on the mouth.

Shaking, Laurel whispered, "How did you find us?"

"Buckey came here straight as an arrow. I guess he did what he's known for and got loose as soon as he could and came to the ranch for help." Hunter smiled down at her, then said, "Notice I didn't call him a hammerhead?"

She rewarded Hunter with a warm, dazzling smile.

"If you're okay, I need to get you safe. Take you out to the ranch because we've got a couple of things to resolve this afternoon." He returned her smile. "Mama is gnawing at the bit to get you started on your new job, plus she wants to order some material for new curtains in your room upstairs." He raised an "I told you so" eyebrow at her.

"And we've got to work out the details of the Valentine's Day festivities," she said.

"I've been thinking about something Stubby said. Why can't we do one big event? I'm thinking you'll be so busy with Mama that the hat shop can wait, so I could donate Bobbie Ray's building to the citizens for a library. With the men's help, we could build shelves, paint it, and have us the best library in the Panhandle." He felt damn proud of himself for giving his friend the credit. "I think you'll be a great leader of the women's group."

"So with a big joint hootenanny, we'll raise enough money for both projects. You're so tricky, Mr. Mayor." Laurel threw her arms around Hunter's neck and kissed him. "I love you so much."

He sheepishly smiled down on her. "And I've been loving you, Miss Laurel, since the day you stepped off the stagecoach and walked into my life."

So the president of the Men's Club and Miss Laurel Dean Womack, the new leader of the Women's Society, forged an inseparable bond stronger than the West Texas wind. They cochaired the most profitable Valentine's festivities ever held in the little piece of heaven known as Farley Springs, in the heart of the Texas Panhandle.

From the Author

To my fictional town of Farley Springs, Texas, the spring of 1887 brought with it the Fort Worth and Denver City Railroad, but the town never became the shipping Mecca that Hunter Campbell dreamed of.

Historical Note

In the spring of 1887, the Fort Worth and Denver City advance building crew of approximately five hundred men camped in tents a mile southwest of the Amarillo Creek bridge to the Frying Pan Ranch pasture in the Texas Panhandle.

Freight service became available in October 1887, and cattle shipping began to focus on the newly platted town of Amarillo as a railhead. The city grew to be the largest rural shipping point for cattle in the nation.

Amarillo became the county seat of Potter County, Texas, in 1887, and today it is still a major railroad shipping point.

Sweet Talk

DeWanna Pace

Chapter 1

Screams of heavy labor stopped, followed by a baby's first cry and a shout of joy from the farmer waiting outside of the log cabin where Dr. Noah Powell worked. *Echoes of happiness*, he thought, wondering if the sounds would ever be part of his own life.

"Give me a minute," Noah told the farmer. "I'll clean up your wife and son, then you can see them."

He worked fast but thoroughly, making sure mother and child were presentable and resting. "You can come in now," he said, opening the door to the man whose weathered face beamed as bright as the first streaks of dawn lining the horizon.

The farmer grabbed his hand and pumped it so hard that Noah felt his lips could have spouted water. "You might want to save some of that, Crenshaw. That boy of yours is going to demand a lot of your stamina just taking care of him. You won't be getting much sleep till your wife's on her feet again."

"Sorry, Doc, I'm just so . . . so . . . it's a boy, you say?"

"A son," Noah repeated, knowing what the once child-less man was really asking. The couple's first two had been stillborns. He was pleased to reassure the man. "Strong and healthy as an ox."

Crenshaw raced past the doctor to gather his wife in his arms, telling her how much he loved her and would till his dying day.

Noah did the one thing he always did at such moments meant for privacy. He turned, gathered his medicine bag, and headed for home and the quiet nothingness that awaited him there.

Sometimes he wished this Panhandle bunch of Texans weren't so bent on populating the prairie, allowing him time to do something about his own particular woes. But the people who lived in and around Longhorn City, Texas, were folks who loved to the fullest, and Noah preferred to live wherever love thrived with a strong voice.

An hour later, exhaustion made stowing away his horse and tack at the livery stable seem longer than usual. The walk down Main Street to his office felt like an endless trek. Silence met him as he opened the door and set down his bag by the medicine cabinet, lit the lamp, and took a look into the birdcage that hung in one corner of the room he used as both parlor and waiting room. "You asleep, little buddy?"

No answer.

"Maybe you're hungry." Noah made his way through the rooms that had become home and office since his return to Longhorn City four years ago. In the kitchen, he caught a brief glance of himself in the glass that covered the doors of the china hutch.

He hadn't combed his hair in two days and it spiked like porcupine quills dipped in tar. Dark whiskers shadowed the lower half of his normally well-shaved jaw. He reached up to rub his chin and wondered if he ought to hang a closed sign on his door for a couple of days and catch up with himself. Eyes that were normally the color of a clear Texas sky stared back tired and intent, searching for sight of the Noah Powell who might have once allowed himself to ignore his better judgment.

He didn't see him there.

This Noah had penance to pay.

Noah turned from his rough image and was glad to see that his housekeeper had replenished the tin of sunflower seeds kept for the bird. He broke open an egg and drained the contents into a bowl, taking the shell, seeds, and fresh water with him.

Wind from an open window fluttered curtains, causing a frightened squawk to come from the parlor. Noah loved to sleep with fresh air, and he would need it if he just went straight to sleep. Which he should since others would learn of his return and expect him to open for business come full daylight. Better to wash up later.

"Turn around, little buddy," he urged his pet, entering the parlor and putting the offerings in trays stationed along the perches in the cage. Noah held his finger up to the tiny blue rump dappled with rainbow-colored feathers. "Tell Doc what's wrong so I can fix it."

The lovebird's peach-colored face rose from behind one wing, where it had been hiding, and a dark brown eye peered at Noah, waiting. A few moments passed and the bird still refused to turn completely around.

"I know you feel bad, fellow, but I brought your favorite this morning."

The bird finally gave Noah a better look. Someone else might just see colorful feathers, but the doctor noticed a few of them had started molting. Amigo's eyes looked dull, without their usual shine. His tiny head didn't bob in its customary manner but tilted slightly as if it hurt to be upright.

Something was wrong and Noah didn't have to be the town doctor to figure out part of the problem. Amigo had started pecking at himself in the mirror hung on one of the perches for entertainment, and the bird had quit making any happy, chattering noises. Instead, he squawked and gave high-pitched squeals.

The traveling peddler who had sold Noah his pet a few months ago warned that Amigo would demand lots of attention and would become grumpy, maybe even sick, when he didn't get it. Noah had thought the man was simply trying to make twice the sale. Now after getting to know Amigo, he realized the peddler knew his business. Amigo needed company.

Something Noah could relate to and understand. But taking care of folks didn't give him much time for socializing and even less time with Amigo. Maybe he should find the bird a better home or a mate. He wasn't being fair, but he'd grown to care for his pet and didn't like the prospect of having to give him up. Noah had bought the littlest member of the parrot family hoping he might teach it to talk and give him some company, but so far Amigo remained mum. At least he was someone Noah could talk to without feeling he was just talking to himself.

The peddler had mentioned that not all lovebirds learned to speak but some did. Maybe the man's route would bring him back to town soon and a lady friend could be found. One that talked and might encourage Amigo to do the same.

"Is that what you need, buddy? A lady friend?" Noah laughed when the bird hopped up onto his extended finger. "You are a boy, aren't you?"

He wished he'd asked a lot more about the species, but he'd been in a hurry the day he'd bought him and hadn't taken the time. His knowledge of animals was limited to barnyard beasts, not the exotic fare brought up from

Galveston. He slowly withdrew his hand from the birdcage and stroked Amigo's head. The peddler had said that it took a few months before the gender could be determined, and even then, it might not reveal itself unless another bird was nearby. "Maybe you need a little *hero* to call your own," Noah pondered aloud, "not a heroine."

A loud rap on the door caused Amigo to squawk and fly off to the top of the secretary that housed ledgers and medical books.

"Doc Powell, you back? My wife, she's about to . . . foal."

Noah recognized the man's voice. He'd already delivered four babies for the expectant father. He'd be adding a couple more this go-round. "Come on in, Mr. Boatright. I'll just grab my bag and head over to the livery to get my horse." Noah looked longingly down the hall at his bedroom and imagined his long, lank body stretched out in the comfort of the four-poster bed, but that would have to wait.

When he left home, it was usually due to an emergency. When he returned, he didn't have to expend any effort looking for keys because he always left the door unlocked. It just made sense to do so and simplified his comings and goings.

The bald rancher rushed into the parlor, his face flushed and his eyes as wide as flapjacks. Disturbed by the interruption, Amigo's squawking became louder.

"Go back inside, buddy." Noah shooed the bird toward the cage, but Amigo refused to obey and continued to shriek. Noah didn't try to make him stop. He didn't believe in silencing anyone.

"I left my boy at the livery." A frown plowed across the rancher's brow. "You take his horse and he'll ride yours." Boatright grabbed the bag from Noah's hand, urging him to hurry. "Y'all can swap out when she's all birthed out."

Boatright had reason to be worried. The twins weren't due till next month and the pregnancy had come too soon after the last one. Noah wrote a brief note, folded it, and put an inkwell on it so his housekeeper would find the message when she cleaned up for him, as she did every other day. "Sorry," he apologized, "had to leave instructions for Mrs. Lassiter, in case this takes a while."

Concern etched the man's face. "You expecting my wife to have trouble?"

Amigo flew to Noah's shoulder and Noah crooned to the bird softly. He had to reassure Boatright, too, even though he couldn't promise there wouldn't be problems with birthing twins. "The *while* I'm talking about has to do with my pet. He's feeling a little puny and I want Mrs. Lassiter to look out for him while I'm gone."

"Give me your word that my wife will make it through. My babies, too." The rancher's concern deepened into challenge. "It's no comfort knowing you can't fix what's yours, Doc, when I'm trusting you with mine. You can handle this, can't ya?"

Noah moved toward the cage, giving a soft whistle, which was the signal for Amigo to return to his home. Instead the lovebird flew away and roosted on the top of the medicine cabinet. "Guess you'll have to find your own way back then, little buddy."

Realizing Boatright was still waiting for reassurance, Noah gathered the mask of unerring judgment he'd worn since returning to Texas. Four years ago he had erred in making a choice and lost someone dear to him—a patient whose death would never allow him to hold the truth back from anyone ever again.

He finally looked the man squarely in the eyes and vowed, "I promise to do the best I can. But if she needs more than my skills, I guarantee you, I'll ask for help."

"From Thurgood?" Surprise etched the rancher's face.

"Especially from him."

"But he's retired and I thought you two weren't talking to each other."

"None of that's changed," Noah admitted, motioning for them to head for the horses at the hitching post, "but my father's forgotten more than I'll ever know about bringing babies into this world. He's still got plenty enough sand in him to save your woman if I can't."

Chapter 2

Dances were never JoEmma Brown's cup of coffee, least of all the one planned for Valentine's Day. The bunch of women sitting in her parlor and betting about which beau would take them to the one planned in Belle Whitaker's barn was even less appealing than the thought of having to attend it herself.

The only reason she would consider going would be if Noah Powell wasn't off somewhere saving the world and had the time to show up at Belle's. Not that she would have a chance to speak with him. Every unmarried woman in the territory would swarm him like bees on bluebonnets. She'd never get her wheelchair within ten feet of the doctor. So why go, when talking with Noah was the only reason she could think of worth spending time in a crowded place of constantly moving people?

"May I help you, JoEmma?" Angelina trilled sweetly from the parlor.

Her approaching footsteps warned JoEmma that her older sister had left Belle and the rest of their guests and was headed her way. Within seconds Angelina's blond head poked around the doorway that separated the parlor from the dining room, where JoEmma worked at the table. With her back to the other women now, her sister's perfectly arched brows knit angrily together over her leaf green eyes.

"What's taking you so long?" she whispered. One look at JoEmma's overalls filled Angelina's tone with exasperation. "Couldn't you have at least changed clothes, for heaven's sake? It's a tea party in there, not a barn raising. I told Hannah before she left to go clean Dr. Powell's place to set out the paisley dress for you. It will bring out the green in your eyes."

The color of her eyes depended on what mood JoEmma was in, and today, the amber hues of her hazel-colored eyes would show more prominently than the green hues. They always did when she was tired. Besides, she didn't care to try to outshine the other women dressed in all their laces and tea gowns today or any other day, for that matter. She had given up years ago trying to match petticoat to ribbon with her sister, and didn't particularly care for being compared as a younger, slightly larger version of Angelina. Sharing the same hair color was about all they had in common. She didn't mind dressing up when she left the house, but JoEmma preferred comfortable clothing while she worked.

"Hannah laid it out and I would have put it on," she reminded her sister, not wanting to place any blame on Mrs. Lassiter, "but I haven't had *time* to change yet. You wanted me to get all of these done, didn't you? Doesn't Belle want to take them with her?"

Completing the last name on the red heart-shaped paper, JoEmma blew on the ink, helping the words dry before placing the heart into the glass bowl with the others. She grabbed the red ribbon she had stitched with lace and created a large, full bow around the bowl. "Here, you take it to them." She offered her sister the hearts. "I'll be there in just a minute."

"You don't have time to change now," Angelina insisted, accepting the container. "They're going to think you're being unsociable."

JoEmma looked at her sister wanting to tell her that she should have spoken up earlier about needing the hearts. Maybe then she wouldn't have had to spend all night and this morning getting them done. Calligraphy took time.

Instead, JoEmma kept silent. Angie was the picture of health and didn't have to deal with a heart weakened from scarlet fever. Didn't have to work in stages. Still, JoEmma relented, no one, not even her sister, who understood how difficult it was for her to do things, should have to make excuses for her.

JoEmma decided to just take a moment's rest to catch her wind before tackling the silly talk shared at such tea parties. "Tell them I have to wash my hands, then I'll be there."

"At least take off your apron," Angie suggested, "and pinch your cheeks. You're looking too pale. We don't want them thinking that I don't watch out for you." She turned swiftly on her slippers and headed back to their guests.

Oohs and ahhs over the decorated bowl echoed from the doorway, telling JoEmma that the others appreciated her efforts whether or not they would understand her delay and lack of tea gown.

A series of chirps from behind her reminded JoEmma that someone else was getting a little perturbed with her delay. She swung her wheelchair around and watched as her pet lovebird rattled the latch that held the door to its cage.

"Says-a-me. Says-a-me. Open up," chirped the bird.

JoEmma laughed, amused by the humor she had taught

her pet. Life got too serious at times and she had to find some way to laugh at her own circumstances, so she took great pleasure in teaching Gabby funny things to say. Their housekeeper had warned her that one of these days Gabby was going to say something embarrassing to the wrong person, but JoEmma knew stern-faced Hannah enjoyed the lovebird just as much as she did. She often found the woman trying to teach Gabby new words, too.

"Says-a-me. Says-a-me. Open up." Gabby echoed the magical command that JoEmma had rephrased from Ali Baba and his old Arabian tale.

"All right, Funny Feathers," she conceded. It seemed everybody was in a hurry today. "But just for a little while, and you have to be on your best behavior. We've got guests."

She opened the cage and Gabby flew out, immediately landing on JoEmma's left shoulder—her favorite place to roost.

"Smch-smch-smch," Gabby chirped, leaning her peach-colored cheek against her owner's.

"I love you, too, little girl, but I've got no time for kisses right now." JoEmma rolled over to the sideboy, which held a decorative pitcher and water bowl. "Got to get my hands washed and get in there before Angie calls in the cavalry."

"Fancy Angie. Fancy Angie. Phew!"

JoEmma laughed and dried her hands on her apron before taking it off and draping it over a chair as she rolled out of the room with Gabby firmly stationed on her shoulder. "You're right," she whispered at the words she'd taught the bird to say when it heard her sister's name. "She's lots of work and a great big phew most of the time."

The hallway announced JoEmma's approach as the chair rolled across the floor, its rugless boards echoing the creak of wheels. She hated that she could never slip quietly into a room, but Angelina wouldn't have let her today even if she could.

"There you are." Angie waved her over to the spot where she'd made space for the wheelchair to complete the circle of settee and high-backed chairs filled with women. "We were just talking about which one of us Noah Powell will ask to the dance. I thought you might want in on that discussion."

All eyes turned toward JoEmma.

"Why should that interest me?" she asked evasively, telling herself to look them in the eye, act like Angie was talking nonsense, and for goodness' sake, not blush.

"No-ah-Pow. No-ah-Pow. Smch-smch-smch." Gabby made little kissing noises, heating JoEmma's cheeks to seven levels of hell. When in blue blazes had Funny Feathers learned all that? She was going to have to have a talk with Hannah about what she could and could not teach the bird.

Angelina stared daggers at Gabby, even though the pet had just confirmed JoEmma's interest in Noah. "Why is that sorry excuse for a hat decoration out of its cage?"

"She's not hurting anyone and she'll stay on my shoulder." JoEmma's voice lowered to warn Angelina not to push the argument. Gabby was a sore subject between the sisters, one that JoEmma refused to bend on. "Let's get on with the tea party."

"She's a cute little thing anyway, Angie," one of the ladies complimented. "I'd like to have one myself."

"No, you wouldn't." Angelina's eyes glinted at JoEmma before turning to her friend and softening. "They're far too much trouble and demand a lot of attention, Carrie. You'd make Bovice jealous spending so much time away from him. Why, that man simply droops when you look anywhere but at him."

A round of feminine giggles and shared tales of other beaux' demands upon their attentiveness made JoEmma wonder if maybe she had been born without a level of sap in her marrow. Her friends oozed syrupy sweetness and flitted from beau to beau like colorful butterflies gathering nectar. She, on the other hand, felt as if she'd been born with a pinch of sourdough and a measure of salt in her veins, and was as congenial as a stinkbug. She realized she was always too hard on herself, but she simply wasn't an oohey-gooey gal like Angie and she didn't know how to act like one.

"Well, I say we make a little bet about whose name is going to be drawn with Noah's." Angelina held up the decorated bowl.

"You probably had her write *your* name on all of them." Though she was challenging Angelina, Carrie Sanders focused her taunt toward JoEmma.

JoEmma frowned at the pouty-lipped woman she'd known since second grade. Carrie had always been envious of Angelina's beauty. "She told me to make one for all of you." Much as it irritated her to do so, Jo Emma defended Angie as well. "And don't be calling my sister a cheat."

Carrie visibly wilted as Angelina returned the honor. "You can be assured that my sister kept it completely fair."

Surprise filled JoEmma at her sister's returned defense of her, easing some of her anger about the verbal attack on Gabby.

Carrie's cheeks reddened. "But I thought you said . . ."

Challenge darkened Angelina's eyes to a deeper shade of green. "What I said was that Belle has asked me to choose the names out of the jar. That would make it very convenient for me to pull whichever name I want to match with his when it comes up, if I were so compelled. And I'm very compelled to pull out my own."

A muffled round of applause echoed over the room as the women clapped their gloved hands. It was no secret that the most beautiful woman in town wanted the most eligible bachelor for a husband. Trouble was, Noah had shown no particular favor to any unattached female since his return to Longhorn City several years ago. Accustomed to having any beau she wanted, Angelina couldn't quite accept the fact that Dr. Powell just wasn't interested. She had set her bonnet to catch him and was determined that her friends would help her achieve that goal any way they could.

"I'll tell." JoEmma didn't realize she had said the words till the applause died and the room filled with silence. It was then that she decided she sounded like she was seven years old again, arguing with them on the schoolyard.

"You told me you wouldn't even be going," Angie countered, scooting her slim hips to the edge of her high-backed chair. "What should it matter to you anyway since you plan on staying home?"

All eyes focused on JoEmma again. She hadn't told them yet that she wouldn't attend. They'd sure enough think she was being unsociable now. All of her softening toward Angie about defending her began to harden with purpose to protect Noah from being manipulated.

"I'll go just to keep things fair," she warned them stubbornly. Let them think what they would. She wouldn't allow Noah to be used that way. If he wanted to take someone to a dance, that was one thing. And if someone's name was chosen randomly out of the bowl, that was another. But to rig the names seemed unfair. Why did none of the other ladies have a problem with this?

"You all have the right to be matched up with him,"

JoEmma argued the point. "Angie's being unfair to each of you and most of all to Dr. Powell."

"An-gie. An-gie. Phew! Pow!"

"Quiet, little one," JoEmma whispered, wishing someone else would speak up for Noah other than Gabby.

"I say we all challenge each other," Belle Whitaker announced. All faces turned to the most respected and wealthiest woman in their midst. She sat at one end of the settee, her golden tea gown, lace fan, and pearl drop earrings adding to the regal presence of moneyed authority. "Whichever of you can convince Noah to escort you to the dance will be the name that Angelina pulls out to match with his heart. Just as we've agreed to match any of you who are escorted by other beaux."

JoEmma began to understand why there was no objection from the others. Angie would be playing matchmaker to several couples.

"I bet he asks me. In fact, I plan to make sure he does." Angelina leaned over and tapped the fan she held on Belle's glove, signaling a call for any takers on the bet.

"You're pretty sure of yourself," Carrie challenged.

"Sure enough that if I don't, I'll come to the dance dressed in . . ." Angelina's head spun around to look JoEmma up and down. "Overalls."

Everyone knew Angelina Brown prided herself in being the best-dressed beauty at any gathering. She would never allow herself to be seen in anything less than the height of fashion. Her and JoEmma's trust fund often suffered the brunt of Angie's overspending on clothes, much to the dismay of JoEmma's more conservative nature. Overspending that urged JoEmma to take up odd jobs here and there to cover expenses above the monthly allotment. The money their parents' deaths had left was just enough to ensure their incomes lasted until both married.

JoEmma did not see that as anytime soon in her own future, if ever. She wouldn't burden Noah with a wife who required more from him than he had time to share. And since he was the man she had set her own mind to marrying when she was ten years old, she'd resolved herself to be a spinster after the scarlet fever had taken her good health. To see him married to another woman would one day be the hardest thing she'd ever had to endure. But if it was to her own sister, to share her future with his but not as his wife, that would be unbearable.

At the moment she had to decide whether she was defending Noah from the women's matchmaking bets or her heart from being broken. The truth would taste sour if she spoke it aloud.

"I'll take you up on that bet." Belle tapped her fan on Angelina's glove. A round of fan tapping took place among all the women except one. No one would back out from the bet. Their word had been given.

"Here, Sister, you can borrow my glove and fan." Angelina began to strip off one glove.

"No thank you." JoEmma waved away the offer, then abruptly hid her hands in her lap, remembering that her bare palms showed the calluses caused from rolling the wheelchair. "I won't be any part of such a bet. You need to make the drawings fair."

If it was fair, she would brace herself for whatever the outcome might be.

"Well, I can see it's time for the sisters to discuss this between themselves." Belle Whitaker stood and thanked her hostesses for their hospitality, signaling an end to the party plans. The other women gathered their parasols and bade their good-byes, preparing to leave.

When Belle grabbed the door handle to open it, JoEmma forgot Noah and remembered that Gabby was still perched on her shoulder. "No, wait!" she shouted.

Her warning came too late.

The door opened.

Gabby took flight.

JoEmma couldn't move fast enough to stop her.

Rainbow-colored feathers soared into the huge blue Texas sky beyond.

Belle offered a quick apology and one of the other ladies said, "A real shame. It was such a pretty little thing."

JoEmma rolled past the kaleidoscope of skirts, rushing down the wooden ramp built to accommodate her own coming and going.

"Be careful, Jo!" Angelina shouted from behind her. "You'll hurt yourself!"

Not sure whether her concern was sincere or just a show for the others, JoEmma dared to stop at the end of the ramp and spun around to see if her sister followed, if she really cared that she might get hurt, if she would actually offer to help.

A mistake.

Angelina just stood there, surrounded by the women, who were trying to reassure her that all would be well. One gloved hand pressed against her lips in dismay.

All for show. JoEmma squelched the hope that had made her look and turned back around to roll the wheelchair down the boarded walk that led to the line of buggies hitched in front of the Brown home. Anger drove her now. Not anger at Angie's lack of true concern but at herself for wanting her sister to care enough.

"Wait, Jo! We can always get you another bird!" Angelina shouted behind her.

"Too late," JoEmma whispered as she maneuvered her way to the street beyond. Angie had taken time to think of something to say that would impress the others with her concern. She had *thought* instead of simply *reacted* with love. JoEmma had wanted her sister to care for her as deeply as she cared for Angie. It simply wasn't on Angie's list of priorities.

Lord, give me enough strength to catch Gabby. JoEmma ignored the rocks and dirt flying up from beneath her wheels, making the calluses sting.

As she caught sight of multicolored feathers flitting from rooftop to branch, she added through gritted teeth, "And please help us both survive my sister."

Chapter 3

A refreshing breeze rustled the curtains in Noah's bedroom, waking him from the deep sleep of exhaustion that had overtaken him when he'd returned from delivering the Boatright twins. He yawned and stretched, waking to the sound of happy chirping from the parlor. The sound hinted that his pet's health was on the mend, and that made the morning seem all the brighter.

Last night Noah had come in so late and in such need of rest himself that he had done little but strip off his worn clothing, take a quick bath, and crawl under the bedcovers. The smell of brewing coffee reminded him that it must be cleaning day for Mrs. Lassiter. No matter what room she happened to be working in, a cup full of coffee was never far behind her.

Coffee. Mrs. Lassiter. You're naked. Reality cleared away the last remnants of sleep, making him reach for the covers to pull around him. But there were none. They lay in a tangle at the foot of his bed. "Mrs. Lassiter? Are you still here?"

"What do you think?" a stern voice replied from the hallway, sounding like a frog learning to croak. "That Texas dust just blows itself into a nice neat pile? Of course

I'm still here, dusting my fool dimples off. And you'd better get your boots and something else but your birthday britches on and go see to that birdcage. It's your turn to change the papers. I've still got to get to Thurgood's by noon."

Too late. She *had* seen him in his altogether. That hadn't happened since he was twelve years old and she'd caught him diving naked in Crawdad Creek on a dare.

"How is he?" Noah asked, hurrying to the armoire to choose a fresh shirt and denims. He decided to wait till patients started arriving to add his usual work clothes of string tie and vest. Apparently, no one was waiting in the parlor to be seen or Mrs. Lassiter would have informed him already.

"*He?* Meaning your father or Amigo?"

"Both, I guess. But tell me about Dad first."

Noah heard something shift across the floor; then a croaky grunt followed as she obviously stretched to reach something higher than her four-foot-two stature allowed.

"When are you going to move these frames down so I can reach them?" she complained. "Nobody shorter than six feet can read them anyway. You need a woman in this house to set things right."

He finished combing his hair and stepped out into the hallway. Sure enough, there she stood tiptoe on a foot stool, round as she was tall, trying to dust medical certificates that needed to be hung lower. He just hadn't had the time. Noah reached over and took the dust cloth from her hand and helped her down the step. "I don't need a woman around here," he teased, dusting the frames. "I've got the best housekeeper in Texas."

"Darn right you do." She pointed to a spot he'd missed. "But you need a woman to teach you things I can't, young man."

"Oh, I don't know about that." He flashed a grin that

usually charmed any female except her. "I've seen you dance with the best of them."

"You bet I can. And speaking of which, you'd best get to deciding which of the town petticoats you're going to ask to Belle's dance. I heard there's some kind of twitter among them over who you'll be courting for the night." Mrs. Lassiter shook a finger at him. "And don't go thinking I'll get you off the hook this time, young man. I've already told Thurgood I'll save all my dances for him, not his son, who has no better sense than to escort an old heifer like me instead of one of those pretty fillies. Wait till I tell him you were butt naked this—"

"Don't, Hannah." Noah rarely used her first name, out of respect for her long service to his parents and then to him. When he did forget to honor her so, it made him feel like a boy in trouble for doing something foolish again. He handed her back the dust cloth. "He already thinks I'm irresponsible. Telling him will only make him unhappier at me. And I promise, I'll figure out who I'll escort as soon as I know if I can actually attend the dance."

"You want to talk about it?" She stood there with her hands on her hips, looking stern but caring, as only Hannah Lassiter could do.

"You know I never decide anything until I'm sure I'm not needed elsewhere," he said evasively, knowing full well that she was talking about his trouble with his father and not his duty to patients who might prevent him from attending the dance.

"Don't twist your tongue at me, young man. You know very well what I mean." She might be short in height but she issued tall orders for the truth.

Mrs. Lassiter had been a part of Noah's life ever since he could remember. At twelve when he'd lost his mother to influenza, it had been Hannah Lassiter's arms that had comforted him. His father had been too caught up in the

role of grieving widower and doctor to realize that Noah
had needed him. A doctor was supposed to understand
death, to accept it as part of the pattern of life. Noah had
needed to share his grief with his father, but Thurgood
Powell had been the stalwart, stoic widower, the image of
professional emotional control. The only break in that
armor Noah had ever seen was when his father was in the
company of the woman who had sustained them both
since that tragic time—Hannah Lassiter. She had become
the protector of emotions his father entrusted to no one
but her.

"There's nothing to talk about," Noah finally answered,
knowing he was lying but preferring not to persuade her to
take his side in the private matter that had arisen between
him and his father four years ago. If she learned it from his
parent, that was one thing. But Noah meant to keep the
family troubles to himself.

"You two are so much alike, you could've hatched from
the same egg." Mrs. Lassiter looked around as if she were
searching for something. "Ahh, there it is."

She grabbed her cup of coffee from a bookcase where
she had set it. Taking a sip, she waddled into the parlor.
"Since you aren't going to tell me about what set the teakettle to steaming between you, you might as well come
see about your fussy feathered friend."

His housekeeper plopped down on the settee and began
to drink her coffee. She looked up over the cup rim, one
dark brow arching upward as he waited for her to take off
the cloth that covered the birdcage. "What? Do you think
I'm going to mess with him today with you home? My
bird sitting is finished until you have to leave again. I did
not hire on to scoop up after that messy little magpie."

Happy chirps came from beneath the cloth that allowed
his pet to sleep easier.

"Magpie? Amigo?" Noah lifted the cloth to discover a

healthier, fuller-feathered lovebird chirping at him. "My goodness, how you've grown, little buddy. You're twice the size you were when I left. And your feathers aren't molting anymore." He faced his housekeeper. "What have you been feeding him?"

"Noah Powell! Open your eyes and take a better look at those squatty legs. How many do you see?"

"No-ah-Pow. No-ah-Pow. Smch-smch-smch."

Startled by the chirpy chatter, Noah peered harder to make sure his eyes were actually seeing what he had counted and his ears certain of what he had heard. "*Four*. He's grown legs and a voice since I've been gone."

"Two of those legs belong to a friend and she's got a mouth on her, that one."

"A girl?" Noah looked a little closer. That's when he noticed how one of the lovebird's wings was definitely fuller on its right side. The smaller set of legs below hinted that the second bird was tucked under the wing of the bigger bird. The one thing he did know about the species was that the female was usually larger than the male. "Amigo, buddy? Is that you under there?"

Amigo's eye peered from beneath the wing where he was being cuddled and repeated part of what the bigger bird had said. "No-ah-Pow."

"Would you listen to that!" Noah could hardly contain his excitement. Amigo was actually saying something. "Whoever she is, she's taught him to speak."

"Love will do that to you." Mrs. Lassiter took another sip of coffee before adding, "Say and do things you never thought would come out of your own mouth."

"Where did she come from?" Noah searched his housekeeper's face and tried to read her expression. She was keeping something from him. Her brown eyes twinkled with definite amusement, as if she knew a secret he didn't. He'd seen that same look many times on his previous birthdays when she surprised him with gifts or when she knew something that would please him and kept him in suspense about it until she thought he was ready to burst. He told her plenty of times that he planned to get his pet a mate. Maybe the peddler had stopped by town. "Did you buy her for me?"

"And add more work for me? No way. I'm not making myself housekeeper to anybody's ark, not even for you, Noah Powell. That she-bird flew in while you were gone. I told you one of these days that something fresher than air would come flying in that window if you kept leaving it open." Mrs. Lassiter took another sip of coffee, then announced, "She belongs to one of the Brown sisters."

Since he shared his housekeeper with the Browns and his father, the woman ought to know of what she spoke. If so, then why hadn't she just taken the bird back home? He could sense she was waiting for him to ask her why she didn't. Maybe he would play the game a little and see what the minx was up to. "How long has she been here?"

"More than a week. How long have you been gone?"

"A day or two more than that. I'm not sure. I lost track of time. Wasn't sure the Boatright twins were going to make it."

"They okay?"

"They are now."

"How are the Boatrights?"

"Mom and Pop are just fine now that the twins are."

"Good. Maybe they'll take some time to enjoy these two before adding to the clan."

Noah nodded, knowing her criticism was a product of once having been widowed and left childless long before Noah ever knew her. He didn't want her dwelling on those sad times, so he steered the conversation back to Amigo's new friend. "You don't think the Browns are worried over the whereabouts of their bird?"

"Oh, I know for a fact that JoEmma has searched high and low, make that *high*, for Gabby. She's even posted a note on the community board offering a reward for her return. She really would like to have her back. Angelina, not so much, I'm thinking."

Now he knew for certain Mrs. Lassiter had some scheme up her sleeve. She had deliberately not returned the bird. She adored the Brown sisters and wouldn't cause either worry on purpose. "Gabby, you say?" he repeated. "That's the bird's name?"

"Gabriella Funny Feathers Brown, officially. Gabby, for short, and because the name pretty much suits her. You'll find out for yourself in a few days."

"All right," Noah conceded, "you've won. You've got me curious as to what you might be up to. If you didn't mean for the bird to stay, you would have already taken her back home. So, since cleaning up after one bird seems to put a burr under your saddle, why did you decide to bird-sit for two?"

"Did I tell you that you are a bright boy, Noah Powell? Always have been. Let's see if you can be a smart man and figure this one out for yourself."

The twinkle in her eyes seemed to intensify as he studied her and tried to make sense of her taunt.

"Okay," he accepted the challenge. "You knew I wanted a mate for Amigo."

"True."

"You knew you could always take Gabby home."

"Again, you're right."

"You saw that she made Amigo happy."

"And healthier. His feathers are sprucing up fine." Mrs. Lassiter added, "I do have a heart, you know."

"You also have some other purpose." Noah tried to think as his housekeeper might; then it finally dawned on him. "You want *me* to take her home."

"Way to hang in there, partner." Mrs. Lassiter's compliment ended with a laugh. "I knew there was a lick or two of common sense still left somewhere in that college-educated brain of yours."

"But you see the Browns every day." He argued the point.

"And *you* don't," she stressed.

There it was—her reason. Mrs. Lassiter was not only playing matchmaker to a pair of lovebirds, but also trying to bring him and one of the Brown sisters together. She'd tried to marry him off for years now, afraid he would end up a confirmed bachelor. Now she'd apparently set her bonnet to marrying him off to one of the Browns. But which one?

"I'm sure they're going to welcome me with open arms, especially when they know I've kept their bird for how long now?" he asked.

"Eight days."

"Couldn't you have simply taken Amigo to their house and let the two birds get to know each other there?" Noah could imagine the younger sister's worry over losing a favorite pet. Being wheelchair bound, she suffered limitations others didn't and that would make every relationship that gave her companionship even more precious. With the older sister, the bird might be a replacement of affection for the parents they had lost to the train accident two years ago. No matter how much this helped Amigo, Noah had no right to keep the female from its truthful owner. "I'll go to the Browns immediately."

"That might mean giving up Amigo," Mrs. Lassiter warned him. "They might want the birds to stay paired, at *their* house."

Noah didn't like the thought of giving up Amigo, but if it was best for the birds, then he would. Maybe the sisters would allow him to visit or maybe keep one of the offspring, if some came along. Noah eyed the happy couple.

A sudden sense of sadness at his own possible loss made him look away. It was only the thought of Amigo's gain that made him set his mind to do what he must. "It's the right thing to do."

"Who knows?" Mrs. Lassiter interjected. "Maybe they'll want *you* to keep the pair. Or even better, want *you* to stay with him."

"Why would they?" He ignored her teasing and focused on Amigo's possible future. He had no qualms about adding Gabby to his household, but if the sisters had come to love their pet as much as he did Amigo, then he couldn't imagine them willing to give her up.

"This is where the birds fell in love." Mrs. Lassiter set her coffee cup down and stood. "Where they feel comfortable in getting to know each other. Talking to each other. That plays a big part in bringing and keeping couples together."

"Let's just hope the Browns agree with you and will be comfortable with discussing that as a possibility once they know how long *we've* kept her away from them." Noah grabbed the birdcage and the night cloth to cover it. "Will you carry the birds while I get Amigo's feed and other toys?"

"Sure." She half rolled to her feet and took the cage. "It's on the way to Thurgood's and I'm finished here anyway. But I won't have time to stay and talk."

"Of course you won't." He grabbed the bow that held her apron in place and gave it a playful jerk, setting it free from around her ample waist. "You just had enough time to get me into this mess."

Chapter 4

"Girls, it's me. I just stopped by to bring you a surprise!"

JoEmma heard their housekeeper's voice and wondered what kind of surprise the woman considered great enough to alter her usual routine of cleaning Dr. Powell's home then heading immediately to the elder Powell's house to do the same. She usually didn't return home to the Browns, where she maintained living quarters, until much later in the day. Hannah Lassiter never let anything, including rain or snow, keep her from those obligations.

Everyone in the county suspected Hannah and Thurgood Powell were sweet on each other, but no one dared talk about it in front of the pair. The couple seemed to want everyone to think their relationship was purely employer and employee, but few were fooled. The surprise must be something extraordinary to make Hannah delay going to Thurgood's.

"I'm in the green room, Hannah," JoEmma called to her from the room filled with a variety of plants and projects she was working on. "Give me just a minute to wipe my hands. I was potting some flowers for Mrs. Kimble. Her joints are acting up again and I told her that I'd get this done and back before she closes up the mercantile."

She only had a couple more pots to complete so it would be a good time to take a break and see what had caused the excitement in Hannah's voice.

"Hurry, girl. You've got a guest."

A guest? Some surprise. JoEmma rolled her eyes heavenward and let out a deep sigh. She wasn't dressed for receiving guests and she didn't have that much time to offer anyone if she intended to meet Mrs. Kimble's time request concerning the pots. It would take her a while to maneuver over the rutted road and balance a tray of pots on her lap. "Ask Angelina to come down and hold the fort for me. She's upstairs trying on her new dress for Belle's party. I'll be there as soon as I can."

Realizing their guest was probably hearing every word, JoEmma decided she needed to offer better manners than the ones she was extending at the moment. "Welcome, whoever you are. You just caught me at an awkward time. I'll be right there."

"Angelina, hurry down, honey. There's a man to see you," Hannah announced.

A man? That would certainly bring her sister running and would give JoEmma ample time to finish the other two pots. Angelina would appreciate time to flirt and show off the dress.

Instead of hurrying, JoEmma returned to the work at hand and began to whistle as she completed her task.

A trill of birdsong echoed from the parlor, whistling back at her.

Startled, JoEmma whispered, "Gabby?"

Hope leapt in her heart as she pressed her lips together and whistled the special command she had taught the lovebird.

A flurry of rainbow-colored feathers flew toward her, and then the bird roosted on her left shoulder.

"Smch-smch-smch."

"Funny Feathers! It is you." JoEmma pressed her cheek against the lovebird. Relief washed through her and threatened to fill her eyes with tears. "Where have you been, little lady? I've missed you."

"I'm afraid she's been holed up at my house," a deep voice echoed from behind JoEmma.

JoEmma's eyes flashed open as she turned to catch sight of Noah Powell standing in the doorway of her workroom. She wasn't sure if the world suddenly spun around because she'd turned so swiftly or if the sight of his handsome face had somehow set her atilt.

There he stood. Six feet two inches of dark hair, eyes the color of the Texas sky on its clearest day, and a smile that warmed her so deeply that she was grateful she was sitting rather than standing because the heat weakened her knees and raced to the tips of her smallest toes. But it was the image of a boy in overalls that swam before her eyes now. A boy who hadn't cared that the other boys had laughed at him for picking her up from the school step where she'd fallen and skinned a knee. He'd lifted her up into his ten-year-old arms and carried her home, with the others making fun of him all the way there. Noah Powell had been her hero ever since.

She dusted her hands against her own overalls and realized, for the first time, why she loved wearing the clothes. Because Noah had.

In his hands now, he carried a burlap sack of something that looked like feed and a couple of small toys. "Y-your house?" she stammered, remembering where he said Gabby had been. "I don't understand."

Hannah poked at him to move aside and stepped around him, setting a birdcage on the table where JoEmma had been working. Inside the cage, a tiny lovebird half the size of Gabby perched on a makeshift branch.

"Here's the male. Noah will do all the explaining."

Hannah pointed, indicating where the doctor could set the feed sack down in the corner. "You can put that there," she told him. "I've got to get to Thurgood's. I'm already late."

Hannah Lassiter left the house faster than JoEmma could ever recall the rotund housekeeper moving. "What is that all about?" she asked Noah as he freed up his hands. "And why have you brought another bird with you?"

He shrugged one shoulder. "Mrs. Lassiter assumes you're going to be upset when I tell you how long I think I've had your bird and it wasn't brought home." He didn't address the issue of the male.

"Why should I be angry with *her*?"

Noah hesitated just long enough not to have to answer. The rustle of petticoats from the parlor warned that Angelina approached and had discovered the identity of their guest. "Dr. Powell, whatever are you doing here?" she asked.

He stepped to one side, making room for her and her buoyant pink dress and layers of petticoats. "Good afternoon, Angelina. My, don't you look lovely."

"Why, thank you, Dr. Powell, for saying so." When she offered her hand, he slightly bowed and pressed a kiss along the tips of her knuckles. "I did want to keep my dress a secret until the Valentine's dance, but I don't suppose there's any harm in showing it to an appreciative gentleman such as yourself."

JoEmma could have lost her lunch in one of Mrs. Kimble's pots if it had been closer to her. Angie was laying it on thick with her sweet Southern belle sidetalk, and all JoEmma could think of was the bet her sister had made with the women. Angelina was wasting no time setting her plan into action and blamed if she didn't look simply beautiful in all the pink bows and lace.

"He found Gabby and returned her," JoEmma informed her sister, her voice sounding as if she was angry with him and not Angelina. "I'm pleased to say," she added in a nicer tone.

"Mrs. Lassiter said Gabby belongs to one of you." Concern etched the doctor's face. "I knew you'd be worried about her."

"Why, of course I was," Angelina hurried to say, stretching her finger toward Gabby to offer a new roosting place.

"Then she's *yours*?" Noah looked a little surprised when Angelina laid claim to the bird.

"An-gie. Phew!" Gabby squawked and moved closer to JoEmma.

Her older sister glared at JoEmma, daring her to correct the doctor's presumption. Instead of answering him, she drew attention to the male bird. "I see that you have one yourself."

"Yes, and that's why I'm here." Noah glanced around the room. "You don't have any open windows in here, do you?"

"No." JoEmma glared at her sister. "I try to be careful about that. Unfortunately, a guest accidentally opened the door, and that's how Gabby escaped."

Noah opened the birdcage's latch and held out a finger to the smaller bird. It stepped up onto his finger and allowed him to give the women a closer look. "This is Amigo," he introduced his pet. "I believe he and your Gabby have become great friends and possibly more than that, I suspect. I don't really know for certain as I've been gone for more than a week and found them together only today. All I do know is that she's apparently been around long enough that she's made him a lot happier than I've been able to accomplish, and his feathers are better since I last saw him. He's even saying some words now, which tells me she's been around long enough for her to teach him. He wasn't talking when I left."

"That's not likely," JoEmma countered. "It takes a

while to teach a bird words, whether the teacher is human or bird."

"Umm . . . ah . . . yes, that's very true," Angelina added. "A week isn't long enough, in my opinion."

Who asked you? JoEmma countered silently but said aloud, "Unless *you've* tried to teach him words." She searched Noah's face. The handsome features made her heart flutter as surely as if a summer breeze had blown across it.

"I have, but he never said anything until now."

"He was waiting for someone he *wanted* to talk to." JoEmma laughed softly at the little bird and held her finger out to him. To her surprise, Gabby pecked at JoEmma's cheek and flew over to Noah Powell's finger, where she joined the male on his perch. Funny Feathers was territorial! "We all open up better to someone we think is special." Then she realized what she had said. "Not that you aren't special, Dr. Powell."

Why did her words twist whenever he was near? "I just meant that it's clear that he's playing games with you or someone else is. If he could talk in a week or so, he could already talk. Has Hannah known all this time that Gabby was at your house?"

"I'd rather let Hannah answer that question for herself."

"Like I said, someone is playing games with you, Dr. Powell. It may be your bird and then again he might have had some help in the matter." JoEmma wouldn't put it past Hannah to play matchmaker, especially if she knew Gabby was safe all this time.

"Oh, now there you go, Sis. He'll think we're ninnies with nothing but bird sense for brains. Doctor, would you care for a glass of tea or some hot coffee perhaps?" Angie linked her arm through his, jolting the hand that held the birds. Gabby flew to a windowpane as if needing escape. Amigo landed on his birdcage near the latch.

"No thank you, Miss Brown." Noah opened the cage door and watched as Amigo retreated inside to safety. "I really only came to talk over what we might do about the lovebirds; then I need to get back to my practice. A few people saw Mrs. Lassiter and me headed this way, so I'm sure word will get around that I'm back in town. I don't like to leave the office unmanned too long."

"What did you have in mind for the birds?" JoEmma whistled for Gabby to return. Instead of flying back to JoEmma's left shoulder, the female lovebird joined the male inside the cage. Nothing else really needed to be said, as far as JoEmma was concerned. Gabby had made her choice already. She preferred to be with her mate. "We can't separate them. That would be cruel now that they've found each other."

"My thoughts exactly." Noah gently moved away from Angelina. "I was hoping we could decide which of us needs to give them a permanent home and allow the other to pay visits. Maybe keep one of the offspring when they come."

"Offspring?" Angelina frowned. "Do you think they have already . . . I mean, how soon do you think that will happen? How many will there be?"

"I don't know much about the species," Noah admitted. "I was hoping you did."

"Me?" Distress flashed across her features until she realized she'd given herself away. "Oh, you know JoEmma, she always takes the care and maintaining of anything living around here as her personal responsibility. And since it's difficult for her to get out and about, I rely on her completely where Gabriella is concerned. I wouldn't dream of hurting her feelings by denying her something that fulfills her so completely. She knows best about Gabby."

Angelina was only half lying. JoEmma supposed

Gabby did belong to them both. After all, she had bought the lovebird with part of the trust fund money, the one extravagance she'd allowed herself in two years. But other than cost, Gabby belonged to JoEmma, heart and soul, and she had studied everything she could get her hands on about the rare bird. "If Gabby starts building a nest anytime soon, then she's getting ready to lay in. She'll drop three to five eggs and it will take about three and a half weeks for them to hatch. They say, since it's her first brood, not all of them will live."

"You seem to know a lot about them," Noah complimented her.

I take care of what's mine, JoEmma wanted to say, but instead she simply stated, "I collect information. It keeps me busy."

"So they should definitely live here." Resignation echoed in the doctor's voice and he bent over the cage. "I'm going to miss you, Amigo," he whispered.

Amigo's head cocked to one side as if he understood and he moved to hide himself in Gabby's protective wing.

"Ahh, little buddy, it'll be okay," Noah cooed. "I'll drop by and see you when I can."

Not with his schedule, Noah Powell wouldn't. JoEmma realized that if the birds didn't live with the doctor, he would seldom have a chance to see them as he hoped. He was gone from home so often that he barely had time to see himself in his own mirror.

JoEmma couldn't do that to Noah. Take away his one companion. She knew how that felt from these days of missing her own sweet pet. Gabby was apparently very happy at Noah's. JoEmma could take care of the birds at the doctor's office. She could go along with Hannah on most days when Hannah cleaned. If they required more frequent visits, he always left his place unlocked, as everybody in town knew. As long as he left her room to get her wheelchair in and out of wherever he kept them, then there was no reason this wouldn't work. She needed to make the offer of bird-sitting for him. It would get her out of the house and away from anything Angelina might plan for Noah if he showed up at their house.

Telling herself that this plan was the best thing for the birds and the best way to keep Noah from her sister's schemes made it easier for JoEmma to brace her heart against losing Gabby for the second time. This time forever. She suggested the alternate plan to Noah.

"You sure this is okay with both of you?" Noah looked from one sister to the other.

To JoEmma's surprise, Angelina's blond curls bobbed in approval.

"It's perfectly fine with us, Dr. Powell. I'll enjoy coming to your home . . . to visit about our birds," Angelina replied. "In fact, I think I'm already looking forward to my first visit."

And what you plan to wear and whom you plan to see you going into his office all gussied up. JoEmma knew just how her sister's mind worked. Instead of ambushing Angelina's plan, she might have just spurred her into winning the race.

"Well, it sounds like we're all in agreement." Noah glanced at the feed sack. "I'll take the birdcage and toys for now and come back for the sunflower seeds later."

"No need." JoEmma eyed her sister and smiled as a devious plan hatched in her mind. "Angelina can carry the birdcage for you and you can get the feed sack. I'll just roll these pots off to the mercantile a little earlier than I planned. Then I'll meet you both at your office. You won't mind doing that, will you, Angie? It will give you a chance to say your good-byes to Gabby."

"I . . . um . . . but my dress. I'll need to change so no one sees my Valentine's dress yet."

"Oh, we can wait, can't we, Dr. Powell?" JoEmma ignored the glare radiating from her sister's green eyes. "He can help me set this tray on my lap so I can put the pots on it for better balance."

When Noah turned to lift the tray JoEmma indicated, Angelina shook a fist at her sister, spun on her heels, and fled upstairs.

"I didn't know your sister was so fond of birds." Noah helped JoEmma arrange the pots on the tray.

"You never know what will strike her fancy. I'm just as surprised as you are that she's offering to help take care of Gabby. She usually doesn't like to get dirt under her nails, much less bird poop."

Noah's eyes met JoEmma's.

Suddenly he found something utterly amusing in the prospect of what might lie ahead.

Chapter 5

"Good, it looks like nobody's here yet," Noah told Angelina, glancing at the waiting room parlor at his office and nodding toward the curved pole that stood in one corner of the room. "Just hang the birdcage on the hook and take off the cloth. They'll settle down once they see that they're home."

Gabby and Amigo were full of chirps and squawks, clearly upset by the way they were being handled by their carrier. Angelina had huffed and puffed with each step as if the lovebirds and their cage had the weight of an anvil. She'd been quite vocal about how it would have been much wiser to have taken a carriage to his office. Not until he mentioned that the walk would allow him to stop at a couple of places he needed to visit before returning to work did she agree to walk instead of ride.

He almost wished he had listened to her and taken a buggy instead. She had made a point of stopping along the way and telling every woman she passed about where they were headed and that they were sharing parenting responsibilities concerning their pets. It was as if Angelina was making sure everyone knew that she would be spending time with him in days to come.

He had thought JoEmma Brown would be caring for the birds, not her sister. He suspected she would do so quietly and confidently, without trying to infiltrate his life with as much ado as Angelina.

If the elder of the two Browns was Hannah Lassiter's choice for him, their housekeeper needed to remember that though he looked forward to bird chatter, he also liked covering the cage when he needed silence. Noah wasn't so sure how he would feel about a too talkative bridal prospect. She might not take to a tablecloth over her head. He'd always considered talking was for sharing words that mattered, not just for the sake of rattling. At least, that's pretty much what he'd learned from his father. He hoped Mrs. Lassiter would drop her efforts where Angelina was concerned.

And JoEmma? The thought echoing through his mind surprised Noah. He hadn't included both sisters in that hopeful wish, and he wasn't sure why other than he looked forward to JoEmma joining them in a short while.

Maybe it was because he'd always enjoyed JoEmma's company. Though she seldom stayed around him long enough to learn much about her, he found what little he had discovered about her to be interesting.

"I can't reach the hook," Angelina complained, half-heartedly attempting to moor the cage to its station. "Would you mind helping me?" she added in a soft plea.

She was a foot and a half taller than Mrs. Lassiter, and the housekeeper had managed to move the birdcage when needed. Angelina was playing coy. Noah set down the sunflower seed bag and guided her hand to the hook to show Angelina that she could actually do it if she tried.

"Thank you, Dr. Powell." Her hand lingered a moment too long with his before her eyelashes dipped then opened to flash green with undeniable attraction. "You're so wonderfully tall."

"And you are flirting with me, Miss Brown." Noah liked Angelina well enough as a person. As a boy, he had looked on her as a possible courting companion. She'd been every young boy's vision of a beautiful girl. There was nothing mean or unflattering about her. He'd simply found her too competitive in collecting beaux, and she had never made him feel that he was anything special to her. Maybe it was nothing more than pure vanity, but he didn't want to waste time being simply a name with many others on her dance card. "I'm very flattered."

"Well, why shouldn't I flirt with you, Dr. Powell?" Angelina swung in a half circle, setting her petticoats to rustling beneath her taffeta skirt. "You have a thriving practice. You're well respected. You're the most eligible bachelor in the territory. You haven't been seen escorting anyone *anywhere*," she stressed as if hinting that there were places he could escort her. "Why . . . there's many a woman who wears her heart on her sleeve for you."

Ahh, she was hinting about the upcoming Valentine's dance. He'd heard that names would be drawn out of a bowl to match couples up at the dance. Each would choose a heart with a name on it and pin it on their sleeve. Whoever's heart you drew was your partner for the evening. Everyone knew the name choosing wasn't always on the fair side of right, but too many women in town liked to play matchmaker. And so far, no man he knew had ever offered to prepare the hearts for any Valentine's celebration.

Though he appreciated her frankness in why he appealed to her, he knew if he didn't encourage Angelina to spend her time on better prospects than him, she would waste what little time there was left between now and the party. She would lose her opportunity to snag a man of prestige who would be flattered by her interest.

"I hear the preparations for Belle Whitaker's dance are

well under way." Noah grabbed the feed sack and started moving out of the parlor and down the hall toward the kitchen. "If you'll come this way, I'll show you where I keep the bird food and fresh trays."

"Is that your bedroom?" The rustle of her petticoats sped up as she moved close enough to get a glimpse at the mess of bedcovers he'd left on the floor.

Noah dropped the sack again, this time just long enough to take a couple of steps to shut the door to his bedroom. "Sorry, I got up in a hurry this morning and didn't make my bed."

"But I thought Hannah did your housework," she said from behind him.

He turned, blocking any further view of his private quarters. It wasn't that he didn't trust her, but she might use whatever she saw there as something to gossip about with her friends. Maybe he ought to take back that last thought. He didn't let anyone near his quarters or in his private life. "I clean my own bedroom. She takes care of everything else."

Noah grabbed the sunflower seeds again and finally deposited the sack where it truly belonged in the kitchen. Next time he would wait to tote a sack around town until he knew exactly what would be done with it. Admiration for the freight haulers who had to lift such cargo day after day filled him with renewed respect.

"You'll find the trays in the lower cabinet of the hutch. I keep plenty of eggs, not for the eggs themselves, but because Amigo likes to chew on the shells to sharpen his beak. I give the egg whites and yolks to the stray cat that pays me a morning visit around daylight, if I happen to be up. I usually try to be."

He didn't know why he was telling her all this. She'd probably never be around to feed the cat that early, but at least she might save the eggs for him till he could feed his visitor.

"Dr. Powell? Are you home?" called a female voice from the front parlor.

Angelina nearly busted her bustle flying out of the kitchen ahead of him as he answered, "I'll be right there."

"No-ah-Pow. No-ah-Pow. Smch-smch-smch," Gabby trilled from the cage as he and Angelina rounded the corner and came face-to-face with a red-haired woman who had her look-alike son in tow.

"Mrs. Rawlston. How are you? Is Roy Lee feeling any better?" Noah eyed his ten-year-old patient. "Have his bowel movements shown any indication of improvement in the past week or so?"

"Yes." She nodded briskly, setting her feathered hat into motion. "I must say, I didn't believe you at all but the frog actually came out, as you said it would."

Angelina looked on in horror. "You mean he—"

"Pooped a frog. Yes, he did. I told him to quit putting strange things in his mouth, but he refused to believe me. He took a dare to see how many frogs he could fit in his mouth and swallowed one." She grabbed her son by the ear as the boy poked his finger into the birdcage. "Just like he's about to get his finger pecked off if he doesn't keep his hands where they belong. Roy Lee, leave those birds alone."

"Says-a-me. Says-a-me. Open up." Gabby rattled the latch. Her bill seemed to be waiting for another poke of the tiny finger.

"Oww, Mama, that hurts!"

"I'm going to make something else hurt if you don't start minding your manners, young man. Now tell Dr. Powell what you did this morning so I can decide whether I need to make you an appointment with the undertaker."

Roy Lee's chin dipped to his chest as he mumbled, "I

put some crawdad eyes in Beth Ann's sandwich when she wasn't looking, and she got so mad she wrestled me and poured some of her daddy's chaw down my throat. I got to spitting it out quick but plenty of it went down and made me spiteful sick. It was all black and gooey and it looked like big ol' lumps mixed with the flapjacks I ate this morning."

Angelina paled noticeably. "I need to sit down."

"Here, dear, let me help you." Mrs. Rawlston let go of her son and helped Angelina to the settee. The boy moved closer to Noah, just to keep out of swatting range of his mother's arms. "Wait till you have a boy of your own. None of this will affect you in the least. Why, by the time you change his first dirty diaper—"

"You ladies enjoy your talk." Noah rustled Roy Lee's red hair. "We'll go see how much his belly's grumbling and be right back."

He gladly escaped with the ten-year-old and took him to the bedroom he used as an operating room. He lifted the boy up on the examination table. "So Beth Ann's pretty upset with you, is she?"

"Naww, she likes me. She told me so."

"Is that why you put crawdad eyes in her sandwich?"

"Yep. I figured I'd see if she was dumb enough to eat them."

"So you'd know if she was the girl for you?"

"Yep. I don't want no dumb girl liking me."

"She didn't eat them, did she?"

"Nope." Respect filled his voice. "She found 'um right off. Said she suspected me right from the get-go." Brown eyes stared up at Noah. "What's a get-go, doc?"

"Don't know for certain, but I think only smart girls can spot one."

"That's what I figure. 'Cause whatever it is, it made sure she knew about them eyeballs and she didn't eat 'um. I still ain't certain how come she had her daddy's chaw so close by, but she used it quicker than I could tell her I was real sorry. Phew! I won't never do that again."

Noah held back a laugh. It sounded like Beth Ann was a lot smarter than even Roy Lee knew. She'd obviously come prepared for possibilities. "So you plan on telling her she's your girl now?"

"On Valentine's Day." Roy Lee rubbed his tummy. "I figure that'll give me enough time to get out of trouble with Ma so I can ask Beth Ann to the dance with me."

"Sounds like a good plan, but I'd like to offer a piece of advice."

"Yeah?" The boy looked at him askance.

"Tell Beth Ann you're sorry before Valentine's Day. She might go with some other boy if you wait."

Noah examined the young Romeo, listening to his belly and breathing, checking to see if he had any temperature. "Have you eaten anything since you lost your flapjacks?"

"Yeah. Some of Ma's blueberry pie."

"You'll live then." He set the boy on his feet and would have given him the usual peppermint stick he offered his other youthful patients but decided to give the kid's stomach a rest. "No need for the undertaker."

"I told her I was tough." Roy Lee strutted down the hall to the waiting room.

When they returned to the women, they found that others had joined Angelina and Mrs. Rawlston. In fact, it looked like a meeting of the Ladies' Church Auxiliary Club had been called. Noah greeted his patients, none looking particularly ill. He focused his attention on Roy Lee's mother.

"My diagnosis is that you need to keep his mouth closed for a while," Noah informed her, "and insist that he only put things in it that are supposed to go in it."

"That's easy for you to say, Dr. Powell." She rose from her seat next to Angelina. "Well, ladies, it's been good talking with you. I hope you all start feeling better. Must be an epidemic going around."

Angelina was the only one of the group who looked even remotely in need of his attention. But he wasn't sure if she was still reacting to the visual Roy Lee had given of losing his breakfast or if she was upset. She looked more like she was pouting.

"I'm next, Dr. Powell." Carrie Sanders stood, lifting her double chins to a determined angle and daring the other women to contradict her claim. "I came in just as you took Roy Lee in to be examined."

"What can I do to help you, Miss Sanders?"

An hour later he had seen all of the women and found none of them to be suffering from anything but a sudden need for attention. Each of them had mentioned the dance and hinted that they were still available. He decided he ought to just escort Angelina to the party and be done with it. If every female in the territory was going to visit him in the next few days to let him know of her availability, he would get nothing done.

To his surprise, Angelina was alone waiting in the parlor when he finished with his last patient. He expected her sister to have joined them by now. "I'm sorry, Miss Brown. I never dreamed I would be that busy. I was hoping to show you and your sister where everything is that I use for the birds, then to see you both home."

"Something's kept JoEmma. I'm getting concerned about her. She should have been here long before now." Angelina looked almost mad, not just concerned. "I wanted us both to be informed of your preferences for Amigo's care."

He suspected she was frustrated by the other women's

appearance at his office today, but there was still a sense of sincerity in her concern over her younger sister and his expectations concerning his pet. "How about I close up for a while and find out what's kept her? You can go along with me or I'll see that she gets home as soon as possible."

"I'm afraid she's overdone herself again." Angelina stood and dusted the wrinkles from her skirt. "I'll go on home and prepare her some chamomile tea. That always strengthens her."

"Let me get a buggy for you." Noah decided that was the least he could do for her since she'd waited so long.

"No, I'll walk. If I ride, I wouldn't be able to lift the wheelchair if I find her along the way home. If I'm walking, I can at least push her home if she's too tired to roll it herself."

Noah watched her walk away, his respect for Angelina Brown deeper than before. She loved her sister. Choosing to walk just now said it louder than any words ever could.

He hurried in the opposite direction, heading for the mercantile a couple of streets away. Looking through every business window that showed activity inside, he saw no one who looked remotely as if they were wheelchair level. No sign of her along the sidewalks. It took him less than ten minutes to get to Kimble's Mercantile. As he stepped inside, he saw her dozing in her chair near the pot-bellied stove that stood in one corner of the store. Coffee wafted from a blue-speckled pot on one of the burners.

Noah wished his boots didn't cause the slats of the floorboards to creak as he walked through the aisles toward her. Instead of waking her, he simply sat in one of the chairs near the stove that the owner provided for customers who whittled or shared stories while they drank coffee.

Mrs. Kimble, a big German woman who looked like a blond-braided Viking of long ago, came in from a back room, saw him, and held a pudgy finger up to her lips to signal silence.

He nodded and folded his arms into each other, crossed his long legs out in front of him. A board creaked beneath his boot. Mrs. Kimble frowned. JoEmma stirred and her head lifted as her eyes blinked open. It took her a minute to focus on him next to her. When she did, her eyes widened in apology. *Brown. They are more brown than hazel*, he decided.

"I'm sorry. I must have dozed off." She glanced at the store owner. "Did we finish the pots?"

"*Ja*, you finished enough. Now you go home and rest yourself, *liebling*."

"I'm taking you home." Noah stood and grabbed the back handles to her wheelchair.

"I can make it there by myself, thank you." Her cheeks stained crimson, making her look even paler. Her fingers flexed and she rubbed her palms together. "I'm okay now."

"Are you trying to tell a doctor his business?" Noah could see that she wasn't up to the long roll of the chair across the roadway. Her hands were obviously sore. Why wasn't she wearing gloves? "I promised your sister that I would make sure you got home, and I keep my promises."

JoEmma gripped the chair as if she were preparing herself for a wild ride.

"Relax," he said as he bent to whisper the word in her ear. She smelled of the earth and honeysuckle she'd been planting in the pots and something he couldn't quite define. The blend of aromas appealed to him and he knew that he wouldn't think of JoEmma Brown ever again without recalling the fragrance.

"Ready?" he asked. "Is there anything else you need to take with you?"

"Just me."

Mrs. Kimble waved her out. "Don't let your young man keep you out too long."

"Oh, but he's not my . . ." JoEmma's words trailed off behind them as Noah rolled her out of the mercantile and down the sidewalk.

"People always assume we're together, don't they?" Noah teased, recalling how his childhood buddies had taunted him for helping her home that day she'd skinned her knee. He'd fought a couple of them for saying she'd fallen on purpose just to get his attention. From that point on, the boys thought of her as his girl and watched what they said about her. He decided to be truthful with her now. "You know Mrs. Lassiter is trying to get me interested in one of you Browns as a bride."

JoEmma's shoulders stiffened, but her words were gentle. "Angelina would have no problem with that. In fact, I'd say that would please her greatly. She'd be a wonderful wife."

"I'm sure she will be one day." Though Noah admired JoEmma for trying to help her sister's cause, he wondered why the younger Brown didn't seem interested in him for herself. He'd always thought JoEmma liked being around him. At least, he'd always felt extremely comfortable with her. Did vanity spur his question even now? "What about you? Have you ever thought about marrying, Miss Brown?"

"If I'm going to take care of Gabby and Amigo, you need to feel comfortable in calling me JoEmma. No formal name for me, please. We've known each other too long for that."

"Yes, we have, and maybe you'll dispense with the Dr. Powell business. I'm just Noah."

"Agreed."

"So answer my question. Will you ever marry, Jo-Emma? I've never known you to have a particular beau. But, of course, I was gone those years at college."

"I had a beau or two until I took the fever, then afterward I wasn't sure how this would affect me. So I found interest in other things like animals and flowers and things I could do at a new eye level once my health put me in the chair. I didn't want to be a burden to a husband. What I can and cannot do is limited, and I wouldn't want to stifle a man's life in any way. Especially an active man who would be slowed down by the things I can't do, and he might feel obligated to do for me."

"I don't recall a time when I haven't seen you working," Noah countered. "You're one of the most active women I know, despite your infirmity."

"Thank you. I try to be." She sounded pleased for a moment before adding, "But just a moment ago, you saw. Every once in a while I just have to turn off for a few minutes, like I'm a light that can be blown out for the night and lit back up in the morning. What if I have no fire at a critical moment when I need it?"

He knew exactly what she meant. That critical moment had happened once to him and he had been as healthy as an ox. But all the fire had gone out of him and he'd given in to pure exhaustion. Not exhaustion of the body. Exhaustion of arguing with a woman about what was best for her. A woman who ultimately lost her brave battle for life because he'd given in and listened to her instead of his better judgment. And because of that, he'd lost his patient and his father's respect.

"You try to forgive yourself if that happens and become more diligent at learning how not to allow yourself that weakness again," he whispered, lost in the sad memory.

A calloused palm reached up and touched Noah's hand. "You do understand."

Those three words bound him to JoEmma as surely as if they'd shared volumes. She had spoken in a language that had touched his heart and made him want to spend more time with her. Made him want to deepen their conversation. She talked with depth, not the shallow talk of others.

It was then he made up his mind that he would attend the Valentine's dance and exactly whom he meant to escort. But first, he would prove she was no burden to anyone. Not even to herself.

He would find out if there was a chance to heal what ailed JoEmma Brown. If not her body, then her spirit.

Chapter 6

When Noah reached his office and started to move past, JoEmma signaled him to stop. "Please don't take me home yet."

He halted his pushing, then gently turned the chair halfway around. Coming in front of the chair to face her, he bent so that their eyes met at the same level. He had positioned her so that she wouldn't be facing the setting sun and she wouldn't be staring up to see him in shadow. His consideration pleased her.

"I promised your sister that I'd bring you right home when I found you. She'll be worried."

"I won't take long, I promise. I would just like to say good-bye to Gabby," she whispered. "Not good-bye exactly, but . . . well . . . you know what I mean."

Understanding shone in the depths of his eyes. "I felt the same thing earlier today about Amigo. Really, JoEmma, if you want to change your mind, we'll take the birds back to your house."

"No, this is best for them. I'll just miss seeing her whenever the mood strikes me. We shared a lot of nights visiting with each other," JoEmma said softly, rolling her chair a few inches closer to the front door of his office. "Shall we?"

Noah opened the door and immediately took back command of the pushing. "This will allow me to take a look at your hands while I'm here. I have some salve that I think will help."

She let her palms rest in her lap, not sure quite what to do with them. He'd obviously noticed the calluses and, being a healer, wanted to help with her pain. Still, she wondered what else he'd taken the time to notice about her. She was no longer a girl with pigtails and skinned knees. Did he find her at all interesting? Pretty?

As he rolled her into his waiting room, JoEmma instantly saw where he kept the birdcage and gave a little whistle.

"Says-a-me. Says-a-me. Open up." Gabby flew to the cage door. Amigo made little kissing noises.

"There you are, Funny Feathers." JoEmma appreciated when Noah immediately rolled her toward the cage, took it down from the hook, and set it on the table next to the settee.

"We'll find somewhere else to hang the cage so you can reach it." Noah sat on the settee to watch her watch the birds.

It was only then that she realized he must be really tired from seeing patients all afternoon then looking for her and rolling her home. "Thanks for everything, Noah. For finding Gabby and giving her a good home. For helping me and Angelina."

"My pleasure. I hope this will allow us some time to catch up with each other after all these years. I've been so busy and you've been . . ." His words trailed off.

"Housebound basically," she interjected, rather than saying what she was really thinking, which was she'd deliberately isolated herself from activities that might make her feel awkward or required too much stamina.

"I was going to say, you've been just as busy with all your projects. Would you like something to drink?" He started to rise but she waved away his effort.

"No thanks. If Angelina's worried about me, she'll have something waiting on me so I best not stay too long."

He nodded. "You know your sister well. She's brewing up something even as we speak."

"Of that I'm certain." JoEmma laughed, not meaning anything that had to do with something to drink.

"She and some of the other townswomen are full of plans for Miss Whitaker's party, from what I could tell this afternoon. I believe they had a gathering of the minds about it here in the waiting room." Noah explained some of what had transpired.

What had Angelina done? Made sure every woman in town knew she was going to the doctor's office? JoEmma regretted even more that she hadn't gotten here any sooner. No telling what was hatched among the hens.

"Don't look so fretful," he teased. "I still have my bachelor status and it's almost sundown, although I'm not sure if it can survive everybody's matchmaking efforts. Mrs. Lassiter can be quite persistent when she sets her mind to something."

"Is that why she didn't bring Gabby home when she found her here? She was playing matchmaker?" JoEmma smiled at the two lovebirds. Amigo was a cutie and the pair looked so sweet together.

Noah exhaled a deep breath, then laughed. "Remember that you said it. I didn't." He picked up the cage and started to unlatch its door, but JoEmma reached out to stop him.

"I wouldn't. At least unless you lock your front door and make sure there is no window open. Gabby might try to escape again."

"You think so?" Noah stood and moved to lock the office door. "I don't usually keep that locked. Amigo doesn't seem to want to explore anywhere but here. Still, I'm not sure my bedroom window isn't open. I'll check. Or if you'd like to go with me, you can see if I need to move anything out of the hallway to give you access to the kitchen, where I keep their food and trays. I'll be just a minute with the window."

JoEmma eyed the birds to make sure that the cage was soundly stationed on the table before she swung her chair around and rolled after him. She got a great look at his lanky height and broad shoulders, admiring his solid stride and easy movement. Noah Brown was a man at his physical best and that made him more attractive to her than all his degrees hanging on the wall above her. He was a smart, healthy man full of life and kind spirit. Seeing such virility made her wish that her heart were stronger, her legs more stable. That she could be a helpmate to him and something much more.

He went through a closed door at the end of the hall. Just as she reached the kitchen, she heard a window slam shut. When he appeared behind her, he gave her a quick inventory of what he kept for the birds and where, how he shared the excess with a neighborhood cat, and that, after tonight, he would start hanging the birdcage in his bedroom.

"It's the only room that people other than me won't be going in and out of," Noah explained, "so I think that's the wisest place to put Gabby to get her comfortable here, don't you? At least until she feels at home and doesn't want to escape."

His private quarters? The thought sent all kinds of images racing through JoEmma's mind, and she hoped her cheeks weren't as red hot above the skin as they felt below. Images of her and Noah in each other's arms, their legs

tangled together. Of his hair all mussed and those broad
shoulders lending her a warm place to cuddle, just as
Amigo had cuddled underneath Gabby's wing.

"Will the bed be any trouble for me?" she asked, trying
to put her thoughts back into a more proper frame. That
didn't come out the way she meant it! "I mean, will I fit?
My wheelchair. Will my *wheelchair* fit?"

"No problem. I don't have much in there but an armoire
and a bed. I'd show you it now, but it's not presentable at
the moment. How about you let me look at those hands for
the time being?"

JoEmma allowed him to roll her to his examination
room, where he stopped long enough to light a lamp to
help with the waning daylight. "They'll be okay. I have
some liniment at home that your father gave me."

"My father? Does he still see you as a patient?"

She heard some emotion in Noah's voice but couldn't
quite discern what it was. Hannah occasionally mentioned
that the two Powell men were having some kind of battle
of wills, but she never really discussed more than her frustration at them both. JoEmma didn't know why father and
son were angry with each other. "Since he took care of me
during my scarlet fever scare, he's always made a point to
look in on me. I think he's really using his visits more as
an excuse to spend time with Hannah. The two of them
should marry, don't you think?"

"He would be a lucky man if they did."

Noah took her palms and turned them over to examine
them closely. "Why don't you wear gloves when you're
using your chair?"

JoEmma shrugged. "They get in my way. I like my
hands in the dirt when I pot plants. I like the way the quill
feels between my fingers when I write. I like to touch the
way things really are. Like this . . ."

She took his hand and ran a finger down the length of

several of his. "Your fingers are warm and smooth and strong and I can feel your heartbeat. A doctor's hand, not a muleskinner's. Oh . . . your pulse sped up." Her eyes met his and held. "You can't feel all of that with gloves on. And it's worth a little pain to feel life, don't you think?"

A profound silence filled the space that separated them, ending any words between them. Noah's lips lowered to press gently over hers, stirring her every sense and sending the exotic taste of temptation blazing through JoEmma. Her arms lifted of their own accord and wrapped themselves around his neck, allowing her to rise gently from her chair so he could deepen the kiss.

She had dreamed of him kissing her for so long that she had imagined it in a hundred different ways. But that had been a ten-year-old girl's limited imagination. She was a woman now and the kiss Noah bestowed upon her stirred such wild yearnings within JoEmma that she knew it would take a thousand moons to send them back to their resting place.

She returned his kiss with the same ardor until, finally, she needed more breath, which demanded she end the exquisite longing.

"You're standing," he whispered.

JoEmma looked down and saw that she was, and the only weakness she'd felt was that her heart might melt from sheer delight.

"We're going to do this again," Noah whispered, pressing a gentle kiss against her forehead now. "As many times as it takes to make you stronger. If you have the strength to stand, even for a few minutes, even during a kiss, we can build on that."

"Don't tease me, Noah." She moved away, sliding back down into the wheelchair. "Not about this."

"I'm not." Noah curved a knuckle under her chin and lifted it so she couldn't look away. "I mean for you to get stronger and you just proved to me that you can. I plan to help you do just that in repayment to you for helping me with Gabby and Amigo."

JoEmma felt crushed. That's exactly what she didn't want—help with a lost cause. It was hopeless and she'd tried so long she'd given up and accepted her fate. She wanted a friend's care to become something more. Something she'd dreamed of since she was a little girl. She wanted to be loved by Noah.

She wished now that she never knew his kiss. Never knew its depth and scope. Never knew what would haunt her now for all the days of her life that remained. All she wanted to do was get away from him. Away from what couldn't be. She wished she had Gabby's wings and could fly away. He was too much of a gentleman to let her go home in the dark without him. She must find a way to force him to take her now . . . before she started crying her eyes out. "And how will you repay my sister for her help with the birds?" Her tongue struck a wicked blow.

It wasn't like her to be cruel and she didn't know she had it within her to be so mean. But the suggestion had its effect. He gave no answer to her question and became all business, grabbing the salve and working it into her palms and wrapping them with fresh linen bandages.

He dropped the jar of salve into her lap. "I'm sending the rest home with you. Use it for a few days and your hands won't hurt so much. And use some gloves when you're traveling about town, at least. Across your floors at home aren't so damaging, but these roadways are."

When he took the bars of her wheelchair to spin her around, she braced herself, thinking that his anger might make the roll home a wild ride. But to her surprise, he was amazingly gentle in pushing the chair.

He allowed her a moment with Gabby, as he'd promised,

but JoEmma was so upset about the kiss that she barely allowed herself any emotion in telling her pet good-bye.

Maybe it was because she knew she could see Gabby tomorrow if she liked. Maybe it was because she knew if she got weepy-eyed over Funny Feathers, then she just might break down and cry for all the things she would never be and had ever missed since becoming ill. Maybe it was because she was scared Noah was right.

She might possibly become strong enough to stand on her two feet again.

Could she accept that his kiss was meant as nothing more than a remedy to make her well?

Fly away home, little bird, she told herself. *Before more than your wings get broken.*

Chapter 7

The silence between them as he took JoEmma home gave Noah plenty of time to ask himself what had compelled him to kiss her. Her hand touching his? The look in her eyes? The sense that if he didn't kiss her, he would somehow miss something that might alter his life forever?

He thought of every moment he'd ever spent with JoEmma Brown. Nothing fancy. Just walking home from school and talking. Sharing a pew in church. Laughing at their toes getting pinched at Crawdad Creek as they sat side by side. All were small slices of life that seemed ordinary to most, but to a boy who had lost his mother and a son whose father rarely talked to him, those slices teemed with a simple sharing that had meant everything to him. There was nothing false about JoEmma. No manipulations. No game playing. Just pure, gentle enjoyment for the true value of life and what it offered.

Noah thought his interest in her had merely been that she touched the doctor of medicine part of him, who valued anyone who valued life. But the urge to kiss her had risen from something other than her expressive words. She had stirred some need within the part of him that was nothing but raw pulsating maleness, a need that had been restrained behind convention for too long. A wish to know how her lips tasted could no longer be held at bay. The desire to breathe in her essence and fill himself with its fragrance had unleashed his arms and drawn her into his embrace when her arms had encircled him. To resist was no longer a choice or within his command to halt. He could do nothing else but draw her even closer than the wheelchair allowed.

"I really think we should talk." JoEmma broke into his thoughts as he rolled her chair up the wooden ramp that provided entry to her home.

"I won't say I'm sorry that I kissed you." He didn't care if it made her angrier to speak his true feelings. He wasn't sorry. He would never be.

"Neither am I," she said, "but it can't happen again."

He wished he could see her eyes. Wished he could read what was not being said in their hazel depths. But all he could see was the back of her head and the rigid set of her shoulders. "It won't unless you ask me to."

He meant the promise he'd just made. He would not take that liberty again though he would spend the rest of the night and many hereafter, Noah suspected, dreaming of their kiss. JoEmma Brown did not know what she had set into motion this afternoon. Not only did he now have the goal to see her up and out of the chair but he meant to find a way to make her unable to live without another of his kisses. A *thousand* more of his kisses.

Maybe enlisting her sister's help would be a way to start.

When her chair reached the Browns' front door, the door swung open and Hannah Lassiter's four-foot-two frame sailed out to meet them. She took one look at the bandages on JoEmma's hands and demanded to know what had happened, how badly she was hurt, and didn't he have any better sense than keeping her out in the night wind so late.

"Don't be hard on him." JoEmma held her hands up to

ward off her housekeeper's attack on Noah. "He didn't do anything but find me and get me home."

She explained all that had happened and that she had been the one who demanded the delay with stopping at his office on the way back. She mentioned nothing of the kiss, and her anger at him seemed gone. As if the kiss had never happened.

Noah wasn't sure if he liked that fact or not.

"Angie's bustle is all in a wad because she's reheated the tea at least three times. I've got supper waiting on you, too."

"I'm sorry, Hannah. You should have gone ahead and eaten without me."

"What, and miss all that lovely gossip about the bloomer brigade and them meeting at the doctor's office?" She stepped aside and let them in. "I've heard her version of the story. Now I want to hear what Dr. Powell has to say about it all. You will be staying for supper, won't you?"

Mrs. Lassiter's invitation was not a question, though she'd tried to be nice enough to offer it as one. She gave him that "young man" expression that meant she was only being nice and he'd better do what she said or he'd hear a tirade the next time she came to clean. She was intent about this matchmaking business.

"I'd love to, thank you." Noah decided he could work this to his advantage. He probably would have just caught a bite to eat over at the hotel diner anyway, so this would just give him more time to set his plan for JoEmma into motion. "Is there somewhere I can wash up?"

"Will you show him, Hannah? I'd like to freshen up myself." JoEmma seemed eager to be alone.

"After you wash your hands, I'll wrap some new bandages around them," Noah offered.

"I can manage." She held up the salve. "I've had plenty of practice before."

When JoEmma rolled into another room, Hannah didn't budge and looked like she might block him from going another step forward. Her pudgy fists knotted on her broad hips. "What have you done to her?"

"What do you mean?" Noah pretended she meant the condition of JoEmma's hands, but he knew she was asking something else. "Her hands were hurting from rolling the chair down the roadway. I merely offered some salve and bandages."

"Waste spit on someone you don't like." One of Hannah's fingers rose to shake at him as she scolded, "That poor kitten rolled in here looking like she'd had all the sand punched out of her. Now I'm asking you again and I expect a reasonable answer."

She asked for it, so he gave her the truth. "I kissed her." The finger stopped in midshake.

"Goodgawdalmighty," she whispered and ran up to him. "Bend down here, young man."

Noah bent and braced himself for the slap that he had initially expected from JoEmma back at his office.

Mrs. Lassiter cupped his cheeks in both of her pudgy palms, gave them a quick squeeze, then planted a kiss right on his mouth. "You finally did something totally right. You are my hero, Noah Powell! I'm so proud of you."

Noah started chuckling, a deep-throated eruption of pure unadulterated amusement. "And you, Hannah Lassiter, make no sense to me whatsoever, but I adore you, too."

She laughed with him, her cheeks stained with a blush that made her look like a plump raspberry and all the more endearing.

"I take it this means I'm not going to be massacred in my sleep before I wake up tomorrow morning for kissing one of your precious kittens?"

"Not since you kissed the *right* one." Her chins lifted indignantly. "I wanted you to prove yourself worthy of figuring out which one of the Browns would be best for you. My intuition proved true, that's all."

"Your intuition?" Noah ignored her indignation and focused on reminding her that he knew her about as well as she knew him. "Intuition is wishful thinking. I've never seen you be wishful about anything, madam. You've always set your mind to having your way, and by jasper, it's going to be that way or else."

"Are you sassing me?" She flashed him a dimpled grin, unable to keep her face stern.

"Yeah," he teased back. "What are you going to do about it?"

She took that same finger that had scolded him moments before and motioned him to go with her. "I'm going to feed you some supper, that's what I'm going to do, and see if we can't get something stirring between those two in there. A little competition always helps to make a heart quit hiding and speak up for what it wants. A little cat fight might just be the call to order here."

Noah linked his arm through hers and let her guide him to the dining room. "You're devious, Hannah Lassiter."

She sighed. "You don't even know the half of it. Just wait till you see what I have in store for your father."

JoEmma sat across the table from Hannah, with Noah to her left and Angelina next to him. There had been no end to the discussion about what had transpired at the doctor's office. One thing was clear. Noah was very much aware of what the women had been plotting. He'd taken it well in stride, if she said so herself, not letting it go to his head like some men might have. She was glad he found humor in it.

She had expected Angelina to be mad about his knowing he was being wooed, but her sister had not won her reputation lightly. Angie acted as if she thought the whole matter quite as humorous as they did.

"Can you imagine anyone being that desperate for an escort?" Angelina reached for her napkin and accidentally touched Noah's hand. "Oh, excuse me."

Puhhleease, JoEmma thought. *Why don't you just reach out and play patty fingers with him?*

"Have either of you girls decided who you're going with?" Hannah cut her roast beef, her eyes focused on the effort rather than on either sister.

Angelina raised her napkin to her mouth and mumbled something incomprehensible.

JoEmma looked at her sister then at Noah. "Uh . . . I . . . uh . . . haven't decided if I'm going to the dance."

"What about you, Dr. Powell?" Angelina asked. "Have all of our matchmaking attempts frightened you off?"

Noah shared a glance with their housekeeper, then shook his head. "Not at all, ladies. In fact, I may very well go. The only way I won't is if a patient requires my services that evening and forces me to be away from town."

"All the babies that were due are born. No one I know is on their deathbed." Hope shone brightly in Angelina's eyes. "Maybe cupid's arrow is pointed in your direction this year. Do we know the lucky woman you have in mind to share hearts with?"

"No," he announced. Angelina's lips lowered into a definite pout to take a sip from her goblet, making him add further, "I mean, I assumed I'd be like every other man there and take the heart that's drawn out of the bowl for me."

Why don't you just get down on your knees and beg him? JoEmma didn't like for Angelina to feel so desperate. "I think that's what we all should do. Just show up and let what happens happen. Nobody escort anybody unless they're already married. That seems more fair and would get rid of all this cooing and wooing one-upmanship that's going on right now."

"I was maybe thinking about asking both of you to allow me to escort you there, if neither of you has a particular beau you would prefer to take you." Noah shared yet another glance with Hannah. "It would take me out of the running if everyone thought I'd already spoken for someone."

"It's the least you could do to help him out." Hannah took another bite of meat and chewed thoughtfully. "Since it was you, Angelina, that let all the women know he was back from the Boatrights and caused the rash of illnesses this afternoon."

Angelina lowered her goblet. JoEmma could see her sister's mind galloping away with plans on how to make this sudden opportunity fit in with her original scheme. "It works for me. I'd love to go with you, Dr. Powell. Thank you for asking."

Sure it works for you . . . at least halfway. Now JoEmma had to attend, too. Not to appease Noah. If she didn't go, Angelina would win by simply showing up with him.

He'd saved himself from matchmaking manipulation only to put himself right back into the line of Angie's fervor to win.

"I guess that means I go, too." JoEmma thought she saw Hannah Lassiter wink at the doctor, but it had to have been a product of her tired imagination. It had been a very long day, a soul-bending kiss, and an extreme effort to remember that she really didn't want her sister to hurt Noah's feelings in any way with what she planned. "Thanks for asking us both."

She rolled her chair back from the dinner table. "I'm

rather tired now. So if you all will forgive me, I'd really like to call it an evening. I want to get up early tomorrow and plan to be at your place by daybreak, Noah, since Hannah won't be cleaning there. That way I can feed the birds, refresh the cage, and feed your cat before church."

"You don't need to come unless you just prefer to." Noah pushed his own plate away, done with his meal. "I'm not going to open the office tomorrow so I can handle Gabby and Amigo on my own. Why don't you get some rest and come by after church?"

"We will take you up on that." Angelina spoke before JoEmma could.

"You never close your office. Not even on Sundays." One of Hannah Lassiter's brows lifted quizzically. "What's so special about tomorrow?"

"If you really must know, I have to make my bed"—he laughed—"and make room for a wheelchair."

"What?" Angelina and Mrs. Lassiter chimed in unison.

Noah explained why he would be making room for the pole and the birdcage in his bedroom rather than the parlor. The bird-sitters would now have to care for Gabby and Amigo in his room.

"How thoughtful of you. I've always been curious about what a bachelor's private quarters might look like." Angelina grinned, looking quite pleased with the prospect. "Since I've never seen one, you know."

JoEmma thought her sister was being too coy and would have admonished her for it, but all she could do at the moment herself was focus on Noah's lips and the fact that they were smiling directly at her and not Angelina. The idea of being in his private quarters with him stirred images that Angelina would find far more than coy if she had access to JoEmma's thoughts. So JoEmma kept her criticism to herself.

Mrs. Lassiter's gaze swept their guest from head to

torso. "That means you're going to have to change some of your sleeping habits, young man."

Something unspoken but electric passed between her housekeeper and the doctor, and JoEmma couldn't fathom its meaning.

"You're right." He winked at the older woman. "At least until our little bird is ready to trust me and not fly away next time."

"Just remember she'll stick around a lot longer if you don't let any kittens in to play."

JoEmma wondered how Gabby and the cat he fed had anything to do with the way he slept.

Maybe he liked to share his bed with a cat.

Chapter 8

Morning went by quicker than Noah had hoped. He was almost finished with cleaning his room and moving out anything but the four-poster bed and the wooden pole that now stood in the corner with the birdcage hanging on the hook. All he had to do now was stow away the rug and leave the floor bare so JoEmma could easily roll around the room.

He had decided to store the sunflower seeds in the corner beneath the cage so she wouldn't ever have to struggle with lifting the sack and he could always be aware of when she might need the supply replaced. He didn't worry so much about her rolling all the way from the kitchen balancing a water tray, but the more he could leave in the bedroom for her access, the easier her job would be.

Now he had to learn to make his bed before he went anywhere so he wouldn't embarrass himself by showing how sloppy he could be. Always being called away gave him plenty of excuses. Besides, he'd always had Mrs. Lassiter to make the rest of the place look good. It had been a challenge the past couple of months learning how to care for someone other than himself. Amigo's care had made Noah aware of how he fell short in other areas of his life, and now preparing his room for JoEmma's ease gave him reason to want to improve some of those shortcomings in himself.

He could start by taking the time to build a bigger cage for the sweethearts, improve their home by making a bookshelf with levels of shelves and perches to allow room for the coming offspring. He'd have to talk with the peddler about getting something that he could use to form a cover for the bookcase that would let in plenty of sunlight and still allow him to see the birds. Yet it would have to provide enough barrier to keep them from flying away. A thin chicken coop wire might be just the thing, but he wasn't certain.

He needed to learn a lot more about the lovebirds as a species and how to care for a possible family of them. Just as JoEmma warned might happen, Gabby was already gathering things that made him certain she was starting to build a nest. He'd gotten close to her when he'd changed out the trays this morning and he'd felt a sting at the top of his head. Next thing he knew, Gabby was taking a string of dark hair and showing it to Amigo before tucking it away in a corner of one perch.

Wanting to protect himself from being plucked bald in the next few days, Noah had gone outside and grabbed a handful of items he thought she might use for nesting material and laid them as an offering in the birdcage. Gabby spent the morning building her nest with leaves, grass, and several threads from the ball of string he kept for the cat to play with when he visited. Noah found a particular humor in the fact that he and Gabby were working their fool heads off all morning while Amigo simply relaxed in the cage, looked on, and chirped, "No-ah-Pow. No-ah-Pow. Smch-smch-smch."

"That's the good life, isn't it, buddy?" Noah teased as he flung the rug up over his shoulder. "Let the little beauty do whatever makes her happy while you practice your sweet talk."

A knock on the front door reminded him that he had forgotten to unlock it. Even though he'd hung a closed sign for the day, if someone desperately needed him, he would open back up. Maybe church service was over and it was the Browns. They should be here anytime. Where had the morning gone? How in the world did Hannah clean the rest of his place so quickly in the same amount of time that it had taken him just to clean and rearrange his bedroom?

"I'm coming!" he hollered, making his way to the door. He opened it and was just about to say he was sorry for having it locked when the words died in his throat. There before him stood Thurgood Powell.

"Dad?" Noah swallowed the word hard. The thought that instantly came to mind was a twelve-year-old's. *Boy, am I glad I cleaned my room.*

"May I come in?" Thurgood took off his Sunday bowler, letting loose a wealth of salt-and-pepper-colored hair that would probably be Noah's fate one day. His father looked healthy for a man over sixty, his blue eyes piercing and intent above the sharp angular features and bearded jaw. If not for the cane he used to help him with his arthritic joints, no one would suspect the dapper-suited man was anything but in his prime.

"I thought it was time we talked."

"Come in." Noah stepped aside and let his father enter the office that had once been his own. "Can I get you some coffee?"

"If it's not too much trouble."

"You want to wait in the parlor or would you prefer the kitchen?" Noah didn't quite know what the protocol should be since making him wait in the parlor seemed too impersonal and the kitchen too personal between two men who had been little more than strangers to each other for several years.

"The kitchen."

Noah led the way, wondering why he suddenly felt so defensive. He worried if the coffee would be the way his dad liked it, if he would approve of what he'd done with the office after being handed over the reins of the medical practice, if he had come to resolve their issues or make a final break between them.

"I suppose you're wondering why I'm here." Thurgood sat down in one of the two chairs at the kitchen table and propped his cane against the edge.

Noah took two cups from the hutch, set one in front of each of them, and poured the cups full. Should he add a saucer? He tried to remember how his dad preferred it. *No saucer. Just a cup.* "I made this about an hour ago. I'll make fresh if you like."

"This will do."

Noah sat down, his hands gripping his cup, but he couldn't have drunk a drop from it if he tried. He was afraid if he lifted it to his lips, his hands would shake the cup dry. He didn't want his father to know how his presence unsettled him so he simply gripped the cup and forced himself to look Thurgood squarely in the eye. "Why are you here, Dad?"

"Mrs. Lassiter has informed me that you're interested in the younger Brown sister."

"JoEmma." Noah needed to personalize her to himself. To both of them. His father was making her sound like one of their patients. She was more than that to Noah. How much more he could only hope at the moment.

"Yes, JoEmma." Thurgood took a sip of the coffee. "I think you've made a good choice."

A compliment? From his father? Noah couldn't remember the last one he'd received and had to think hard

to remember even the silent pats on the back his parent
had offered when he achieved something at school or college. The memory came suddenly, full blown and full of
irony. It had involved JoEmma even then. The day he'd
carried her home from school with the skinned knee. His
father had seen the other boys taunting him as he carried
her safely home. When Noah finally reported home and
learned that his father had witnessed his act of kindness,
Thurgood rustled his hair and said, "Good boy, son."

Noah had helped JoEmma because it was the right thing
to do and *she* had always been kind to *him*. The fact that
the deed had made his father proud of him had made Noah
feel like the heavens had opened up and poured sunshine
on his soul that day.

"You always liked JoEmma," Noah remembered aloud.

"She's got a good heart. Comes from a fine family."

"Is this your way of telling me that you approve of my
interest in her?"

"It is."

It seemed that their conversation was a train struggling
uphill one chug, one sentence at a time. Maybe they were
simply out of practice in talking to each other. Noah didn't
know what it was that made it so difficult for them to feel
comfortable with conversation between them, but it had
always been this way. No, the difficulty had started after
his mother died. Then the conversation was so rare and so
brief that Noah had thought his father had gone mute with
grief. He decided maybe now was the time to put into
action his plans for JoEmma. Maybe his father would be
willing to speak more if it concerned her.

"Speaking of her good heart, you won't mind me asking
what you know about her state of health at the present?"
Noah broached the subject cautiously and waited. His
father was a retired doctor, after all, and might not violate
patient privacy.

"That shouldn't matter if you care about her."

Emotion from a stoic man? Noah felt a little envious that his father defended JoEmma so quickly. He'd obviously spent the last several years making sure he kept up with JoEmma's progress. He couldn't remember another person in the territory his father had come out of retirement for.

Noah didn't like what he was feeling. It wasn't JoEmma's fault that Thurgood Powell showed more interest in her than he had in his own son. He was being childish and that would get him nowhere. All it had ever done was put more distance between them and stop any conversation that might have started between them.

"I care enough," Noah finally answered his father's reprimand, not wanting to share exactly how he felt about JoEmma. That was purely between her and him. "That's why I'm asking. I want to know if it's her heart that keeps her in the wheelchair or if she has something else she's dealing with physically."

"Doctor to doctor, it's her heart. I'm not telling you anything that isn't already common knowledge and she's told others herself. Father to son, I'll tell you that I think it's her belief that she's a burden to others that keeps her chairbound. If she worked at it, she could strengthen those legs and that would strengthen her heart as well. She just hasn't found enough purpose yet to push herself into trying to improve more quickly. She practices standing and walking but not enough."

"But if she were not in the chair, she could prove to *herself* she's no burden. That doesn't make sense."

"To you it doesn't. To her it does. Have you ever known anyone afraid of success?"

Noah thought about it. Yes, he supposed he did. "Yes. They're afraid if they're successful, they still won't get what they want, so it's easier not to challenge themselves to be better."

"Your JoEmma unconsciously remains a burden to herself because she's afraid in the end that she still won't get whatever it is she truly wants. She's never been able to compete with her sister."

My JoEmma? She could be. The kiss had told him that he wanted her to be. If he could only encourage her to believe that whatever she really wanted, he would help her get it. If he could somehow urge her to open up to him about what was so important to her that she intentionally denied herself better health, then he might find a way to make it all possible. Noah dwelled on the wisdom of his father's words. The answer to everything seemed to lie in getting JoEmma to speak up.

He had to thank his father, not only for finally coming to visit but for being truthful about JoEmma and confiding in him. It was the finest conversation they'd shared since his youth. "I appreciate you talking about her with me, Dad. It means a lot." Noah dared to share something more with his father. "*She* means a lot to me."

"Good." Approval echoed in Thurgood's tone. "That's what I came to hear. Hannah told me that she heard wedding bells in your future. I didn't believe her. I wanted to see for myself if you really were starry-eyed or if it was just a figment of her matchmaking imagination. I can see Hannah has diagnosed the situation correctly. The woman can be hardheaded at times about things she wants. She knew I wouldn't ask her to marry me and she wouldn't accept until we were both sure you had someone to really take care of you, not just your office."

Thurgood wiped the coffee from his mustache and looked sternly at his son. "You rely too much on Hannah, son. And frankly, I'm not getting any younger waiting on you to get smart enough to realize that you need more than a profession to make life worth living."

"So, that's why she's being so stubborn this time." Noah saw it all more clearly now. "She's in a hurry to be a bride herself."

"And she wants what she wants when she wants it."

For the first time in a very long time, he saw that Thurgood Powell was a man who had been bested . . . by love. "And we both know what she wants most."

"*Her* way," they echoed in unison.

The two shared their first laugh as grown men together.

Years of loneliness washed away in that moment of sharing. Noah felt pounds lighter as if a burden had been lifted from his shoulders and the love he'd always felt for his father formed a lump in his throat as he tried to swallow it back, afraid it might make him cry the tears he had refused to shed all those years after his mother's death and his father's estrangement.

He wanted the air between them to be pure once again, needing to put to rest the foul stench of the last words they'd shared four years ago before they had treated each other with silent indifference. Though he didn't want to lose the sudden camaraderie between them, he had to make things right again. "Dad, I want you to know I'm sorry that I didn't come to you in time to save Cousin Jenny. I honestly tried to persuade her to let me bring you in but she begged me—"

"You don't have to say anything more, son. I know. When I visited your cousins after I retired, they told me that you did everything possible for Jenny. They also told me that Jenny made you swear on your mother's grave not to leave her, even if it meant coming to fetch me. Betsy and Will insisted that they were too scared to come get me themselves for fear that they wouldn't see their daughter alive again if they did. And they were right. You all were right for staying there and being there with Jenny in her last moments. I simply overreacted with grief of not knowing that I had been needed. Of not being able to say goodbye to that precious girl. Of having more grief added on to the other grief that I still wasn't coping with well."

His hand reached out and patted Noah's shoulder. "I said some cruel things to you the day you came home from Jenny's. I thought you were so upset with me about going into myself and leaving you all alone since your mother's death that you had deliberately not consulted me about your cousin. That you were too afraid to talk to me about her or anything else, for that matter. After all, I was. Angry at my life as it was. Angry at death for taking your mother away from me. Angry at myself, Noah, because if you had been able to come to me, I wouldn't have been there to hear you. And even though I knew I was the one at fault, I wasn't man enough to admit I was wrong. Instead, I took it out on you and drove us even farther away from each other than before. You did right by staying with Jenny and doing what you could to comfort her going."

His eyes met Noah's and held them intently. "I want you to know I'm sorry, son. Sorry that I wasn't there for you when your mother died. Sorry that you felt you couldn't talk to me because you thought I didn't have time for you anymore. Sorry that I've made you think that I consider you anything but the wonderful doctor, man, and son who others have had to tell me you are. I could have been, and should have been, learning that on my own. I'm most sorry for the years we've spent apart." His voice broke as he added, "L-look at the time I've lost with you."

Thurgood pulled Noah to him. Noah's arm reached up slowly to wrap itself around his father's shoulder. He closed his eyes and breathed in the essence of the man who had always been his own personal hero, the man he'd modeled his own life after, the man he had wanted to make so proud of him.

Thurgood began patting Noah's back and saying, "I love you, Noah. Please forgive me. I'm so very sorry for hurting you."

Noah's other arm went up to complete the hug. Tears that had lain deep in his heart for seventeen years rushed up to spill from his eyes onto shoulders not as physically broad as Noah once remembered, but strong enough to make amends.

A twelve-year-old voice quivered in the throat of a twenty-nine-year-old man as Noah found the best words of forgiveness he could offer his father. "I love you, too, Dad."

Chapter 9

"Good grief, how long is this going to take?" Angelina sat down on Noah's bed in exasperation and held the soiled paper away from her body as if it were a rattlesnake ready to strike. "I thought you said there was nothing to it."

"You're the one who told Noah that Gabby was yours and you would help take care of her." JoEmma ignored her sister's look of exasperation and turned to spread fresh paper inside the bottom of the cage. "It takes however long it takes."

"But I thought he would be in here with us," she whispered even though the door was closed to his bedroom and they couldn't be heard, "and I don't like having to deal with bird droppings."

"Nobody does. That's just part of what you've got to do if you're going to keep them healthy. And Noah's with his dad for the first time in years. Let him be."

"What do I do with this?" Angelina rattled the paper. "It stinks."

"Put it in that basket next to the bed. I'll take it out when I'm done with everything else." JoEmma had expected Angelina to eventually tire of coming with her to take care of the birds but not on the first day. Her sister had been prepared to make a great show of effort if Noah had stayed to watch, but with him out of their presence, Angelina was already back to her usual practice of letting someone else take care of the actual work.

Not that JoEmma really minded. At least she knew the cleaning was being done right and Gabby and Amigo wouldn't suffer from Angie's lackluster efforts.

"Look at them. Aren't they cute together?" She watched as the lovebirds flitted about the room, one spotting a new place to roost and calling the other over to investigate its comfort while JoEmma changed out the cage lining. "They're showing each other their new surroundings."

"Not much to it." Criticism filled Angelina's tone behind her. "I thought a bachelor's private quarters would be more . . . interesting. A bed, a pole, and a trash basket? There's not a place to hang your corset even if you had a mind to let him woo it off of you."

"What kind of man do you take Noah for?" JoEmma finished putting in the clean trays and filling one with a scoop of sunflower seeds, the other with some water from the ewer balanced beside her in the wheelchair. She was surprised that Angelina might consider him one of those fancy gambler sorts who traveled through town and stayed long enough to make his next stash and woo a new female conquest with his flashy clothes and the dexterity of his fingers. That kind of man held a particular fascination for her sister, but JoEmma considered his sort a walking woman-trap. Not Noah. He didn't have it in him to be anything but forthright.

No, what he had in him was a certain way with a soul-searing kiss. "Noah's not home enough to need more than this," she defended his practicality.

"Dr. Powell is male enough, don't fool yourself, Sister." Angelina deposited the paper in the basket. "But I'm beginning to think that after the Valentine's dance, I should start setting my cap elsewhere."

Full-blown anger fired through JoEmma, making her swing around to face her sister. "Make up your mind, Angelina. Either go after him as your beau or don't. But don't accept his offer to escort you, then dishonor him by trying to charm someone else there. I won't have it. I'm tired of you thinking you can have anyone you bat your eyelashes at, then tire of them and move on. I won't allow you to do it to Noah. Not now. Not ever."

"Whoa!" Angelina held her hands up to ward off her sister's attack, her slippers shifting suddenly to tuck themselves beneath the folds of her skirt. JoEmma had rolled the chair so close that the wheels pinned the hem of Angelina's skirt and wouldn't let her move any farther backward.

"Owww!" Angelina yelped, her hands flying to the top of her head as a flutter of rainbow-colored wings flashed by her blond hair and flew somewhere behind the bird's true owner. "That hat decoration plucked my hair!"

"Better her than me," JoEmma warned, wanting to yank out wads of her sister's hair for being so knuckle-brained about Noah. "Maybe it's best you don't come here anymore, Angie. You don't want to deal with the birds. Gabby has plans to use your hair for her nest. And after you win your stupid bet, I don't want you hanging around Noah or his place ever again unless you are in dire need of a doctor. Do you understand?"

"Roll back," Angelina said quietly.

"Why?" JoEmma had expected a full verbal assault, not something so calmly spoken from her sister.

"I said, roll off of my hem so I can leave. Your chair is holding me down."

JoEmma rolled back, the anger slowing from its rapid course through her veins.

"All you had to do was tell me you were really in love

with him." Angelina rose and shook the hem of her skirt to straighten it. "I would have never made the bet nor agreed to him escorting us both. I would have stepped aside."

"Of course you wouldn't have." JoEmma didn't believe her.

"Whether you believe it or not, I wouldn't offend you deliberately." Angelina grabbed her bonnet where she'd placed it on the bed when they first entered the bedroom. "I thought you showed interest in him because you know how competitive I am and that I would try to win his favor for that reason. I thought you were playing matchmaker, like Hannah has been these past two years. Trying to see me married so that we don't run out of the trust fund money and I won't have to take employment doing God knows what to earn my keep. I don't have all your many talents, you know. I'm just pretty and that gets me only so far."

"When I asked you to draw the hearts fairly and not match yourself up purposefully with him, you thought I was *competing* with you? That doesn't make sense." JoEmma never quite understood Angelina's way of thinking, but then they were two totally different types of women.

"I'm stubborn. You know that. If you tell me what to do, then I intend to do quite the opposite. Perfectly logical reasoning."

I was born different, JoEmma decided, once again realizing that if such reasoning was logical, then it had to be something not within her makeup. "I guess I'm different from you. I mean what I say," she told her sister.

"Yes, you do. You just don't speak up for yourself enough. Not to me. Not to others. Certainly not to Dr. Powell."

"It's none of your business," JoEmma argued.

"No-ah-Pow. No-ah-Pow. Smch-smch-smch," the two lovebirds chirped simultaneously.

"It's apparently everybody's business." Angelina's gaze slanted to the birds. "Even they know how you truly feel about him. You've fooled nobody but yourself and apparently me, for a while. Now that I know, I insist that you do something about it. Let me help you do something about it. You just might find yourself spoken for by Valentine's Day."

"I won't play games with Noah, and don't act like you really care." JoEmma couldn't deal with her sister's sudden concern. It hurt badly enough that pursuing any feelings she had for Noah would come across as competition with Angie. That was the last thing it would ever be. "No one's watching and you won't get anything out of saying you'll help. He's not a prize to be won. Leave me alone. Leave him alone."

Something dulled Angelina's eyes for a moment before they suddenly shimmered with tears. "I'll get something I've wanted for a long time, Jo. I'll see you well and happy. Believe it or not, I'm telling you the truth now. I want nothing more than I want that at the moment."

Sister eyed sister in silent regard. JoEmma's heart clenched as she realized she'd been too hard on Angelina. Maybe too critical for too long. Her elder sister was being sincere at the moment. JoEmma felt it to the bone, to the depths of her damaged heart. She'd hurt Angie deeply by accusing her of wanting to take rather than give something to her.

Sadness had caused the tears welling in her sister's eyes. Sadness that the bond that had once been strong between them had been frayed by envy and mistrust. JoEmma recognized that sadness, for she had it every time she ever wanted Angelina to show how much she loved and cared for her. Angie had simply done things her own way and her way wasn't JoEmma's. That didn't make her any less of a sister. It just made her different.

JoEmma was wrong this time and admitted it. "I'm sorry, Ang. I'm silly and do stupid things sometimes. Maybe I'm even just a little jealous of you."

"You have reason to be, you know." Angelina's chin tilted at a haughty angle and her eyes twinkled amid the shimmer of tears.

"It's hard to forget when you keep reminding me, Angie."

"An-gie. Phew! An-gie. Phew!" Gabby chimed in.

The sisters laughed together, easing the tension between them. Both had returned to their more comfortable roles— older sister bossiness and younger sister defiance. Each now with a better understanding of the other.

"Just what does she mean when she says that?" Angelina stood and tried to get closer to Gabby, but the love-bird flew into the cage and hid behind one corner of the perch where a rather large nest was being constructed.

"Phew!" Amigo echoed and joined his mate at the nest.

JoEmma laughed and told her sister that she had taught Gabby to say the word whenever she heard Angie's name and that it meant Angelina could be exasperating at times.

"Then all's fair," Angelina announced, sticking her face close to the cage. "JoEmma-just-wait," she chirped in a babylike voice, trying to get the bird to repeat the words. "Heh-heh-heh," she laughed.

JoEmma smiled. "What is that supposed to be . . . a threat?"

"Like I just said. Just wait and see." When Gabby moved from the nest and flew toward the latch, Angelina quickly swung the door closed. "No, ma'am, you aren't getting any more of my hair for your nest, Hat Decoration. What do you have to say about that?"

"Smch-smch-smch."

JoEmma started giggling. "I think she just told you to kiss her blue-colored rump."

A knock on the door told them the men had finished with their own talk.

"Come in," JoEmma encouraged, feeling good that Angie had laughed right along with her.

"Are the birds in their cage?"

Noah's concern pleased her and reassured JoEmma that even when he was alone with their pets, he would be cautious with Gabby. She assured him the duo was secure from escaping.

"You two sound like you're having a wonderful time in here." He looked pleased at the prospect. "I didn't know taking care of birds was such a hoot."

"That would be for owl sitters." Angelina kept her face straight as she uttered the pun.

"Good one, Sis." To Noah and his father, JoEmma added, "She's cagey sometimes with her humor, but it always has a seed of truth in it."

Noah glanced at one sister then the other. "Are we missing something here?"

JoEmma shrugged. "Not any of the birds. Just a few old misconceptions that have flown out the window. Right, Angie?"

"Right, Sis."

Thurgood Powell tipped his bowler to the women. "I think it's time to leave these two ladies to what they were doing, son. I believe they're perfectly fine and don't need us to step into something that we won't remotely understand no matter how much sense we try to make out of it. Good day, JoEmma. Angelina."

"An-gie. Phew!" Amigo chirped.

"JoEmma-wait," Gabby added. "Heh-heh-heh."

JoEmma nearly fell out of her wheelchair giggling.

"So Hannah's not addlepated after all." Thurgood tapped his cane on the hard wood floor. "I thought she'd been stirring up some wild concoction of a story about teaching two little lovebirds to talk to each other so that she could get two bigger lovebirds to do the same. Now I know what her intentions were. I take it one of those birds is yours, son, and the other belongs to one of the Browns."

"To JoEmma," Noah replied before Angelina could contradict him.

"Good, so you know the truth." Angelina stood and dusted off her skirt. "No more poop paper for me, thank Heaven."

JoEmma laughed. "Ahh, Funny Feathers was looking forward to adding blond hair to her nest."

Angelina patted the top of her head and moved toward the door. "It will have to be yours, I'm afraid. I plan to keep the rest of mine." She waved her hand, encompassing the room. "It's been a pleasure, Drs. Powell, both of you. I didn't realize you were such a practical man, Noah. If you ever need to refurnish your private quarters, just call on"—she eyed JoEmma—"my sister. She's got a good eye for decorating things."

"You don't need to rush off, Miss Brown."

"Oh yes, I do. It seems I may have to buy a pair of overalls." Angelina's gaze met JoEmma's and held. "And as Gabby suggested to me a minute ago, Sis, smch-smch-smch. In other words, kiss . . ."

"I understand, loud and clear. Don't say another word."

Chapter 10

The next few days went by too quickly. JoEmma wasn't sure she was ready for the Valentine's party tonight at Belle's but she'd promised Noah she would go with him and Angelina. Every time she'd tried to bring up a conversation to the contrary, he'd been too busy taking care of patients to talk to her. Now that she had changed her mind and had reason to want to go, it seemed this morning would prove to be like all the others. Too busy for him to stop and talk to her.

She had stalled around taking care of the birds as long as she could, and it was long past time to head home and start preparations for the party. She had to help Angie with her hair and find something presentable to wear herself. Hannah was becoming suspicious about why JoEmma was taking so much longer than usual and had checked on her twice already. She wouldn't be put off a third time.

It was almost time for Hannah to head over to Thurgood's place to clean, and she would not leave until she knew what was causing the delay. JoEmma knew her well enough to realize that her housekeeper thought she was ill. She couldn't let her think that or Hannah wouldn't attend the dance with Thurgood. That was not an option. Noah's father planned on proposing to Hannah tonight and presenting her with a ring. He'd enlisted JoEmma's advice about the possible size to fit his future bride and sworn her to secrecy. Noah didn't even know he was about to get a new mother.

Though she had once dreaded going to the dance, JoEmma wanted to be there to share in Hannah's great surprise. She just didn't want to go without Noah knowing about the bet the women had placed. He deserved better than that. He deserved the truth. He was certainly aware of the matchmaking attempt, but she would be no true friend if she didn't tell him the full extent of the bet.

"Are you about done with those birds?" Hannah Lassiter called from the other side of the door. "Are you not feeling well, Kitten?"

"Stand up. Puhleease," JoEmma whispered to herself one more time, willing her legs to stand up from the wheelchair one last time. They trembled as she tried, shaky from the countless times she had practiced standing all morning and every one since the day of her and Angie's talk. At home she couldn't practice without stirring her housekeeper's curiosity. Here at Noah's, the privacy of his bedroom allowed her alone time to work on improving her ability to move better. At least the morning hadn't been a complete failure. Not being able to talk with him had given her extra practice time.

"Did you say stand back?" Hannah's croaky question made JoEmma aware that the woman must have heard at least part of what she'd said.

JoEmma plopped down in the wheelchair, needing the rest and to catch her breath. "I said it's okay to come in," she fibbed, making a mental promise that she would confess the fib at a later date to Hannah and apologize for it.

The door opened and the rotund housekeeper waddled in. "You are ill, aren't you?" Worry filled the woman's tone. "You're all flushed and out of breath. Did you try to lift the feed sack? You know it's too heavy for you."

JoEmma shook her head. "I'm fine. It's just a little warm in here with the window and door closed. I need a little air."

The housekeeper waddled over to the window. "I'm just about ready to leave. If you like, I'll walk with you partway." She started to open the window, then paused and glanced at the birds. "Is it all right if I open this? Is Gabriella secure?"

JoEmma's gaze swept to the birdcage and she was assured she had latched the door to the cage. Gabby couldn't escape. She doubted Amigo would even try to unlatch it, if he could. Gabby's sweetheart rarely moved inches away from her, he was so enamored of his mate. "They're both locked in. The room needs to air out a bit anyway."

"Good. Noah asked if you had a moment to talk before you go. There are no more patients for now and he wants to discuss something about tonight."

The sound of Noah's footsteps coming down the hall sped up JoEmma's pulse to a much faster beat than before. She looked toward the door in anticipation, listening as Hannah raised the window. His handsome face brought with it a smile that flashed white against his angular features. She had dreamed of those lips since the day he'd kissed her, and the sight of him smiling at her made her heart feel as if it might leapfrog out of her chest.

"Good, you're still here." Noah's gaze swept over her, softening as it blazed a trail from the top of her head to the hem of her overalls. "You're sure looking pretty today."

"Thank you." If her face was flushed from the exercise, it surely burned bright from the pleasure of his compliment. He wasn't just being polite. His attention had returned to her lips and lingered there.

JoEmma no longer cared that everyone might think she

was competing with Angelina for Noah's favor tonight or any other night, for that matter. Since she told her sister the truth about the way she cared for him, JoEmma had decided their kiss was worth whatever it took to make herself no burden to Noah.

Finally putting away her stubbornness had made her see herself as others might, and frankly, she hadn't liked what she saw. She had been insecure, afraid that if she did get better, then she still wouldn't be enough for Noah. Out of fear, *she*, not the scarlet fever, had kept herself infirmed. She realized she had to chance losing so that she might win. She had to bet on herself.

Come hell or high water tonight, she would show Noah and everyone else that this was a new JoEmma Brown. A woman who would let nothing, particularly herself, stop her from getting what she wanted. No . . . what she *deserved*. To love and to be loved.

"I'd like to know what you're thinking right now."

The huskiness of Noah's voice made JoEmma aware that she'd drifted off into her thoughts and he was still watching her face intently. "Oh, just that I'm very happy that we got Gabby and Amigo together."

"You mean *I* did," Hannah reminded them from across the room.

"Ahhh, so you finally confess." Noah chuckled.

"It all worked out for the best." Hannah dusted her hands together. "You really need to take a cloth to those windows. It's getting dusty in here."

"Hannah . . ."

"Oh, quit complaining. You wouldn't know what to do if I ever let up on you anyway, Noah Powell. Besides, I'm gone now. Out the door, if you will see JoEmma home after your talk."

"Just a minute, Hannah," JoEmma called.

The housekeeper stopped in her tracks. "I bought you a

dress for tonight." JoEmma hoped that wasn't irritation creasing Hannah's brow. "I hope you don't mind. I thought it looked just like you, and I think Dr. Powell will think you're the prettiest girl there."

One of Hannah's brows arched high. "Kitten, I haven't been a girl in a whole lot of years, but thank you just the same." Curiosity got the better of her and she suddenly sounded more girlish than she was willing to admit. "How pretty is the dress?"

"Not as pretty as you, but it will do you justice."

"As long as Thurgood thinks so." With that, the woman spun around and left the room to the younger folks.

She had never been alone in a man's bedroom with him before, and the fact that it was the man she loved made JoEmma all the more aware of how his presence filled the room. He looked handsome in his white shirt, string tie, and vest that he wore to see patients. His scent was pure Noah—a mixture of medical remedies, soap, and something infinitely masculine. Try as she should to leave his private quarters, something kept her here immovable in her chair and waiting for Heaven knew what.

"W-what did you want to talk about?" she began, hoping that her voice would quiet the rush of sensations heating her every pore.

"May I sit?" Noah asked, motioning to the bed.

He must have been tired from the morning's activities. "It's your bed, after all," she whispered.

He sat across from her and reached for her hand. JoEmma didn't pull away from him as she might have even a few days ago. She meant to show him she'd had a change of heart. No, she had a strengthening of heart and purpose.

"I want you to know that I'm taking you and Angelina to the Valentine's dance, JoEmma, but it's you I wish were on my arm alone tonight. I've wanted to tell you that when we were alone, but the time hasn't presented itself till now."

"Maybe we can go somewhere together, just the two of us, sometime in the future. I'd like that, Noah."

His eyes searched hers. "You mean it? You'll stop trying to match me with Angelina?"

"I promise."

"You'll quit thinking you're too much trouble for me to have any interest in you?"

"I can be a handful at times."

"It's a heart-full I'm wanting, JoEmma." His lips moved toward hers, then halted barely an inch away. "And I promise not to kiss you until you're sure you want the same thing I want."

She wanted him to kiss her now. Would have asked him to. But she had that moment saved for a very special time when she could show how much she wanted another of his kisses and so much more. "Give me a little more time, Noah. That's all I need."

"No-ah-Pow. No-ah-Pow. Smch-smch-smch," Amigo chirped.

"Stand up. Puhleease," Gabby chimed in.

Noah's attention shot from JoEmma's lips to focus on the birds in the cage behind her. Puzzlement creased his brow. "Where did she hear that from?" he asked.

JoEmma rolled her chair forward and headed for the door, not wanting him to see evasion in her face. "Angelina, probably. You know how she's always complaining."

It wasn't a lie, exactly. Angie had been helping her practice standing all week. Her sister had said it was so that JoEmma might walk down the aisle someday and that had been plenty of motivation to keep practicing.

"Got to go now. Don't forget to shut that window so they won't get out if Amigo decides to open the latch again. Little Lockpicker."

"Says-a-me. Says-a-me. Open up," Gabby chattered.

"You stay out of this, Funny Feathers. Don't encourage him."

Noah laughed, got up, shut the window, and hollered for JoEmma to wait. "I told Hannah I'd see you home."

"Last one there has to sit next to Angelina in the buggy and she's wearing at least a dozen petticoats."

"No fair. I'm pushing." Noah grabbed the bars of her wheelchair. "You're ahead of me already."

"More than you know, Noah," JoEmma teased, nearly squealing with pleasure from the secret she was holding from him until tonight. Then she remembered . . . she still hadn't told him about the bet. He'd done all the talking.

"Hannah, the Powells are here," JoEmma informed her from the bottom of the stairs. "Are you and Angie about ready? We don't want to be late."

"Coming," Hannah yelled back. "I'm not used to all this fluff and puffy stuff."

She appeared at the head of the stairs looking like a cherub in white lace and silk, the long dress flounced and flowing, the mutton sleeves puffed so perfectly the top of their edges nearly touched Hanna's earlobes. Ruby earrings and a brooch added just the right touch to bring out the brown of her eyes and give her a dash of Valentine color.

Thurgood stepped forward, his cane leading him across the wooden floor to the foot of the stairs. "My dear, you look simply ravishing."

"I do, don't I?" Hannah patted one side of her hair. "And so does your dapper self." Her cheeks were flushed from the elder doctor's compliment, and she looked regal as she made her way down the stairs to accept the arm he extended her.

"We look good enough to get hitched," Hannah announced, linking her arm through his. "Now let's get that buggy moving. I've got on my dancing shoes."

"Hannah, you don't," JoEmma said, then saw that the housekeeper wasn't joking.

Hannah lifted the bottom of her hem and showed them she was wearing her favorite worn kid boots beneath the fancy dress. "They're worn in good and nobody will notice them anyway. Better than those fancy toe-tighteners you bought for me. Take 'um back for all the good they'll do me."

The men laughed, knowing to argue with her would do little good.

"Angie, you coming?" JoEmma called, focusing her attention on getting their last dallier downstairs. How much longer would it take her sister to finish dressing? She'd not come out all afternoon from her room, but she hadn't let either her or Hannah help even though they'd both offered.

JoEmma had been given too much time to get ready. Looking her best for a party was definitely more work than anything she'd done in a long time regarding her appearance, but she was no primper. She'd slapped on her emerald paisley, combed the tangles out of her hair, tied a matching ribbon to hold back the top of her hair so it wouldn't get in her eyes, and pinched her cheeks to make them look not quite so pale. That was the sum total of her preparations. But then she was not on anybody's most sought after list.

A door opened upstairs.

Everyone's gazes swung around to view what they knew would be one of the loveliest beauties at the party and the prettiest dress.

Suddenly Angie appeared . . . dressed in overalls! Overalls that had lace sewn on the straps, around the edges of each pocket, at the waist, and the leg hems. Angelina had prettied them up until they looked almost fashionable.

"Close your mouths, everybody, and quit staring. I made a bet and I mean to keep it. I just intend to keep it in my own way."

"But you didn't lose," JoEmma reminded. "You don't have to wear them."

"Oh, but I do."

"Lose what?" Noah asked. "The fact that she bet I would escort her to Belle's?"

"You know already?" Relief washed through JoEmma. She had practiced a dozen ways to tell him and none of them seemed right.

"I had a feeling about it that day all the women showed up in my office pretending to be sick. Then others dropped by, none of them any less healthy than the first ones. I knew for sure that you were involved with some sort of bet, Angelina, when you were so eager to accept my wish to escort you both. I heard about some bet between the women. I just didn't know which women until that day. And I didn't know what the consequences would be if I didn't take you to the party."

He directed his last statement to Angelina. "Like JoEmma said, if you want to change out of those, she and I will wait for you. Dad and Mrs. Lassiter can go on ahead of us."

"I'm going just like this," Angie announced. "Let's grab the cookies and be on our way."

Noah and JoEmma grabbed the desserts that had been assigned for the Browns to bring to the festivities and all made their way to the buggies. When they reached the one Noah would be driving, he placed the cookies in the back and turned to help JoEmma out of her chair.

"Just a moment." She held up one hand to ward him away. JoEmma handed him her box of cookies, and when his back was turned, she stood from out of her chair and waited.

Noah turned and astonishment filled his face. "You're standing."

She nodded, smiling at him. "I've been practicing. I wanted to surprise you."

"You have. May I lift you up or do you want to try on your own?" He didn't quite know what to do with his hands.

She laughed. "I'm not that strong yet. You can lift me, if you like."

He swung her up into his arms and gently set her in place on the front seat, whispering in her ear, "I like it very much, Jo."

She thought it might be difficult for him to deal with her chair but Noah had no trouble arranging it in the back. Angie sat behind her and Noah, munching on a cookie all the way to the party.

Lanterns lined the roadway on both sides, blazing a trail for visiting wagons and buggies to find their way to the Whitaker Barn. The dance would last into the wee morning hours, and the lanterns would light everyone's way back to town. Or at least give better light to those who imbibed too much of Jug Mason's moonshine and needed a point in the right direction to start their way home.

The local moonshiner had offered to put some "shine" to the punch, provided some of the local cowboy bachelors agreed to dance with his three daughters, Half-pint, Gal, and Keg. Most men around Longhorn City didn't find them particularly homely, but each of the Masons had a certain "fragrance" that came with them from minding their papa's still every day.

Music and laughter filled the air as the doctors and their ladies entered the throng of people dancing in the barn. Dresses twirled in time to the rousing reel being shouted by the fiddler. Male hands clapped like thunder to the rhythmic beat, and an occasional "Yee-haw" rent the air.

Moving through the crowd in the wheelchair would have proved daunting for JoEmma if she'd been forced to move on her own. Noah wished that the Whitakers had laid down some boards and sawdust to dance on, but they'd elected to simply muck out a huge dancing arena in the middle of the barn instead. The raw floor made it hard for JoEmma to maneuver.

A glance at her hands made him smile. She'd worn gloves to protect her palms, as he'd advised. "Where do you want to go?" he leaned down and asked her. "Do you think you'll be more comfortable near the punch and cookie table or over by the bales of hay where everyone's resting."

"Help me reach Belle, wherever she's at. I can't see through this throng."

Noah found their hostess near a table decorated with a red cloth and that had a bowl of paper hearts at its center. "Hold on," he announced, steering JoEmma in that direction. "Excuse me. Pardon me. Man on a mission. Wheelchair coming through."

Bodies dodged and parted, allowing them to reach Belle.

"There you are!" Belle smiled at JoEmma. "I had hoped you would come, after all. And my, don't you look beautiful."

"Yes, she does," Noah agreed.

Belle glanced up at him, her brow lifting quizzically. "And Angelina, where's she? We've been waiting for her to—"

"I'm right behind them." Angelina joined her sister at the table.

"You're wearing overalls." Belle's gloved hand shot up to press against her lips as if she was dismayed.

"I lost. Plain and simple. Noah and JoEmma are here together. I just hitched a ride with them."

"We are?" Noah looked at JoEmma, searching her face for any sign of reluctance. "Here together as a couple?"

He found none there.

She nodded and smiled. "If you want to be."

"I definitely want to be. Now and for many Valentine's Days to come."

"Then that settles that." Angelina grabbed the bowl of hearts. "Let's get this matchmaking on the road. The night's not getting any younger."

"But first, Angie, we have one couple in particular who needs pairing." JoEmma wiggled her finger, making Angelina bend down to listen to her whisper.

What were the two up to?

"Really?" Angelina gasped. "Oh, that's wonderful." She cupped her hands to her lips and shouted, "May I have your attention, folks? Stop the music!"

When it stopped, she continued, "It seems our former doctor, Thurgood Powell, has a special announcement he would like to make. Dr. Powell, the floor is all yours."

The people around Thurgood and Hannah Lassiter suddenly moved backward as Thurgood sank to one knee in front of his housekeeper, though it was difficult for him to do so. "Hannah Lassiter, would you do me the honor of marrying me? Of becoming my bride? Of making this the happiest Valentine's Day of my life?"

Hannah looked down at him. "Stand up, puhleease, you big hunk of Hippocratic Oath. Of course I'll marry you."

A round of applause sounded throughout the barn. Congratulations echoed over the crowd. Noah rolled

JoEmma over to the newly engaged couple, knowing she would want to add her best wishes as well.

"Do you have it?" Thurgood asked as JoEmma approached.

"Right here in my pocket." JoEmma brought out a box tied with a tiny ribbon of red that ended in a heart shape and handed it to Noah's dad.

They all watched as Thurgood offered the box to Hannah. "A symbol of my deep affection, my dear."

Hannah unlaced the ribbon and looked inside. She took out the gold ring and smiled. "Put it on my finger, Good Honey."

Thurgood did as he always did, exactly what Hannah Lassiter wanted him to do.

"Now kiss me like you mean it."

And he did that, too.

"You knew about this?" It was JoEmma's lips that held Noah's attention now, not his parent's. "And you didn't tell me?"

"One of my surprises for tonight," she said, her eyes shining with something more than tears of happiness for Hannah.

"One of? Are there more? I thought you had told me everything back at your—"

"Noah. Just shut up and kiss me. Like you want me forever."

She didn't have to tell him twice.

Epilogue

Angelina Brown had her way with the hearts that night, making certain that JoEmma's and Noah's paper hearts were drawn out together and that Thurgood Powell's and Hannah Lassiter's were matched as well. She even made sure that Gallon Mason was paired with the man of her papa's dreams, the local barrel maker.

Angelina herself caught the eye of a visiting gambler who had attended Belle's dance and was ready to give up his old ways and settle down somewhere with a good old farm girl. Wearing overalls had been a sure bet after all.

Thurgood and Hannah put other couples to shame, attending every dance given for the next three years.

Amigo and Gabby procreated to the best of their feathered ability, producing a long line of healthy, talkative offspring that filled the homes of Longhorn City, Texas, with lively echoes of "smch-smch-smch."

JoEmma was not only standing but walking on her own now, helping Noah chase after their two-year-old chatterbox of a son, and listening to all the sweet talk that made the life and love they shared together worth living.